BOWIE'S GOLD

BOWIE'S GOLD

Evan Lewis

COVER BY
GARY CARBON

STEEGER BOOKS • 2022

Mr. Bowie and I wish to salute the following folks, heroes all, who helped out on this one. In pretty much alphabetical order, they are:

Drew Bentley, Jackie Blain, Gary Carbon, Jack Edmondson, Rob and June Edwards, Christine Finlayson, LaVonne Griffin-Valade, Ron Ianitello, Kassandra Kelly, Becky Kjelstrom, Nancy LaPaglia, Doug Levin, Ann Littlewood, Marilyn McFarlane, Matt Moring, Will Murray, Cap'n Bob Napier, Angela M. Sanders and Brian Trainer.

And, most of all, my lovely wife Irene, without whom this book would never have seen the light of day.

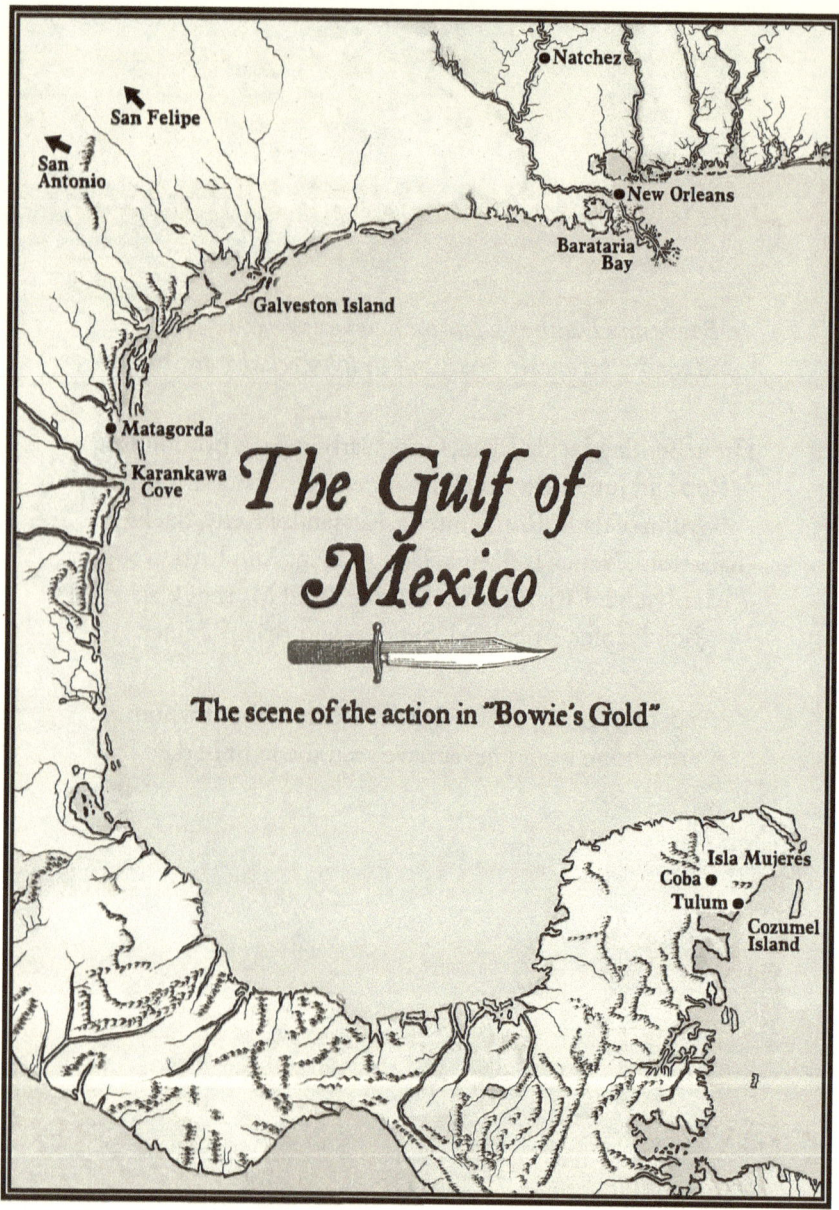

The Gulf of Mexico

The scene of the action in "Bowie's Gold"

Natchez

San Felipe

San Antonio

New Orleans

Barataria Bay

Galveston Island

Matagorda

Karankawa Cove

Isla Mujeres

Coba

Tulum

Cozumel Island

PART I
VENGEANCE

CHAPTER I

"Little more than a savage."

"COME, MR. BOWIE. Won't you show us the knife?" The former governor of Louisiana slid a stack of gold coins toward the glittering pile at table's center. "Raise five hundred."

"Yes, James, please do." The judge on Bowie's left studied his cards a moment before dropping them in disgust. "Lord knows this game is not providing me much amusement."

The tobacco baron on Bowie's right made a sound that was half growl, half harrumph. "I'm out. But I, too, would like to see this fabled blade."

James Bowie eyed his three jacks and two queens. He fingered five coins from his own dwindling stack and pushed them forward. "Call."

When no one spoke, he glanced up to find them all looking at him.

He hesitated. The plush gaming salon of the Hotel Monock, favored haunt of the most distinguished men of New Orleans, was no place to be brandishing a knife. Particularly a knife with a ten-inch blade designed to open a man from gut to chin.

"Here." The ex-governor plucked a gold piece from his stack. "I'll even pay for the privilege." He flicked his thumb, and the coin glittered as it spun through the air.

Bowie caught the coin and closed a fist around it. "A knife, gentlemen, is much like a sword. It should not be unsheathed unless one intends to use it. And I earnestly hope I shall never have to use it again."

"By God," the judge said, "I almost believe he means it."

The former governor accepted the return of his coin. "You still intend, then, to seek Brent's seat in Congress?"

"I intend," Bowie said, "to win it. And I hope I may count you gentlemen among my supporters."

Congressman William Brent was now in his third term, and voters had become increasingly dissatisfied with him. His latest opponent—a blowhard Democrat named Overton—had been favored to defeat him, a prospect that played no small part in Brent's decision not to seek re-election.

After an uncomfortable pause, the tobacco grower said, "But what of your health? Have you truly recovered from that—that incident?"

"I'm strong as an ox," Bowie lied, "and twice as handsome. The six months abed gave me time to reflect upon my sins, and I've come forth a new and better man."

Bowie hoped at least part of that was true. The "incident" had been a huge setback in his quest for respectability, but had carried a hidden blessing.

Seven months earlier, on a humid afternoon in September 1827, his dreams had nearly gone to smash. On hand to witness a duel between a friend and another gentleman, he'd become embroiled with a personal enemy with friends of his own. As a result, he'd taken three pistol balls to the body and been run through four times with sword blades. One of those blades had pierced a lung, as he was still reminded with every breath.

That he lived was astonishing enough, but in the process he had buried his knife in the vitals of his chief opponent—killing him on the spot—and severely wounded another. The Sandbar Fight, as the newspapers called it, had tarnished his reputation as a gentleman. Over the past few months, Bowie's name had become synonymous with dueling and sudden death.

But he had discovered, to his surprise, that while his newfound notoriety was off-putting to some high-minded voters, their less sophisticated neighbors heartily approved the notion of sending a knife fighter to Congress.

And that fact, he knew, was not lost on his present companions.

The ex-governor examined him with shrewd, probing eyes. "I find you a most formidable individual, Mr. Bowie, and believe you may be just the man to represent our interests. So yes, you shall have my support."

The judge nodded. "And mine."

The tobacco grower raised a glass. "Let's make that unanimous."

AGLOW WITH SUCCESS and fine bourbon, Bowie found the scene almost magical. Pipe and cigar smoke formed a hazy cloud above the players, muting the light of the great crystal chandelier. Waiters drifted like wraiths between the tables. To his ears came the murmur of a dozen conversations and the gentle clink of coins and chips, punctuated at intervals with cries of exultation or dismay.

As play progressed, Bowie lost steadily but with much grace. He was skillful enough to win when he wished, but today's foray into the heart of New Orleans respectability was not about winning at cards. Having found favor with these three gentlemen, he peered through the haze of smoke in search of others to help advance his campaign.

Snatches of conversations in French and Spanish identified the Creoles, who still considered themselves the city's aristocracy. The Creole families, having come to Louisiana during the time of French and Spanish rule, held less influence than they once had, but were still a contingent to be reckoned with.

These were outnumbered by the more boisterous Americans, who owed their social positions to wealth rather than breeding. They were sugar growers, shipping magnates, mill owners, manufacturers, physicians, barristers and landlords, and all, by their very presence here, proclaimed themselves to be among the city's new elite.

"I hear Lafitte is dead again," the ex-governor remarked.

The judge emitted a snort. "What is it this time? I suppose hanging is too much to hope for."

"Sadly, yes." The tobacco baron made a sour face. "Something about malaria, I believe."

Bowie's thoughts took him far from the gaming room and its distinguished company, back to the island stronghold Lafitte had called *Campeachy*. The sandy bank had teamed with jeering pirates, while Bowie himself sat nailed to a log in the lagoon, face to face with a man determined to take his life. Among the crowd he noted the saucy blonde cause of the duel, and the livid, snarling face of his opponent's brother, Renato. And overseeing it all, amusement curling his lips, towered the figure of Jean Lafitte himself.

"What say you, Bowie? Did you ever encounter the black-guard?"

In his mind, Bowie ducked as his opponent's blade flashed past his head, nicking his ear.

"Mr. Bowie, are you with us?"

Quick as lightning, he returned the thrust, grinning as blood spurted from the other man's arm.

"James! James, for God's sake!"

A hand gripped his wrist, and Bowie nearly lashed out, but some instinct warned him, and he blinked, shocked to behold his gaming companions regarding him with mouths agape.

"Good Lord, James." The former governor fanned himself with his cards. "The way you were gripping that knife, we feared you were about to slaughter us all."

Bowie glanced down, relieved to see the knife still sheathed at his hip. With effort, he loosened his grip on the smooth wooden handle and returned his hand to the table.

The scene at Lafitte's base on Galveston Island had played out eight years earlier, but its aftermath, involving the saucy blonde wench and the pirate Renato, still haunted his dreams.

"Your pardon, gentlemen," he said lightly, "I believe you were speaking of Lafitte. For my money, he was dead the last time we heard of him, and dead the time before that. These continuing rumors are the work of idle minds."

"I must agree," the former governor said. "Lafitte is indeed dead, and piracy died with him."

Bowie lit a cigar to hide his smirk. The ex-governor was a fool, but there was no profit in saying so. Lafitte was dead, he had no doubt. But piracy, as he well knew, lived not upon the seas, but in the hearts of men.

IT WAS MERE minutes later—and Bowie's equilibrium had not yet returned—when a new and entirely unwelcome voice came from the table behind.

"That bumpkin Bowie," the voice said, "troubles me not at all. Lord knows, the man is little more than a savage, prancing about with that ridiculous toadsticker of his."

Bowie turned to cast a hard eye upon the new arrival. It was General Walter Overton, one of the aging heroes of the Battle of New Orleans, and Bowie's main rival in the coming election.

Dropping his bulk into a vacant chair, the man continued, "Thankfully, his bid for Congress has died a'borning, because that scoundrel Brent has reneged on his pledge to retire. 'Duty to his constituents,' he says. Balderdash! The man has been suckling at the public teat so long he cannot bear to be weaned."

Bowie was out of his chair in an instant, already reaching for the man's collar.

"What a state of things!" Overton droned on. "Men of character who will not stoop to low and dirty intrigue are shunned as being out of fashion, while the most blatantly corrupt are—"

The man gasped for air, his fat face purpling as Bowie yanked him out of his chair.

"This news of Brent," Bowie gritted. "How did you come by it? Speak, damn you!"

"James." The ex-governor was at his side. "A man can hardly speak while being strangled."

Bowie's red fury abated not at all, but he saw sense in the words, and loosened his grip.

"Now," he said, "you will tell me more of Brent."

Overton sucked in great draughts of air, his eyes bulging from their sockets. The only sounds escaping him were whimpers.

"It may also serve," the ex-governor said, "to sheath your blade. Unless, of course, you feel compelled to use it."

And Bowie realized, to his horror, that the knife was in his hand, quivering like a thing alive, its point an inch from Overton's nose.

CHAPTER 2

"Your ears on a necklace."

RENATO GRIPPED HIS brush with a firm but supple wrist, applying a deft stroke of glimmering gold. Leaning back in his chair, he examined the canvas with a critical eye. This was a fine day's work. *The Last Great Terror of the Gulf,* it would be called, a bold and graceful prince of pirates, wide of shoulder, trim of waist, and up to his kneeboots in treasure.

The booty as yet had little definition, appearing almost a hillock of molten gold, but that would soon change. Renato hoped it would include a little of everything: goblets, vases, necklaces, crowns, statuary, and his personal favorite—chests spilling over with glittering coins.

"Er, ah, Cap'n…"

Renato scowled up at the burly buccaneer posing against the ship's rail. The man's attire was truly magnificent. A shining breastplate of hammered silver, a flowing red velvet cloak and a wide-brimmed hat adorned with a band of rubies. But the vision was marred by the man's brutish features, dull and common as mud.

"Cap'n, sir, by yer leave, might I be returning to my station?"

Renato wrinkled his nose. The fellow's fist-like face and harsh voice had driven his muse away. "Go, damn you. But see that you remove that clothing and stow it in my cabin. And take care, LaChaise. Should I find the slightest rip or stain, you'll be wearing your ears on a necklace."

As the oaf lumbered off, Renato laid his brush aside and

examined the painting yet again. Fine as it was, it would be vastly improved once he filled in the face—a task that could only be performed in a mirror.

Renato slipped a hand into his coat pocket and extracted the smooth oilskin pouch holding the key to his future. The pouch contained a map, the object of a five-year search, that would make him the richest man in the western world—perhaps wealthier than all the kings of Europe.

The map held the secret to the treasure the vaunted Lafitte had sought—and failed—to find. Lafitte, who had deemed himself Prince of Pirates, had slunk off to die on a forlorn island, while most of his contemporaries had been driven to ground. The once great Dominique You now prowled the streets of the French Quarter, selling tired tales for the price of a drink, and Renato's own stepfather, the famed Renato Beluche, had switched sides, helping Simón Bolívar rout the last privateers out of Cuba.

The true pirates of the modern day, Renato knew, were the rich merchants of New York and London. They had usurped the smuggling trade that once belonged to the buccaneers. That he himself still thrived was a credit to his cunning, and his nimble ship's ability to navigate the shoals and coves lining the Gulf of Mexico. For the past few years he had plied his trade between the mouth of the Mississippi and the shores of Texas, always alert for word of the map that was his by right, the map that would lead him to his destiny.

The map had come to him only recently—and at great cost— and he had not yet had an opportunity to study it in detail. He was about to do just that when he heard the telltale clack of Faraday's boots on the deck behind.

Returning the oilskin pouch to his pocket, Renato fixed the man with a glare. "Mr. Faraday. I gave orders we should make for Texas at all possible speed. Why are we still at anchor?"

"Your pardon, Captain." In place of a bow, the man offered a barely perceptible nod. "We are taking on provisions, and it will be late afternoon before we're fit to sail."

Faraday wore ragged burlap trousers and a simple blouse of once-white cotton—hardly an outfit to rival Renato's gold-trimmed frock coat, plumed tricorn hat, black silk breeches and silver-laced boots. His straw-blond hair, blowing free in the wind, paled beside Renato's black-lacquered curls. Still, the man had a certain presence, and Renato had already begun to regret appointing him quartermaster.

Faraday was a shade too handsome, dimming Renato's luster with the ladies—and a shade too tall, forcing Renato into heels higher than he liked. But the man's ultimate offense lay in becoming too popular with the crew.

He recalled the first time he had seen Faraday, a gangly youth barely in his teens. He'd taken the boy under his wing, taught him the ways of pirating, even saw him as a substitute for his dead brother Rayón. But those hopes were long gone.

It was at times like this he missed Rayón most. True, he'd been only a half-brother, but twice the man of any now among his crew. And Rayón would still be with him if not for that backwoods braggart Bowie and the lordly ways of Lafitte. But Renato would soon have his vengeance on them both. The treasure would bring him power Lafitte had only dreamed of. And from the height of his glory, he would reach down and obliterate Bowie and all his kin.

But for now, he was stuck with Faraday.

"I am not well pleased," he said. "I wish to lay hands upon my treasure without delay."

"The men and I are equally eager, Captain." And when Renato merely stared at him, Faraday added, "to claim our own allotted shares, of course."

Renato recalled a favorite saying of his famous stepfather. *Dead men require no shares.*

"Oh, of course," he agreed. "You and the men shall get all that you deserve."

THE SCHOONER *L'INTREPIDE* lay at anchor in a secluded cove on Barataria Bay, fifty miles south of New Orleans. The place had been ideally suited for Lafitte's headquarters, accessible to the city by small boat, but shielded from the Gulf by two barrier islands. By 1814 it had become an open marketplace for smuggled goods and slaves, popular with citizens eager to avoid the heavy duties imposed by the state. But in that year, a fleet of U.S. ships and gunboats had made a concerted attack on the bay. Jean Lafitte, along with his brother Pierre and most of their four hundred-odd men—Renato included—escaped on pirogues into the bayous, but a good number were captured, along with more than two dozen pirate vessels.

Renato's mouth still watered at the thought of that lost booty. Thousands of dollars in silver bullion, gold coins and paper bank notes. Uncounted gallons of wine, brandy and other spirits. Warehouses full of silk, cigars, chocolate, coffee and other merchandise.

Following the raid, the Lafittes had moved their base of operations to Galveston Island and prospered anew. Illicit trade in Barataria Bay did not end, but was greatly diminished, and now, more than a dozen years later, it was one of many places Renato found refuge from his enemies.

At one end of the bay was a Cajun trading post, and Renato found it convenient to exchange stolen cargoes of tobacco, cotton and other items for necessities such as gunpowder and spirits.

While boats ferried such goods back and forth, shore parties filled casks of fresh water and baskets of fruit from the shore.

Renato found the process maddeningly slow. He paced the deck, finding fault at every turn, and damning men, beasts, fishes, the sun, the moon and all the gods in the heavens.

And he was in this frame of mind when an apparition climbed over the rail to deposit itself on deck.

The thing appeared to be a woman, but that could hardly be. The Cajun women on this stretch of the coast were tawny, rough-skinned creatures, and the plump and toothless slatterns found in nearby taverns were equally undesirable.

The vision before him, slim-waisted with delectable curves above and below, was coiffed, rouged and adorned in a hooped gown, looking for all the world like she'd stepped from a New Orleans bordello. Her features were delicate, her skin smoothly pink, her hair lustrous as black pearls, and her eyes startlingly green. When she smiled at him his heart forgot to beat.

"What?" he said haltingly. "Who? How?"

Then reality came crashing upon him as another apparition stepped over the rail, one he recognized and had hoped never to see again.

"Andre!" he snarled. "You dare show your face upon my ship?"

The man was altogether as hideous as the girl was fair. His coat was ragged, his trousers stained, and his hat appeared to have been regurgitated by an alligator. In face as well as form, he resembled nothing so much as a giant toad.

Andre had been a fixture among the pirates of the Gulf for decades, but always as a creature of Lafitte's. After the great poseur died, the man had even sailed for a brief time with Renato himself. But he'd been unable to control his tongue, constantly veiling criticism as advice, as in *That's not how Lafitte woulda done it*, or *as Lafitte always said…* Renato soon had his fill of the blatherskite, and had him cast ashore.

The thing called Andre performed a mock bow. "Beggin' your pardon, Cap'n Renato, sir. On me own hook, I'd never have come, but when me dear daughter learned ye was anchored here, she was afire to meet thee. She's heard much of your exploits, see, and when she wants a thing it's beyond me to deny her."

"Daughter?" Renato was dumbstruck. "This—this beauty is your daughter?"

"Mariette, dear," Andre said, "the gentleman deserves a proper greetin', does he not?"

And as Renato stood rooted to the spot, the vision floated toward him. Placing white-gloved hands upon his chest, she stretched to plant a wondrously soft kiss upon his cheek. The sweetness of her perfume made his head swim.

"I am so pleased to meet you, Monsieur. It has long been a girlish dream of mine."

The next few minutes were a daze. Renato readily acquiesced to the lady's request to see his cabin, where she greatly admired his paintings. Twitching in every nerve for want of her, he poured large goblets of wine.

"Oh, Monsieur Captain! That is far too much. I suspect you wish to make me tipsy."

"Nonsense," he said. "This is nothing." And to demonstrate, he downed his own glass to the last drop.

"Well," she said, ever the coquette, "only if you will join me."

And he quickly refilled his goblet, while she sipped at her own.

Several glasses later, she removed her dress, while he doffed his coat and trousers.

Her elegantly soft arms were about his neck, her lips tantalizingly near, her heart beating in time with his own, when he felt himself slipping away, tumbling into the depths of her enormous sea green eyes. And then he knew no more.

CHAPTER 3

"You call me a liar?"

BOWIE'S BLOOD BOILED as he made his way down Bourbon Street.

He had spent the past two years cultivating men of influence and ingratiating himself to voters throughout the southern parishes of the state, and he would not see his political hopes fall prey to the mercurial whims of Congressman William Brent.

Bowie had come from nothing, raised wild in the bayous where men were esteemed for their ability to wrestle bulls and alligators. After years of arduous work, he and his brothers had established a large cypress plantation near Opelousas, complete with a sawmill. After engaging in certain profitable activities with Jean Lafitte—an enterprise they would just as soon forget—they had devoted their efforts to land speculation and politics.

His brother Rezin had recently been elected to serve Avoyelles Parish in the state legislature, and John reelected from nearby Catahoula. James, ever eager to best them, had set his sights on Washington. Having gained the support of several wealthy landowners, he had convinced Brent to step aside.

His troubles began in late 1826, when *the knife* became fixed to his hip. After being shot in the breast in an encounter with a particular enemy named Major Norris Wright, Rezin convinced him he must thenceforth carry a formidable blade for his protection. While a pistol might misfire, Rezin pointed out, a knife would not.

The chosen weapon was a crude, single-edged hunting knife, with a blade nine inches long and an inch and a half wide. Bowie had fashioned a sheath that almost disguised it as the weapon of a gentleman. But it was not, as he well knew. Once the point pierced flesh, a twist of the wrist would cut the heart strings of an opponent, as it had done to that same Major Wright in the Sandbar Fight.

Reports of the fight had appeared in newspapers throughout the South—and beyond—making Bowie both famous and infamous. Everyone wanted to see and touch the knife, and it seemed prudent to show them something worthy of admiration. So, during the long months of recovery, he'd found a blacksmith worthy of the task.

The new knife was ten inches of shining steel, with a cross-guard to catch an opponent's blade, and a curving clip point near the tip. The curve was honed sharp as a shaving razor, and the mere sight of it had already made men think twice about challenging him.

Over the past few months he'd taken great pains to reassure supporters he was still fit to serve them in the nation's capital. But his new reputation was proving both a blessing and a curse. He was no longer just a man—he was *a man with a knife,* and he sometimes felt the blade was wielding him, rather than he the blade.

The fact that he had unsheathed it at the Monock Hotel still troubled him. He had not meant to draw it. He had not even *known* he had drawn it.

The thing seemed to have a mind of its own.

HUGO TAMARAND'S OUTER door opened onto a small, dark-paneled room containing several cabinets and a single desk strewn with papers. Behind the desk, a florid-faced man with thick spectacles scribbled numbers into a ledger, his ferret-like eyes darting from papers to book and back again.

When the clerk failed to acknowledge him, Bowie cleared his throat.

Without looking up, the man said, "Your purpose?"

"I must see your employer," Bowie said. "On a matter of great importance."

"Out of the question. Mr. Tamarand sees no one without an appointment."

"In that case, I require one. Immediately."

The florid-faced man dipped his pen in an inkwell, blotted the tip, and proceeded to transfer more numbers into the ledger. "You misunderstand me, sirrah. Mr. Tamarand grants appointments only at his own pleasure. If he wished to see you, you would have been summoned."

Bowie felt the knife calling to him. *I am the answer*, it said, *to every question.* He clenched his fists. He would not succumb to it again. He could not. Not with his entire future in the balance. Planting his knuckles on the desk, he leaned over the scribbling man.

"It occurs to me," he said in a deathly quiet voice, "that I neglected to give you my name."

Still the clerk did not look up. "You are welcome to keep it. And take it with you when you go."

"The name is Bowie. James Bowie."

For several seconds more, the man continued working. Then his hand began to shake, as if from palsy. Beads of sweat trickled down the slope of his skull. At last, he angled his gaze upward. "Ah."

"I have just recalled," Bowie said, "that I *do* have an appointment. Now. Do you wish to call me a liar?"

Color fled the man's face. "I will inform him you have arrived." He rose and turned toward a door on the rear wall.

"Let's inform him together."

Bowie followed him into a hallway lined with small offices containing other pinch-faced men hunched over ledgers.

Bowie felt a measure of shame at bullying this little man. It was an act unworthy of a gentleman. Still, it was good to know his reputation had practical application. And once ensconced in Congress, such threats would no longer be necessary.

The name of Hugo Tamarand was spoken in hushed tones within Louisiana political circles. Ostensibly, his business was shipping, but his true source of power was the behind-the-scenes manipulation of Louisiana politics. Anyone with aspirations in the state had to deal, soon or late, with Hugo Tamarand. Even Andrew Jackson, it was said, had recently come hat in hand, seeking Tamarand's favor in his bid for the Presidency. And when Congressman William Brent promised to step aside, he had couched his words with the catchphrase, *Should it please Mr. Tamarand.*

Loath to prostrate himself before any man, Bowie had avoided seeing him. But he must know the truth of Brent's intentions.

At the end of the hall, the clerk rapped knuckles delicately against an unmarked door.

"Go away," issued a thin voice from within.

The clerk exhibited an elaborate shrug.

Bowie guided the sputtering fellow out of the way and strode inside.

The clerk shrilled, "Mr. Tamarand, sir! This ruffian forced his way in. I assure you I—"

"That will be all, Smythe," the voice said. "I will see him."

Bowie's eyes swept the room in search of the speaker. The padded chair behind the massive, marble-topped desk was vacant. Behind it rose row upon row of leather-bound books. In one corner stood a shining globe of the earth, fully a yard in diameter, and next to it stood half a man. *Half,* because the great Hugo Tamarand, despite the giant shadow he cast over Louisiana, was hardly larger than a boy.

The fellow's skull was bald, and gleamed pink in the lamplight. Indeed, his entire face was pink, and his side-whiskers, as long as Bowie's own, had the look of peach fuzz. His formal dress, a florid scarlet cravat over a satin waistcoat, made him appear the mere parody of a man.

Bowie felt even more the bully. "Your pardon, sir. I fear I have behaved badly."

"On the contrary, Mr. Bowie. Compared with your actions this afternoon at the Hotel Monock, it would seem you have shown uncharacteristic restraint. I must thank you for not slicing poor Mr. Smythe's throat."

Bowie swallowed. So the man knew him, and was remarkably well informed. "That was regrettable," he said, "but I was provoked."

"Yes. So I understand. And I expect you had a similar excuse for that celebrated killing on the sandbar."

Bowie bit back his response. Any answer he gave would sound lame.

Tamarand threw open his coat. "I assure you I am not armed. I hope you feel no provocation from *me*."

"It's about Brent," Bowie blurted. "He promised me his seat."

"Did he now?" Tamarand's eyes were gleaming steel balls. "And did you truly think it his to give?"

Bowie held his tongue, feeling foolish.

Tamarand climbed into the overstuffed chair behind his desk. Somehow it made him appear even smaller. "Please sit, Mr. Bowie. I dislike looking up at people."

Bowie found a straight-backed chair across from the desk. His knees rose at an ungainly angle, and he realized Tamarand could now look down upon him.

"Brent gave me his word," Bowie said.

Tamarand reached for a long-stemmed pipe, tapping its contents into a small silver bowl. "Yes. I persuaded him to reconsider."

"May I ask why?"

Stuffing a pinch of tobacco into his pipe, the little man lit it from a candle and puffed it to life. For a long moment, he examined Bowie through the smoke. "Mr. Brent, I regret to say, has been unwise in his investments. Quite simply, he cannot afford to leave office."

Bowie was stunned. Money flowed freely in Washington, and had a way of sticking to the hands of public officials. That was no small factor in his desire to join them.

"You persuaded him," Bowie said. "May I assume his debt is to you?"

"I must say, sir, you are unusually direct. But it happens directness is a quality I admire. Your assumption is correct."

"How much does he owe?"

"A great deal, I'm afraid."

"How much?"

"There is such a thing, Mr. Bowie, as being too direct."

"I wish to pay it," Bowie said. "With his debt paid, he would be free to retire."

Tamarand turned his pipe, using the stem as a pointer. "You have much to learn of politics, I fear. Whatever the amount of Mr. Brent's actual debt, his presence in Congress is of far greater value. To put it bluntly, he is an asset I am not prepared to lose."

So he's in your pocket, Bowie thought. Things were much clearer now.

"How much will it take? How much to release him, and run me in his stead?"

Tamarand's mouth hung open. "You are an unusual fellow, Mr. Bowie. I am not unaware, of course, of your current difficulties with the General Land Office. It seems they suspect you of forging a number of old Spanish grants."

Bowie bristled. "Unproven charges. And in any case, such pursuits are behind me now."

Tamarand eyed him keenly. "Do not misunderstand me. The fact that you have engaged in such activities and so far eluded prosecution is a point in your favor. I am also not unaware of certain dealings you had with the pirate Lafitte. With proper grooming, a man of your audacity and moral fluidity might do quite well in Washington." He puffed on his pipe, eyeing Bowie keenly through the smoke.

Bowie waited. To this man, everything had a price.

At length, Tamarand said, "I am sorry to dampen your hopes, but I'm afraid you would find the amount quite beyond your reach."

"How much?"

Tamarand twisted his pink lips. "I could not possibly consider less than a hundred and fifty thousand dollars."

Had Bowie been standing, he would have staggered. Even if he and his brothers were to liquidate all their property and borrow against future prospects, they would be hard pressed to raise half that amount. "Not impossible," he said, "given time. But the election will soon be upon us. The most I could offer on such short notice is seventy-five thousand."

"I might look favorably on a hundred and twenty-five thousand."

"Eighty-five," Bowie said, "with one month to gather the funds."

Tamarand's eyes gleamed. The man was enjoying this. "A hundred and fifteen, with a good faith deposit of twenty thousand."

Bowie drew a wallet from his jacket pocket, sliding a thick stack of bills into his hand—money entrusted him by his brothers for a land deal in Arkansas. "Ten thousand dollars," he said, "toward a total of a hundred thousand, payable one month from today."

Tamarand's eyes fixed on the cash. "Mr. Bowie, we may make a congressman of you yet. Provided you raise the rest of the money."

"Do you doubt I can?"

"I believe you can," Tamarand said with obvious amusement. "It will be interesting to see if you will."

CHAPTER 4

"Your head on a platter."

RENATO AWOKE TO a scratchy tongue licking his cheek. He yawned, the yawn becoming a groan, and blinked into the piss-yellow eyes of a hairless cat.

"Ah, Princess," he said, his voice thick and slurred, "can it be that you are jealous?"

The cat made the low gargling noise that passed for purring and strutted about the cabin, sniffing at this and that.

Renato massaged his temple. He felt as if he had been dragged to Davy Jones's Locker and back. He must have given Andre's daughter a magnificent ride.

"Mariette," he said, "you must meet my other princess, the one you have now dethroned."

But the girl was nowhere to be seen, and the only sign she had been there was her wine glass, still nearly full.

Renato ran his tongue about his mouth. It tasted peculiar, and as the fog lifted from his brain the realization struck him like a blow. He had been drugged!

At first in confusion, then with growing alarm, he stumbled to his frock coat and thrust fingers into the pocket, encountering only lint. In panic, he wrenched all the pockets inside-out, and clawed at the coat until it lay mangled at his feet.

Then he burst from the cabin, reached the deck in a single bound, and roared, "Where is she?"

The deckhands nearly jumped overboard in fright, while Mr. Faraday, cool-as-you-please, inquired, "Where is who, Captain?"

"That hell-bitch of Andre's, you dolt! What has become of her?"

"Oh," Faraday said. "Her. She and her father left hours ago, saying you gave orders not to be disturbed. So, ever acceding to Your Lordship's wishes, we were careful to let you rest. Now that you are greatly refreshed, I'm sure you'll be pleased to learn we have entered the Gulf, and are on our way to Texas."

Renato felt his head was about to explode. He gripped Faraday by the neck and lifted him one-handed from the deck.

"You bungler! You fool! They stole my map. You shall turn the ship at once, returning to that cove, and set men after them. I'll have their heads for this—or I shall surely have yours!"

HOURS LATER, BACK in Barataria Bay, Renato was still in an ill humor, and his mood was reflected in the crew. Their movements were lethargic, and he sensed them furtively watching him.

As they left the Gulf, they'd sighted a tempting prize—a well-laden merchantman moving ponderously toward the mouth of the Mississippi. But the stolen map was worth a thousand such prizes, and Renato had been afire to send search gangs ashore. It had now been more than an hour with no word.

Renato sat tensely on the church pew he'd stolen from a Spanish freighter and had installed on his quarterdeck. Angels and cherubs adorned the arms and back of the bench, intermixed with images of crosses, flowers and bleeding hearts. While not in the least devout, he recognized the power in such icons, and it impressed the men to see him amid such heavenly company.

On his lap lay a yellow-backed book, one of many he'd appropriated from passing travelers. On the flyleaf he'd sketched the vague beginnings of a map—all that he could remember from his brief perusal of the original. In his mind's eye, the image had been clear, but as he drew, the lines became blurred, and the features elusive.

That it represented a bay on the Texas coast, he knew, and it was hauntingly familiar. Renato had come to know the inlets and coves of the Gulf coast intimately—but from a ship's deck, not looking down upon them like a god in the sky.

The map depicted a cove shaped rather like an old crone's breast. At the tip of the cove, a sagging nipple pointed directly at a bold black X. There had also been drawings of animals, and a host of connecting lines, but he could no longer envision them.

Hearing the determined tread of Mr. Faraday, Renato turned the book to a random page and pretended to read.

Faraday stopped in front of him. "Captain."

After half a minute of feigned interest, he looked up to find a smirk on the quartermaster's face.

"A good book, Captain?"

Renato was about to deliver a suitable reply when he noted the title atop each page. *The Faerie Queen.*

Renato's cheeks grew warm. He snapped the book shut. "I had no idea you could read."

"Some," Faraday said, not without pride. "Mr. Quayle's been teaching me."

"Quayle reads too? Then I fear civilization is doomed."

"No word from the search parties, Captain. Shall I send more men?"

Renato shook his head. "I am going below. You will notify me the instant there is news."

IN HIS CABIN, Renato hurled the book aside, cursing himself for not noticing the title. It would be the talk of the ship within the hour.

The book hit the bed, spilling a number of newspaper clippings onto the blanket. Renato bent to retrieve them. They were accounts of a battle involving James Bowie, the man he hated most in the world, and he had saved them for future perusal.

Eight years had passed since Bowie had murdered his brother Rayón, but Renato's rage had dimmed not a whit. Even the spectacular vengeance he had visited upon the girl responsible had done nothing to sate him, and he'd followed Bowie's activities, planning for the day they would meet again.

Bowie, the story went, had been one of a large party transported to an unnamed beach near Natchez, Mississippi to witness a duel. The duel itself came to nothing, but in the aftermath, Bowie, a supporter of one combatant, had an altercation with members of the opposite party—first with a man named Crane, then with two brothers and a particular enemy named Major Norris Wright.

Renato scanned the accounts, focusing on underlined passages from various articles to refresh his memory.

Crane observed Bowie with a drawn pistol. He thereby shot him first. Bowie exclaimed, "Crane, you have shot me, and I will kill you if I can." He then drew a large butcher knife and endeavored to put his threat in execution, but was prevented by Crane by a blow from the butt of his pistol, which brought him to his knees.

Good!

Bowie then discovered Major Wright, who had arrived from the woods at the scene of action, in company with the two Blanchards. They both fired, Wright one or two seconds first, and both with effect. Mr. Bowie was shot through the breast.

Even better!

Wright then fled. Bowie drew a knife and pursued him, and when within about ten feet of him, he received a simultaneous fire from the two Blanchards; one of the balls took effect in his thigh and cut him down; observing which, Wright wheeled, when he and Alfred Blanchard drew their sword canes, rushed on and commenced stabbing Bowie who was prostrate.

Renato smiled, savoring the image.

But this, he knew, was where the reading became less pleasant.

Bowie scuffled for some seconds until he had gained his seat. He then reached up, caught Wright by the coat, drew him down on him, and plunged his knife in his bosom, a stab which went to his heart. He died instantly.

Renato tossed the clippings aside in disgust. Some of these

accounts had appeared in *The New Orleans Argus*, which was prestigious enough, but others were from *The Niles Register*, a paper circulated throughout the entire plaguey United States.

That such a brief incident should earn Bowie fame was an insult he could not abide. Renato had been raiding ships and settlements on the Gulf for years. It was his name that should be on men's lips in taverns and clubs. To see this upstart farmer so lionized was the height of injustice.

Soon, Renato vowed, once his treasure had been won, he would exact the terrible vengeance that was his due, and newspapers everywhere would trumpet his achievements.

Came a rap at the cabin door.

"What is it, damn you?"

"Quayle has been sighted, Captain." Faraday's voice. "He's on his way from shore."

"Have him await me on deck."

Slipping a key from around his neck, Renato unlocked the iron strongbox he used as a night table. The box was the most secure spot on the ship, and it was here he kept his most choice possessions. Among them was a note written in his father's own hand—and a delicate miniature of his mother, painted by that same gentleman.

Before inserting the book, he took a last look at the rough map, but had nothing to add. His memory of the rest was entirely gone.

RENATO WAS BACK on deck to see the his rotund bosun clamber over the rail. The man was slack-jawed, slovenly, and dumb as a stump, but he was the one crew member Renato could trust. Quayle knew nothing of loyalty or honor. He knew only fear—and feared Renato far too much to betray him.

"Quayle, you piece of weasel shit, what kept you so long?"

Quayle touched his forelock. "Your everlastin' pardon, Cap'n. Some of the local folk was hard to catch, and then couldn't speak 'til they regained their senses."

"Spit it out, then. What did you learn?"

"Andre was seen, Cap'n. Him and the girl. They wished to buy a pirogue, but no one would admit to selling them one."

A pirogue. Such a small boat could only mean they hoped to slip into the bayous and wind their way to New Orleans.

"And that was all you learned?"

Quayle winced before answering. "No, Cap'n, no. Others allowed as how they might have taken passage on that merchant-man we seen earlier."

"Did anyone see them board?"

"Not for certain sure, Cap'n, but boats was seen to ply back and forth from shore."

So Andre and the bitch had fled into the swamps, bound for New Orleans. Or they had gone aboard that slow-moving brig, with the same intent. That made sense. To seek the treasure, they would need a ship and crew, and those were easiest found in the city.

"Where are the rest of the men?"

"They took boats, if you please, sir, and headed into the bayous."

That covered one possibility. The fat merchantman was one he must deal with himself.

"Mr. Faraday! What are you waiting for? If we don't catch that brig by sunset, I'll have your head on a platter."

CHAPTER 5

"I shall call you 'Jim.'"

BOWIE'S BOOT HEELS rapped the wooden planks as he strode purposefully along the wharf. The dockyards followed the great bend in the Mississippi, and the masts of a hundred ships snaked off into the distance like a forest of barren trees. Officers and overseers barked orders in half a dozen languages. Stripe-shirted sailors strained on ropes, hoisting cargo from ships' holds. Burly dockworkers trundled handcarts to and from waiting wagons.

Bowie hurried on. Each step brought a twinge in his lung, a parting gift from the sword of Major Norris Wright, but he could not be troubled by pain. He must raise ninety thousand dollars in thirty days or his congressional career would be over before it began. He and his brothers owned great tracts of land, but to see both men and overcome their reluctance to sell would consume most of the thirty days.

Collecting debts owed him was equally problematic. The odds of his debtors having funds at hand were slight, and there was every chance he would encounter gentlemen to whom he himself owed money.

At length he spied the red and yellow flag of Spain atop the mast of a brig. A group of gentlemen in tall beaver hats watched liveried grooms struggle to keep four spirited horses in check. Bowie admired their strong, clean lines. They were thoroughbreds all, and coming down the gangplank was the most impressive of the group, a great black stallion with a blaze of white across its face.

The well-dressed gentlemen crowded around, running hands over their flanks. One was arguably a thoroughbred himself, standing head and shoulders above the rest. He wore a camel hair coat of the latest cut and a broad brimmed white hat with an eagle feather.

Bowie hurried forward, executed a brief bow and extended a hand.

"Mr. Neville," he said, mustering all his grace. "My compliments on an exemplary group of animals."

Fletcher Neville chewed his cigar a moment before taking the hand. His grip was firm, but the shake tentative. "Do I know you, sir?"

"Indeed," Bowie said. "My late friend Reuben Kemper introduced us at the track in Alexandria. My name is—"

"Bowie. Yes, I remember. You won a fair amount of my money that day, if I am not mistaken."

"Luck," Bowie said truthfully. The horse he had backed had bested Neville's filly by little more than a nose. "I trust there are no hard feelings."

"Not at all," Neville said. "I admire a man canny enough to beat me at my own game." He removed the cigar from his mouth and pointed it at Bowie. "Though it does make me wary of him in future."

Neville commanded one of the richest cotton plantations in the state, and was known to be somewhat mercurial, prone to invest vast sums on the merest whim. If any man in Louisiana could be Bowie's savior, Fletcher Neville was that man.

"I heard a story about you, Mr. Bowie."

Bowie attempted a smile, dreading the sordid tale that was sure to come.

"I heard," Neville said, "that you are running for Congress."

Bowie's smile became genuine. "I am indeed. And I intend to win."

Neville studied him critically.

The man's neatly coiffed black hair and strong, jutting jaw made Bowie uncomfortably aware of his own unruly red locks and dimpled chin.

"What sort of congressman would you make, Mr. Bowie?"

"A great one. And one who would not forget his friends."

"Hm. If true, it would certainly distinguish you from that scoundrel Brent. I suppose you would not be averse to accepting a modest donation to your campaign."

Bowie could not believe his luck. Neville was making his case for him. "You are more right than you know, sir. Truth to tell, it was for that reason I sought you out today."

Neville turned to the tweedy, bespectacled man at his shoulder. "Levin, see that Mr. Bowie receives a check in the amount of…" he twirled his cigar in the air, "five thousand dollars." Then, catching Bowie's eye, he raised an eyebrow at what he found there, and said, "No, make it ten."

"You are most generous, sir. So generous that it pains me to admit my need is considerably greater." Seeing Neville's eyes grow hard, he rushed ahead. "I ask no further donation, of course, but if you could see your way clear to a personal loan, I am confident that within a few months I would be able to—"

The sound of a whip crack brought both their heads around. Opposite the dock, before a tavern whose sign read *Satan's Crypt*, stood a burly giant with a braided horsewhip in his hand. Facing him in the street, next to a wagon laden with kegs, was one of the tallest black men Bowie had ever seen. The fellow wore only white-duck trousers and a red rag about his neck, and his chest shone like a newly polished riding boot.

"How much?" Neville demanded.

Bowie found his mouth dry. Now that the moment had arrived, he could barely form the words.

"How much do you need? Clearly you came here with an amount in mind."

The number was barely more than a whisper. "Ninety thousand."

Neville raised an eyebrow. "You presume a great deal on so slight an acquaintance."

"If I overreach," Bowie said, "it is only due to zeal."

The whip cracked again. No blow had yet been struck, but Bowie could see it coming. The slave betrayed not the slightest trace of fear. And with the girth of two men, the man with the whip was clearly one to be feared. A well-greased mustache flared out onto mottled cheeks, and thick brown stubble covered his fleshy jaw. Bowie knew him to be the tavern's proprietor, a man he'd heard addressed as Heckmann.

"Move, you black jackanapes! That wine does me no good sitting on a wagon."

Bowie turned away. He was no stranger to slavery, but he had never tolerated brutality. Still, this was no time to involve himself in the troubles of others.

He found Neville watching him.

"Well, Mr. Bowie, you do not lack brass, I'll grant you that. And no one can accuse you of doing things in small measure. But not all I've heard is favorable. I believe you have earned quite a reputation as a brawler."

"I'm a new man," Bowie said. "I've put violence behind me now."

"I see. And exactly when did this reformation begin? Yesterday, perhaps, right after you almost slit a man's throat in a respectable hotel?"

Bowie could offer no defense.

"Is that how you intend to conduct yourself in the halls of Congress?"

"Certainly not," Bowie said, hoping that was true.

"I must say I am not convinced. On the other hand, a knife at the throat may be exactly what some of our legislators need, if applied with moderation and restraint."

"Those," Bowie said solemnly, "are qualities I sincerely aspire to."

Neville eyed him steadily. "For ninety thousand dollars, even in the form of a loan, I would expect a certain allegiance."

Bowie pursed his lips. This felt like selling another piece of his soul. But a seat in Congress was practically a license to print money.

"As you may know," Neville said, "I also have interests in Tennessee. I backed a fellow there in the last election—a backwoodsman named Crockett—because I thought he could be useful." He gave Bowie a piercing look. "He has now decided he is his *own man*. I should hate for that to happen again."

The whip cracked a third time. Not the sharp warnings he had heard earlier, but the thick, obscene slap of a quirt biting into human flesh. Bowie turned, wincing at the angry welt across the black man's chest.

Heckmann's whip shot forward again like a great snake.

Bowie flinched, hand straying without thought toward his hip.

But as the lash raked the slave's shoulder, a black hand shot up. Like a trained serpent, the whip coiled around the slave's arm, and Heckmann was caught like a fish on a hook.

Over Bowie's shoulder, Neville said quietly, "The fool."

Bowie wondered which man he meant.

The slave's courage was impressive, if not mere stupidity. And no matter what Heckmann did next, he would lose. If he killed the man, he would be out a great deal of money. But if he did not, his power over this and any other slave would be forever forfeit.

Heckmann yanked a long-barreled pistol from his belt. "Release that whip, or I'll splatter your brains on the street."

"Shoot, then. I shall suffer no further indignities from you." The slave's voice was rich and weighty like an orator's, and smacked of aristocracy.

"Shoot," Neville said softly. "Shoot and be done with it."

The wharf had grown still. Sailors, dockworkers and slaves alike stood frozen, waiting to see what Heckmann would do.

What he did was sputter. "Wh-Why you damned sassy ape!" His arm shook as he strove to level his pistol on the black man's chest.

Bowie sprang forward, covering the yards between them at a gallop. Heckmann's pistol exploded as Bowie slammed into him, and the ball crashed through the staves of a barrel. Wine gushed as Heckmann went sprawling to the cobblestone street.

The man was up in an instant, hand reaching for another pistol.

Bowie's blade flashed from its sheath, catching the morning sun. Before Heckmann could bring the gun to bear, Bowie had him by the throat, the knife biting into his chest.

Heckmann glared into Bowie's eyes. "Who the devil are you, to meddle in my affairs?"

"A man who hates bullies. But for the record, the name is Bowie. James Bowie."

Heckmann's face drained of color. "I don't care who you are. No man stands between me and my property."

Bowie smiled grimly. "I see two possible solutions. One, I stick you like a pig and foul the river with your corpse." The blade dug deeper. "Or two, I relieve you of your problem."

"So that's the way of it." Heckmann sneered. "You'll either murder me or steal my slave."

"Killing a snake is hardly murder. But it needn't come to that. I'll give you a fair price."

When Heckmann ran out of curses, a crafty gleam came into his eyes. "He's worth at least a thousand."

"He may have been once," Bowie said, "but he's been ill-treated. You'll take four hundred."

"Four! That's robbery!"

"If it's more than your life is worth, so be it."

The man's eyes went dull as stones. "Six hundred cash, and not a penny less."

"Five," said Bowie, "and you'll accept a note. I assure you I'm good for it."

With a great scowl, Heckmann agreed, and Bowie lowered the knife. From the onlookers came a smattering of cheers, but an equal number of jeers. And as if a spell had been broken, the dock returned to life.

Bowie's eyes sought Neville, but all he caught was the back of the man's jacket disappearing into a carriage. An instant later the carriage and horse trailers went rumbling off down the wharf.

Bowie watched them go. The ninety thousand was now certainly lost to him, and likely the promised ten thousand as well.

He turned to face the slave.

The black man stood as if rooted to the street, the tail of the whip still coiled about his arm. "You will most assuredly regret that," he said in his orator's voice. There was no threat in the words. He was merely stating a fact, one he seemed to find amusing.

Bowie grinned tightly. "I already do. What's your name, fellow?"

The man straightened, making himself even taller. "I am Mr. Samuel Frost Gideon."

"An impressive name. And you're an impressive man, Sam. But I've no use for a slave. I'm granting you your freedom."

The man's head drew back. "I prefer to be addressed as 'Mr. Gideon'. And my freedom is far too valuable to be tendered upon a whim. Until I can earn it, I shall not accept it at all."

Bowie felt his heat rising, but detected a faint smile on the black man's lips. The rascal was baiting him. Shaking his head, Bowie emitted a gruff laugh. "I'll play your game, for the moment. I shall call you Mr. Gideon, and you shall call me—"

"'Jim,'" the black man said firmly. "I shall call you 'Jim.'"

CHAPTER 6

"Can you not even die properly?"

T HE TWELVE-POUND BOW-CHASER
boomed a warning shot, sending a quiver through *L'In-trepide's* deck. Renato smiled as the iron ball burst through the smoke, clearing the bow of the other ship by scant yards before geysering into the sea.

He stroked the neck of the hairless cat perched on his shoulder. "What say you, Princess? Will she fight or flee?"

The brig was a two-masted merchantman, her square white sails climbing high into the azure sky. She rode low in the water, signifying a heavy cargo, perhaps sugar or cacao.

"Your silence speaks wisdom, my dear," he told the cat. "We shall have them either way."

Raising his gold-mounted telescope—inscribed to its previous owner by the King of Spain—Renato brought the brig into focus. She bore only three small guns per side, no match for *L'Intrepide's* six 9-pounders. And instead of preparing to fight for their lives, her slack-jawed crewmen stood idle, awaiting their captain's decision.

The cat's needle-sharp claws pierced the wool of Renato's coat. "What is it now, Mr. Faraday?"

The voice behind him said, "Oh! Um. Your pardon, Captain. I—I mean the men—have concerns."

"Which is it? You—or the men?"

Faraday looked pointedly at the other ship. "She's American."

Renato eyed the stars and stripes flying from the brig's mainmast. "A wondrous deduction, Mr. Faraday. However did you accomplish it?"

"It troubles the men," Faraday said. "The American navy has largely ignored us of late, but such an attack may force their hand."

Renato bristled. "You think I fear the navy?"

"It's not a matter of fear," Faraday said. "They're bad for business. Besides, we don't know Andre and the girl are aboard."

"And we don't know they are not." Renato snapped the telescope shut. "Mark me well, Mr. Faraday. I will do whatever it takes to recover that map, and no amount of carping from you or the men will dissuade me."

It had been a full day since the theft, and the bitter tang of the drugged wine was with him still. His rage had grown stronger by the hour, to the point he now desired vengeance nearly as much as the treasure itself.

A flurry of activity erupted on the brig's deck, as the Americans rushed for their guns. Their captain had chosen to fight. Renato's lips curved into a grin. "We will put a full broadside into her rigging. But take care. I wish to capture, not sink her."

At Faraday's order, the pirates scurried to their stations. "A surly lot," Renato whispered to the cat. "But we require their services, like Faraday's, for a short while longer."

The ship came about to the music of ports creaking open and guns rumbling out. The Americans had run out their own guns as well, but the brig's movements were sluggish. A sleek schooner like *L'Intrepide* could dance rings around such a heavy-laden scow.

Renato could now read the faded letters on the merchantman's hull. *Old Hickory.* Named for the so-called hero of the Battle of New Orleans. Renato snorted. He himself had been as much responsible for that victory as the horse-faced General Jackson, and what had it got him? A pardon for past crimes and not a penny more. Little wonder he and his mates had soon returned to piracy.

"Starboard guns," Faraday bellowed, "fire!"

The three 9-pounders erupted in a single explosion that shook the deck, and the cat disappeared into the hold. Renato peered expectantly through the smoke, but a moment later fell to swearing. *L'Intrepide* had risen on a sudden swell, and with the guns already aimed high, the chain-shot sailed harmlessly over *Old Hickory*'s topsails.

"Again!" he roared. "Quickly!"

Wheels rumbled and curses flew as the men heaved the guns back into position. The delay allowed *Old Hickory* to bring her own weapons to bear, but Renato sneered his contempt as her balls tore up the sea more than twenty yards short of his hull.

L'Intrepide's guns answered in a rolling thunder, and a moment later, the brig's mainsail came loose from the mast.

Renato gloated.

Orange flame billowed from *Old Hickory*'s side. The first ball whistled high over *L'Intrepide*'s deck, tearing a small hole in the mainsail. The second shattered the rail near the stern, and a man screamed.

Renato sniffed. Gunners such as those would not last a day under his command. He was still gloating when a third ball scorched the air above his head, gusting his hat to the deck. Cursing at the broken plume, he nearly fell as the ship took a sudden lurch to leeward. He spun to see the tiller roaming free. They were adrift!

Renato raced for the quarterdeck. The helmsman was nowhere in sight, and he found the tiller whipping about like a thing alive. A hideous scream brought his head about. Near the shattered rail lay the helmsman, flopping about like a giant tuna. The man clutched a bloody stump that moments before had been his left leg.

Renato stared in horror as blood spurted from the stump, spraying his own silk breeches.

"Damn your eyes!" he snarled. "Can you not even die properly?" Leaning heavily on the tiller, he thrust out a boot and rolled the wretch over the side.

L'Intrepide's guns began firing at will. It started well, as a ball tore through the American's foremast. Then *Old Hickory* rose on a swell, exposing her hull below the waterline, and Renato cursed as two shocking great holes appeared in the brig's belly.

Old Hickory shuddered before falling heavily back to the sea, water already rushing into her hold. Knowing they were doomed, the Americans raised stricken faces to the pirate ship and scurried away like frightened chickens.

Renato swung the tiller hard to starboard, and the schooner began to close the distance. "Mr. Faraday! Is it too much trouble for you to keep a man at the helm? See to it at once, then prepare for boarding!"

As the ships came side and side, *L'Intrepide's* men snatched up swords and belaying pins. Grenades and smoke bombs arced over the narrowing gap, fueling the chaos on the other deck.

"A hundred British crowns," Renato bawled, "to the man who brings me Andre and the girl!"

Grappling hooks sailed out to snag the brig's rail, and the ships crunched together, a plaintive shriek of wood upon wood. Screaming their bloodlust, Renato's men flooded onto *Old Hickory's* deck. A handful of Americans showed fight, but the rest hurled themselves over the rails, preferring sharks to the wild-eyed buccaneers.

The merchantman rode ever lower in the water, but the lure of Renato's gold drove the pirates on. Faraday and a dozen others disappeared through the hatch, and Renato held his breath in anticipation.

Almost at once, pirates clambered back onto deck, all jabbering at once in a mad chorus of curses. Some held cloths to their noses, and a few staggered to the rails and vomited into the sea.

When Faraday himself appeared, Renato drew a pistol and blasted a shot into the air above their heads. All conversation ceased.

"Mr. Faraday! What is it? Have you found our fugitives?"

"No, Captain. They are not aboard." The man spoke with a hint of rebuke. "And there is no cargo worth the taking."

Renato choked back his anger. It would not do to challenge Faraday now.

"What, then, made her captain so eager to evade us?"

Faraday glanced down into the hold, his features wrinkling in disgust. Then he squared his shoulders and growled a single word.

"Slaves."

CHAPTER 7

"God's own terror."

"JIM BOY, IT pains the soul to hear ye don't trust old Andre."

Bowie watched the man drain his tankard and slam it to the rough oak table. Andre's one good eye reflected the burning coals of the tavern's stone fireplace. He did not look at all pained.

"You're a pirate," Bowie said. "Name one man fool enough to trust you."

Andre wiped foamy lips on the back of a sleeve. "A livin' man, you mean?"

"Yes."

"Does me brother count?"

"You don't have a brother."

Andre raked gnarled fingers through his beard, and a spotted weevil poked its shiny head tentatively to the surface.

"What about me daughter?"

"*You* have a daughter?"

Without looking, the old pirate caught the weevil expertly between thumb and forefinger. He held it close to his one good eye, examining it like a rare gem, then popped it into his mouth and crunched with great gusto.

Bowie's tongue curled. He was already regretting this distraction. Upon leaving the wharf with his unwanted slave, the man had hailed him in the street, wishing to offer a proposal. Andre represented a past best forgotten, and being seen with him could soil Bowie's already damaged reputation. But Andre had been one of the few to show him friendship on his visits to Lafitte's island, and he deserved the courtesy of a hearing.

They sat now in The Black Ship, a waterfront dive catering to dockhands, sailors and cutpurses, and Bowie was disturbed by the realization he felt more at home with such men than with politicians and plantation owners. The slave Sam—Bowie refused to think of him as *Mr. Gideon*—had been left to his own devices in the alley. With luck, the man would simply wander away.

"I recall a time, Jim Boy, when you was not so choosy as to your companions."

"Men grow," Bowie said. "Men change."

"Not I, me lad. I'm the same as ever was."

Bowie shook his head. "You're fatter. And you smell worse."

"And you're tricked out like a window dummy. If not for that cavernous cleft in your chin, I'd not have known ye."

Bowie bristled. "This suit was fitted for me in Washington City—just last month—by the personal tailor of John Quincy Adams."

"The name's familiar. Some great criminal, is he not?"

"He's the President," Bowie said, and when the man merely squinted, added, "of the United States."

Andre nodded. "As I said." He raised a hand to signal more ale.

"Truth, old man. Why are you here?"

Andre glanced up over Bowie's shoulder, face lit like a man given a reprieve.

"Another round, gents?"

A flame-haired barmaid leaned a hip against the table, smiling down upon them.

"Angela is the perfect female. She always knows what a man wants." Andre grinned up at her. "Set 'em up, darlin'. Me friend here can well afford it."

The barmaid turned crinkling eyes on Bowie. "I know what *you* want, too. You want this old canker to pay for his own."

"You're a mind reader," he told her, "but I am used to disappointments." He pressed a coin into the woman's palm.

As she swayed away, humming to herself, Bowie held Andre's eye. He knew the man well enough to expect only scraps of truth, but this time he sensed something serious behind the banter.

"Talk," he said. "What do you want of me?"

The merriment went out of Andre's eye. "I need help, and that's gospel. I'm after a treasure too big to handle by meself."

Bowie could imagine no treasure large enough to compel a man like Andre to share. "That part of my life is over," he said. "I'm going to be a congressman."

Andre snorted. "And what is that, but an overdressed pirate?"

Bowie could not help but grin. "Not a great deal, old friend. But these men plunder on a much grander scale."

"No grander than this, Jim Boy. Nothing is."

"Even if that were true, why come to me?"

"I need a fightin' man, Jim. You was always that, but now I hear you're God's own terror. That story of your fight up Natchez way, it was…"

"Exaggerated. What's all this about treasure?"

"I have a map, Jim Boy, a map leading to a mountain of gold. And others wants to steal it from me."

"And did you happen to steal if from them first?"

Andre looked shocked, confirming Bowie's suspicion.

"Tell me the rest of it, you old pirate. And quickly. Why do you need me?"

Andre's voice became a whisper. "It's them damned Kronks. Most men piss themselves at the thought of them blasted cannibals. But not you, Jim Boy, not you."

"You're going into Karankawa country? That's madness. No treasure is worth that."

"This one is, Jim. It's more than a man could dream of. Lafitte called it the richest of the ages."

Bowie considered this. Andre been close to Lafitte, but if all the tales could be believed, Lafitte's treasures lined the Gulf coast from Louisiana to Texas and around the tip of Yucatán.

The barmaid returned, leaving two more tankards, and Andre's was empty in an instant.

Bowie pushed his bench back. "You waste my time, old man. I have much to do."

"Wait, Jim, please. I'll show ye the map."

"All right. Show me."

"I don't have it on me. It's with me daughter, for safekeepin'."

"Your daughter? You truly have a daughter?" The notion that an old reprobate like Andre could sire a daughter almost passed belief. And the image Bowie conjured up of such a crea-ture—squat-bodied and squinty-eyed, with a twisted potato of a nose—made Bowie shudder. "Never mind. Who did you steal it from?"

Andre mumbled a name, too low to catch.

"Who?"

Andre raised his eyes, and Bowie saw fear there. The old man's mouth opened again, but before he could speak, the tavern doors crashed back against the wall.

On one side of the wide doorway, a pug-faced pirate with a wide mustache cocked the hammer of a Spanish blunderbuss. On the other, a bald giant cleaved the air with a cutlass.

Between them strode a tall man in a faded blue frock coat. Each hand carried a long-barreled dueling pistol.

The barmaid said, "Welcome, gentlemen. I'll thank you to keep your weapons to yourself during your stay."

The tall pirate showed his teeth in a travesty of a smile. Some-thing about the man tugged at Bowie's memory. It was the eyes he remembered—soulless eyes, dead as knotholes in a board.

As the dead eyes touched his face and moved on, Bowie

turned to check on Andre, finding he'd slid out of sight under the table.

When he turned back, the tall pirate was aiming a pistol barrel like an accusing finger.

"You, sir, are somehow familiar. Who are you and what is your business here?"

Grasping his cane, Bowie stood to shield Andre. "I might ask you the same."

"We are merely innocent travelers, seeking another such as ourselves. Perhaps you have seen him. A short, wide, troll of a fellow with a wooden eye and a beard full of maggots."

"I've seen no man with maggots in his beard," Bowie said, hoping that was true. "I suggest you seek him elsewhere." As he spoke, Bowie toyed with the silver pommel of his cane.

The tall man said, "I place you now. You are Jim Bowie, the celebrated knife fighter."

"You are mistaken. I am James Bowie, candidate for U.S. Congress."

The bald man let out a lusty snort. "Christ, Nacio! This bleeder's nothin' but a fop. Why are we wasting time on him?"

Nacio. Bowie remembered him now. One of the many villains he'd met on Lafitte's island.

"Don't let the fancy dress deceive you." Nacio's tone was faintly mocking. "He has killed many men with that knife of his, including Renato's brother Rayón."

Renato. A cold fist closed about Bowie's heart. His right hand itched for the knife, but he fought to resist.

The pug with the blunderbuss sucked in his breath. "He done Rayón? He's *that* one? Cor! Maybe we should—"

"Shut your hole, Darby." Nacio addressed the tavern's clientele. "The *congressman* will remain. The rest would be wise to depart. Now!"

Almost as one, a dozen odd men slid from their seats and

skittered toward the exit. Angela gave Nacio an indignant look and vanished through the doorway behind the bar.

The bald pirate with the cutlass began circling to Bowie's right, while the man with the blunderbuss edged down the bar on his left. Bowie eyed the funnel-shaped barrel of the blunderbuss without affection. The gun was designed for a huge .75 caliber ball. That alone was enough to blow a man in half, but they were often loaded with spikes and nails.

"Nacio!" The bald man shouted. "Andre is here!"

"Then take care," Nacio replied. "We'll be paid handsomely for him—alive. And be wary of Mr. Bowie's fancy cane. I suspect it conceals a blade."

Bowie exhibited a tight smile. "This simple thing?" He twirled the cane as if for Nacio's inspection. "It is innocence itself." Pressing a hidden catch, he sent the weighted shaft hurtling like a javelin, spilling the man with the blunderbuss over backwards.

Bowie spun about, the slim steel sword flashing in his hand. The bald pirate crashed through the tables like a buffalo, cutlass already slashing toward Bowie's head. Sparks stung his cheeks as the two blades clashed. Then Bowie stared at the six-inch stub of his sword as the longer portion clattered to the floor.

Pug-faced Darby was stooping to retrieve the blunderbuss. Bowie must finish one of these men quickly or be caught between them.

The bald man decided the question with a bellowing charge, cutlass poised like a cleaver. Bowie sprang at him, arm raised as if to catch the blade on his broken sword. But at the last instant, he fell to one knee, the cutlass singing over his head, and thrust the tip of his shortened blade deep between the man's ribs.

Bowie whirled to find Darby approaching, the blunderbuss riding before him like a small cannon.

Nacio, meanwhile, had flushed Andre from beneath the table, and the old man was putting up a bold front with his rapier.

The call of the knife—that sweetest of siren songs—was stronger than ever. By force of will, Bowie drew a small pistol from his coat. The gun was not accurate at more than several feet, but it was a gentleman's weapon.

As Darby advanced, Bowie cocked and fired in one smooth motion. Powder flashed, followed by a loud metallic click. A misfire. Then Darby's eyes darted to something over Bowie's shoulder.

Bowie dodged as the heavy cutlass bit deep into the tavern floor. Behind him towered the bald man, Bowie's broken sword still protruding from his chest.

There was no time for amazement. Bowie flung himself at Darby. He had one hand around the man's neck and the other diverting the blunderbuss when the blast came, and the bald giant's head vanished in a shower of blood and brains.

Then Darby went berserk, and it was all Bowie could do to avoid his gnashing teeth. Bearing down with both hands, he squeezed Darby's neck until his eyes popped from their sockets, and he heard a sharp crack.

"That will be enough!" The voice was Angela's, and Bowie saw her level a pistol at Nacio. The dead-eyed pirate had Andre by the scruff of the neck, dragging him toward the door.

Nacio raised his own pistol and the two guns spoke together. Bowie saw Nacio duck, while his ball caught Angela full in the face and flung her backward.

Head roaring with blood, Bowie charged like a bull. The knife was in his hand, swinging back in great glittering arc. As Nacio's next ball screamed past his ear, he brought the blade up from his knees and buried it to the guard under the pirate's ribs.

Powered by rage, the blow lifted Nacio off his feet, arms flailing helplessly at his sides. Then, as the man's weight returned to the blade, Bowie ripped upward before thrusting the gutted remains to the floor.

Heart pounding, he rushed behind the bar, and stopped short, riveted by the sight. Angela lay in a pool of red, one eye having devoured the ball from Nacio's gun.

Fire still raging within him, Bowie wiped his blade on Nacio's coat and slammed the knife into its sheath. He found Andre leaning heavily on the bar and steered him back to the table. Remarkably, their tankards had not been upset in the fight.

"Sit." Bowie's voice was deathly cold. The rage still burned within him, but he was in control. Just. "Those were Lafitte's men. Is that old devil really dead?"

"Did ye hear the story of him sunk by a British sloop off the Gulf of Honduras?"

Bowie nodded. "It sounded false."

Andre returned the nod. "The truth of it is, he lived another three years and died of disease on the *Isla Mujeres*."

"The Island of Women?"

"Aye. Saw the grave meself. Fitting, is it not?"

"Then who set those men on you? Who did you steal the map from?"

Andre shook like a man with ague. "I swear, Jim, I thought I'd lost them in the bayous."

Bowie slammed a hand to the tabletop, making the tankards dance. "Who?"

Andre worked his mouth, but the name was too low for Bowie to catch.

"Who??"

"It's Renato," Andre croaked. "He has an oar in this too."

"Renato." A flood of images swept through Bowie's mind. Campeachy and the Maison Rouge. A woman, young, blonde and saucy. Renato's brother strapped to a log with blood spurting from his jugular. And finally, the scarred face of Renato himself, crimson with fury. "Where is he?"

"I don't know, Jim, on my mother's soul. But he's after me, and he's sworn you'll feed the sharks to avenge his brother."

"That was a fair fight," Bowie said. "What Renato did to the girl afterwards is another matter entirely."

Andre's eyes grew wide, and he upset his bench in his haste to back away.

The knife was out of its sheath again. The heavy blade came thundering down into the table, shooting splinters into the air. Foaming ale flowed from Bowie's upset tankard, spattering the floor.

"I have an election to win," Bowie said. "But once that's done—we'll see who feeds the sharks."

CHAPTER 8

"He carried their heads off in a sack!"

L'INTREPIDE LAY AT anchor in the narrow inlet where she had spent the night. Tall palms danced lazily in the morning breeze, bringing the mingled scents of gardenias and orange blossoms. It was a welcome break after the bitter, sweetish stench of the slave ship. Renato had ordered the clothing of all concerned thoroughly washed, then had the schooner's decks scoured with lye.

The ship was quiet but for the muted chorus of wails and moans drifting up from the cargo hold. The noise had not stopped since the previous afternoon, when the slaves had been rescued from the merchant ship. The pirates had time to free only eight of the estimated four hundred crammed horizontally into the shallow slave deck of *Old Hickory*, and the sound those left behind made as she slipped beneath the waves had been picked up by the ungrateful wretches aboard *L'Intrepide*, as if they echoed the tormented souls of the damned.

Renato shook the thoughts from his head. It was a slave's lot to suffer. This was surely as Fate intended, or it would not be so. If the group in the hold continued that hellish noise much longer, he would have their lips sewn shut.

Renato had hoped to awaken to the news that one of his search gangs had returned. Three gangs were out, working their way up the bayous toward New Orleans. Andre's was a familiar face there, and most men would sell their own mothers for the price of the reward.

He cast a final look at the shore. "We've waited too long, Faraday. Prepare to make sail."

"As you command, Captain. But you should know, the men are uneasy."

"And what have they to be uneasy about?"

"The slaves, Captain. They are eager to be quit of them."

"It has only been one night."

"One night too many," Faraday said with heat. "What with the smell, and that incessant caterwauling, the men got little rest last night."

Renato laid a hand on his sword hilt. "If any desires me to sing him a lullaby, he may come forward now."

Faraday's voice rose in pitch. "Another night like the last, and we may face a mutiny."

"These men have run slaves before. They'll cease complaining when their pockets are lined with coins."

Faraday remained defiant. "Many feel the risks are now too great. Some have even come to feel that slavery is… wrong."

"Wrong? A crew of bloody pirates arguing ethics?" Renato peered closely at Faraday. "You're not one of those ridiculous abolitionists, are you?"

Faraday's face darkened, but he made no answer.

"Er, Cap'n Renato, sir?" The squeaky voice belonged to Quayle.

Renato turned, anticipating his breakfast of fresh fruit and Madeira, then noticed the man was empty-handed and quivering.

"What's wrong with you, Quayle? Where the devil is my breakfast?"

"It's the fruit, Cap'n. It's ah, gone."

"Gone?"

"It's vanished, Cap'n. Disappeared. All of it."

In a single motion, Renato grasped the man by his lapels and lifted him off the deck. "All of it?"

"Aye, sir!" Quayle's feet beat the air spasmodically, like a man with the St. Vitus dance.

"There were at least two crates of oranges. A bushel of apples. Sacks of bananas. How could it be gone?"

Quayle appeared about to expire from terror. Renato dropped him squirming on the deck and turned his wrath on Faraday. "Were those slaves not shackled and guarded?"

Now it was Faraday's turn to squirm. "We've no shackles 'aboard, Captain, but they were well secured with ropes. No guard seemed necessary."

"Not necessary. And yet a vast amount of fruit has vanished in the night. You will get to the bottom of this at once, Faraday. If there is so much as a seed of evidence our black guests were responsible for this pilferage, I will hold you personally accountable."

Faraday stood, teeth clenched, his body quivering like a bowstring.

"Go."

As Faraday marched stiffly toward the cargo hatch, Renato could not resist a grin. It would be worth an entire shipload of fruit to see the impudent fellow get his comeuppance.

A pistol shot echoed hollowly in the narrow inlet. On the beach stood three men. An evil-looking bunch, Renato thought. Obviously three of his own.

He took up his speaking trumpet. "You found them?"

One man cupped his hands and shouted a word that could only have been "No."

"Then go. Return when you have."

The man shouted again, and the final word seemed to be "News."

Renato thrust the trumpet at Quayle. "Send a boat for them. And pray their news is good."

IN HIS CABIN, Renato dropped into an overstuffed chair and chased dark thoughts around in his skull.

Damn Faraday and his talk of slaves! The risk of slave running had risen in the past few years, it was true, but so had the profits to be realized. Other conditions had improved as well. In Renato's youth, slavers had cut their journeys short by scooping up hapless blacks from all the isles of the Caribbean—including even Haiti. Renato had seen the disastrous effect the witch doctors from that scabrous country had on his crewmates. He himself did not believe in such superstitious nonsense, but he had seen entire ships lost due to the poisonous fear of Voodoo.

Thankfully, slavers had learned to steer wide of the cursed place, finding more complaisant pickings in Africa.

Still, the blacks on board *L'Intrepide* were becoming a distraction. Renato would gladly dump the troublesome bastards into the sea if he had not already taken a stand. He could not show weakness by acceding to the demands of his crew, especially when Faraday might be seen as their champion.

Life had been much simpler when he was a mere freebooter, with nothing but drink, women, and booty on his mind.

After a timid rapping sounded on the door, Quayle ushered in the leader of the search party.

A beefy man with his arms covered in tattoos snatched off his hat and touched his forelock.

"Your name is Bendix." Renato made the name an accusation.

"Aye, Cap'n."

"Why, against my orders, have you presumed to return empty-handed?"

"We brings news, Cap'n. Of Andre, and Nacio."

"Speak, then, and pray it pleases me."

Bendix rushed to get out the words. "We got the story from a stevedore, who had it from a keelboatman, who—"

"Bugger that! What have you learned?"

"Nacio's dead, Cap'n. The others as well. And more."

"Small loss. What of Andre and the girl?"

"Well, Cap'n, a stumpy one-eyed pirate were seen at the Black

Ship tavern. Andre, for certain. But you'll never guess who else was there."

"Bendix, do you have a death wish?"

The man's rabbit-like eyes said he did not. " 'Twere that famous knife fighter," he said quickly. "Big Jim Bowie."

"Bowie!" Renato spat the name. The face of his dead brother flashed before him, and his head swam with blood.

Bendix rushed on. "The way we heared it, Bowie was set upon by a dozen or more pirates, and the battle raged until a river of blood ran into the street." Warming to his tale, Bendix acted out the part of Bowie, slashing the air with his crumpled hat. "The pirates came at him like a pack of hungry wolves, but Bowie was a demon! His mighty blade was everywhere at once. He lopped off their heads and gutted 'em like hogs. Then, after hanging their entrails from the rafters, he carried their heads off in a sack!"

Renato stared, galled beyond belief. "These dozen bodies. You saw them yourself?"

Bendix shook his head. "Most of the bodies was gone. Nacio was there, with what remained of Darby and Mendez, and Nacio himself were split open like a—"

"Never mind. Had they truly been disemboweled?"

"Well, not exactly, Cap'n, but—"

"And were their heads missing?"

Bendix scratched his own bedraggled scalp. "Why no, Cap'n, else we wouldn't have knowed them."

Renato rolled his eyes. "And what of Andre and Bowie?"

"Why, we don't know, Cap'n. They was gone, and no one could tell us nothing."

"And you heard nothing of the map, or the wench Mariette?"

Bendix grinned and bobbed his head. "That's so, Cap'n!" The imbecile seemed relieved to be able to answer in the affirmative.

Renato frowned. Much as this man deserved a flogging, there was a nugget of treasure here. Bowie had become a man of note, and tongues would wag at his passing, making Andre all the easier to find. And Bowie's involvement smacked of destiny. Renato was being shown the hand of Fate, and would not squander the gift.

Footsteps sounded on the stairs, followed by a knock.

"Come, Faraday."

The quartermaster's face was pasty white, like a man condemned.

"So," Renato said almost happily, "did the blacks eat our fruit?"

"I don't believe so." Faraday's voice was flat. "I questioned them quite closely. They speak a sort of pidgin French when they want to."

"Then surely they saw the culprits."

"They spoke of faint noises and flitting shadows. But that's not what I came to tell you."

"You mean you've found the fruit?"

"No. It's not about the fruit. It's about the slaves."

"Then out with it, damn you. What about them?"

"I asked where they were from," Faraday said, and stopped, his eyes glassy as the windows of a vacant house.

"And what answer did they give?" Renato said, acid in his voice. "London, Paris, Constantinople?"

Faraday's head rocked repeatedly from side to side, as if denying the truth of his reply.

"Haiti," he said. "They are from Haiti."

CHAPTER 9

"I choose knives."

BOWIE SLOUCHED AT a table on the walk before
a bistro on the Rue Charteris. In his hand was a half empty
tumbler of bourbon, and between his teeth a half-smoked cigar.
He was not normally a smoker, nor was he overfond of hard spirits, but he knew men who swore by both as aids to thinking, and
present circumstances called for extreme measures.

Thus far, the experiment had yielded naught but a warm
stomach and a dry throat. The more liquor he consumed, the
further he seemed from an idea, but the less he cared.

His fundraising skills left much to be desired. So far, he had
succeeded only in spending five hundred dollars he did not have
on a slave he did not want, while further sullying his already
questionable reputation.

The unwanted slave sat against a lamppost at the edge of the
walk. He appeared to be sleeping, but Bowie suspected he was
dreaming up further mischief. It would be wise to dispose of him
as quickly as possible, but given this man's temperament, forcing
him back into service would be tantamount to a death penalty.

As if the fellow sensed Bowie's thinking, he chose that
moment to speak.

"What compelled you to do it, Jim?"

Buying time for thought, Bowie said, "Do what?"

"You clearly have no desire to own a slave, so why did you
rescue me from that vulgarian?"

"If you were a free man, I'd tell you. Are you ready to accept your freedom?"

This brought a deep laugh. "When the time comes, Jim, you shall be the first to know."

Why *had* he done it, Bowie asked himself. The answer took him back eight years, to his first meeting with Jean Lafitte. He wished now he could erase all that followed, but he'd been young, unworldly, and impatient to make his fortune.

The Bowie brothers, having seen their plantations all but destroyed by a hurricane, were desperately in need of cash. When they learned of Lafitte's operation on Galveston Island, a place he called Campeachy, they seized upon a plan to reclaim their fortunes.

Many of the ships captured by Lafitte's captains carried slaves, but the difficulty was in getting them to willing buyers in the States. While slavery was legal in the South, the importation of new slaves was not, and the American Navy had grown ever more watchful.

Eyes full of dollar signs, the Bowies purchased slaves in bulk from Lafitte, then transported them by various means into Mississippi or Louisiana. Once within U.S. borders they turned the slaves in as captured contraband, and collected a finder's fee. The slaves were then put on public auction, where the Bowies used the reward money to purchase them legally, and sold them to plantation owners for many times their original investment. Their first such venture had netted in excess of ten thousand dollars.

At first, while saddened at the fate of the unfortunate blacks, young Jim had consoled himself with the fact they were better off than if left to the savage mercies of the pirates. In the Bowies' hands, they were at least well fed and properly treated. But that bit of self-deceit could not withstand the soul-crushing misery he witnessed, and he was soon plagued by a level of self-loathing he had never dreamed possible.

Though slavery was a way of life in the South, he was now

thoroughly disgusted with it. And it was this revulsion, more than anything, that prompted his ill-timed "purchase" of Sam from the tavernkeeper, dashing his chances with Neville.

A voice interrupted his thoughts, and Bowie blinked to see two Creole dandies striding past the cafe. Bowie had encountered many of their ilk, and found them, as a class, to be perfectly useless. Though born and raised here in New Orleans, they presumed superiority by way of their French or Spanish bloodlines, and devoted their lives exclusively to pleasurable pursuits.

One man nudged the other, and Bowie was not surprised to see an exceptionally attractive young woman crossing the avenue. She was a petite brunette, her thin cloak half-concealing a gown of rose-colored silk. A demimonde, no doubt, the sort of woman a wealthy man would keep for his mistress.

Perhaps this was just the inspiration he sought. He began a mental list of gentlemen who might be approached here in the city. But as he visualized each placing money into his hand, he saw yet another slice of his independence slipping away.

Still, it was against the Bowie nature to give up. That much had been inherited from his fierce Scottish ancestors. He might suffer failure, but always sprang back more determined to succeed.

A sharp cry interrupted his thoughts. Halfway up the block, the demimonde struggled in the grip of the taller Creole, her tiny fists hammering his chest.

"Let—me—go!"

Before the words faded, Bowie was up and running. Without conscious thought, his fist crashed into the jaw of the tall man. The fellow spilled into the street, while his companion leapt to his attention. Glaring down at them, Bowie felt a gentle touch on his arm.

"My Lancelot." The woman's voice was honeyed, with a delectable hint of French. "You are a godsend."

For a moment, Bowie found himself unable to speak. He was no stranger to women, but this one was so exquisite as to take his breath away. Not more than five-and-twenty, she was so slim he could have circled her waist with his hands, and her features were smooth and delicate as a cameo.

She raised a gloved hand, touching a silken fingertip to his lips. "Please, good sir. I am greatly in your debt. I would hear the name of my hero."

"James," he managed. "My name is James."

"James." In her mouth, it sounded like *Shames*. "The supplanter. An apt description under the circumstances, would you not agree?"

The mass of ebony curls framed her features to perfection, and her scent was like a breath of wild roses. He realized she was looking at him queerly, and he recalled she had asked a question.

"Supplanter?"

"One who replaces another, as you have so effectively replaced that beast who affronted me."

"Ah."

Hearing a groan, he saw the taller Creole being helped to his feet, eyes fixed on Bowie in a mixture of astonishment and rage.

"You, sir! What is the meaning of this outrage?"

Bowie turned back to the young lady. Such an elegant creature was not for the likes of him, and it seemed advisable to make his exit. "You should be on your way," he said softly, and turned to leave.

"No. Please, James. Don't go."

"Indeed," said a deeper voice. "Don't run off, Monsieur. You have much to answer for."

Bowie inspected the young Creole. He was soft-skinned and weak-jawed, in a peacock blue Spencer jacket over a black velvet waistcoat and apricot cravat. His fawn-colored pantaloons were strapped beneath sharp-toed shoes. A tailor's dummy come to life.

Bowie was painfully aware of his torn jacket, and the dried

blood on his sleeve. "Our business is finished," he said curtly, "unless you plan to accost this lady again."

"Accost her?" The man's cheeks were livid. "What mummer's farce are you two playing at? This...this *trollop* stumbled against me, and I merely sought to steady her."

"It would seem," Bowie said coolly, "that you require another lesson in manners."

"From you, sir? A common street ruffian? If you had an ounce of breeding, you would meet me on the field of honor."

Ruffian. The word struck home. "A duel? You are challenging me to a duel?"

The Creole produced a bit of white pasteboard. "My card, sir. You may have your seconds call upon me."

Bowie ignored the card. "Why wait? Let's settle things here and now."

The two dandies sniffed at this snub of proper protocol. "As you are obviously a cretin," the tall man said, "I too wish to conclude this as quickly as possible. This lady addressed you as James. Have you a surname as well, or are you uncertain as to your parentage?"

"The name is Bowie. James Bowie."

He waited for the usual reaction, for the man's face to grow taut, and his bravado scuttle away deep inside.

Instead, the fellow merely smirked. "Bowie. An oafish name, to be sure. It quite suits you."

Bowie sighed. Here was an instance in which his reputation might serve him well, and this popinjay had never heard of him. Still, he had no wish to kill the man.

"As for weapons..." Bowie slid the massive blade from its sheath. "I choose knives."

The tall man looked as if he'd swallowed a lemon. "That is hardly the weapon of a gentleman."

"But I am merely a ruffian, am I not? So I offer a ruffian's conditions. We enter a pitch-black room, armed with knives. The man who emerges will be considered the victor."

The fellow's friend began to sputter. "But that is preposterous!"

Bowie held the eyes of the tall man. "Those are my terms. Unless you prefer to apologize."

The Creole's eyes flared, then cooled, and a look of petulance crossed his face. He inclined his head. "I offer my apologies, Monsieur."

"Not to me. To the lady."

The man stiffened, but he hesitated only a moment before rotating to face the woman. "My deepest regret, Mademoiselle, for any discomfort you experienced."

Bowie raised the knife again. "And for your insulting words as well."

With visible effort, the fellow said, "And for my irresponsible tongue."

The young woman's eyes gleamed. "Accepted."

Bowie nodded toward the far end of the block. "Now be on your way."

The two regarded him a moment from half-lidded eyes. The tall one went so far as to peer down his nose. Then they strode up the walk, and Bowie turned back to the girl.

Her smile warmed him down to his heels. With other women, he would have taken that as an invitation. With this one, it was likely no more than a smile.

Doffing his hat, Bowie executed a short bow. "Your servant," he said, and turned away, striding deliberately back toward the bistro.

The lady's scent stayed with him, and he knew he would later regret his abrupt departure. But this was no time to be chasing after women, especially one so clearly beyond his means.

Reaching his table, he noticed her scent had grown stronger

rather than weaker, and turned so quickly the young lady nearly bumped into him.

She did not appear at all flustered. "Mr. Bowie. James. You must allow me to thank you properly."

"Your smile was more than sufficient, I assure you."

Her blush matched the pink of her lips. "No, I insist. At least allow me to join you for a cup of tea."

Bowie could hardly refuse. Not unhappily, he held a chair for her. As was his custom, he reserved the seat next to the wall for himself, affording a clear view of his surroundings.

Catching a smirk on Sam's face, he shifted his chair slightly, placing the young woman between them.

Her cloak fell away from her shoulders, revealing a low-cut gown and slender bare arms.

Bowie's mouth was suddenly dry.

"Tell me, James, do you make a habit of rescuing young damsels in distress?"

"More frequently," he said, "they require rescuing from me."

Her lips twisted prettily. "I am almost inclined to believe you."

"What do you suppose got into that Creole puppy? He did not look the sort of man who would have to force himself upon a woman."

She looked down at the table. "Men are rarely what they seem. It takes more than fine clothes and pretty manners to make a gentleman."

"Too true," Bowie said, reflecting on his own experience.

A fancy carriage trundled over the cobblestones, the horses' trappings jingling, and Bowie watched it pass, wondering if it held the benefactor he so urgently required.

Suddenly his scalp prickled. Instinct told him he was being watched. Making no show of alarm, he let his eyes drift across the street. There, on the opposite walk, was a scowling face. The face was brown as a nut, and square-shaped, with wide, almost rectangular eyes. It was visible only a moment, then gone, but struck him with such malevolence to be seared onto his mind's eye.

"James."

The soft voice brought his eyes back to the table.

The girl extended a hand, poised like the head of a crane. "What is it, James? What troubles you?"

Bowie took the hand gently. He was almost compelled to brush it with his lips, but settled for a moment of warm eye contact. The scowling face still disturbed him.

"You have yet to tell me your name."

"As you are my Lancelot," she said, "it is only fitting you call me Guinevere."

"Tell me, Guinevere, do you have any particular enemies?"

Her eyes widened. "What a peculiar question. Do you?"

"Yes."

She arched her eyebrows, but Bowie said no more, waiting.

"There are always men," she said, "some more persistent than others. I am not always so fortunate as to have a protector at hand."

Putting the question of the scowling man aside, Bowie ordered tea, and they chatted for a time. She lived in the French Quarter, and proved quite fluent in all the latest styles and gossip. At length, she surprised him with a question.

"Is it true, James, that you are seeking the congressional seat now held by William Brent?"

Bowie choked on his tea. He found it hard to credit that this delightful creature would trouble herself with the sordid scuffle of politics.

"It is indeed," he said. But something compelled him to tell her the truth. "Or at least, it was."

"Was?"

"I fear this electioneering requires more funding than I dreamed. I am in need of a wealthy benefactor."

Guinevere—if that was her name—cocked her head to

the side, appraising him. "You would make a fine statesman, I believe. And an exceedingly handsome one. How much money do you require?"

"A fortune," he said simply. "An amount so great, I am ashamed to name it."

Surveying the street in both directions, she drew her chair closer and leaned across the table, providing a glimpse of her lovely bosom.

Her voice was barely above a whisper. "Perhaps we can help each other, James. I feel you are a man I can trust."

Bewildered now, Bowie merely nodded.

"I would like to show you something. Something you must swear to keep secret. Do I have your oath?"

Bowie hesitated. There was something decidedly odd here, but she *was* quite lovely. "You have my word."

After another careful inspection of the street, she reached into her bag, extracting something wrapped in a black velvet scarf.

Bowie waited, intensely curious. His scalp prickled again, and he glanced quickly across the street to find the same scowling face. And this time, he caught sight of a short, white-clad figure darting into the shadow of a doorway.

"I would ask," the girl said, "that you inspect this out of sight of prying eyes."

Bowie still probed the dark doorway. "Any eyes in particular?"

"Any at all," she said, and slid the object toward him.

He coiled his hand around it, pulling it onto his lap. The thing was perhaps ten inches in length, and remarkably heavy.

Another glance across the street revealed nothing, but he knew he was still being watched.

Beneath the cloth, his hand encountered something cold and metallic. Frowning, he leaned back and lifted a fold of the scarf. And could not contain a gasp.

Peering up at him was the intricately formed head of a serpent, its coiled body disappearing into deeper folds of velvet.

The serpent's jaws stretched wide, small golden fangs poised to bite.

The workmanship was flawless, but at the same time repellent. He wanted to cast the foul thing from him, but something stronger than dread compelled him to probe deeper.

Bowie looked up at the girl. Her lips were parted expectantly, and her eyes bright as emeralds. Behind her, the white-clad figure scuttled toward them. He stopped a good six feet away, glowering for all he was worth, but presenting no immediate threat. He was little more than four feet tall, and within the square-shaped head, his face was flat as a board. The girl seemed unaware of his presence.

"This a friend of yours?" Bowie asked, nodding toward the brown man.

The girl glanced over her shoulder. "Oh, la. That's just Pacal. He doesn't bite." And when Bowie gave her a doubtful look, she added, "Much."

Careful to keep the man at the edge of his vision, Bowie returned to the object in his lap. He turned the last fold of velvet, and once again, he gasped.

The body of the snake extended another three inches, terminating in a second head—a mirror image of the first. But protruding from its jaws was a blade of glittering black stone. The edge was uneven, and the surface far from smooth. Evidently it had been chipped from a length of obsidian. Bowie touched a thumb to the edge, producing a drop of blood.

Again, he felt the urge to cast it from him. Instead, he wrapped his fingers around the handle. The gold was deathly cold in his hand—far colder than the humid evening should permit.

Something touched his arm, and his head shot up. He had forgotten the brown man. But it was the girl, standing, leaning across the table. Still motionless in the street, the man called Pacal watched. "James. James, are you alright?"

Bowie stared at her a moment before nodding.

"You had such a look on your face. I feared you had done yourself injury."

Bowie released his grip on the golden dagger. Working by touch, he hastily wrapped it and pushed it across the table at her.

"What is that thing?" His voice was hoarse, and he downed the rest of his tea.

The girl stuffed the bundle back into her bag. "Merely a sample. A king's ransom is waiting, James. And you shall have a handsome share, if you help me retrieve it."

Bowie's eye narrowed. Something about this sounded all too familiar.

Wrapping fingers about her slender wrist, he said, "Who are you?"

The girl's eyes flashed. "James, please…"

Something moved behind her. The scowling man had reached the edge of the walk. Bowie locked eyes with him, sending a warning.

"Who are you?" he asked again.

Busy watching both the girl and the brown man, Bowie almost failed to notice a looming presence on his right. But even before the hearty voice rang out, he had recognized the sour and fetid odor of Andre.

"Jim Boy! I've been searching for ye high and low. And here I find ye with me own sweet daughter, Mariette."

CHAPTER 10

"I will hear no more of Voodoo!"

MORNING FOUND *L'INTREPIDE* moored at Grand Terre, the easternmost of the barrier islands guarding the entrance to Barataria Bay. It was now a waiting game, and Renato chose to wait with brush in hand, applying his genius once again to his masterpiece, *The Last Great Terror of the Gulf.* The encounter with Andre and his whore of a daughter had provided new inspiration. At the bottom of the canvas he'd added two severed heads. One was round as a cannon ball, with a bulbous nose, a vacuous expression and a vermin-infested beard. The other had lustrous black hair, fiery red lips, and a serpent coiling through empty eye sockets.

Hearing the clack of Faraday's boots, he pierced the man with a glare.

"I trust you bring good news, or you would not dare disturb me."

Good news would mean a sail had been sighted coming from the east. Andre's best route to the treasure led by ship down the Mississippi and west into the Gulf, and *L'Intrepide* would be waiting to pounce. And if the murdering braggart Bowie had joined the doomed venture, the result would be all the sweeter.

Faraday eyed him coolly, almost insolently, and Renato was tempted to shoot him on the spot.

"Good or ill is for you to decide, Captain. The lookout reports a sail, but not the one you seek."

"What sail? Where?"

"A sloop has anchored on the bay side of Grand Isle. He recognized it as the *Catalàn*."

"*Catalàn*?" This was news indeed, and far from good. "I warned Suárez I'd gut him if I found him here again."

Suárez, a man of large appetites but little ability, was another of Lafitte's former captains, now preying on remote settlements and small fishing boats to survive. The man was no rival to Renato's operations, but he was a nuisance, attracting the notice of navy patrols.

"Your orders, Captain?"

"Have him watched. And alert me if he stirs."

Faraday nodded, but did not depart. There was something else. There was *always* something else.

"Out with it, damn your eyes. What do you have to say?"

"You will not be pleased."

"When am I ever pleased?"

"Quayle was afraid to tell you. There are no eggs. And no ham. The food vanished sometime in the night."

As Renato seethed, Faraday said, "I must tell you, sir, that I have heard whispering from the men."

"And what do those layabouts have to whisper about?"

Faraday had trouble meeting Renato's eyes. "There have been other strange occurrences. Some believe it the work of Voodoo."

"*What* strange occurrences?"

"A chicken's head was found on deck this morning. And feathers. But no corpse."

"A hungry crewman, no doubt. One who values his stomach more than his head. I suggest you catch him."

"There's more," Faraday said doggedly. "The master's mate has broken out in boils, and one of the topmen has grown a goiter."

Renato snorted and spat over the rail. "The men have done little but weep and wail of late. I have a simple solution. The next man who speaks of Voodoo will be shot and tossed overboard. You'll be amazed how quickly the others forget their ills."

"There must be another answer."

"Then you had best be about discovering it. I will hear no more of Voodoo."

IN HIS CABIN, Renato went to the strongbox. If there truly was thievery aboard, he should look to his own valuables.

The miniature of his mother was there on top, an exquisitely rendered portrait in a frame of filigreed gold. His mother had been the most desirable woman in the city of Cap-Français, and his father a painter of great renown. She'd loved him fiercely during his brief stay in the island nation of Saint-Domingue. But at the advent of the first black rebellion, he had fled to his native France, never to return. Renato, then called Pierre, had begged her for the great man's name, but to her the subject was closed.

He was nearly eight before she took another lover, the famous buccaneer Renato Beluche. It was from Beluche that he took his name, shedding his mother's choice like an ill-fitting shirt. It was Beluche who gave him a younger brother in Rayón, and Beluche who taught him to be a man.

Returning the miniature to the box, he moved a hand among the other articles. And found something missing. *The Faerie Queen.* The book with his vague memory of the map was not there. He rummaged about, making sure, then fell to searching the rest of the cabin.

He worked frantically, with growing desperation, but as before—when seeking the original map—it was nowhere to be found.

"Faraday!" The force of his voice brought dust raining from the deck above. "Faraday! To me, at once!"

Arriving, the man eyed the shambles of the room—blankets, clothing, maps and weapons strewn every whichaway in a mad scramble. "Ah," he said, "you have been redecorating."

Renato spun to face him, and Faraday jerked back as if struck. Whatever he had seen in Renato's eyes had chilled him to the core.

Renato's voice was like a blade scraping bone. "This thievery has gone too far. You will find the culprit quickly, or pay the penalty yourself."

Protest was written on the man's face, but so was fear. The fear won out. "Aye, Captain. At once."

"Then why are you still standing there?"

"I, uh, I bring other news, Captain. The lookout has sighted another sail."

"Andre?"

"Most assuredly not. It's a navy ship." Faraday gulped visibly before adding, "The *Medusa*."

Renato was enveloped in a sudden sweat. To pirates, *Medusa* was the most feared ship on the Gulf. She was every bit as fast as *L'Intrepide*, and several times more deadly.

Borrowing an idea from a captured Puerto Rican privateer, her builders had placed a huge 18-pound gun square in the center of her deck. On land, it would have been called a siege gun, for its power to shatter castle walls. Mounted on a swivel, the fearsome weapon could fire from either side, sending a ball nearly twenty inches in diameter crashing into an opponent a mile away.

Medusa was a pirate hunter, and it had taken every ounce of his cunning to evade her as long as he had. Now, at the worst of times, the devil ship was back to plague him. If Andre and Bowie came along now, he would be helpless to follow.

"You have been given a reprieve, Mr. Faraday. For now. This current emergency must be dealt with at once, or our dreams of treasure will vanish like so much smoke."

CHAPTER II

"I hope to give them indigestion."

"**I** AM MOST GRATEFUL, Monsieur James, that you have agreed to help us." The musical voice was Mariette's, but the soot-smeared face, visible under an oversized watch cap, betrayed no hint of the beauty she had displayed the previous evening—and the ragged coat and trousers hid every curve of her figure.

"I've agreed to nothing," Bowie said. "You promised me a look at your precious map."

He tried not to sound petulant. It had been her curves, in addition to the evidence of the hideous golden dagger, that had brought him to this battered brig named *Lucinda*, docked at the foot of Barrack Street. Mariette's only explanation for her change in appearance was that she did not wish to excite the curiosity of the ship's captain and crew.

Andre looked sideways at Mariette. "Is Jim Boy not as I described, daughter? A lad who knows what he wants, and goes after it straight as a blade."

The three sat at a small table in a cramped cabin, faces lit by the lamp swaying from a beam. The ship's cargo was dimly visible through the cabin doorway: picks, shovels and blankets; sacks of coffee, sugar and salt; kegs of rum, gunpowder and ten-penny nails.

Andre refilled his cup from a bottle of mulled wine. "Join me in a drink, Jim. It'll soothe your spirit."

Bowie answered with a curt shake of his head.

A cultivated voice said, "I would be pleased to partake, if you can offer a decent vintage." The lanky slave Sam leaned against a bulkhead, head lost between the beams of the upper deck. "I trust Jim would have no objection."

Bowie winced, saying nothing.

Andre's eyes looked fit to burst from his head. "What—what—what—?"

Bowie stopped him with a hand. "Don't ask. Show me the map."

"In a moment," Mariette said. "We await the final member of our company."

"Another?" Bowie examined the little brown man hunched cross-legged in the corner. "By my way of thinking, there are too many here already."

Mariette had called the little monster her servant, but offered no further reason for his presence. Bowie had been shocked to discover that along with a flat face, the fellow had a peculiarly shaped skull. His head, wide in front and back, would measure no more than a hand-width on either side. Perhaps a pinched brain accounted for his sour disposition.

"The man we await," Mariette said, "is my Uncle Frederic. It was he who arranged passage on this fine vessel."

Bowie perked his ears. If a man of means was involved in this scheme, perhaps he could be persuaded to front the sum to pay Tamarand, making this treasure hunt unnecessary. "Now I am intrigued," he said. "I look forward to meeting him."

Andre made a sound midway between a cough and a laugh. "I would be surprised, Jim Boy, if you've not already met. His reputation exceeds even your own."

"Frederic?" Bowie plumbed his memory. "I recall no one of that name."

Mariette wore a peculiar grin. "That is his given name, but he is better known as Dominique You."

Dominique You. *Capitaine Dominique.* Bowie had never met the man, but he was a well-known figure in the city. He had once been Lafitte's strong right arm, and one of the most feared privateers of the Gulf.

When the British attacked Louisiana, You, along with Lafitte and others, had lent his skill as a gunner to the American cause. Some said he was the man most responsible for Andy Jackson's decisive victory at the Battle of New Orleans.

Like all the buccaneers involved, *Capitaine Dominique* had been granted clemency. But while most returned to piracy, he had settled down as a law-abiding citizen. Or so it seemed. He had many friends, and rumors persisted he was still involved in the smuggling trade.

Bowie fixed Andre with a hard look. " 'Uncle Frederic.' Am I to believe Dominique You is your brother?"

Mariette answered for him. "*Capitaine Dominique* is my uncle in name only. As you know, my dear father is away much of the time," she paused to pat Andre's arm, "on *business*. Uncle Frederic has been like a second father to me."

Uncle. Bowie caught himself wondering if that was as far as the relationship went.

"I fear I must insist," he said. "Show me the map, or I'll be on my way."

Mariette's eyes flashed. "Very well." From somewhere within her ragged coat she produced a flat oilskin packet and placed it on the table.

Andre hunched over it, eyes gleaming.

With careful hands, Mariette unfolded the packet and smoothed the crinkled paper.

Bowie leaned forward. The map was badly stained, and torn at the edges, but clearly depicted a long narrow island, behind which stretched a bay. At the near end of the bay, almost opposite the opening from the sea, was a circular cove. And near the cove, a bold black X.

Bowie placed a finger on the mark. "The meaning of this is plain enough, but what are we to make of these other figures?" His finger traced a circle on the map, indicating four crude images above, below and to either side of the X. "A fish, a turtle, a snake, and some sort of bird."

Sam peered over his shoulder. "So-called treasure maps invariably utilize such enigmatic markers. Their meaning is rarely evident until one reaches the site."

"How—?" Bowie stared at him a moment, then shook his head. "Never mind."

He found the brown man at Mariette's side, his wide-set eyes devouring the map.

Bowie covered it with his hands. "What is your interest here?"

If the little man understood, he gave no sign.

"Away with you!" Bowie said in French.

The brown man twitched, but still betrayed no comprehension.

Bowie tried Spanish. "Back off, or I'll throttle you like a chicken."

The brown man jerked erect, one hand flashing to his throat, and he slunk angrily away.

"His wits may be addled," Andre growled, "but he savvies Spanish well enough."

Mariette turned stormy eyes on Bowie. "What did you say to the poor fellow?"

Bowie ignored the question. "What do you know of that little demon?"

"Nothing at all, save that his name is Pacal, and that he came highly recommended."

"Recommended by whom?"

Mariette's eyes flashed again. "My Uncle Frederic, whom I trust in all matters."

A mark against *Capitaine Dominique*, Bowie thought. He turned to Andre. "You said this supposed treasure lies in Karankawa country. This bears little resemblance to Galveston Bay."

"Right you are, Jim Boy. It's not Galveston." Shielding his

lips from the brown man, Andre mouthed a word. The silent word was "Matagorda."

Bowie had heard of the place, an extension of Austin's colony somewhere south of Galveston.

He found Mariette regarding him steadily. "Well, Monsieur James, does this meet with your satisfaction?"

"The map looks real enough," he admitted, "though I've yet to hear of one actually leading to treasure. And I still question the role of Dominique You."

"He has earned the right to accompany us. It was he who alerted me to the map, allowing me to steal it."

It took a moment for the words to sink in, but when they did, Bowie sat bolt upright in his chair. "What do you mean *us?*"

Andre sat gaping, equally surprised.

"But of course," Mariette said sternly. "The map is mine. Did you truly think I would turn you two rogues loose with it?"

"Girl, ye cut me to the bone. One would think ye don't trust your own father."

"If I did, would I truly be his daughter?"

Andre's hands wove circles in the air. "We simply cannot take you, little one. Cannibal country is no place for a lass. I'd fear to go meself, if not for Jim here."

"I must agree," Bowie said. "You'd make a tasty morsel for a family of Kronks."

"In that case, I hope to give them indigestion. But I'm going. That's final. So is Uncle Frederic. And Pacal."

Bowie thrust back his chair and stood, towering over the table. "No, by God. Sailing off on this quest with two moss-grown pirates would be folly enough. Taking a pampered girl and her evil-eyed servant is utter lunacy."

Mariette pointed her pretty nose at Sam. "I notice you are taking *your* servant."

"He's not my servant. And he's going nowhere but my brother's plantation. As for myself, I was mad to even consider this venture. I'll finance my campaign here in Louisiana, or not at all."

Ignoring their stricken looks, Bowie turned toward the cabin door. But at that moment the ladder creaked, and a thickset man in a sea-green frock coat filled the passageway.

"Uncle Frederic! Thank heaven you've come."

The man was half a head shorter than Bowie, and half a lifetime older. His hair was the color of cold steel, and tied in a queue. His clothing was frayed and long out of fashion, but his bearing that of a king.

A long-necked bottle swung carelessly in his hand, and Bowie caught the sharp tang of cheap wine. Great the man may be, but he smelled like a common street sot.

Before introductions could be made, a voice called from the deck, "Yer pardon, gentlemen. A man's here asking after *Capitaine Dominique*."

Bowie saw You's eyes narrow. Andre swore softly.

"Send him away, Uncle," Mariette said. "Let us be off before trouble develops."

You thumbed his whiskers. "I'll tell Captain McQuiddy to make haste, but Dominique You hides from no man." And nimble as a monkey, he sprang up the ladder and through the open hatch.

Bowie caught Mariette's look of distress. "I believe I'll take the air," he said gruffly, and followed.

THE TATTOOED MAN facing You had pirate written all over him. Such men, like wolves, traveled in packs, and Bowie felt a tingling in his gut.

The dock to *Lucinda*'s west was stacked with barrels. To the east, wagonloads of cotton awaited unloading. In the street, heavily-laden carts rumbled past. Nothing seemed amiss. But there was that *feeling*.

"I recall the fat rogue," You was saying, "but haven't seen him in an age. Why come to me?"

The tattooed man squirmed. "Everyone knows you and him was close to Cap'n Lafitte. When I heared he was hereabouts, I hoped to collect an old debt."

"If you truly know Andre," You said, "you know that's a forlorn hope."

The pirate laughed hollowly under You's scrutiny.

Still uneasy, Bowie followed the conversation with only half an ear. *Lucinda*'s crew bustled about the ship, hauling lines and making things fast. Her captain, a rotund fellow named McQuiddy, watched between puffs on a long-stemmed pipe.

Dominique You said, "Your name is Bendix, is it not? You served on my corsair *Le Pandoure*, until I had you marooned for filching rations."

At this, several crewmen turned sour glances on the tattooed man, whose face turned violet. Even a landsman like Bowie knew that to steal from one's shipmates was a seaman's greatest sin.

McQuiddy's men were alert enough, but could they be relied upon in a fight? Aside from six small cannons and a few belted daggers, the only weapon on deck was a cutlass in a rusty scabbard nailed to the mainmast.

Sensing movement behind him, Bowie found Sam at his shoulder.

"These vessels were designed for men of stunted growth," he said, gingerly touching his temple. "Were you serious about sending me to your brother's plantation?"

"We'll discuss that later," Bowie whispered. "Can you handle a weapon?"

The black man's nose wrinkled. "I am quite expert at cleaning and loading a gentleman's dueling pistols."

"Well and good. But can you fight?"

"Violence begets only violence," the black man said, "and I have seen all I care to."

"Yes," Bowie said with finality. "I'm sending you to my brother."

A softer voice said, "I can fight." And up through the hatch came the ragged apparition he knew was Mariette. "Who do you wish me to kill?"

A flash of movement took his eyes to the cotton wagons, and he was rewarded with the sight of a head peering over the bales. Just as quickly, the head sank from sight.

"Fetch your father," Bowie told the girl. "We're going to need his sword."

A WILD CRY erupted from the dock.

Bowie could have sworn the scream was that of an enraged catamount, but it issued from a gaudily-clad figure charging from behind the barrels. Other attackers burst from various hiding places, while on *Lucinda*'s deck, the pirate called Bendix bobbed to escape the sweeping arms of Dominique You. Mariette leapt for the rusty cutlass hanging from the mast, and Andre drew his rapier, bellowing like a bull. Sam's looming presence merely melted away.

Knife in hand, Bowie raced for the gangplank. He preferred the solid surface of the wharf to the unsteady deck of the brig.

Locking eyes with the screaming pirate leading the charge, he felt the bloodlust emanating from the man. And knew him. He was named Hector, another close friend of Rayón. Though not Renato, he would do until the time came. Gone were thoughts of Congress, of Mariette and treasure. All that remained was blind fury, a world consisting of himself and the man hurtling toward him.

With scarcely a yard between them, Bowie ducked under the pirate's saber, his knife darting for the man's breast. Hector caught the blade on his hilt, and metal shrieked. The shock coursed up Bowie's arm, and it was all he could do to retain his grip.

On the brig, Andre had been cornered by two men in the bow, but his rapier spun a steel web, keeping them at bay. Dominique You crossed blades with Bendix, while Mariette fenced with a skeletal man on the main deck.

Bowie saw Hector's saber on course to split his skull. Too late to parry, he deflected the blow with an arm and lunged forward, his knife seeking the man's throat.

As if warned by some sixth sense, Hector dove sideways, stumbling away as the blade cleaved the air.

A cry from the brig halted Bowie's pursuit.

Mariette was pinioned from behind by a hulking brute, while the skeletal man hacked at her cutlass, trying to disarm her.

Bowie bolted for the gangplank, but had taken scarcely a stride before a knot of brown-skinned fury sprang to Mariette's aid. The little madman Pacal landed on the big brute's back, ripping into him like a wild beast.

From behind came the telltale cock of a pistol. Hector was on his knees, his weapon leveled on Bowie's chest.

Blade balanced between thumb and forefinger, Bowie sent the knife darting like a shard of sunlight from his hand. Hector was equally quick, deflecting the blade with his gun barrel.

Bowie charged like an enraged bear, arms outstretched to wring the man's neck. But with a desperate swing, Hector brought the brass hilt of his saber thudding into Bowie's jaw.

Bowie went limp and crashed to the dock. Hector was on him in an instant, a boot pinning his neck to the wharf. His eyes flamed as he balanced the point of his sword on Bowie's chest.

Bowie lay as if caught in a nightmare, his limbs refusing to respond. Dimly, amid the near-constant ringing of blades, he heard shouting from the ship.

"Hector! Look out! You's lighting a fuse!"

You's lighting a fuse. Nonsense words, Bowie thought. Then the meaning came clear, and he spied Dominique You crouched over one of the ship's 6-pounders, a flaming match in his hand.

Hector had seen this, too. Quick as a snake, he raised his pistol and fired. *Capitaine Dominique* jerked upright, clutched at his shoulder and toppled backwards.

The rest of the deck was in chaos. One of Andre's opponents was down, and he battled the other in the bow, while the emaciated man was hard-pressed by Mariette. The hulking giant danced madly about, striving to pry the brown-skinned savage from his back.

Hector glared down at Bowie. "Now," he said, "time to pay for Rayón."

"Perhaps not," Bowie countered. "I suggest you look behind you."

Hector snorted. "That ruse is old as Moses. Nothing can save you now."

And Bowie smiled.

Orange flame blossomed from *Lucinda*'s side. A screaming hail of grapeshot scorched the air, and Hector went rigid, collapsing on Bowie's legs.

Behind the smoking 6-pounder stood Andre, wearing a silly grin.

Dominique You lay slumped on a coil of rope while Mariette fussed over him. Two of the pirates lay still on the deck, and the others flew off in different directions along the wharf.

Andre tipped his hat. "Ye gave me a scare, Jim Boy. Is that bastard dead?"

Bowie kicked at one of Hector's boots, and heard a moan.

"Close," he replied. "Demons are hard to kill."

"Then finish him quickly. We're about to cast off."

Bowie stood over the prone figure, the knife eager in his grip. It would be easy now. One turn of the wrist, and Hector's life-blood would seep through the cracks in the dock. Surely the man deserved no less.

"Kill him, Jim. Hurry!"

Bowie grimaced. He had slit the throats of helpless hogs and cattle, but a human being was different, even one so inhuman as this. Still, the man was a tool of Renato's, and had tried to prevent him seeking the treasure that would buy his seat in Congress.

The realization that he now believed in the treasure gave

Bowie a start. The evidence had been building, it was true. Renato's pirates, the golden dagger, the map, and finally Dominique
You. But until this moment he'd thought he could resist the call.

"It's now or never, Jim Boy!"

Though riddled with grapeshot, Hector refused to die. The
man coughed, shook himself, and regarded Bowie through slit-
ted eyes. "I bested you," he wheezed. "You should be dead."

Bowie could not disagree. He had been lucky. But luck was
part of the game.

"Still," the pirate said, "your time is coming. Renato will surely
send you to Hell."

"And you'll be there to greet me." Bowie readied the knife for
a quick and decisive stroke.

"By God," came a voice from the street. "That's Big Jim
Bowie, or I'm a Dutchman."

"Bowie? The knife fighter? You're daft."

Bowie saw a dozen or more onlookers shuffling forward,
curiosity overcoming fear.

"That's him, alright. See the size of that blade?"

"James!" Mariette's voice, pleading. "Hurry! We're underway!"

A glance confirmed this. *Lucinda's* sails belled. The gangplank
was being pulled in, the mooring ropes coiled.

Bowie's heart pounded. The knife handle was slick with sweat,
and he took a firmer grip.

A bystander let out a long hiss. A woman squeaked and
caught her breath.

Bowie glared at the gawking citizens, and knew he could not
do it. Not like this, in cold blood, before a crowd of witnesses.

From further away came angry shouts, and he saw more of
Renato's men rushing to Hector's aid.

With a snort of disgust, Bowie sheathed his blade and
galloped for the ship. He hit the edge of the dock running,
shoved off with all his strength, and sailed into the air. He

focused on Mariette's frightened face as his heels cleared the brig's rail and skidded across the deck.

It seemed his momentum would carry him off the opposite side, but a strong black arm steadied him, and a deep voice spoke softly in his ear.

"For the briefest moment there, Jim, I feared for your immortal soul."

CHAPTER 12

"The fish will drink your blood."

MEDUSA.

Like an evil phantasm, the ship had haunted Renato's dreams. Now she was here, and her very presence might help Andre and Bowie steal his treasure. *Medusa* must be dealt with, and quickly, or all would be lost.

Renato had chased the others from his cabin so he could concentrate, and now lay on his mattress, staring at the underside of the deck. What would his famous step-father do?

With her monstrous gun, *Medusa* was too heavily-laden to enter the bay. And should *L'Intrepide* come out she would be blown from the water before her own guns could reach the foe.

Renato plumbed his bag of tricks, discarding plan after plan, until his temple throbbed with the effort.

Came a light rap upon the door.

"Go away!"

Another rap, lighter still. "It's me, Cap'n. Quayle."

"Damn your eyes, Quayle, you have broken my concentration, just when I was on the cusp of a plan!"

"Apologies, Cap'n. You wished to know if there was any movement from *Catalàn*."

"And was there?"

"Why, no, Cap'n. She ain't budged a inch since first we seen her. Figgered you'd want to know."

Renato was about to curse the fool when he felt a spark, then a sizzle, and within moments a full-blown plan had flared up within his brain.

"Quayle," he said, "remind me to have you flogged at the earliest opportunity. For sheer stupidity. But first, you will send Mr. Faraday to me. At once!"

THE PIROGUE RENATO'S men had stolen from the Cajuns was a tight fit for six, especially when one of the six was LaChaise.

"Damn you, LaChaise! If I feel your bony knees in my back again, we'll find out how bony they really are."

"Sorry, Cap'n." The man did not sound sorry. "Nowheres else to put 'em."

LaChaise, Quayle and the others with him were a sorry sight, dressed in rags and smeared with mud and blood. Their fleshy parts were decorated with angry red splotches, and—to add authenticity—the men inflicted with goiters and boils were featured prominently in the bow. Renato himself, his mirror had assured him, looked equally atrocious. He would have much preferred to have this play enacted without his presence, but could not trust his feeble-minded men to perform it properly.

"Row, you sluggards," he growled. "We are preserving our fortunes, not larking on a Sunday picnic."

The pace increased a bit, but with Andre's ship liable to pass by at any moment, the pirogue's progress was maddeningly slow.

At last, rounding an outcrop of Grand Isle, they sighted *Catalàn* riding at anchor. The sloop's crew had been lazing about, but came swiftly alert at the pirogue's approach.

"Now," Renato told Quayle, "empty that bottle into your mouth, and quickly!"

"But Cap'n, it smells."

"So do you, wretch. Drink, or the fish will drink your blood."

Quivering with revulsion, Quayle put the bottle to his lips and filled his cheeks.

"Suárez," Renato called, drawing the name into a wail. "Help us, please!"

Catalàn's pirates merely stared, repugnance growing until their captain jostled them aside.

"Keep your distance! Who are you, and what do you want here?"

"Do you not know me, old friend? It's Renato!"

Renato hid a smile. *Old friend* was laying it on thick, but supplied the proper degree of desperation. When he and Suárez last met, they'd done their best to kill each other.

"State your purpose, and smartly," Suárez demanded, "before I blast your stench out of the water."

"As you see," Renato whined, "we find ourselves in dire straits. While moored in the bay, the men had sport with some of the women, and this foul sickness ran through us like a plague." He poked Quayle in the back, and the fat bosun turned his head, spewing a stream of black slime over the side.

Catalàn's men gagged, and one could not help vomiting in return.

"Half my crew heaved their guts out and died, while others went mad and dived overboard. We are the last of *L'Intrepide*'s crew, and beg your favor to take us away from this evil place."

Suárez digested this with narrowed eyes. "Had you gold to make it worth my while, I might consider towing you to another cove. But *Medusa* was sighted lurking about, making that impossible."

"We saw her as we passed the channel," Renato offered, "heading east, and doubtless returning to the city. Should you slip out now and make for Texas, she would never catch you."

"Perhaps," Suárez admitted. "But there is still the matter of gold."

Renato put dejection on his face. "Alas, I have none at present. But I have vast amounts cached along the Gulf, and you can trust me to reward you once we're safe."

Suárez at last displayed a smile. "Alas, *old friend*, I know precisely how far I can trust you." He turned to his men. "Make ready to sail, at once! I feel the call of Texas."

"But what of us?" Renato pleaded.

Suárez peered at him as if his presence had already been forgotten. "I would prefer not to waste powder and shot on you, but if you're still in sight when we're ready to depart, I will surely do so." Then, smiling hugely, he turned away.

Fighting the urge to cast a parting insult, Renato gave quiet orders, and the pirogue was soon scooting away, far more rapidly than it had approached.

BACK ABOARD *L'INTREPIDE*, Renato waited eagerly for the signal. A man posted near the channel between the islands would fire a shot once *Catalàn* had passed into the Gulf—a sound sure to reach the sharp ears of *L'Intrepide*'s lookout.

The signal came sooner than expected.

"A shot!" the man in the crow's nest called. "I just heared it, Cap'n!"

Renato pictured *Catalàn* turning west into the Gulf, and began counting the minutes until it would be too late for Suárez to turn back. Two of the 9-pounders were already loaded and run out, and a man dispatched to the opposite end of Grand Terre had confirmed that *Medusa*—contrary to what he'd told Suárez—still lay hidden at the eastern end of the bay.

When time enough had passed, he gave the order:

"Fire the guns! Now!"

The first 9-pounder roared out its song, followed by the second, and the twin blasts re-echoed about the bay.

Renato could see the result in his mind's eye.

Alerted by the guns, *Medusa* would emerge from hiding, and quickly sight *Catalàn*. The sloop would be well within range of her 18-pounder, and nature would take its course.

Every man on *L'Intrepide* knew the same, and the ship was eerily quiet for the space of nearly five minutes. Then the silence was split by a boom so loud it seemed like thunder from the heavens.

Renato smiled.

The *Catalàn* was no more, and *Medusa*'s captain, with a feeling of accomplishment, would surely return to base in New Orleans.

Come to me, Andre, Renato prayed. *Bring that damned Bowie with you. And we shall have a reckoning.*

CHAPTER 13

"It has bewitched you."

BOWIE DID NOT like ships. He preferred the elegant Mississippi riverboats, which were little more than floating hotels and gambling salons. *Lucinda*, by contrast, was cramped, rough-hewn, and plagued with the odor of unwashed bodies. And though this stretch of the Mississippi was wide and smooth, the brig never ceased to rock, making him long for solid ground.

The scenery, too, left much to be desired. The surface of the river was broken only by mudbanks and bulrushes. Along the shores, alligators sunned themselves, sliding in and out of the ooze. The land on either side—flat for as far as the eye could see—was broken only by the occasional barns and huts of sugar plantations.

And it had become all too familiar. Bowie had recently returned from Washington City on a ship only slightly better appointed than this. Armed with testimony and affidavits, he had lobbied officials of the State and Treasury Departments—unsuccessfully—to settle a particularly nettlesome land claim, and the queasy feeling had barely left him. Just the thought of it made him weary.

Sleeping quarters aboard *Lucinda* were mere hammocks of rough and soiled canvas, hung in tight rows beneath the main deck. But Bowie, weary to the bone, tumbled into the nearest and was instantly asleep.

And *dreaming…*

Blue sparks flew as the blades clashed again and again. Rayón, his dark face contorted, feinted left and thrust right, almost faster than the eye could follow. Bowie parried, deflecting the point of the pirate's poniard from his heart, but the blade sliced through the flesh beneath his arm, loosing a red shower across the surface of the lagoon.

Bowie had no formal training with sword or knife, but to the young Bowie brothers, fighting had been a form of play. Studying Scottish and Spanish sword manuals, they had adapted the lessons to whatever weapons they had at hand, and spent countless hours facing off in furious mock-battles.

What Bowie faced now, though, was no child's play. He and Rayón straddled a floating log, face-to-face, less than a yard separating them. Both were stripped to the waist, breeches fixed to the log with square-headed nails, and there they would remain until one of them was dead.

Rayón slashed wildly at Bowie's head. Bowie ducked, and the man's knife cleaved nothing but air. Off balance, Rayón was unable to stop his lunge, and Bowie felt the log rolling to the side. Desperately, he flung his weight in the opposite direction, saving them from toppling into the water.

A chorus of raucous cheers came from the three score pirates assembled on the bank of Galveston Isle.

The buccaneers were brawny, hard-eyed men, bristling with weapons and clad in fantastic combinations of finery and squalor. They were a wild-eyed and riotous lot, reveling in this death sport involving one of their own.

Standing stiffly apart was Bowie's brother Rezin, grim-faced, with thick dark hair and long side-whiskers. He nodded slowly, and Jim read the meaning. *Remain focused*, the nod said, *and you may yet prevail.* Hunched at his elbow, the stocky rogue called Andre displayed a crooked smile and winked.

The women watching were mostly hard-faced slatterns, but one among them was young and fresh, fair of hair and skin. Bowie tried to catch her eye, but she stood downcast, slim hands clasped before her. She had been animated enough the night before, responding openly to his attentions, never hinting that this man Rayón had laid prior claim to her.

Seeming to draw strength from his friends' encouragement, Rayón surged forward in a flurry of flashing steel. Bowie twisted and weaved, barely managing to deflect his cuts and thrusts.

A stinging pain bit his right hand, and the knife nearly leaped from his grasp. Rayón's weapon had scraped the length of Bowie's blade and cut deep into the flesh between his thumb and forefinger.

Bowie regretted his lack of crossguard. His knife was designed for carving meat, while Rayón's poniard was twelve inches of razor-honed Toledo steel, with a guard of braided brass.

Bleeding freely, Bowie reeled to his right, just as Rayón lunged in the same direction. This time, there was no saving them. The log rolled with their weight, tipping both into the chilly water.

By the time the log was righted, Bowie's lungs were near bursting, and Rayón spurted a stream of brackish saltwater full in his face.

"Continue!" The French-accented voice cut through the oaths and catcalls of the mob. This was the notorious Lafitte himself, atop a rock that placed him head and shoulders above the crowd. Of all present, he alone appeared clear-eyed and sober, clad in a wine-red greatcoat and blue silk breeches tucked into silver-buckled boots. But like the others, he clearly found this grim drama irresistible.

"Enough of this farce!" This second voice, raspy and grating, came from Rayón's brother, Renato. "This oaf has no rights under our laws. He should be roasted like a rabbit over a slow fire."

Renato's nose was sharp as a knife and hooked over a tight lipless mouth. He might have been cruelly handsome save for the crooked scar on his cheek, and the yellowish tint to his skin.

Lafitte laid a hand on his pistol butt. "Monsieur Bowie, along with his brother, is my guest, and shall be granted the courtesy we extend to our own. The match will continue." His voice was not particularly loud, but his tone said he would brook no argument.

Renato growled, eyes blazing, as hands hauled him back into the fold.

Bowie glanced at his brother, seeking strength. Rezin wrapped the fingers of his left hand about his right wrist, holding it fast. Bowie read the meaning, nodded his thanks, and nearly lost his life, as Rayón's poniard darted toward his throat. Bowie turned the blade on his own, forcing Rayón's arm back, and quick as a cobra, his left hand shot out and caught Rayón's knife-wrist in a vise-like grip. At the same time, he thrust his own blade toward Rayón's heart, forcing the man to grasp Bowie's wrist as well.

Bowie smiled grimly. This was Rezin's advice—to clinch and deny the advantage of the pirate's longer blade, making this a battle of main strength.

Bowie stared deep into Rayón's eyes and saw the seeds of fear. Sweat poured from the man's forehead as he exerted all his power to divert the butcher knife. Bowie now brought his full might into play, forcing the tip of his blade ever closer.

Rayón gasped, expelling a cloud of sour breath as the butcher knife pierced his skin. The veins swelled in his temples and his eyes seemed about to pop. And still, Bowie pressed on.

The shouts of the crowd had faded to low growls and muttered curses when a ball whistled past Bowie's ear and burned a furrow across his shoulder.

A great hubbub broke out on the beach. Space had cleared around Renato, who stood defiantly, a smoking gun in his hand. His face was dark with fury, his eyes like burning coals. On the rock above towered Lafitte, the black muzzle of his own pistol trained on Renato's breast.

"Seize him!" barked Lafitte. "He will answer for this later. But for now, let us see the finish."

Without warning, Rayón lunged forward and struck like a viper, opening a deep gash in Bowie's chest and slashing up across his cheek.

Bowie gasped, pain lancing through him. Licking dry lips, he caught the salty tang of his own blood.

And with that first taste of blood, everything changed. The sounds of the mob faded. His vision narrowed until his entire world was the log, the flashing knives, and his maddened opponent. He could no longer feel his heart. It was as if he were now living between the beats.

Rayón's movements seemed sluggish. Bowie waited, watching the poniard's slow approach. Thrusting Rayón's arm aside, he brought the butcher knife hurtling down like a stroke of lightning. Rayón threw up a futile hand, and the knife flashed through it, filling the air with severed fingers before slicing deep into the man's neck. Striking bone, Bowie twisted the blade and jerked upwards, severing the jugular. Blood spurted as from a fountain, and Rayón's body went slack.

Only then did he hear the shouts and curses from the water's edge. Above the din rose the keening wail of a wild beast. Shaking the blood from his eyes, Bowie saw a figure frothing at the mouth and flailing in the grip of a dozen men. Had the creature not been clothed as a man, Bowie would have thought him some demon freshly escaped from the Pit. And that was not far from the truth, as the man was Rayón's brother, Renato.

Lafitte stood serenely atop the black rock, eyeing Bowie with grim admiration as the pirates forced the wild man to his knees.

Bowie looked to the blonde girl. For an instant she favored him with a saucy smile. But before he could smile back, her flesh began to whither, the golden locks shriveled from her head, and her face became a hideous grinning skull atop a crumbling skeleton.

BOWIE AWOKE WITH a start, bathed in sweat. He did not recognize his surroundings. The room swayed drunkenly, and he seemed somehow confined. From out of the darkness came the snorting of a savage beast, and Bowie feared he had slipped into some new nightmare. Then a shaft of light played across the hairy face of Andre, eyes closed, lips blowing in and out, in a nearby hammock.

Bowie had suffered the nightmare many times, but this was the most vivid. Once Renato had been dealt with, he prayed the blonde girl would release him from her spell.

Rolling from the clammy hammock, he found his boots and carried them past Mariette, who still slumbered, then climbed the ladder to the deck.

The air was salty and brisk. They had left the river, then, and now sailed along the Gulf. Bowie moved toward the bow with wide, careful steps. The Gulf coast was green and inviting on his right, while on his left was an endless expanse of blue. Bowie was used to being in control at all times, and did not like trusting his fate to the vagaries of the untamed sea.

Finding an upended keg, he sat, staring out toward the western horizon. For better or worse, his hopes of high office now depended on this mad treasure hunt. The one positive development was that Dominique You had been wounded too severely to accompany them, and been offloaded at the first opportunity.

Almost without thought, Bowie slid the knife from its sheath and began cleaning it, applying oil from a bottle kept in a watch pocket. How long he sat there he did not know. Then he heard a soft voice.

"I never imagined I could be jealous of a knife."

Bowie looked down at the blade. He had almost forgotten it was there. "I was just cleaning it."

"I could use a cleaning like that. The way you stroke it, caress it like a mistress. It's as if you worship that hideous thing."

Mariette still wore the baggy seaman's outfit meant to disguise her as a boy. Only her sparkling green eyes and musical voice betrayed the woman within.

"There's nothing hideous about it. A knife is a tool like any other. It just needs proper care."

"It is an evil toy," the girl said. "I fear it has bewitched you. Even when you're not fondling it, it's always at your side. My God, you even sleep with the thing."

Bowie hadn't thought in those terms, but there was truth in what she said. The blade was more reliable and trustworthy than any woman. Had it truly become a mistress?

"If you'd seen the things I've done with a knife, you'd be less jealous."

"I've heard stories," Mariette said. "But was it truly you doing those things, or the knife itself?"

Bowie met her eyes. "Is there a difference?"

The girl's mouth twitched, and she seemed to shiver. Then, with a last glare at the blade, she drew the blanket tightly about her shoulders and strolled back toward the stern.

Bowie tried to see the knife through her eyes. Its ten inches of steel had had been polished to a near mirror-like finish. How could she not find it beautiful? She couldn't see that the edge had been honed to cut through bone as easily as butter. Couldn't know the tip was capable of ripping a man in two.

The knife was a tool, it was true, but it was also a magnificent mankiller. As was Bowie himself. The two were now irreversibly linked, as if they had been forged together.

He turned the knife in his hands until the blade caught his reflection. The image was distorted, but he could discern a man with deep-set blue—almost gray—eyes, long sandy side-whis-kers, unsmiling lips and a grimly angled jaw. The man looked as dangerous as the knife itself.

A peculiar clicking noise took his eyes up through the rigging. There, clinging to the mainmast, was the brown demon Pacal, waving a thin arm frantically toward the long island Bowie recognized as Grand Terre.

Scalp tingling, he hurried to the rail. At first he could see nothing, but as his eyes relaxed he caught the gleam of a sail emerging from between Grand Terre and its sister, Grand Isle. The ship was turning to follow them, and Bowie's heart quick-ened at the sight.

His lips tightened, and he somehow knew.

Renato, you are mine at last.

PART II
DEMONS

CHAPTER 14

"A demon!"

THE SAIL APPROACHING Grand Terre had spoken in a voice Renato alone could hear. *Your destiny awaits,* it said, *you have but to take it.* He knew, without understanding how, that this small brig carried his precious map—and those who had dared steal it.

At the moment, the brig had the luck of the wind, keeping it tantalizingly out of reach. But once the wind changed, *L'Intrepide* would strike her prey like a hawk upon a swallow.

Renato stood at the prow, filled with the need to slash and kill that always preceded such an encounter. He was addicted to the thrill of the chase, the smoke and thunder of the guns, the sweet taste of hard-won victory. The need had intensified to the point that, as a newly-made captain, he had decapitated his own first mate for no greater offense than being slow to deliver a telescope. Luckily, he had soon found his second calling—his one other passion—in the paints and brushes inherited from his birth father. Without that release, he would long since have slain his entire crew.

Today, however, he was far beyond painting. At the approach of determined footsteps, he said, "How quickly, Mr. Faraday, could you fetch me a telescope?"

Faraday stopped out of striking distance, hand fingering his neck. Finally, he said, "My apologies, Captain. The wind does not favor us."

"The wind will change. It always does."

"The men are not so certain. They begin to believe we are accursed."

Renato laughed, a short ugly bark. "If you speak again of Voodoo, you do so at your peril."

Faraday fidgeted. "Even you cannot deny the sky."

Renato glanced at the heavens. The clouds had been dark and menacing for the past hour, while the ship they pursued seemed to race in a beam of sunlight. "We have seen bleak skies before, without blaming it on heathen magic." As he spoke, a fresh breeze whipped at his cheek. "You see, Faraday? The winds are with us after all."

The man remained gloomy, downcast. Something more troubled him.

"We have another problem, Captain. It's…it's the water."

Renato surveyed the dark sea separating them and the other ship. The brig was still far off, but they were gaining. "Do you think the sea against us, as well as the skies?"

"Not the sea. Our drinking water. It's nearly gone."

"Impossible. We filled more than a score of casks just this evening past."

"That we did. But most of it is now awash in the hold."

Renato stood as a stone, inwardly boiling. This could be naught but sabotage—or sorcery. "The slaves? Did they see nothing?"

Faraday hesitated. His mouth was tight.

"Damn it, man. Speak before I relieve you of your tongue."

"They cowered together, quaking, their eyes wild. One of them babbled the same two words again and again."

Renato felt icy fingers run up his spine. "What two words?"

Faraday swallowed hard. His voice trembled. "*Evil spirits.*"

BOWIE CLUNG TO the rail, guts churning. He was not cut out to be a seaman. Since first sighting the other sail, *Lucinda* had been skimming over the water light as a ballerina. Now, with the change in the wind, she fell into the trough of each great choppy wave, the sea hammering the hull with force enough to rattle his teeth.

At the same time, the sails of the pursuing ship belled with new wind and seemed to burst ahead. A dark flag became visible atop the schooner's mast.

Bowie looked to the crow's nest, where a crewman peered through a spyglass.

"Two skulls," the man droned, "against a field of black. One white and grinning, the other red as blood, with a down-turned mouth and Xs for eyes."

Bowie swung to Andre, hunched next to him at the rail. "That flag. Is it him?"

The old man nodded. "There now be no doubt."

"Two skulls, one bloody. You pirates are not a subtle lot."

Andre squinted at him. "Renato crafted it himself. The white skull is his. The red is a man ye may have cause to recall."

The old man continued to eye him until Bowie said, "Rayón."

"Aye. Do ye begin to measure the man Renato has become? He's not one to forget a grudge."

The face of the blonde girl swam up from Bowie's memory, and his knuckles grew white on the rail. "Nor am I."

From the bridge, Captain McQuiddy shouted for his men to make more sail.

Bowie and Andre were immediately put to work on the capstan, a yard-tall iron contraption at the center of the deck. Inserting wooden poles into slots, they put their backs to the task, turning the thing like a wheel, and a sail began climbing into place.

Pacal raced past, toting an odd collection of rubbish, and Andre said, "It was madness to bring that brown demon with us. We should feed him to the fishes now, while Mariette is below."

The strange little fellow had been racing about for the better part of an hour collecting bits of straw, dirty cloth, barrel staves, soup bones and anything else he could scavenge or steal. What had begun as a mere pile of trash was now taking on the shape of a scarecrow with an oversized head and mismatched arms sticking out at the sides.

"Probably an idol," Andre said. "One of his damned heathen gods."

"Heathen or not," Bowie said, "Mariette desires his presence. I wish I knew why."

After applying his latest acquisitions, Pacal scurried back into the hold. The man's fervor was disquieting, but Bowie could think of no excuse to halt the project.

He studied Renato's approaching ship. There was still time for men to address any gods they might have. Bowie's parents had raised him to fear a higher power, but experience had taught him to rely on his own head and hands. A man who deferred to his god in times of danger would likely meet that deity sooner than he wished.

"If we catch the wind again," Andre said, "we may yet escape."

"I hope we don't," Bowie said. "This feels like running to me, and I'd as soon stand and fight. It's time Renato and I came to conclusions."

"Ye're mad, Jim Boy. Renato will blast us from the water long before our puny guns are in range."

"No, he won't. He wants that map, and won't sink us until that's in hand. And there's the little matter of vengeance."

"Me own fate will be no more than I deserve," Andre said, his voice cold as the grave. "But I pity poor Mariette at the mercy of that monster."

Bowie thought again of the blonde girl, and felt a stab of guilt. He had not considered Mariette in those terms. He could not bear the thought of her sharing the same fate as that other young woman.

Pacal flashed by with more pieces for his scarecrow. His small hands moved over the body of the bizarre figure, stuffing, tucking, wrapping it with twine.

"Whatever Renato's plans for you and Mariette," Bowie said,

"he'll have to face me first, and I intend to win. After that, he'll be shaking hands with Old Nick."

Andre seemed about to comment, but stopped, nose twitching.

The pungent scent of smoke reached Bowie just as the cry went up.

"Fire on deck!"

RENATO ADMIRED THE dark plume rising from the brig. The smoke boiled up through the sails, flattening into a purplish-gray ribbon as it stretched across the heavens. The brig itself bobbed like a cork, caught in rough water, while *L'Intrepide* closed the gap between them.

"What think you, Cap'n?" This from Quayle. "Some kinda trick?"

"More likely a fire in the galley," Faraday said. "If it reaches their powder, it will save us the trouble of killing them."

Renato turned on him, scowling. "I hate a pessimist." He trained his telescope on the brig. A knot of furious activity roiled around the source of the smoke, and at the center was a flickering spot of flame. Renato squinted, wishing his sight was better. He knew what he *thought* he saw, but could scarcely credit it.

With a studied snort, he handed the glass to Quayle, who had the best eye of any man aboard. "See for yourself."

Quayle pressed it to his mottled face. "Cor!" he said. "I canna believe it!"

"My feelings exactly," Renato purred.

"What the devil is it?" Faraday asked.

"It looks," Quayle said, "like they's burning someone at the stake!"

BOWIE BEAT FURIOUSLY at the blazing scarecrow with his jacket. Fiery bits of refuse showered upon him, but he seemed to be merely fanning the flames.

Andre raced up, flinging water on the pyre. Where it struck, the flames hissed into smoke, but the bulk of the blaze raged on. Finally two crewmen engulfed the burning figure in a spare sail and toppled the whole mass onto the deck. They performed a frantic dance as smoke and ashes burst from both ends.

Spotting Pacal peering from behind a powder keg, Bowie snatched him up and dangled him over the rail, legs kicking the air.

"What in seven hells is wrong with you?" he demanded in Spanish.

Pacal glowered and spat out a series of clicks.

Bowie shook the man until his eyeballs bulged, but no other response was forthcoming.

"Let that poor man down at once!" Mariette's voice was shrill and imperious.

Bowie gave him another shake. "He tried to set the ship afire. If I don't kill him, the captain and crew will."

Several hard-eyed seamen were already offering suggestions as to how.

Mariette's glower included them all.

"If you throw him over, you'd best do the same to me."

"Why? What has he done to earn your loyalty?" A shocking thought occurred to Bowie. "Was that fire lit at your command?"

Mariette gave him a pitying look. "You are a bigger fool than I thought. Confine him if you must, but if any harm comes to him, you'll wake tomorrow with a slit throat."

"AIEEE! A DEMON!"

One of Renato's least-favorite pirates, a rat-faced knave called Sharky, gestured wildly at the air above him.

"Faraday! Silence that man."

Faraday grasped Sharky by the neck, but he continued pointing toward the rigging. "It was there! Putting the evil eye on me, it was!"

"Faraday!"

The quartermaster clapped a hand over the man's mouth and dragged him bodily back to the quarterdeck.

Renato pressed a pistol to the fool's forehead. "Now, Sharky my boy. You will tell us what all the fuss is about. And if I hear any more talk of..." he lowered his voice to a whisper, "*demons*, I shall surely lose control of my trigger finger."

Once the rat-faced man's mouth was uncovered, he seemed to have lost interest in speech.

"Out with it," Renato growled, "before your brains stain the deck."

The words came out in a gush. "I seen something, Cap'n. Truly I did. It was up there grinning at me, but by the time I called out it was gone."

"Gone where?"

Sharky's tongue darted this way and that. "I know not, Cap'n. It just vanished."

Renato dug the barrel deeper. "And what did this *person* look like?"

"I only seen his eyes, Cap'n. Big ones they were, and bright as the fires of..." his voice trailed out, the unsaid word sending a shudder through the men.

Renato steeled his countenance. Strange, inexplicable things were happening aboard his ship, but he could not show concern.

"Mr. Faraday. Our friend Sharky is suffering from heat stroke. I suggest some solitary employment below decks, such as swabbing out the bilge."

As the sniveling wretch was led away, Renato turned his attention to the brig. The fire was out, but she still made very little way, while *L'Intrepide* leapt through the waves like a dolphin.

Quayle suddenly stiffened, and lowered the telescope. "Cap'n sir! I sees him!"

"You sees—you *see* whom?" Renato demanded. "If you say a demon you are going into the sea."

Quayle showed his few remaining teeth in a crooked smile. "No, Cap'n. It's someone you're craving words with. That old toad Andre!"

CHAPTER 15

"Like a hurricane."

THE CLOSER RENATO'S ship loomed, the faster Andre moved. He was everywhere at once, checking gun emplacements and scouring the ship for powder and balls.

Shockingly, *Lucinda's* hands had instantly deferred to his judgment. Andre had apparently earned a reputation as a master gunner, and these men knew it. To Bowie, this was akin to discovering a pig could fly.

Andre had formed three gun crews and insisted on practice sessions. He deemed *Lucinda's* 6-pounders mere pop-guns compared to Renato's, but vowed that if she went to the deep she would take a goodly number of pirates along with her.

After fifteen minutes of drills, Bowie had learned all he wanted of operating a cannon. Having no experience, he was assigned the job of Rammer, a task requiring only muscle. After each shot, he swabbed out the muzzle with a sponge. Mariette, as Powder Monkey, then supplied gunpowder and ball to two crewmen. After one poured the powder, Bowie rammed down the charge. The other rolled the ball into the muzzle, and Bowie rammed down the shot.

Mariette, surprisingly, seemed in her element. Her eyes danced as she exchanged jests with the seamen. While Bowie found this strangely disturbing, he took comfort in the fact she had allowed him to bind Pacal securely to the port rail.

One person Andre had not drafted into service was Sam,

who sprawled at the foot of the mainmast, attention rooted in a small leather-bound book.

Ignoring Andre's complaints, Bowie strode wide-legged across the rolling deck. When his shadow fell across the pages of Sam's book he stopped, fists on hips, and glared.

The fellow continued reading, oblivious to Bowie's presence. His legs were crossed, one bare foot swaying to some inner music.

"Mr. Gideon. Is this how you plan to meet your maker? Lolling about with your nose in some lurid novel?"

The man held up one finger as his eyes moved down the page. "Good morning, Jim. Have you ever read Virgil in the original Latin? I would be pleased to recite a passage."

"If you try it," Bowie said, "I'll toss you over the side. If you refuse to fight, the least you could do is make us breakfast."

Sam's grin faded. He craned his neck, peering past Bowie as if transfixed.

Before Bowie could turn, a deep boom echoed over the waves. Something screamed through the air not six feet from his side, and the port rail next to Pacal vanished in a shower of splinters.

"FARADAY!" RENATO'S SHOUT cut through the ragged cheers of the men. "I ordered a shot across their bow. Is this an example of your shooting?"

Faraday dipped his head, clearly embarrassed. As well he should be. The shot been off target by a good twenty yards.

The brig would soon come within range of his 9-pounders, and Renato worried over the accuracy of a broadside. Men still jittery from Voodoo and Sharky's demon could not be trusted to fire on the brig without sending it to the bottom of the Gulf.

"Mr. Faraday, have the men shorten sail and bring us about. I wish to put chain shot into their rigging. And this time, I will aim the gun myself."

At Faraday's command, men began scurrying up the ropes and along the spars to the topsails. Renato was reminded again of Sharky's demon, and fought off the chill, warming himself with thoughts of long overdue retribution.

A tug on the side of his coat announced the return of Princess. "You are just in time, my dear, to witness another victory. Would you like Andre's nose for a plaything? Or would one of his daughter's ears be more to your liking?"

He had just raised his telescope when he heard a loud snap, a brief cry, and a plunking splash. He had heard such sounds before, and felt a stab of annoyance. Without turning, he listened for the words that would surely come.

And come they did, from several throats at once.

"Man overboard!"

"MAN OVERBOARD!" THE gleeful shout came from *Lucinda*'s lookout, gesturing wildly toward the oncoming pirate ship.

Through the spyglass, Bowie studied the frantic activity on *L'Intrepide*. Men in the rigging plopped to the deck, while others scrambled to the stern, pointing and waving their arms.

A broad-shouldered man in a black frock coat stood unmoving in the prow, an island in the swarm of activity. Bowie's blood burned. This could be none other than Renato.

Lucinda's crew laughed like doomed prisoners granted a reprieve. The repeated phrase "man overboard" rose to the blue heavens like a prayer.

Mariette was caught up by Captain McQuiddy in a twirling dance of celebration. As she broke away, her lips spread in the first genuine smile Bowie had seen from her.

Running to Bowie, she wrapped arms around his neck, swinging until he was forced to put an arm around her waist. She felt slim and soft under the rough clothes. "Is it true? Are we saved?"

"So it would seem," he said, feeling slightly deflated.

"Can you doubt it? Renato must stop to rescue his man."

Bowie nodded, pretending to be pleased. He had steeled

himself for the showdown with Renato, and now it would be postponed.

"Jim." Andre gripped the rail, staring intently at *L'Intrepide*. The schooner was closer now, and showed no sign of slackening speed.

Bowie raised the glass again. Renato was still motionless on the deck, staring across the waves as if straight into his eyes.

"What's wrong?" Mariette cried. "Why hasn't he turned back?"

Andre's face was grim.

"He don't intend to."

RENATO FOCUSED ON the floundering brig, shutting out the chaos behind him. He was too near his goal to be balked by the slip of a clumsy fool's foot.

"That were Portwood!" a man shouted.

"My cousin!" cried another. "I sees him, Cap'n! He's waving for help!"

"The demon!" Sharky squealed. "The demon musta done it!"

"Shorten sail and prepare to come about!"

These last words, from Faraday, jarred Renato into action. "Belay that!" His voice was like a pistol shot. All activity came to a halt, the crew goggling like mindless apes.

"Captain!" Faraday's voice rang with indignation. "We must send a boat for him."

"*Must*, Mr. Faraday? Are you giving the orders now?"

Renato willed him to say *yes*. It would be the perfect excuse to shoot him.

Faraday quivered with righteous rage, but his lips remained tightly shut.

A man appeared behind him, a tall, well-built fellow with rage purpling his face. His name, too, Renato recalled, was Portwood. "That's my cousin, Cap'n. You have to save him!"

Renato eyed him coolly. The fellow's right hand was perilously close to his saber. "I *have* to?"

The tall man glanced about as if gauging support from his crewmates. "Aye, Cap'n. You do."

Renato had rehearsed such a scene many times in his mind, but the speaker had always been Faraday. This fellow would be less satisfying, but would serve the purpose. For now.

The pistol sprang from Renato's belt like a rattlesnake. The powder flashed, the butt kicked in his hand, and while the gun still roared, a blue hole gaped in Portwood's face, a scant inch from his nose.

"JESUS, MARY AND Joseph!" Andre rubbed at his eyes, then pressed the spyglass back to his face. "I can't believe it. Renato shot one of his own, and the bugger's dead as yesterday's breakfast."

Mariette put hands to her cheeks. "Not Mr. Faraday, I hope! He was the only handsome one of the lot."

Bowie shaded his eyes, straining to bring the tiny figures on the other deck into focus. "Is it mutiny, then?"

"We'll soon see. Renato's just rolled the dice. If we've any luck, those rogues will turn on him and hack him to pieces."

"And if they don't?"

Andre's tone was grim. "Then he'll be comin' at us like a hurricane."

Bowie stole a look at Mariette. If he failed to kill Renato, she would be a corpse within the hour. He could not let that happen.

"Quickly!" Andre rapped. "We must get off a round before their guns come to bear."

Bowie nodded at the 6-pounders. "Can these toys really do them any harm?"

"Only if we hit something vital—like Renato's head."

"And how likely is that?"

"About as likely," Andre muttered, "as a whirlpool openin' up and suckin' 'em to the bottom of the sea."

RENATO PEERED THROUGH the pistol smoke at the crumpled body before him. His nose twitched. The man had loosed his bowels in a final show of contempt for the living.

The tension on deck was electric. This was the critical moment. If his men had time to think, they could unite behind a new leader and butcher him where he stood.

"Mr. Faraday. Remove that stinking carcass at once. We will then swing about and load the starboard guns with chain shot."

Faraday went white as his shirt. He wanted badly to take the measure of the men, Renato knew, but feared to look away.

Renato saw hands creep toward hilts and gun butts. Furtive glances were exchanged. They ached to act, but none dared make the first move.

"Mr. Faraday!" Renato's voice was a whipcrack. "Now!"

Faraday winced, and was lost. "Trainer! Napier! Toss that corpse to the sharks. Yazzolino, get a bucket and swab up those brains. And be quick about it, damn you!"

As the men named sprang into motion, Renato turned his back, heart hammering beneath his coat. The men had placed their hopes in Faraday, and seen him back down. Until a new champion arose, they had no will but to obey.

L'Intrepide was already coming about. The guns were loaded, but had not yet come to bear when the lookout squawked from above.

"Cap'n! They're lightin' fuses!"

The sharp crack of the brig's guns told Renato they were mere 6-pounders. He squared his shoulders and clasped hands behind his back, smirking as two balls churned up the sea well short of his hull.

"Prepare to fire!"

Men crouched over the black iron barrels, torches at the ready. Renato judged the rolls of the two ships, and raised his arm, waiting for the perfect moment.

"Ready!"

Lucinda's sails stood out white and fragile against the powder blue sky, and Renato could already picture them crashing down upon her passengers and crew.

"Fire!"

CHAPTER 16

"Worse ways to die."

"TAKE COVER!"

Fire blossomed from three points along *L'Intrepide*'s side, and even at this distance, the roar smote Bowie's ears like a thunderclap.

Men cursed, yelled, and scrambled in all directions. Even the placid Sam deigned to react, glancing up from his book with a look of mild annoyance.

Bowie spied Mariette near the foremast, bandaging Pacal's limbs. He ran three steps and dived headlong through the air.

Balls whistled overhead, followed by a mad chorus of snapping ropes and cracking timbers. Bowie sailed over the brown man, cradling Mariette beneath him, and tumbled to the deck, shielding her body with his own.

A storm of broken spars and splinters showered over them, and the deck itself leapt as a yardarm crashed down. One end of the huge timber slammed across Bowie's back, sending him reeling. A moment later he and Mariette were smothered in plummeting folds of canvas.

"Mariette! Are you—?"

A stream of lurid French cut him short, and Bowie had to smile. She was at least well enough to be angry.

All around them were muffled shouts and curses. From out of the din came Andre's voice. "Mariette! Jim! Be ye alive?"

Bowie roared back, and presently the constricting weight melted away. When the last fold of heavy canvas was pulled aside, he rose and blinked into the sky where the topsail had been.

Mariette's watch cap had come off, spilling her luxurious hair over her shoulders, and *Lucinda*'s crew was agog, realizing at last there was a female in their midst.

Bowie looked away. Glaring at him with undisguised venom was Pacal, apparently damaged no worse than before. Sam, likewise, seemed unharmed, though he stalked the deck as if in search of something. Perhaps his wits, Bowie thought. Or his courage.

The deck was a shambles of fallen ropes and spars. Crewman staggered about, surveying the wreckage with defeated eyes. And from across the waves, turning toward them once again, came *L'Intrepide*, her black flag of vengeance looming ever larger.

Bowie turned to Andre. "How bad is it?"

The old man's face was haggard, blood streaming from a gash in his temple. "They shot away half our foremast. Even if we had room to run, our speed would be cut in half."

"So what do we do now?"

"Little we can do, Jim Boy, but fight and die."

"I suppose it's too late," Bowie said, "to buy your lives with the map."

Mariette shook her head. "Even if it weren't, I would never give Renato the satisfaction. Before he takes me, I'll swallow it whole."

And have your gizzard slit as he fishes it out, Bowie thought grimly. *Unless I kill him first.*

L'INTREPIDE'S DECK RANG with the coarse cheers of the crew.

Renato allowed them their moment. They had done well enough, and not put the map at risk.

He raised his telescope. The man directing the brig's clean-up effort turned his head, and Renato caught his breath. *Andre—the betrayer!* Renato weighed his options. He could have the skin

flayed from the little toad's body. He could keelhaul him, dragging his stubby form over the coral reefs. He could stuff him into
an iron maiden and hang him from the yardarm as an example
to his men. Perhaps all three.

This pleasant reverie was cut short as he spied the man working next to Andre—a broad-shouldered fellow in a white shirt
and tan waistcoat. There was a quick, fluid quality to his movements. Renato's heart began to pound. Then the man's features
came into view. The heavy brow, deep-set eyes and dimpled chin
were just as he remembered. *Bowie.*

Renato examined his old foe with new eyes. The gangly
youth had grown into a formidable man. His hair was cut to
the latest style, with side-whiskers extending halfway down his
ruddy cheeks. His clothing, despite its state of disrepair, looked
well-tailored and expensive.

Still, the man's reputation was obviously overinflated. That
error would soon be rectified.

"Mr. Faraday! Prepare hands for boarding!"

The pirates snatched up clubs and swords, tucked knives into
belts, checked the prime of pistols. They smelled blood, and
could be depended upon to do what they were best at.

"Cap'n, sir! Look!"

Renato did, and smirked as the proud stars and stripes came
slinking down in surrender.

"ARE YE DAFT?" Andre's howl trailed him as he scurried for the quarterdeck, halting toe-to-toe with McQuiddy. "Ye
strike your colors after the first paltry broadside?"

McQuiddy thrust out a whiskered chin, pugnacious as a bulldog. "Back off, you old buzzard! No man questions my orders."

"This is how ye pay favor to your great friend Dominique You?
By handin' us over to that butcher?"

McQuiddy's faced grayed. "It pains me to say it, but it might
be the only way to save my ship."

"Save your ship? Be ye mad? Renato'd lay torch to your blessed ship just to light his pipe!"

"That's as may be, but he's a capricious sort. No telling what he'll do."

Andre threw up his hands and stomped away, lips flapping curses.

"So he's given up." Bowie's voice was flat. He eyed the schooner coursing toward them. "It's down to you and I." He put a hand to his hip, and the big blade flashed out, brilliant in the harsh sunlight.

Andre nodded in solemn salute. His thin rapier sang from its sheath and traced a figure eight in the air. "You and me, Jim Boy."

"You forget me, gentlemen."

Behind them stood Mariette, a pistol in one hand and a cutlass in the other.

Andre said, "Darlin', no, you can't…"

"She might as well," Bowie said. "There are worse ways to die."

He surveyed the crew. While some still worked to clear away debris, most stood slump-shouldered, watching the approaching schooner.

"A proud lot of mighty seamen," he said. "Do none of you have the grit to match this slip of a girl?"

A few men eyed their captain as if seeking permission to fight. But as McQuiddy's head moved side to side, all fell silent.

"So that's how it is," Bowie growled. "Two men and a girl against a shipload of bloody pirates."

"Two men, a girl and one superb baritone," added a rich voice.

Swaggering toward them came Sam. Without pausing, he plucked a dagger from the belt of a downcast sailor.

Bowie was unable to suppress a grin. "So, Mr. Gideon, you've finally found your courage."

The black man's teeth gleamed. "More to the point, I've lost my Virgil. A falling spar struck my hand, and that exquisite volume was swept overboard." He twirled the dagger and sent it flying to the mainmast, where it stuck and quivered. "Men responsible for the death of poetry, even indirectly, merit no mercy."

"Splendid," Mariette said. "Now we have them outnumbered."

Bowie trained the spyglass on *L'Intrepide*. Renato, too, had a telescope pressed to his face. Their magnified gazes locked on one another, and it was as if a lightning bolt quivered in stasis between them.

Then Renato lowered his glass, revealing a scabrous smile.

Bowie's breath hissed between his teeth. Save for dreams, he had not seen that face in more than eight years. There were more lines than he recalled, and sharper angles. But there was much the same: The yellowish tint to eyes and skin, the livid red scar from nose to jaw, the thin horseshoe mustache framing his lips in a perpetual scowl.

The schooner was now less than a hundred yards away. Bowie had thrown rocks with deadly accuracy farther than that, and wished he had one now. One good cast would knock the leer from Renato's face.

"Oh!" Mariette said. "Perhaps Pacal will join our little band."

The brown man squatted alone near the fallen topsail. Mariette called to him, and he rose slowly to his feet. But rather than join them, he tilted his head back and stretched his arms to the heavens.

The cry that escaped his lips was like nothing of this earth. It began as a bone-chilling wail and rose to an ear-splitting screech, as if the man's twisted soul spewed from his body and spread its madness across the sky.

RENATO'S NAPE-HAIRS TINGLED. Perhaps *L'Intrepide* was not the only ship playing host to demons this day.

As the eerie shriek faded into the wind, his pirates stood mute at the rail, eyes hollow and faces pale.

"A song to warm the heart," Renato called out. "One of their crewmen screaming like a ravaged woman!"

His sneering laugh was echoed by a handful of men, but their jovial mood did not return.

Faraday approached, rubbing his hands. "Beg pardon, Captain, but now that they've surrendered, what are our orders?"

"You'll never be a leader, Faraday. You've no imagination." Renato strode to the mast. "You men, attend me well! Our enemies toy with us, feigning surrender. Do they think us fools, to be gulled by so old a trick? Once we close, you've leave to glut your swords on every wretch aboard, with the exception of three."

The big man LaChaise took the cue. "Which three, Cap'n?"

"The first you know well—Andre the traitor. The second is his vile offspring, she of the mannish clothes and flowing black hair. The third is…" he checked himself, realizing Bowie's name could have a demoralizing effect, "that lumbering ox in the white shirt. They are to be captured, if possible, but by all means left alive." Renato now played his trump card. "With those three in our hands, the treasure will soon follow, and within the week, every man among you will be rich as a lord."

LaChaise cheered, followed by others, and in a matter of moments the coarse jests and eager faces were back.

Renato allowed himself a smile. The death of Bowie would be a suitable subject for his next painting. Perhaps he would even prepare a woodcut for submission to *The Niles Register*.

As for the girl, she was quite fetching, despite her tainted blood. He could either kill Andre and Bowie first and take his time with her, or have them bound and forced to witness the proceedings.

Renato smacked his lips. The life of a pirate was hard, but had its compensations.

Confidence surged through him. That he had seriously considered the possibility of Voodoo at work on his ship now seemed fantastic. It was cunning, strength of will, and might of hand that determined a man's fate, not mummery and super-stition.

And as he thought these things, he heard a faint sputtering somewhere behind him. It was almost like the hissing of a snake. But surely there were no snakes aboard *L'Intrepide*. It was more like...yes. He had it.

The burning of a fuse.

BOWIE COULD NOT believe his eyes.

One moment the pirates hung wild-eyed on the boarding lines, while Renato strutted about, curling his mustache like the villain in a melodrama. An instant later, the schooner's deck erupted with the force of a volcano.

The would-be boarders shot twenty feet through the air to plummet into the sea. Renato himself seemed to hang suspended above the deck before being engulfed by a huge ball of fire and smoke.

L'Intrepide's mainmast leapt upward, straining its ropes, then toppled forward, crashing through the spars of the foremast. Sails fluttered down amid a rain of rope, tackle and shattered timber. The falling mast, having demolished everything in its path, slammed to the deck, projecting from the prow like the lance of a jousting knight.

The pirate ship floundered out of control less than thirty yards from the brig. The sea between the ships boiled with frantic pirates, clinging to the bodies of their less fortunate mates. Of Renato there was no sign. The spot he had occupied was now covered in heaps of fallen sail.

Through the ringing in his ears, Bowie heard his own voice. "What the hell?"

Andre crossed himself. "Hell is right." He turned to stare at Pacal, who still stood with face and arms outstretched to the sky.

"You don't think that lunatic sicced his gods on them?"

"What else would cause their powder to blow at so oppor-tune a moment?"

Bowie shook his head, at a loss for words.

"Hard a-port!" Captain McQuiddy's voice rang with command.

Lucinda turned sluggishly, her remaining sails filling with wind.

"What's happening?" Bowie demanded. "We're not leaving?"

"Aye, Jim Boy. That be it exactly."

"No, by God! We can't! I must be sure Renato's dead."

Andre shook his head. "A pretty thought, but it'd be madness to linger now. A single shot from one of them guns would sink us sure."

"All the more reason to strike quickly." Without waiting for a reply, Bowie charged to the quarterdeck.

"Get me aboard that ship," he demanded. "I have unfinished business with Renato!"

McQuiddy's face blanched, eyes fixed on the blade quivering inches from his nose. "Impossible. We must flee while we've half a chance."

"Just set me aboard. Then you can sail away to Hades, for all I care."

"I dare not!" Sweat glistened on McQuiddy's brow. "If we get that close, the men in the water will try to board us."

"But half of them are already dead!"

"If true, they still outnumber us two to one. Be reasonable, man!"

Bowie swung away, eyeing the dark expanse of water between the ships. He could swim that distance easily, even if he had to gut a few pirates along the way. An odd movement caught his eye, and he blinked. For moment, he thought he'd seen a small creature bound from head-to-head in an effort to get back to the crippled ship.

"James." Mariette materialized before him. "Please. We—I need your help with the treasure."

The ships were pulling steadily apart. He must dive, and quickly, or miss his chance.

"I'm sorry." He slipped carefully around the girl, not trusting himself to her touch. He'd flung one leg over the rail and was about to dive when a voice squawked from the water below.

"Help! A rope, please, a rope!"

Close to the hull, a rat-faced pirate clung to the back of a corpse.

Bowie glared down at him. He could not be troubled with such a rogue as this. Not while Renato may yet live.

Gentle fingers curled around his arm. "James, please. I know him. He's not as bad as the others."

Bowie looked longingly at *L'Intrepide*'s deck. Still no sign of life, and now nearly out of range. And the hand on his arm was wondrously soft.

Long after the half-drowned rat had been plucked from the sea, Bowie stood motionless at the rail, eyes fixed on the receding hulk of Renato's ship, torn between the ebon-haired girl at his side and the blonde wraith who haunted his dreams.

CHAPTER 17

"What madness is this?"

RENATO WRITHED IN a world of pain and darkness, interrupted only by brief periods of even more intense agony. His mind roiled with barely glimpsed faces that leered at him before whirling back into the void. His ears howled with the unrelenting wails of others in anguish. His nostrils flinched at the stench of charred flesh and the pungent odor of blood. More than anything, he felt like a pig being roasted on a spit.

There was only one possible conclusion. He was in Hell.

During one of his more lucid moments, he heard an anxious voice. "Mr. Renato! Mr. Renato!" He knew that voice. Quayle. So his squalid little bosun was here too.

Renato seethed. This was the height of injustice—a great captain of buccaneers landing on the same level of the Underworld as a cheap and common villain like Quayle. But if he and Quayle were in Hell, perhaps Rayón was as well.

"Rayón! Brother, are you there?"

Rayón did not respond. Instead, he heard the annoying rasp of Quayle.

"Mr. Renato, sir! Can you hear me?"

He could now make out Quayle's pitted teeth and bulbous nose. Realizing he was flat on his back, he struggled to rise. "Help me up, damn you!"

Quayle tugged at his arms, and Renato gasped. It felt as if the man's hands were on fire. Reeling, he grasped Quayle by the collar and pulled him close. *Zounds!* His hand stung with the contact, but the pain was only half as bad as the odor. The man's stench in death was as repellent as it had been in life.

"Where is Rayón! Tell me, damn your eyes! Where is he?"

Quayle's voice shook. "Why, he ain't here, Mr. Renato. He's dead."

"Of course he's dead, fool. So are we!"

"Let go, Mr. Renato! Please, you're breaking my arm!"

That was good. It was some small compensation that he could inflict pain as well as receive it. He could now make out other figures around him. All the faces visible belonged to members of his crew. This was a strange sort of afterlife.

With a start, he recognized his surroundings. This was not Hell, after all, but the crew's quarters aboard *L'Intrepide*.

"Quayle! What's the meaning of this?"

"Tended you myself, I did, three days and more." A small note of pride entered Quayle's voice. "No one believed you'd live. No one but me."

"Three days!" Renato was thunderstruck. "What of Andre and the girl—and that damned Bowie?"

Quayle cringed. "The brig's gone, Mr. Renato. Sailed off right after the explosion. Six men drowned, and others already dead, but you—"

"Damnation!" Renato recalled the white-hot blast, the deafening roar, and the deck erupting beneath him.

He was still reeling from this vision when another fantastic site hove into view. A hulking black man clad only in soiled cotton breeches ambled up and stood goggling at him.

"Curse you, Quayle! What madness is this? Why is this black rascal roaming free about my ship?"

Quayle drywashed his hands. "The men decided, sir. They was afraid of the Voodoo."

"The men decided?" Renato was incredulous. "Saints preserve us. What else, pray tell, have *the men* decided?"

"Well, sir, when they thought you'd die, they took a vote."

"A vote? Since when is this a democracy?"

"Some said it were your fault, Mr. Renato, as you'd refused to release the slaves."

"Damn you, Quayle! Why do you persist in calling me *Mr.* Renato? You'll address me properly or see your skin flying above the mast."

"I was getting to that, sir, really I was. You see, you ain't cap'n no more. You're a prisoner."

No longer captain? It was preposterous. Unthinkable. Renato clutched the fool by the throat, to wring the truth out of him.

Quayle let out a squeal that would have raised the dead. He thrashed madly about, trying to free himself.

"Speak, you little twat! Why are you feeding me these lies?"

Renato heard footsteps, and almost rejoiced. Maybe now he could talk to someone with a brain.

Instead, he saw a belaying pin flashing toward his head. His world went white, then he plummeted back into blackness.

CHAPTER 18

"Men are often ridiculous."

AT FIRST, THE coastline had been no more than a dark line above the blue plane of the sea. But as the sun dipped ever closer to the horizon, the land grew up to meet it, and the flat line evolved into hills sprouting patches of green, tan and brown.

Bowie breathed deep as *Lucinda* finally passed behind the barrier islands into Matagorda Bay. The biting wind had slackened to a breeze, and the fresh scent of greenery was sweet after the unrelenting tang of the Gulf.

Along the darkening shore, fields of tall, swaying grasses were broken only by scattered patches of scrub wood. Beyond the grassy plain, a distance of at least a mile, stood rows of huge live oaks and stands of pecan trees.

To Bowie, motionless at the rail, it was as if the land were being newly formed before his eyes. A newborn country. That was Texas, a place of wide-open spaces and infinite possibilities, where life balanced on the edge of a blade. A land too wild and free to ever be thoroughly tamed.

Bowie had felt its pull since his first visit, when he had joined General Long and his tiny army of filibusters in a mad scheme to wrest Texas away from Spain. The enterprise had ended in prison and death for Long, but to Bowie it had been his first grand adventure. He'd left home a wide-eyed youth and returned a man to be reckoned with.

Now, nine years later, Texas called to him again, daring him to come and be tested. It would be only a matter of time, he knew, before he answered that call and made this land his home.

Bowie tensed as someone touched his arm. But the fingers were soft, and could belong only to Mariette.

"What do you see out there?"

"My past," Bowie said, "and my future."

"I thought you were going to Congress."

"I am."

"Why?"

"*Why?*"

"Yes. Why do you want to be a congressman?"

Bowie flushed. It seemed a silly question, but the answer was hard to put into words. "Why, for respect, of course. And power. I've been to Washington, and seen those men operate. They make money hand over fist."

"Is that all you want from life? Wealth and power?"

The question made him uncomfortable. "At present, I have little of either."

"At the end of this journey," she said, "you will have wealth beyond imagining. Will that not give you the power you desire?"

"Perhaps."

She eyed him shrewdly, as if she were peering into his soul. "And perhaps," she said, "you are not as vain and avaricious as you pretend. Perhaps you are one of those dreamers who think they can serve their constituents better than those who have gone before."

"That's ridiculous."

"It is, isn't it? But men are often ridiculous."

As she flounced away, Bowie realized he'd been thinking little of wealth and power of late. He'd been consumed with the need to see Renato dead, and the blonde girl avenged.

It had been three full days since the encounter with the pirates. Three days of regrets and recriminations, wondering if Renato were dead or alive. A part of him hoped the yellow-skinned bastard had been consumed by the hellish blast that ripped the mainmast from *L'Intrepide*'s deck. But on a deeper level, he longed for another chance to meet him face-to-face and blade-to-blade.

The time on board *Lucinda* had not made a sailor of him, but he'd gained an appreciation of McQuiddy's ability to guide his crippled ship to the very place indicated on Mariette's map.

Bowie's eyes flicked back to the shoreline. Something had caught his eye. A movement. Nothing he could identify, just a hint of motion inconsistent with the breeze.

Bowie peered into the shadows, probing for further movement. Texas was a land teeming with wildlife. It might have been a deer, a coyote, even a wild boar. He would have thought no more of it, but for the prickling sensation on his scalp.

He would have to be on constant alert. This was Karankawa country, where a man stood to lose far more than his hair. His last visit to this area had resulted in tragedy. A group of slaves he'd been guiding had escaped in the night, and he'd found only bodies and bones, grim evidence of the Indians' deviltry.

A tinkling laugh floated over the deck. Mariette sat on an upturned powder keg, her face aglow with merriment. Her dark tresses now danced free in the wind, and her mannish attire seemed snugger, hinting at a figure not evident before.

Bowie found her an enigma. She had seemed warm enough after the escape from Renato, but the more attention he paid her, the less it was returned.

Entertaining her was the unwelcome refugee from *L'Intrepide*—the man called Sharky. Whatever interest she had in him, it was surely not his looks. His eyes were spaced no more than an inch apart, leaving scant room for a brain, and his wart-covered nose hooked over a mouth nearly devoid of teeth. His back was bent in a permanent crook, and his arms and legs seemed attached at odd angles.

Bowie was not yet sure what to make of the man's story. That Renato had acquired unwanted slaves from Haiti was credible enough. But the tales of stolen food and a demon in the rigging smacked more of ignorant superstition than of magical forces.

Farther down the deck, Pacal's eyes were fixed on Sharky with a malevolence heretofore reserved for Bowie himself. He, too, would bear watching. What had possessed him to create that fiery scarecrow? And had his ear-piecing scream been somehow connected to the explosion on Renato's ship? The little monster had other strange quirks as well. He ate enough for three grown sailors, and always did it somewhere below deck, too bashful to eat in front of the crew.

"Sweet bleeding Jesus!" Andre burst through the hatch from the lower deck to confront McQuiddy. "What treachery are you up to now?"

Bowie sighed. Andre had been full of complaints and unwanted advice to the point McQuiddy threatened to have him put in irons. Bowie moved toward the shouting, thankful this leg of the journey was nearly at an end.

Andre thrust a finger heatedly back toward the entrance to the bay. "If our destination is back there, why in the sweet by-and-by are ye sailing in the wrong direction?"

McQuiddy's boot rapped a tattoo on the deck. "I've already explained that, you loathsome wretch!"

Bowie halted behind Andre. "Perhaps you could explain it to *me*."

McQuiddy spat a stream of evil fluid expertly over the side. "Devil take me if I ever again accept passengers. As I've told your aged companion, my ship is in no condition to touch down in hostile territory. Her maneuverability is limited, and her armament in an even sorrier state. That spot you're so anxious to visit is known as Karankawa Cove. Does that not suggest something to you?"

McQuiddy paused to glance back at the channel they had entered. "I've a peculiar pain in my shoulder. It's from an old wound, but has long since ceased to ail me—except when danger is near."

Andre sucked in his breath and peered this way and that with shaded eyes.

Bowie himself had no use for magics and portends, but knew better than to question a man's instincts.

Recalling the movement he'd seen, Bowie's hand strayed to the butt of his knife. That Renato and his gang of cutthroats could be on their trail so soon after that crippling explosion seemed unlikely, but here in Karankawa country, trouble was never in short supply.

"I saw nothing," Andre blurted. "Like as not it's just your yellow streak showin' again."

McQuiddy puffed up, his face growing crimson, then let his breath out in a hiss.

"If you're not taking us to the cove," Bowie said, "where *are* we going?"

McQuiddy waved an arm. "At the end of this bay lies the little city of Matagorda. We need a safe place to reprovision and make repairs, and I believe that's our best hope."

"A city?" Mariette had appeared at Bowie's elbow. "We're visiting a city? How delightful."

"Best lower your expectations," Bowie said. "In Texas, all it takes to comprise a city is two hogs and an outhouse. And last I heard of Matagorda, that's all it was."

"That's as may be," McQuiddy said. "But a schooner full of New Yorkers put in there a while back, and it's said to be a thriving community."

Andre, who had been steaming like a teakettle, finally burst. "This is no time for sight-seein' in some backwater village! What if Renato is comin'? Ye think he'll fear to enter that cove?"

"I pray he does come," Bowie said. "And that I'll be there to greet him."

BY THE TIME the settlement came into view, the sun was a blood-red ball over the dark mass of the mainland. In the dim light, Bowie made out a cluster of small cabins of unhewn

logs and clapboard roofs. Between the shoreline and the settlement, a line of flickering torches cast dancing shadows over the
landscape.

"A welcoming committee," Bowie said. "And quite a crowd."

Mariette beamed with anticipation. Andre merely growled.

Bowie began to pick faces out of the gloom. They were mostly
men, at least two dozen in all, none of them smiling and most of
them armed with muskets, rifles and pitchforks. Beyond them
huddled a small cluster of women and children.

"Halloo the settlement!" McQuiddy's voice rolled from the
speaking trumpet, sharp against the distant boom of the Gulf.

"Keep your distance," a man called back, "if you value your
lives!"

"We're peaceable!" McQuiddy proclaimed. "And Americans.
Mine's a trading vessel out of New Orleans, with goods you may
welcome. Might I come ashore?"

After a brief conference, the answer came back. "You may. But
come alone. And if we like not your looks, you may be staying
permanent."

"Just myself, and a man to row me," McQuiddy agreed.

As the boat was lowered, Bowie moved to the captain's side.
"I'll do the rowing, if I may."

"I'm not sure that's wise," McQuiddy said.

"What's that supposed to mean?"

"It means," the captain said, "that these people are unlikely
to be soothed by a man famous for killing."

"Then you underestimate me, Captain. I'll wager these folk
will find me more palatable than one of your common seamen."

McQuiddy scrutinized him. Having donned a spare shirt and
managed a morning shave, Bowie knew he looked reasonably
presentable.

"Very well, but you'll leave that young sword of yours behind.
This is a trading vessel, not a pirate ship."

Bowie gripped the handle, prepared to surrender the knife to

Andre, but the thing would not budge. He tugged harder, but the blade seemed to be glued to the sheath, and the sheath to his hip.

"I believe I'll keep it." He held McQuiddy's eye until the man nodded.

"I must insist, however, that you let me do the talking."

Bowie smiled, making no promises, and dropped into the small boat. Talking was a politician's job, and if he expected to sway opinion in the halls of Congress, he could surely do so here in the wilds of Texas.

ON THE BEACH, the greeting party formed a partial circle around them. At the forefront was a tall, robust man in a coat of English rather than French cut, indicating he had recently come from New York. A good third of the rest were attired in similar fashion, while others wore rough homespun or loose Mexican blouses and pantaloons. The women, looking nervous but defiant, wore dark wool cloaks, and bonnets cinched tight beneath their chins.

McQuiddy performed a half bow. "Angus McQuiddy, captain of *Lucinda*." Bowie had not seen the man smile before, and the effort made him look unnatural. "I've coffee, tools and other provisions you may find useful."

"We're unfamiliar with your ship." The leader's voice was hard as flint. "How do we know you're not pirates?"

"You see my flag, surely?"

A man laughed harshly. "Ah, surely. Just like the one Renato flew."

Renato! This, then, explained the sour faces. "If Renato is your enemy," Bowie said, "I'm pleased to call you friends. There's no man on earth I'd rather kill."

The eyes of the group now focused on Bowie.

"And who might you be?" The leader's voice remained stern.

Before Bowie could answer, someone cried, "Look! Two of Renato's men, or I'll be shot!"

The man pointed up at the pale faces of Andre and Sharky peering over the rail.

"Aye!" Another shouted. "I remember them all too well!"

All guns now swung to the ready. Those nearest Bowie and McQuiddy centered on them, while the rest drew bead on the ship.

Bowie spoke calmly, as if addressing a gathering of friends. "Those two once sailed with Renato, it's true, but they've seen the error of their ways. If it would please you, though, you're welcome to hang the skinny one."

Sharky yelped, his face vanishing from the rail.

Mutters ran through the crowd, as interest settled once more on Bowie.

The leader said, "Suppose you tell us who you are, sir, and why we should believe you."

After a distinct pause, Bowie said, "The name is Bowie."

Men exchanged surprised looks.

"James Bowie, of Natchez?"

"I've spent time there. But I'm equally of Kentucky, Arkansas and Louisiana, and sorely tempted to join you brave folk as a resident of Texas."

A man said, "If you're really Jim Bowie, show us the knife."

"Aye," said another. "And quickly."

With a knowing wink at McQuiddy, Bowie put a hand to his hip and let the knife flash into view. With a score of torches to feed it, the blade shimmered like a tongue of fire.

Men gasped or cursed. A woman cried, "My Lord!"

The leader lowered his rifle, causing the others to follow suit. "It's smaller than I thought. From the tales men tell, I expected nothing short of Excalibur."

Bowie dipped his head. "I fear I'm no Arthur."

"That the blade that killed Major Wright?"

Bowie adopted a modest grin. "A gentleman never tells," he said, and the tense atmosphere dissolved into laughter.

Many in the group moved closer. Smiles began to appear.

The leader addressed his flock. "If Mr. Bowie vouches for those two men, I say we allow them ashore. But he must also take responsibility for them. What say you, sir? Will you be accountable for their actions?"

Bowie was careful to mask his misgivings. He ran a thumb along the edge of the blade. "If either misbehaves," he said solemnly, "I'll skin him alive and feed him to the Kronks."

Holding the grin firmly in place, he glanced up at the scowling face of Mariette. That was one promise he hoped he would not have to keep.

CHAPTER 19

"A will-o-the-wisp."

RENATO WOKE TO the salty brine of sea water rushing up his nostrils, stinging his eyes.

With it came the raucous laughter of his crew. Laughter aimed at *him*.

"Ah, it seems His Royal Highness is back from the dead." The voice was Faraday's, but rang with a sarcasm the man had never before dared.

Renato blinked. Yes, that was Faraday, and next to him Quayle, clutching an empty bucket. But what was Faraday doing in that fine wool coat of midnight blue—the pride of Renato's own closet?

He struggled to move, but found himself lashed to the foremast. Above him, an odd assortment of sails twitched in the flaccid wind. The mainmast was gone, and *L'Intrepide* limped along like a fish with one flipper.

The men eyed him as if he were some new kind of animal. Worst of all, they seemed completely devoid of fear.

The horror of Quayle's words came rushing back. He was no longer captain! His command had been ripped from him—just when he needed it most. And Faraday wearing his coat told the rest of the tale.

Renato bared his teeth and snarled. "I don't know which of us looks more ridiculous, *Mr.* Faraday. Me as a prisoner, or you in the costume of a captain."

Faraday slammed a vicious backhand to the side of his face, and the contact sent waves of unbelievable agony through him.

"That's *Captain* Faraday to you. Now if you're quite ready, Your Lordship, we'll proceed with the sentencing."

"Sentencing? What bloody farce is this?"

"The men and I wish to do things right and proper. You slept through the trial, I'm afraid, but you're in time to hear the verdict."

Faraday leveled an accusing finger at him. "Charge the first. That you knowingly attacked and sank a vessel under American flag, putting us afoul of the U.S. Navy."

Growls of agreement came from the crew.

"Charge the second. That in sinking said vessel, you drowned a hold full of slaves from the devil isle of Haiti, putting the curse of Voodoo on us all."

"Aye!" someone shouted. "An' he buggered Quayle, too!"

Renato's face burned. "That is a damned lie."

"Well, you could if you'd wanted," added a wag. "Everyone else has!"

Faraday grinned, waiting for the laughter to subside. "Charge the third. That said curse was aggravated by the continued imprisonment of those few blacks we rescued."

Renato snorted.

"Charge the fourth. That said curse made our provisions disappear, and summoned a demon who flung Portwood into the sea."

"Good Lord! You believed that fool Sharky?"

"Charge the fifth. That you refused to lower a boat for Portwood, thereby abandoning him to the sharks."

The men's faces were now stony cold, all joviality gone.

"Charge the sixth. That you murdered his cousin in cold blood, for no greater offense than wishing to aid his kin."

"He challenged his captain. You all saw it. I could do no less."

"And finally, seventh and most damning of all, that ignoring all signs and portends, you proceeded to attack the *Lucinda*, causing our ship to blow asunder and kill half our friends and brothers."

"Bilge and blather," Renato said. "It was sabotage, pure and simple. Someone aboard this ship was clearly in league with Andre."

Faraday sniffed that away.

"After due deliberation, you were found guilty of all charges." He paused dramatically. "The penalty, quite naturally, is the most grisly and unpleasant death we can devise."

Renato was determined to keep up a bold front. "If it's my life you want, why all the ceremony? Why didn't you slit my throat as I lay unconscious?"

"There were so many volunteers that we had to draw lots. But Mr. Quayle made a convincing appeal for your life."

"It would appear Quayle has more brains than the rest of you combined. Are you now ready to end this jest and release me?"

"You misapprehend, *Mr.* Renato. Your death sentence stands. But first, you have a service to perform."

Renato just stared.

"As Quayle reminded us, you've amassed a considerable fortune over the years. You're going to guide us to your hidey-holes."

Renato forced a laugh. "What trinkets I've stashed away would barely keep you in rum and whores for a week, while the treasure on that map will make you all kings for life."

"Bah! A will-o-the-wisp. You'll live until we've found your hidden troves, and not a moment longer."

"You've clearly no head for bargaining," Renato said. "If I'm to die anyway, why should I aid you?"

"As you've taught us well, there are many ways to die."

Renato knew this was true. But Faraday had underestimated him. He was not afraid of death, no matter the method.

"Do your worst, dogs. You'll get not a cent of my savings."

Someone in the rear clapped hands and yelped, "Ha! I'll be collecting them debts now, if ya please." The burly LaChaise strutted forward, palms extended.

Faraday flipped a coin to the gleeful man. "LaChaise insisted you'd not be swayed by ordinary threats. But he suggested one method he thought would be effective."

"It will avail you nothing. I'll still not talk."

Faraday's smile was extremely discomforting. "LaChaise told a tale we found hard to believe—until he explained it involved the death of that plaguey brother of yours. We all know how balmy you are on that subject."

An icy ball formed in Renato's stomach.

"The tale," Faraday went on, "involved a certain young wench you blamed for Rayón's death. According to LaChaise, you—"

A hoarse cry ripped from Renato's throat. "Enough!"

"What? You don't wish to hear it? Well, no matter. We've arranged the same circumstances for you, in case you're still reluctant to—"

"Enough, damn you! I'll guide you to my holdings."

"Yah!" LaChaise's shout rose above the hubbub. "I wins again!"

Renato slumped against the mast. Feeling vaguely disconnected from reality, he mumbled directions to a relatively meagre horde of booty on the Texas coast, and did not come fully alert again until he heard Faraday speaking.

"Now that His Nibs has been so obliging, there's one more thing we should bring to his attention."

Renato was too spent to summon more anger. One more thing? What more could possibly matter?

The men snickered, nudging one another. Faraday wore an especially sadistic grin.

"Damn you all to Hell," Renato growled. "Have done with it."

Faraday snapped his fingers, and a man stepped forward with something shiny in his hand. It was Renato's own shaving mirror, the one he used to finish his self-portraits.

"See for yourself, *Mr.* Renato. We're all desirous of your opinion."

Renato glared into the glass, eager to get this final indignity over with. He narrowed his eyes, forcing himself to focus.

At first, he felt only confusion. Then he nearly laughed. This was no mirror after all—but a cruel joke. Someone had painted an impossible image on the glass to mock him.

He began a snarl—and stopped. The lip of the fantastic image had moved in concert with his own! He shook his head in denial, and this, too, was mimicked by the head in the glass. What he was seeing was horribly real.

His eyebrows and eyelashes were gone, along with half his mustache and half the lip that had borne it. The entire left side of his mouth was peeled back in a rictus of living death, exposing blackened teeth and gums. What had been a bold and commanding nose was now a twisted blob hanging akimbo beneath parched and bulging eyes. One ear had shriveled like a piece of dried fruit, while the other was reduced to a scorched hole in the side of his head. What little hair still clung to his skull was clumped in small tufts amid a sea of poached and scalded flesh.

As Renato goggled, the eyes in the mirror rolled up, and he saw no more.

CHAPTER 20

"Old Beelzebub himself."

BOWIE POURED A jar of Matagorda moonshine down his throat. His eyes bulged, his nostrils flared, and he felt steam spouting from his ears.

A coonskinned trapper named Ianitello clapped him heartily on the back. "Good stuff, eh? Made it myself, I did."

Bowie forced his lips into a smile. The concoction smelled like horse droppings, tasted like composted squash, and carried more kick than a blunderbuss.

"Sweet as milk and honey," he proclaimed. "A fine beverage for the ladies, but what do you gentlemen drink in these parts?"

Ianitello's eyes popped. Bowie returned the clap on the back, laughing, and all around the fire joined in.

The group numbered close to thirty men. Some squatted on rough logs circling the firepit, while others stretched full on the ground. Still more gathered around the outskirts, jars and tankards glistening in their hands.

Someone said, "C'mon, Jim. Tell us about your latest duel."

Bowie raised a hand. "Now, boys. You know I'd never participate in anything as unseemly as a duel."

This display of false modesty brought more laughter. Despite the wild stories Bowie himself had marveled at, the closest he'd come to a formal duel was his savage encounter with Rayón.

He regarded the men's faces, craggy and bright in the firelight, and for the first time in weeks felt at home.

Matagorda's residents were roughly divided into three camps.

Those nearest him were the newcomers, still clad in the latest styles of New York and New Orleans. These men were wide-eyed and optimistic, with little understanding what they were truly up against.

A second group, discussing matters of trade with Captain McQuiddy, were the established colonists, most hand-picked by Stephen Austin himself. What store-bought clothing they possessed was frayed, and patched with homespun. These men were pragmatists, having learned what was truly needed, what they could fashion for themselves, and what they could do without.

The men of these first two groups had held various occupations in the States, but most were now resigned to being farmers or ranchers. At present, Texas needed tanners, blacksmiths, gunsmiths and doctors, but little else.

Aloof on the far side of the fire, clad in well-worn buckskins, were the true frontiersmen. In the States they had been hunters, soldiers, gamblers and outlaws. Of everyone present, they were most likely to have their fingers on the pulse of the Indians, and therefore those Bowie was most eager to speak with.

Towering above this group like a buffalo in a herd of sheep was a man more famous than Bowie himself—Big Strap Buckner. Tales of his exploits had traveled all the way to the States. One had him wrestling a giant ox to the ground with his bare hands, while another said he'd tied a knot in the Devil's tail. Bowie had scoffed then, but now found the stories harder to discredit. The man's arms were thick as tree trunks, and his shoulders broad as an oxen-yoke. It would be wise to stay on the fellow's good side.

Matagorda's handful of women had taken Mariette to one of the rough log houses, doubtless to quiz her about the latest fashions in New Orleans. Andre and Sharky had wisely elected to spend the evening aboard *Lucinda,* while Sam—after a brief foray ashore—had shown the rare good sense to join them. The little madman Pacal had not been seen since their arrival, and

Bowie would be content to learn he'd gone scampering off into the wilderness.

One of the recent arrivals said, "Tell us true, Jim, how's old Andy Jackson doing?"

Another chimed in. "Is he gonna throw those thieving bastards out on their ears?"

Bowie grinned. Many thought the election of 1824 had been stolen when Jackson had won the popular vote, but the House of Representatives chose John Quincy Adams as President. Four years later, Jackson was back for a rematch.

Bowie himself was no admirer of Jackson, but knew his audience. "He'll have the votes, all right," he said. "And if those fools in Congress deny him again, I'll personally go to Washington and carve my vote in their hides."

For the next hour and more, the news-starved colonists peppered him with questions about doings back in the States. It was understandable they would hunger for news of the land they'd left behind. But Bowie had burning questions of his own.

Of foremost importance were the whereabouts and disposition of the Karankawa Indians. If they were fishing near the coast, it would be necessary to swing inland to reach the treasure cove. But if they were off hunting in the woodland, it would be safer to proceed through the tall grasses of the coastal plain. Bowie could only hope they were not on the warpath, angered by the flood of new colonists from the States.

The man to talk to, he reasoned, was Strap Buckner. Taking another swallow of the ghastly moonshine, he moved off in the direction of the frontiersmen, but the tall, robust leader of the community stepped into his path. The man's name was Edmondson, and he'd been introduced as the *auyomento*, or mayor, of Matagorda.

"What do you think of our town, Mr. Bowie?"

"Impressive, I must admit. And sure to grow. I hear there's over a thousand folks in Austin's colony now."

"Closer to two," Edmondson said proudly. "We're growing

like wildfire. Talk up in San Felipe is they'll soon have a city hall, a jail, maybe even a newspaper. And Steve Austin's brothers are working on a cotton gin."

"Better yet," piped a red-faced man in a beaver hat, "Israel Waters has damn near finished his distillery!"

When the cheering stopped, Bowie said, "Mr. Edmondson, I hesitate to impose on your hospitality, but I must ask a favor."

The man's smile was genuine. "Glad to be of help, sir. What can I do for you?"

"My friends and I would like to do a little exploring tomorrow, and would be much obliged for the loan of horses."

Edmondson pursed his lips. "Horses, you say. How many would you be needing?"

"There are five in my party."

The mayor looked at his feet, rubbed the back of his neck. "I, ah, believe it would be possible to spare two. This is rather short notice, you know."

Bowie nodded, striving to remain friendly. "Does the shortage of horses have anything to do with two of my men being ex-pirates?"

Edmondson flushed. "That's a difficult subject, I'm afraid."

Bowie saw he would get nothing further. "Two horses, then, will be much appreciated."

"See me in the morning." The man's voice held a hint of apology. "You'll get two of our best."

Bowie eased around the fire to join the frontiersmen. He was ten feet away when his nose began to twitch, a reminder that these men were scornful of such civilized notions as bathing.

"Thought I'd never escape the small talk," he said by way of introduction. "I hoped to pick you gents' brains on the true temper of things here in Texas."

Buckner stared down at him before taking a hand-rolled cigar from between his teeth. "Didn't seem to pain you all that much, playin' the hero to those greenhorns."

"I'll take that as a compliment to my acting ability."

"If you're so shy and retiring," Buckner said, "maybe you should have stayed in hiding with your pirate friends."

"If you don't mind my asking," Bowie said amiably, "what exactly do you have against those two?"

"Thing is, we do mind. It's entirely our business, and none of yours. That a problem for you?"

"Not yet," Bowie said. "Mind telling me a little about things here in Texas?"

Buckner chewed his cigar, eyes narrowed and thoughtful. "Such as?"

Bowie sensed it would be unwise to ask directly about the Indians. "For starters, how're you getting along with the Mexican government?"

"Depends who you ask. Charlie, here, thinks things are just dandy."

A mustachioed man stuck out his chin and said, "Well, I do, Strap, and that's a fact. I been freer here than I ever was back in the Carolinas."

"Charlie's right about that," another opened up. "I come down with Austin in '22 and ain't paid a cent of taxes yet. These folks wantin' us to break off and join the Yoo-nited States plumb got their heads in their asses."

The moonshiner Ianitello bristled at that. "Here now, Clem Yarrow! You sayin' I wear my ass for a hat?"

Bowie studied the face of Buckner. The man's freckles, in keeping with his size, were big as five-cent pieces.

"And what do you think of all this, Mr. Buckner?"

The man extended an enormous hand. "Call me Strap."

Bowie intended to give it a firm shake, but his fingers would not reach around the palm. "Jim."

Buckner's hand covered Bowie's entirely. "I hear you like to wrassle."

Bowie felt as if his bones were cracking. "Used to play rough and tumble with my brothers, but I sort of outgrew that."

"Shame," Buckner said. "Then that talk of you wrasslin' gators in the swamp was all lies?" He spat the final word, and the implication was clear—that the lies had been Bowie's own.

The big man was deliberately trying to provoke him. "I can top that," Bowie said with a wink. "I hear you once battled Old Beelzebub himself to a draw."

Buckner's huge chest swelled even larger. "Who says it was a draw?"

Buckner released Bowie's hand, grinning as the others praised his wit.

Bowie flexed his flattened fingers. It appeared his best approach was to appeal to the man's vanity. "Seriously, Strap, I'd value your opinion. Are you sensing trouble with the Mexicans—or anyone else?"

"I've said this before," Buckner began, "and I'll say it to you. Trouble is coming. It's only a matter of when. Sure, Spain was glad to have us here, at first. Hell, they'd been trying to tame the Indians for two hundred years, with nothing to show for it but a handful of worn-out missions. About the time we began to prosper, the Mexicans decided it was time to kick the Spaniards out. Both sides have been too busy with each other to pay us much mind, but once they sort things out, they'll be coming for us."

"Could be it's already over," Charlie said. "Heard just last week that Santy Anny beat back Genr'l Barradas down at Tampico. With a man like him on our side, we got nothin' to fear."

Buckner shook his head. "You always were full of shit, Charlie. Santa Anna's on nobody's side but his own."

"Damn straight." Ianitello spat a stream of tobacco juice into the fire. "Somebody oughta scalp him and blame it on the Kronks."

"Maybe the Kronks *will* get 'im," Clem Yarrow opined. "Way they been actin' up, wouldn't nothin' they do surprise me."

Bowie snapped at this. "What do you mean? What have they been up to?"

Yarrow propped a foot on a log and seemed about to launch into a long complaint. But before he could speak, angry voices came out of the darkness. Two men scuffled into the firelight, dragging a third between them.

Edmondson, the mayor, sprang to the forefront. "What's all this?"

The men came full into the firelight, letting their burden fall to the earth. "We caught this damned rascal skulking about behind the Wilson place."

Bowie peered at the pear-shaped form on the ground, a leaden ball forming in his gut.

While Edmondson rubbed his jaw, Strap Buckner bulled forward, towering over him like an oak to a sapling. "Let's have a look at the bugger."

Careful not to touch his knife, Bowie followed.

Buckner caught the captive's scraggly hair between thumb and forefinger and jerked his face into the light.

A hiss went through the settlers.

The captive's face was purple, his beard matted with blood. His one good eye was half open and fixed pleadingly on Bowie.

"Evenin', Jim Boy. Havin' a nice party, are ye?"

CHAPTER 21

"The walking dead!"

SOMETHING WAS SCRATCHING Renato's face. It hurt like the very devil, but at the same time, it was somehow pleasant.

He blinked his eyes, willing them to open, and winced from new waves of pain. He tried to raise a hand to stop the scratching, but his arm refused to obey.

He forced his eyes open, then wished he had not—for he stared into the face of a demon. Two malignant eyes regarded him from a head no larger than a fist, but covered with charred and blackened flesh.

The thing's mouth opened, revealing sharp yellow teeth, and emitted a sound midway between a screech and a squall. Its breath smelled like a rotting corpse.

"Princess!" Renato gasped. "What has happened to you? Why do you look so…" And then his situation came rushing back with the force of a hurricane. The explosion, the journey through Hell, the farcical trial, the leering faces of Faraday and the men. He'd hoped it was all the foulest of nightmares. But here he stood, bound to the foremast, a prisoner on his own ship.

The cat withdrew its claws from his coat and leapt off to seek new entertainment, leaving Renato reeling. His dreams of everlasting glory lay dashed to shards.

Hearing muted voices, he discerned two dark shapes standing in the prow. The men's backs were to him, mere shadowy outlines against the gray horizon.

The two spoke an odd sort of pidgin French. He caught only scattered syllables, but the word most repeated was "ship." Craning his neck, he strove to see what the two were looking at, but could divine nothing on either side but the dark sky and the darker line of the sea.

"What is it? What ship? What the devil is out there?"

Four huge round eyes regarded him from the darkness. Two sets of gleaming white teeth appeared, growing ever larger as the faces approached.

Renato gave a snort. Two of the rescued Haitian slaves roamed free-as-you-please about his deck, while he himself was trussed up like an animal for slaughter.

"What have you seen?" he demanded. "Is there another ship out there?"

The slaves stared dumbly at him, their bright eyes fixed on his face. Their lips trembled, and their shoulders quivered. Renato had spent his entire adult life instilling fear in others, and could not fail to recognize it now. But why these two should fear him, helpless as he was, was a thing he could not fathom.

"What's wrong with you?" he asked. "Are you bereft of your wits?"

The men continued to stare, but their terror was giving way to another emotion, something akin to revulsion—or pity.

Renato snarled. These poor wretches should be awed by his fierce and manly countenance. But as the picture of his own cruelly handsome features came to mind, it began to twist, to change, to melt like wax and reconfigure itself into a charbroiled fright mask.

The image in the mirror! His mind had blocked it out, unable to accept that indignity on top of all the others. But that, too, he now knew, was horribly real.

One of the Haitians shrieked, pointing at something out of Renato's sight. The two jabbered wordlessly, eyes wide with terror, as Princess leapt from the deck and clung to Renato's chest, thrusting her face into his own.

"Zom-bie," one man stammered. "The walking dead!"

But this particular terror was short-lived, as his companion was jabbering again, a black arm gesturing forward toward the prow.

Renato forced himself to concentrate. He would have the rest of his life, short as that may be, to bemoan his disfigurement. What mattered now was what these men had seen on the horizon, and what it might mean to *him*.

"There," the man said, eyes wide with alarm. "Ship comes. Closer!"

CHAPTER 22

"A tough little nut."

TIME SEEMED TO stop as Bowie stared down at Andre's battered and bloody form. He forced a smile, said, "Hello, old man. You always did know how to make an entrance." He took the pirate's arm, hauling him to his feet.

"Not so fast," Buckner snapped. "This man's a prisoner."

"Prisoner?" Bowie addressed the group at large. "What crime has he committed?"

A low growl rolled through the colonists.

Buckner said, "Likely planning to snatch one of our women."

Holding Buckner's baleful glare, Bowie displayed Andre to the group. "I ask you, gentlemen, does this look like a man who needs to steal his women?"

This garnered a smattering of laughs, but most faces remained grim.

Strap Buckner betrayed no amusement. "If he wasn't up to mischief, what was he doin' behind the cabin?"

Bowie squeezed Andre's shoulder. "How about it, old man. Care to explain yourself?"

Andre looked sheepish. "I'd come ashore hopin' to purchase a bottle, when the call of nature come upon me. I'd just opened me breeches when these two oxen fell upon me. Lucky for them I was without me sword."

"Sounds reasonable to me," Bowie said. "Anyone object to that?"

Buckner thumped his chest with a huge fist. "I do. He stands trial. Then he hangs."

Bowie felt the call of his blade. He could not let these men execute his friend, but this was their land, and he could not afford to alienate them.

He addressed all who would meet his eye. "I don't know you men personally, but I know Texans. You're men of honor, and fairness runs strong in you. If you mean to hang my friend, you need more cause than choosing a poor spot to relieve himself."

For near a full minute, the only sound was the soft crackle of the flames. Then the breeze brought the haunting refrain of "Barbara Allen" from the cabins. Mariette and the women were singing.

With a practiced eye, Bowie identified which colonists bore weapons, and which were most likely to use them. If it came to a scuffle, the best course of action would be a quick retreat to the ship. Once on board, he could plead his case from behind a cannon.

One man said, "Hell, Strap. He was only taking a piss."

"He's right," said another. "If that's a crime, we're all of us guilty."

Buckner's face grew tighter. "It's a damn sight more than that, as you well know." He turned to Bowie, a grim smile on his lips. "But Mr. Bowie spoke of honor. Perhaps he'd like to test his against mine."

Bowie stiffened. "You're challenging me to a duel?"

Buckner nodded toward Bowie's hip. "We settle our differences man to man. Are you afraid to face me without your toy sword?"

Bowie drew the knife from its sheath and flung it point first into the earth. Buckner outweighed him by at least eighty pounds, all of it muscle and bone, but it would be unseemly to enforce his will with a blade.

"If you want to fight," he said. "Let's have done with it."

"Fine," said Buckner, and without preamble, unleashed a backhand swing at Bowie's head.

Bowie ducked, feeling the *whoosh* of air above him. Springing up, he bounced a flurry of jabs off Buckner's stomach and straightened with an uppercut to the jaw. A normal man would be seeing stars, but Buckner merely smiled, while the force of the blow rattled down Bowie's arm, jarring him to the teeth.

Long arms sailed out and caught him by the shoulders. It was like being caught in a vice. Bowie watched helplessly as Buckner's knee swept up and plowed into his face.

Bowie staggered, but did not go down. When his head cleared, he saw the big man standing with hands on hips, astonishment plain on his face.

"Damn!" Buckner said. "You're a tough little nut."

Bowie shook himself. "Now that the handshaking's over," he said, "what say we start the ball?"

Buckner's answer was a sudden rush.

Bowie dodged a huge fist and delivered a roundhouse right to the side of Buckner's head. The crack of teeth was loud, and the big man's nose ran red, but the punch slowed him not a whit.

Rocking back, Buckner sent a boot toward Bowie's crotch. Bowie took the blow on his hip and got both hands under Buckner's ankle. Grunting with exertion, he moved in, thrusting the leg ever higher. At last Buckner's other foot left the ground, and he crashed onto his back, sending a tremble through the earth.

A chorus of gasps escaped the crowd.

"Good God! Strap's down!"

" 'Tain't possible!"

"Never thought I'd see the like!"

Bowie shook the sweat from his eyes, praying the battle was over. But that was not to be.

"Now you done it," Ianitello said. "You gone and made him mad."

The big man was back on his feet, teeth bared and glaring red hate. Buckner wrapped both hands around a log that had served as a campfire bench, tore it from the earth, and brandished it above his head. Illumined by the firelight, he presented a fantastic image, an enraged giant out of ancient myth.

Bowie's knife, within easy reach, called to him like a lover. But he must finish this battle with honor—or die trying.

Gripping the log like a club, Buckner unleashed a ferocious swing. The log came racing toward Bowie with force enough to swat him clean out of the clearing, and he jumped back as the tip scraped a layer of hide from his chest.

He needed a weapon of his own—and quickly. Bolting past Buckner, he barreled straight for the fire, plucking a five-foot limb from the flames.

He heard a bellow from behind. Looming over him, Buckner's massive frame blotted out the moon and stars. He held the log high above his head, poised for a killing blow.

Bowie's limb was puny compared to Buckner's log, but had one small advantage—it was still burning. Spinning about, he thrust the tip like a spear at Buckner's face

Roaring, Buckner released the log to shield his eyes. For a moment it seemed to hang suspended in the air, then came plummeting down with enormous force on the crown of Buckner's skull.

A great *whoof* burst from the big man's lips, and his eyes rolled up in their sockets. He toppled forward and thundered to the earth like a felled tree.

Bowie dropped the burning limb. The hoots and cheers of the colonists filled his ears. He saw men dancing and clapping each other on the back.

He turned away, pained in every limb. Blood ran freely from the gashes in his chest.

"Tolerable nice fightin', Jim Boy." Andre was at his side, grinning through his beard.

Bowie realized he still did not know what he'd been fighting for. He meant to find out, and soon, even if he had to squeeze it out of Andre himself.

Then from out of the darkness stepped Mariette, her face white and strained. She eyed Bowie as if he were a stranger—one she had no desire to meet.

Stung by the look, Bowie sought words to explain. But she was looking past him, eyes growing wide. The colonists gasped and swore.

Strap Buckner was back on his feet, advancing with great lumbering steps, his face a mask of blood.

"Strap, wait!" Bowie called. "Let's call it even." But he knew the man would never give up. Like Bowie, Buckner had become a legend in his own time, and was now a slave to his reputation.

The giant Texan advanced, his steps shaking the earth. Then the colonists were looking away, back toward the cabins, and Bowie heard shouts of anger and alarm. And even Buckner turned to stare.

Up to the fire rode five Mexican soldiers. White crossbelts over their blue uniforms identified them as lancers. And atop the leading stallion, a dark-faced man in a flat-brimmed hat leveled a flintlock at Bowie's chest.

CHAPTER 23

"Fiiiire!"

RENATO CURSED HIS poor eyesight. The two Haitians had run away, but after much straining, all he could discern was a tiny smudge of gray between sea and sky.

"Sail ho!" he shouted. "Rouse yourselves, you worthless scum!"

No response. They were all still hungover from celebrating his downfall.

At last a shape loomed over him, and he looked into the face of yet another slave.

"Out there!" he said in French, pointing with his head. "What is it? A frigate? A sloop? A brig?"

The Haitian shrugged. "Ship," he said.

"Is she square-rigged or lateened?"

The man looked again at the horizon, his head nodding. "Yes," he said. "Ship."

Renato grimaced. Clearly, he would get no more from this fellow. He stared at the distant smudge, willing it to come nearer. The possibility that Andre and Bowie might be so close maddened him above all else.

He scowled back toward the stern. The crew should have been roused by now. An alarm should have been given.

The quarter moon threw a faint light over the ship. He could see the crow's nest empty, and a dark form slumped over the tiller. Scattered about the deck were other snoring crewmen, including his fat little bosun.

"Quayle! Wake up, you worthless canker!"

Quayle rolled over and launched into a perfect impression of a hog snorting for its supper.

Renato tried the helmsman. "Murray! Damn you, man, bestir yourself!"

Two full minutes of cursing brought no better results.

Renato stewed. There was one cry guaranteed to bring all but the most besotted from their slumbers. But to employ it meant assuming the role of a lowly deckhand, a position he found demeaning.

Squinting hard at the mystery ship, he almost believed he could make out a squareness in the sails. If it truly was *Lucinda*, this was the time to be upon her, before she could escape again.

Wetting his lips, Renato raised his head and unleashed a cry he knew would penetrate to every inch of the ship. "Fiiiire!"

Even before the cry ceased, the sleepers began to stir. The helmsman's head jerked aright, whipping this way and that. In a trice, men poured from the hatch, boots thumping onto the deck. The air was thick with snarled questions and muttered oaths. Someone shouted, "Summon Cap'n Faraday at once!"

Captain Faraday! Renato sneered. The notion of that self-righteous prig occupying his cabin, his very bed, turned his blood to bile.

After too long a time, the prig himself finally emerged, clad in a French officer's greatcoat and gold-braided hat. If nothing else, the man had learned the importance of keeping up appearances.

Faraday harrumphed his way forward and surveyed the scene. "What's all this about a fire?"

"There is no fire," Renato said coolly, "merely a sail these laggards were too stupid to notice."

"Sail? What sail?"

"There, Cap'n!" Men jabbed grubby fingers toward the western horizon.

Faraday peered out over the waters, a downward curl to his lips. "The telescope. I'll have it in my hand."

Renato gnashed his teeth. He had mouthed those same words on many an occasion.

Accepting the scope, Faraday peered out at the distant sail. The men grew quiet, eyes shifting between him and the approaching ship.

"Holy Mother of God," Faraday gasped. "It can't be. Not now!" He lowered the glass, his face drained of blood.

Quayle crouched at his side. "Beg pardon, Cap'n. What did you see?"

Faraday's mouth moved, but no sound came out.

Renato could wait no longer. "Hell's teeth, man! What ship is it?"

Faraday shook himself. He stretched his neck and swallowed.

"*Medusa*," he said, his voice a croak. "The ship is *Medusa*."

CHAPTER 24

"I would be breaking your neck."

MIND RACING, BOWIE stared into the pistol barrel. The man holding it, whose epaulets identified him as a sergeant, was quite close, and Bowie's knife was on the far side of the fire, a lifetime away.

The other four soldiers had lowered their lances, and now formed a rough triangle with the sergeant at the point.

Bowie performed a sweeping bow. "Welcome, *Capitán*," he said in courtly Spanish, flattering the man with a promotion in rank. "You honor us with your presence."

The sergeant eyed him owlishly. "I believe you are well aware of my rank." The man spoke decent English, but his accent was atrocious. "I am Sergeant Enrique Rosario Bartolomé Gutierrez of the Federalist Republican Army of Mexico."

"Such a lot of names," Buckner said, "for such a small man."

"Do you not realize," Guitierrez demanded, "that dueling is against the law of the republic?"

Seeing Buckner's brow grow dark, Bowie spoke quickly. "You misapprehend us, Excellency. My large companion and I were merely engaged in a friendly contest of strength."

Pointedly examining the blood streaming from Buckner's nose and Bowie's ribs, the sergeant gave a snort. He surveyed the gathering. "Who is *auyomento* of this village?"

Edmondson stepped forward. "I have that honor."

"Then I fear you have been derelict in your duties, Señor. You have allowed a pirate ship to anchor in your harbor."

"You are mistaken, Sergeant. Captain McQuiddy here is a respected trader from New Orleans, and among his passengers is the famous Mr. James Bowie." He nodded toward Bowie, causing the sergeant's eyes to follow.

"Famous for what?"

Bowie said quickly, "He does me too much honor. I am a simple land-trader, once fortunate enough to find my name in the newspapers." He kept his eyes locked on the man's face, hoping the colonists would not betray him with laughter or smirks.

With a sniff of dismissal, the man turned back to the mayor. "Then surely you have collected their taxes." He extended a gloved hand, palm up.

"Taxes? With respect, Sergeant, that's a matter you must discuss with Mr. Austin up at San Felipe."

"You may depend upon it. But in the meantime, I am discussing it here with you."

From the corner of his eye, Bowie saw Andre shift his weight, edging behind one of the settlers.

A lancer gave a sudden start and kneed his mount next to the sergeant, speaking in low tones.

A fresh gleam lit the sergeant's eyes. "It has come to my attention that you are harboring a criminal." He aimed a finger at Andre. "This man is a notorious pirate who has long preyed upon our ships and citizens. It is my clear duty to hang him."

"This man is in our custody," Edmondson said. "His guilt or innocence has not yet been determined."

"Of his guilt, there can be no doubt. But I may consider letting him off with a fine. Shall we say five thousand pesos?"

"Five thousand? We haven't half that sum in the entire settlement."

Bowie regretted his empty pockets. This was mere extortion, but Andre was guilty of more piracy than this man would ever know.

Buckner thrust out his huge chin. "That's robbery, pure and

simple. I command the local militia, and I'll not surrender this pirate to you or anyone else."

The sergeant shifted his aim to Buckner's chest. "I advise you not to interfere, Señor. You would be breaking the law."

"No," Buckner said, "I would be breaking your neck."

Guitierrez backed his horse a step.

Bowie swore under his breath. There was little chance now of catching the man off guard, but he had to try. "Your pardon, Sergeant. Would the amount of that fine be open to negotiation?"

The man's eyes slid over him. "You wish to make a counter offer?"

Bowie edged closer. "Would you perhaps settle for a thousand American dollars?"

The man's eyes gleamed. A thousand dollars was worth far more than five thousand pesos.

"You will forgive me, Señor, but you do not look like a man with that amount of money."

"Not on my person, but if you'll accompany me to yonder ship. . ." Bowie left the suggestion dangling.

Gutierrez turned for a brief glance at *Lucinda*, and Bowie sprang like a panther. Grasping the man's crossbelt, he yanked with all his strength, and the sergeant yelped, flopping sideways in the saddle. Bowie tugged harder. The man squalled like hog, but still refused to fall.

Holding fast to the crossbelt, Bowie peered over the horse, and gaped. Buckner had one enormous hand encircling the sergeant's leg. The two had the hapless Mexican caught in a game of tug-of-war.

Bowie glowered up at Buckner. "Let go, you lummox!"

"You let go, little man!"

Bowie applied more force, heaving on the crossbelt with all his might. Buckner responded with a mighty tug of his own.

Gutierrez screeched in terror as he rocked in the saddle. His great black stallion began to snort and buck.

The lancers, having overcome their shock, urged their horses forward. Bowie and Buckner let go at the same moment, and the terrified stallion sunfished, sending the sergeant toward the stars as if shot from a catapult.

Bowie's hand flashed to his side, then he remembered the sheath was empty. But before the first soldier reached him, Andre was there, placing the knife in his hand. As the soldier's lance sought his heart, Bowie slashed upward with his blade. A crimson shower erupted from the man's arm, and the lance fell from a nerveless hand.

The second lancer reared his horse, hooves pounding the air above Buckner's head. With a speed belying his size, Buckner ducked under the hooves and placed one massive hand on the stallion's breast, holding both horse and rider at bay.

As the last two lancers neared, Buckner gave a great heave. With a bellow, the horse toppled backward, slamming into the others, and all three crashed to the earth, taking their riders with them.

Two of the men lay stunned, but the third, leg pinned beneath his mount, drew a pistol and leveled it at Buckner. The big man bent low and charged, but the lancer had a clear shot and a steady hand.

Bowie flipped his knife, catching it by the spine, and it flew like a bolt of lightning, striking the man's pistol as it discharged.

When the smoke cleared, the lancer lay shrieking on the ground. Buckner's huge right foot hovered over his skull, poised to crush it to jelly.

"Enough!" Edmondson's voice cut through the din. A half dozen settlers were at his side, weapons trained on the soldiers. "Leave him be, Strap. We'll have no killing here tonight."

With a grimace, Buckner brought his foot crashing down next to the lancer's head.

Bowie took stock. Sergeant Gutierrez sprawled near the fire, dazed but still conscious. One lancer lay groaning with his leg at an odd angle. Another clutched his jaw, while the man who had nearly lost his head lay curled in a fetal position. Of the soldier whose horse had bolted into the darkness there was no sign.

Edmondson addressed his people. "I believe these Mexican gentlemen have learned what it means to interfere in our affairs."

Andre let out a hearty laugh, echoed by several colonists.

Buckner wasn't laughing. The big man glowered at Bowie, eyes gleaming red. The message was clear. Their business was not yet finished.

Bowie swung to face him. He ached in every bone, but would fight to the death before giving up his friend.

Buckner's lips cracked into a horrible smile.

"Strap!" Edmondson's voice was sharp as a blade. "The fighting is over. And as you may recall, Mr. Bowie just saved your life."

Others spoke up.

"He's right, Strap. Let it go."

"Save it for the Kronks. Or the damned Mexes."

"Yeah, Strap," called Ianitello. "Texas needs all the fighters it can get."

At last the fire left Buckner's eyes. "I hate being beholden to any man, so we'll strike a bargain. You may have this pirate's life, though why you value it I cannot fathom. In return, I owe you nothing. No thanks, no debt of any kind. Agreed?"

"Agreed," Bowie said. "But I do claim one additional honor." He paused, watching Buckner's eyes narrow. "I've the right to say that like Old Beelzebub, I fought Big Strap Buckner and lived to tell the tale."

Buckner snorted.

Bowie began to laugh, and his mirth spread quickly through the colonists, until the earth trembled with the deep belly laughs of Strap Buckner himself.

CHAPTER 25

"How do we know you won't butcher us?"

MEDUSA!

Renato's gut churned. In her present condition, *L'Intrepide* could neither fight nor run. And he himself, bound as he was, would be denied even a warrior's death. If he survived, he'd be dragged back to New Orleans, tried in a puppet court and strung up on the waterfront until the flesh rotted from his bones.

The men's strident voices brought him back to the crisis at hand. Every word dripped with anger, fear, desperation or doom. Some lined the rail, squinting against the sun and fighting over the telescope. Others hung from the rigging, reporting activity aboard *Medusa*. Still more sat with heads bowed, contemplating their sins.

Renato kept his silence as arguments boiled around him.

"We should make for the coast. Slip into a shallow cove like we always done."

"Not a chance of it. They'd run us down within the hour."

"Then we stand and fight!"

"You're daft! With that monster gun, they'd blow us to Hell."

"Belay that bickering!" This, surprisingly, came from Quayle, "It ain't for us to decide. Cap'n Faraday will get us out of this. What say you, Cap'n, how we gonna whip those Yankee-doodles?"

All turned to Faraday, who gaped back with vacant eyes.

"C'mon, Cap'n, tell us your plan!"

"What's a'matter, Cap'n? Don't be bashful, now."

"Don't rush me." Faraday was like a man stricken with palsy. "I'm thinking."

"Sakes alive, Cap'n! It's past time for that."

"Aye, Cap'n! We gotta do something, afore they blast us to bits!"

Faraday hooked a finger in his collar. "Having weighed all options, I see only one course of action."

"What'd I tell you?" Quayle squeaked. "I knew he'd have a plan!"

"What is it, Cap'n? What'll we do?"

Renato studied Faraday's face. He knew what the traitorous fool's answer would be. He had known it well before Faraday himself.

Faraday drew Renato's cutlass from his belt. His face was deathly white. "We've only one choice," he said. "We must lay down our arms and surrender!"

He released his grip on the sword, and in the stunned silence, the clang of steel on the deck was loud as the crack of doom.

Renato knew what was coming. There would be howls of protest. The men would turn upon each other like animals. Faraday might even find himself hanged from the yardarm. But in the end, *Medusa* would capture his ship, perhaps even sink her, and the survivors would be carried away in chains.

Before any of that could happen, he broke the silence with a long, bloodcurdling laugh. "Is that what you want, laddies—to have your necks stretched, or your bones rot in prison?" A dozen men shouted disapproval, and Renato bulled on. "If you want to live free, with gold in your pockets and rum in your bellies, you've only one choice. Cut these ropes and swear your oaths to me once more. I'll see you free of these Navy dogs and make you rich as kings!"

"Three cheers!" Quayle squeaked. "Three cheers for Cap'n Renato! Hip-hip—"

A score of mouths drew breath, but Faraday cried, "Wait! If

we make you captain again, how do we know you won't butcher us out of spite?

Renato smiled, reveling in the effect his grisly new countenance had on the crew. "The answer to that, Mr. Faraday, is simplicity itself. You don't."

CHAPTER 26

"Nothin' left but soup bones."

"**MY GOD, MR. BOWIE,** come to your senses! No sane man goes a' purpose into Karankawa coun- try." The speaker was Curly Dan Withers, who'd been one of Strap Buckner's entourage at the welcome party. Of Buckner himself, there had been no sign since the previous evening.

Bowie paused in arranging the packhorse. The man was far from wrong.

"He means no offense, Jim." This from Edmondson, ever the diplomat. "The way those savages are acting of late, it's become a death trap."

Bowie returned to his task. The colonists had been more than generous. With the gray packhorse, they'd provided a mustang for Bowie and a buckskin for Mariette, along with blankets and camp tools.

"The Kronks have always been devils," Bowie said. "How has that changed?"

"They've gotten all spooky-like." Curly Dan spat a stream of tobacco juice. "Afore this, they've always shifted about. Now a band of 'em has staked out some kind of holy ground, and got their backs up somethin' fierce."

Bowie had heard as many tall tales as any man, and this smacked of imagination. He looked at Edmondson and raised his eyebrows.

The mayor ran fingers through his silvering hair. "Old Jim Batson, who'd had a cabin out on Palacio's Creek, had his stock run off and crops burnt out. And the last hunting party went out that way was driven back by a storm of arrows. Whatever's happening out there, it's not normal."

"One good thing about the Kronks," Curly Dan said. "You can smell 'em afore they smells you. Worst god-awful stench in creation. Damned if they don't stink even worse'n a bunch of God-damned nig—" The man's grating voice stopped abruptly, and Bowie looked up.

Curly Dan took a step back, resting a hand on his pistol butt. His bulging eyes were fixed on a point over Bowie's shoulder.

Sam was there, working his hands as if about to strangle a chicken. "I suffered enough such effluvia in Louisiana," he said, "and will suffer no more."

Bowie hid a grin, wishing he could let this drama play out. Curly Dan was perhaps the foulest smelling human in his experience, but this was no time to anger the colonists.

"Mr. Gideon," he said, keeping his tone light, "I've a favor to ask. Would you kindly inform Andre and Miss Mariette we are ready to depart?"

Sam glared at him a moment before returning his scowl to Curly Dan.

"While you're at it," Bowie said, "warn them not to step on any snakes. We can't afford unnecessary delays."

Sam's eyes narrowed in understanding, and he stalked off toward the cabins.

Bowie watched a gang of sailors with a team of borrowed horses drag a live oak trunk across the clearing toward *Lucinda*. McQuiddy was wasting not a moment to begin repairs.

Bowie was about to mount when three men staggered into the clearing. The first two were strangers to him: a black-bearded fellow in grimy buckskins and a thin Mexican in a calico shirt. But close upon their heels came the gnarled collection of gristle and bone known as Sharky.

Sharky carried an empty bottle, which he flung backhanded into the trees. He blinked at the morning sun and peered around the clearing. When his eyes met Bowie's, his knees buckled and he nearly went down.

"It would seem," Bowie told the mayor, "that not all your colonists are above consorting with pirates."

"That's as may be, but those two are none of ours. Hinkle and Sanchez, they call themselves. Drifted in a week or two ago, and I've asked Strap to keep an eye on them." Edmondson lowered his voice. "It's bad manners to ask, but do you mind telling me why you're so keen on this venture?"

Curly Dan's ears seemed to grow longer. Without apparent movement, the other colonists loomed closer.

Bowie chewed his lip. These men deserved some sort of explanation, but he couldn't tell the truth without starting a mad scramble for gold.

As he hesitated, the mayor said, "If Mr. Bowie doesn't care to discuss the reason for his journey, that's his right. It was rude of me to ask."

Bowie opened his mouth, still unsure what to say.

"Mr. Bowie is just being gallant." Mariette approached, arm-in-arm with Andre. "He is making this trip for *me*."

Andre's face was mottled and red, while the girl was positively glowing. Her cheeks were pink and her eyes bright. A skirt of butternut and brown gingham flowed from her hips, while a snug white blouse accentuated a ripe and fetching bosom. Bowie felt a dryness in his throat.

Then the meaning of her words sank in. Did she really intend to tell them of the treasure?

"Mariette, I don't think—"

" 'Shaw, Mr. Bowie. No reason we shouldn't tell these gentlemen the truth. I've already informed the ladies."

Bowie blanched. He had visions of an entire army of settlers— women, children and all—racing off toward the cove.

"You see," Mariette said, "Mr. Bowie has agreed to help me rescue my brother from the savages."

Curly Dan let out an explosive grunt, while the rest sucked in a collective breath.

"My poor brother Barry was wintering in Capano when he fell afoul of those nasty Karankawas. Once word reached New Orleans, my father enlisted brave Mr. Bowie to guide us here. We intend to bargain for Barry's release."

Bowie stared, speechless. She was the coolest, most proficient liar he had ever seen. At her side, Andre beamed with fatherly pride.

The colonists shifted their feet. One coughed into his hand.

Curly Dan, less delicate than the rest, decorated the dirt with tobacco juice. "Beggin' pardon, Miss, but if them Kronks've had your brother that long, there ain't nothin' left but soup bones."

"Dan!" Edmondson said. "My God, man, what's wrong with you?"

"That's quite all right," Mariette said, a catch in her voice. "I realize the odds we face. But I know in my heart my dear brother is alive, and Mr. Bowie has sworn not to rest until we find him."

Edmondson gazed at her in reverence. "We admire your courage, Miss. But you can't know what you're getting into. Why not remain here, while we find volunteers to accompany Mr. Bowie?"

"You're too kind, sir, but this trial is my own, and I must trust in the Lord—and Mr. Bowie's strong right arm—to see me through."

Bowie saw Sam leaning on a corral post. His face was a mask of stone, but his eyes danced with merriment.

Bowie swung a leg over the mustang. They'd best be underway quickly, before these folks declared Mariette a saint. "Time we were going." His words sounded harsh after the gentle speech of the girl.

Men moved to help Mariette, but she put a foot in the stirrup and swung aboard as if born to the saddle.

Bowie stared as Sharky appeared, weaving to a halt beside the packhorse. "Where do you think you're going?"

Sharky was taken aback. "Why, with you o'course, Cap'n sir."

"Not a chance. You're not needed. Much less wanted."

Sharky quailed. "But I can't stay here. These blighters will hang me sure!"

"And the world will be better for it. But if you object to the idea, stay on board *Lucinda*."

A gentle hand touched Bowie's arm. "James, please. The sailors hate him, too. He won't be safe there."

Bowie met the girl's eyes. "And we won't be safe with him along. He'll likely murder us in our sleep."

Sharky waved his hands in denial. "Oh, no, Cap'n! Never that! You can trust me like a brother."

"Please, James, let him come. For me."

Bowie pressed a palm to his forehead. Why did this girl have such power over him? And why did she have a fondness for such scabrous little companions? It was beyond reckoning.

"For you," he told Mariette. Then to Sharky, his voice low but firm, "But if you ever again liken yourself to my brothers, I'll chop you into fish bait."

With that, Bowie tossed a salute to the colonists and guided his horse onto the trail south. He had one thing to be thankful for—that little nuisance Pacal had not materialized. With any luck, they were rid of him for good.

Mariette fell into line behind the packhorse, with Andre and Sharky following close afoot. Sam had still not moved, but Bowie was confident he would join them as soon as his distaste for the colonists overcame his petulance.

From behind rose a chorus of good wishes and fond farewells, and Bowie caught one last exchange.

"I still say they're mad goin' into that country," came the voice of Curly Dan.

"No argument here," Ianitello replied. "But if any man can make it, it's Big Jim Bowie."

"Bull feathers! Wouldn't matter if he was Hannibal, Hercules, or Jesus Christ hisself. If he rides into that nest of devils, he ain't never comin' out."

CHAPTER 27

"I'll slice his knickknacks off."

RENATO STRAINED AGAINST the foremast, making a great show of the fact his hands were securely bound behind him. Though the position had become familiar, the circumstances were dramatically different. He was now here by design, and no longer alone. Strapped to the mast at his side was a plump figure with long golden curls, a purple silk gown and an ample bosom. And joining them on deck were two freshly shaved men in landsman's clothing, seated and bound to the iron capstan.

Renato himself wore a three-piece suit, complete with paper collar and cravat. Save for the artistically applied smears of soot and blood, and—of course—his grisly new visage, he was the very picture of a prosperous merchant.

A hundred yards away, *Medusa* sat with loosed sails, drifting ever closer. Her captain was being cautious, approaching from the stern to prevent being the recipient of a surprise broadside. Clearly, the man was no fool.

Renato cursed silently. Normally, he relished a wily opponent, but just this once he had hoped for a cocky young tyro.

Medusa's huge 18-pound swivel gun pointed directly at *L'Intrepide*. A single shot from that massive weapon would blast the pirate ship in two, plunging Renato and his crew to the bottom of the Gulf.

This was the crucial moment. Would *Medusa's* captain be wise enough to shoot first, or would he pause to investigate?

The two hours since sighting the naval vessel had been frantic. It was imperative the ship look as if it had fought a losing battle, then been left helpless and adrift. Torn sails that had been painstakingly restitched were hastily undone. The scorched and jagged wreckage of the blast that had destroyed the mainmast was collected and scattered haphazardly about the deck. The two 9-pounders that had been righted with backbreaking effort had been overturned once again.

The small band of slaves had been retied in the hold. If his plan succeeded, the navy men would not see them at all.

Of greater concern was his own band of cutthroats. Over a score remained, and hiding places aboard the ship were limited. A more than cursory examination of *L'Intrepide's* hold would surely bring them to light.

Renato's chief worry was that someone would recognize his ship. *L'Intrepide* had been spreading terror for more than a decade, and a freshly applied stripe of yellow paint around her hull was a poor disguise. He had no such qualms about his own appearance. No one acquainted with the dashing Renato of old would know him beneath the travesty of a face he was now forced to wear.

In any case, he would live or die, as always, by the power of his wits. The trap was laid. All now hinged on the behavior of the mouse, in the person of this American captain.

A stream of extremely unladylike curses spewed from the figure at his side. "By all the gods, Cap'n, I almost hopes they shoots us. If we survive, I'll never live this down."

"Keep your voice down, Quayle, and act like a lady in distress. If those sailors suss you out too soon, you'll get your wish."

Quayle's voice dropped to a hiss. "If one of them mateys so much as pinches my tit, Cap'n, I'll slice his knickknacks off. Swear to Jesus I will."

"And if we're caught due to your blubbering, I'll give you the same treatment. Now close your yap and try to look fetching. And whatever you do, keep that homely phiz of yours averted."

Bound with their backs again the capstan, the two men disguised as clerks began to snicker.

"And that goes for you two as well."

The snickering stopped, but the men's shoulders continued to shake with mirth. Renato let them be. From a distance, LaChaise and the tow-headed pirate named Moring might appear to be crying, which was all to the good. He just hoped that when the time came, they would be competent enough to slip their ropes and pull the hidden pistols from their clothing.

Medusa was closer now, and Renato could not help admiring her. Like *L'Intrepide*, she was a schooner. But to compare the two was to liken a fox to a panther. Where *L'Intrepide* was light and agile, the navy vessel was sleek and strong. *Medusa* had been designed for a single purpose—to hunt and kill pirates, and her success was already legendary.

American telescopes were now trained on *L'Intrepide*, and Renato could feel their scrutiny. He did his best to appear helpless and abused, which in his present condition was not difficult. He was used to inflicting pain, not suffering it himself, and each sway of the ship caused the rough cord to bite deeper into his wrists.

A quick count revealed at least forty blue-clad sailors crowding *Medusa*'s deck, and it was evident many favored shooting first and investigating afterwards. A man with a torch stood eagerly over the touchhole of the 18-pounder. The fact that he had not yet been allowed to act gave Renato hope the American captain was a man of compassion—and therefore his inferior.

Still, the size of that gun gave Renato an odd feeling in his stomach, as if he had swallowed a bowlful of beetles.

For a man who laughed at fear, he did not feel much like laughing.

CHAPTER 28

"Like the hounds of Hell."

"**M**E BEARD'S ITCHIN' like blue blazes." Andre turned in the saddle, peering back over the bony shoulder of Sharky, who straddled the rump of the same horse. He scratched vigorously at the bird's nest beneath his chin. "We're bein' followed, sure."

Bowie flicked a glance over their back trail. "Maybe your little pets are just throwing a square dance."

The old pirate snorted. "Them buggers is always jiggin' about." As if to affirm this, two stripe-backed weevils poked to the surface before scuttling back into his whiskers. "This itch is a different sort, and's never failed me yet."

Bowie studied the surrounding terrain. He'd had the same feeling for the past hour. Since leaving Matagorda they'd moved steadily southward through a wide grassy plain, broken only by occasional spurts of mesquite and yellow-flowered acacia. The grass grew higher than a man's head, and even on horseback they could barely see over the top. The path they followed had been forged by the hooves of many horses, but was now half covered in new growth. The bee in the Karankawas' bonnet had slowed southbound travel to a trickle.

A half-mile to the left, stands of sturdy live oak marked the edge of the mainland, while a mile or more to their right, giant cottonwoods lined the fringes of the inland forest.

The arrangement envisioned by the colonists, in which Bowie and Mariette would ride while the others walked, had proved too slow, and they had doubled up on the mustang and buck-skin, with Sam crowding onto the packhorse with the supplies.

Bowie plucked at his shirtfront, separating the damp cotton from his skin.

"How can you be sure we're being followed?" Mariette's breath was soft on his neck. "We've seen no sign of anyone." She pressed tighter against his back, making him conscious of the twin points of impact. This was a source of heat he did not mind.

"That's how the Kronks operate," Andre said. "Ye don't know they're about until there's an arrow stickin' out of your back."

"Don't worry, father. I'll avenge you." Mariette grasped a handful of gingham skirt and raised it over her boot, expos-ing the butt of a small pistol. Bowie noted with horror that the hammer was cocked.

"Great leapin' Jesus." Andre's face was white. "Tell me ye haven't been carryin' that all this way. Ye could have blown your foot off."

"I'm lucky by nature," Mariette declared. "If I weren't, I'd be whoring in some bordello on Beacon Street, or worse, raising a shopkeeper's babies—rather than adventuring with you charm-ing gentlemen."

Bowie held his tongue, resolving to never again trouble himself over this young lady's sensibilities.

He turned to examine their back trail, plainly marked by bent and broken grass. On either side, the damnably tall shoots danced at the whim of the breeze. He might as well be staring out over the surface of the sea, trying to guess what dangers lurked below.

"Lord, Jim Boy, would ye kindly not dally?" Andre's voice was a whine. "I can't bear the thought of those savages gnawin' on me bones."

"I don't know what *you're* worried about, old man. You're the last of us any cannibal would want."

"Ye thinks so, hey? Look what they got to choose from. Ye're mostly muscle, and your manservant back there looks dry and stringy. This insignificant carcass behind me ain't nothin' but scabs and gristle. And me little Mariette, well, tasty as she'd be, she ain't nothin' but a mouthful." Andre paused to pat his ample belly. "A robust man like meself would feed a score of them savages for a week."

"I say, Jim," Sam's baritone broke in, "is it true these aborigines are possessed of a distinct olfactory presence?"

"You mean do the Kronks stink, like Curly Dan said?" Bowie wrinkled his nose. "Yes, Mr. Gideon. Indeed they do."

Sam made sniffing noises. "I detect the aroma of anacua, elm, pecan and grape, in addition to the spoor of the blue heron, opossum and pocket gopher, but I can ascertain nothing that could to be attributed to homo sapiens."

Andre swung about, his face mottled. "Ye damned jackanapes! Are ye insultin' me again?"

Bowie silenced him with a hand. "You catching any Karankawa scent just now?"

Andre tested the wind, his big nostrils gaping wide. "Can't say's I do." His tone was reluctant. "But they'd be sly enough to stay downwind."

Bowie shook his head. "The way this wind swirls about, we'd have picked them up by now."

"So if it ain't Kronks behind us, who might it be?"

Bowie saw several possibilities. Renato and his rogues, if any still lived, would stop at nothing to find the treasure. The Mexican lancers he and Buckner had manhandled would be itching for vengeance. Then there was that annoying little Pacal, whose disappearance was still unexplained. It was also possible one or more colonists had felt compelled to help rescue Mariette's imaginary brother.

This last reminded him of a long overdue question, and he swung to Andre and Sharky. "It's time you two told us a tale. Why do those settlers hate you?"

While Sharky turned several shades of yellow, Andre remained all innocence. "Their foibles are beyond me, Jim Boy."

Bowie would not be put off. "Talk," he said, "or you're walking. And we won't wait for you."

Andre sighed. "Ah, well, I suppose it must be told. Two summers past, Renato and us sailed into Matagorda Bay with a fresh cargo of goods. We had much to offer—stuff we'd liberated from a Spanish trader, and Renato was in a great sweat to turn a profit. He'd heard the settlement was growin', and figured the colonists was ripe for swindlin'."

"So," Bowie said, "Renato sailed an armed vessel full of stolen goods, manned with the scum of the seas, into a port of god-fearing pilgrims. Not an auspicious beginning."

Sharky eyed Bowie as if he'd spoken a foreign tongue.

"That about covers it," Andre said. "They were wary, but badly in need of our wares, and Renato offered generous prices by way of reelin' them in."

"Generous?" Bowie gave a short laugh. "That's not the man I knew."

Andre shrugged. "He was in one of his grandiose moods. Lafitte had just died, or so he thought, and he seen himself as assumin' the crown, so to speak. Anyways, the mornin' after we arrived, three of his scalawags got restless and slipped away. We didn't know they was gone 'til the ruckus started."

"What ruckus was that?"

"We hears shots in the distance, and come boilin' out of the cabins in time to see them three pirates burst into the clearing draggin' a Indian girl. They was runnin' like the hounds of Hell was after 'em, and wasn't far wrong. Next thing we knows we're dodgin' a hail of arrows. We all jumps for cover, and those with guns starts blastin' into the brush. In the confusion, the girl gets loose and scampers off, and the savages just sorta melts away."

"So what happened next?"

"Soon as the settlers sees the Kronks are gone, they turn on us, demandin' we clear out of their harbor."

"And how did Renato take all this?"

"Nearly had smoke pourin' from his ears, as ye might imagine."

"Did he put up a fight?"

" 'Twere a near thing. But the settlers makes noises about firin' our ship if we don't vamoose. Renato's so mad he's beyond givin' orders, so we all retreats to the ship, draggin' him with us."

"So you left."

"Fast as we could, leavin' some of his goods behind. Before we'd cleared the bay, the three responsible was hangin' from the yardarm. Renato left 'em there 'til the stench was more than he could bear, then had 'em tossed to the sharks."

"And did he return for revenge on the settlers?"

"The thing stuck in his craw, that's sure," Sharky put in. "But no, we never went back."

Bowie frowned. "So what's the rest of the story?"

"What do ye mean, the rest? That's all there was."

"I can understand the settlers hating you, even wanting to hang you. But if that's all that happened, why were they so close-mouthed about it?"

"I've not a clue, Jim Boy. Swear on me mother."

Bowie peered around the old man at Sharky. "And I suppose your charming shipmate doesn't know either."

Sharky bobbed his head. "That's it exactly, Cap'n Bowie. I knows less than nothing."

This brought a snicker from Sam, and Bowie closed his mouth over his own retort.

"I'm reminded, Jim," Andre said, "how grateful I am that ye joined us on this expedition. I know ye're not just here for the gold."

The remark caught Bowie unprepared. If not for gold, what the devil *was* he doing here? He hoped the old pirate didn't think he was sniffing after his daughter.

"Ye're a good friend to me, Jim Boy. Better than I am to you."

Bowie looked closely at him, but Andre dipped his head,

averting his eyes. The man's statement was hard to argue with, but left him puzzled.

They rode awhile in silence, while Bowie's discomfort grew. A sharp crack, like the breaking of a twig, sounded from somewhere behind, and a flock of birds took sudden flight not ten yards off their back trail.

Andre buried a hand in his whiskers, scratching again.

Reaching a sudden decision, Bowie reined the mustang and slipped to the ground. The grass immediately blotted out his view of the horizon, and his sense of menace increased. "I'll lay back and find out who's after us. The rest of you ride on, and I'll catch up when I can." Doffing his hat, he placed it on Mariette's head. "If anyone's watching, they should think I'm still with the party."

Mariette's eyes were huge. "What if it's Renato and his crew? You wouldn't stand a chance."

"If it's truly Renato," Bowie said, "*he* won't stand a chance." He gave Mariette's mount a firm slap on the rump, causing it to leap ahead of the others.

Turning off the trail, Bowie was instantly enveloped by tall grass. Moving quiet as an Indian, he headed north, parallel to the trail. He soon found what he was seeking—a clump of grass grown up around a scraggly mesquite bush. The spot would afford him some slight cover, and not be parted by a fickle wind. He eased to the sandy earth and made himself as comfortable as possible.

Working quickly, he primed and loaded his pistol, then slid his knife from its sheath.

The gleaming blade, more than half the length of his arm, seemed to shine with a light of its own.

He was much like the knife, he reflected. Sheathed, he was the witty and courteous James, who dressed well and lived well, enjoying beautiful women and polite society. Unsheathed, he was the savage Big Jim, terrible in his rage and lethal to his

enemies. He tried to keep the two sides separate, but was finding it increasingly difficult.

A knife had saved his life, it was true, but it had also stolen it.
For better or worse, the thing had become an extension of his
body, his character, even his soul.

Was it his imagination, or did the blade sing to him now,
calling out for blood? Turning it slowly in his hand, he caught a
distorted reflection of himself—a grim-faced warrior as savage
as any in this wild land.

And despite the heat of the day, he felt a sudden chill.

CHAPTER 29

"That infamous devil Renato!"

"**A**HOY THE SHIP!" The call, made tinny by a speaking trumpet, rang clearly across the waves.

Renato fought back a grin. A small victory. The American captain had chosen to talk rather than shoot.

"God be praised!" Renato used his best New England accent. "Our deliverance is at hand!"

"You will please identify yourself. What ship are you?"

"Help! They've murdered my crew!" Renato did not want to sound too coherent. A ready answer would arouse more suspicion than a frenzied one.

"We'll be pleased to aid you, but you must first identify yourself."

As the ships drifted closer, Renato got his first clear look at his adversary. *Medusa*'s captain was tall, towering above his crewmen, with wide shoulders and a narrow waist. Blond muttonchop whiskers hid his expression, but his eyes were firm and uncompromising.

Renato was now able to speak without shouting. "Thank the Lord you've come. My poor daughter is near dead of thirst."

"What ship are you?"

Renato shook his head as if clearing a fog. "*Abigail Adams*," he said, naming the famous mother of the current American President. He had no idea if there were such a vessel, but hoped it would command some degree of respect. "We were beset by the foulest of pirates!"

After a long pause, the answer came. "This is Captain Charles Bentley of the *U.S.S. Medusa*, at your service. Whom am I addressing?" The man's deep, powerful voice carried cleanly over the waves.

"The honorable Horace P. Worthington, late of New York. You are indeed our savior, sir!"

There was a spate of conversation aboard *Medusa*. Renato could imagine the name passing from lip to lip, as each man plumbed his memory. It had a ring of power and authority— the sort of name men would feel they should recognize or be deemed ignorant.

"Who attacked you, Mr. Worthington?"

"The bloodiest pirate who ever sailed the seas. The Hawk of the Gulf. That infamous devil Renato!"

There was more hushed discussion on *Medusa*. Then, "Who? Who did you say?"

Renato stared, struggling to form words.

The shoulders of LaChaise and Moring began to shake.

"Renato the Terrible!" The words came out in a roar. "Renato the Bold!"

After another moment, Captain Bentley said, "Renato Beluche? I thought he retired years ago."

Renato bristled at the mention of his stepfather. "No, by God, not Beluche! This was his namesake—a fiend more ferocious than Morgan, Blackbeard and the Lafittes combined!"

"I see." Bentley's tone was maddeningly condescending. "Some petty scoundrel trying to make a name for himself. Everyone knows all the great pirates have been scourged from the Caribbean."

Renato burned, drawing blood from his tongue. On the heels of his recent indignities, this was too much to bear. He fought to regain his Yankee accent. "This Renato fellow is the Devil incarnate, I assure you! Pray you never cross his path!"

Bentley's answer was laconic. "I'm sending a party to determine your situation."

On *Medusa*'s deck, men set to uncovering a jolly boat. Renato forced a deep breath. If the sailors searched his ship, they could not help but discover the pirates below.

"Begging your pardon, Captain, but there's a delicate matter we must address."

"And what might that be, sir?"

Renato put just the right amount of reticence into his tone. "As I said, Captain, it is...delicate. It would be better discussed in private."

"Plenty of time for that, Mr. Worthington, once we've ascertained your needs."

"It's not merely my own needs I'm thinking of, Captain, if you get my meaning."

"No, I am afraid I do not."

"Well, it's like this, my good sir. That fiend Renato made off with my cargo and what he thought were all my worldly possessions. But I've still quite a pretty sum, if I do say so, and—meaning nothing against your noble sailors—it would be unfair to subject them to temptation. 'Twould be better far if you and I discovered it together, allowing me to show my gratitude in proper fashion."

Bentley's face seemed to close down, and he turned away.

Renato sweated, striving to appear earnest and disarming. He'd put it plainly enough for the dullest fool to understand. He could only hope the man's sense of greed was keener than his wit.

The seconds dragged into minutes. Action around the jolly boat had stopped. Captain Bentley stood on his quarterdeck, holding conference with an officer who appeared to be his second in command. The eyes of *Medusa*'s sailors roved incessantly between Bentley and Renato, bright with speculation.

Renato crowed within. The mouse must be preparing to take the bait.

At last Bentley stood away from his subordinate and spoke again. "You have my assurance, Mr. Worthington, that your valuables will be safe. Any thanks you wish to express will be

discussed at the proper time." To his officer he said, "Lieutenant Goble, you will take four men and determine the extent
of damages to Mr. Worthington's vessel. I'm sure I can depend
upon you to see that his personal property is respected."

Renato was stunned. He had read about such individuals in
books. He had even once met a man who claimed to know one,
but the fellow was a notorious liar and Renato had discounted
the tale. Now, at the worst possible time, he was forced to admit
such a person could truly exist. Captain Bentley was that rare
being he had so long believed a myth—an honest man.

This development not only left Renato's carefully laid plan
in ruins—it shattered his faith in human nature. Like a sleeper
trapped in a nightmare, he watched as the jolly boat was lowered,
and the competent-looking Lieutenant Goble moved slowly
among the sailors, clapping hands on the shoulders of those
who would accompany him.

A chill gripped Renato's heart. The rough hemp scratched at
the raw skin of his wrists, and he could now fancy it tightening
about his neck as well.

CHAPTER 30

"If I was a Injun, you'd be dead."

HUNKERED BEHIND THE gnarled clump of mesquite, Bowie wiped his brow with a sleeve. The merciless sun had already dispatched the wispy ocean clouds, and now seemed intent on burning the blue from the sky.

He had eased the pistol's hammer gently back, wincing at the faint click, and returned the knife to its sheath to prevent a giveaway flash of blade. There was still no scent of Karankawa on the wind, but all his senses told him someone was near.

Bowie found himself strangely ill at ease. He feared no foe, savage or civilized, singly or in groups. Nor did he have any particular fear of death. But he was responsible for others now, and his survival mattered. In any case, he did not like this laying in ambush. He preferred to look his enemies squarely in the eye.

The enemy he most wanted to see was Renato. Bowie's failure to avenge the blonde girl weighed more heavily with each passing day. He could not have acted differently in his battle with Rayón, but if he'd had an inkling of Renato's plans for the girl, he'd have given her protection.

Upon hearing of her death, he should have set out immediately to kill Renato. But that would have meant abandoning his brothers and putting their current moneymaking operations at risk. And therein lay the guilt. He had allowed avarice to override his responsibility to the girl.

In the years since, he had done his best to atone for that indulgence. He'd made it his business to take the side of the underdog, to defend others from men of Renato's ilk. The resulting confrontations had made him stronger, and enhanced his reputation, but failed to erase the shame in his heart.

There was only one way to lift that burden. He must remove Renato from this plane of existence by the same means Renato had employed upon the girl.

Bowie was contemplating the details of that reckoning when he heard the whisper behind him.

"If I was a Injun," the whisper said, "you'd be dead."

Bowie was careful to make no sudden move. "That mean you don't plan on killing me?"

"Not at the moment. But no promises."

Though now certain of the speaker's identity, it still came as a shock to see the huge figure squatting on his haunches a scant yard away. The man seemed bothered not at all by the split lips or purple bruises inflicted the night before by Bowie's fists. Bowie himself felt like he had been trampled by wild horses.

"Buckner. How in blazes did you sneak up on me?"

"Hell, little man. You was quivering head to toe like you was fit to blow. Any troubles you'd like to share?"

Bowie cursed himself. He had allowed his preoccupation with Renato to put his life at risk. And the fact that this particular man had caught him at it made it all the worse.

Buckner raised a finger to his lips and pointed back down the trail.

Listening intently, Bowie caught rustling in the grass and the wheeze of heavy breathing. The sounds were made by a single human being—and a clumsy one—traveling on foot. A horse would have made less noise.

Buckner's huge hands worked open and shut in anticipation. His sky-blue eyes gleamed, and his entire body seemed to emit waves of compressed energy.

The tall grasses parted, and through them slouched a stocky figure in grimy buckskins. The man had taken no more than a step when he stiffened, his eyes goose-egged, and he wheeled about, running breakneck back the way he'd come.

Bowie sprang after him. He had seen enough to recognize the fellow—one of Sharky's late night drinking partners, the man named Hinkle.

Speeding along, Bowie heard a great ruckus off to his right. Strap Buckner was bulling his own path through the grass, making this into a race. Bowie turned up the speed, legs pumping with long, even strides.

Ahead, he caught sight of Hinkle's galloping heels. Bowie was nearly upon him, readying himself for a leap, when Buckner exploded onto the trail, slamming into Hinkle with the force of a tornado. The smaller man left the earth, windmilled through the air and crashed down somewhere in the distance.

Bowie followed the howls of pain, arriving to see a hand the size of a coal shovel pluck Hinkle from a blackjack thicket and dangle him by the scruff of the neck.

Circling wide around Buckner, Bowie peered back toward Matagorda. The grass swayed lazily in the breeze, and he heard nothing but the chirp of swallows and the distant cry of a heron. It seemed Hinkle had been traveling alone.

"Thanks for your help, Strap. But what the blazes are you doing here?"

Buckner snorted. "I come to ask you that very thing."

Hinkle began making harsh squawking noises.

Bowie raised his voice. "Didn't the others tell you about the young lady's brother?"

"They told me. Some of 'em even believed it. Me, I know hogwash when I hear it."

"What makes you think it's hogwash?"

Hinkle, still dangling, cried, "Hey!"

"You ain't so big as your reputation," Buckner said, "and you travel in poor company, but you ain't fool enough to go gallivantin' into Karankawa country on so hopeless a mission."

Bowie had to smile. "That almost sounds like a compliment."

Buckner growled. "The settlers hereabouts are under my protection. I can't have you stirrin' up the Kronks, and runnin' off while the rest of us pay the piper. That won't never happen again."

"Goddamn it, Buckner!" Hinkle shrieked. "You set me down!"

Buckner turned a curious eye on Hinkle, as if he'd forgotten the man was there. He looked back to Bowie. "What shall we do with this jasper?"

Bowie stroked his chin. "How about we truss him up and leave him as dinner for the Kronks? Sort of a peace offering."

Buckner smiled horribly, and Hinkle looked about to faint. "No!" he wailed. "You're in danger! I come to warn you!"

Buckner said, "I don't know. He looks none too tasty. We give those red devils bellyaches, it'll just make 'em madder."

Bowie made a show of examining his knife. He pressed the point into the soft flesh under Hinkle's chin, watching a thin red line trace down the blade. "Maybe I'll just open him from chin to brisket. Leave him for the wolves."

Hinkle held himself very still. "Didn't you hear me? They're after the gold! And the girl!"

At the word *gold*, Buckner's eyes flicked to Bowie. Then, with a broad smile, he said, "Here's a trick you'll like." He wrapped a hand over the top of Hinkle's head, covering it from ear to ear. "I'll pop his skull like a melon."

"Wait! Wait!" Hinkle squawked. "I'll tell you everything!"

Bowie jingled his purse. "Five dollars says you can't do it."

"Ten," Buckner replied.

Hinkle's body shook violently. Then his face went slack, and his body hung limp.

Buckner let him fall to earth.

"Fainted," Bowie said.

"Not only that," Buckner said, nose twitching, "he pissed himself." He turned his head, squinting at Bowie. "Now what was that he said about *gold*?"

Before Bowie could answer, a pistol shot sounded in the distance.

He whipped about, staring off toward the south, toward Andre, Mariette and the others. More shots ripped the air, and Bowie felt them almost as if they had entered his own breast.

Then he was running, barreling through the grassy jungle like a maddened buffalo, straight for the sound of the shots.

CHAPTER 31

"Is there pox aboard that ship?"

A S T H E F I R S T sailor threw a blue-trousered leg over *L'Intrepide*'s rail, Renato adopted his oiliest manner. "Bless you, my man! You're my salvation. Free me quickly and I'll see you richly rewarded."

Renato had picked his mark with care. The fellow was tall, with thick spectacles, and walked as if he had a toothache in his heel. As their eyes met, Renato congratulated himself. The man's face held revulsion, but an even greater dose of compassion.

The tall sailor was reaching for the ropes when Lieutenant Goble's voice cracked from the jolly boat. "Mr. Paschelke! You will touch nothing until so ordered."

Renato regretted his decision to be bound so securely. The logical first act of a rescue party would be to free him, and he could not risk the discovery of slipknots. But his plan was already veering off course. He had hoped to lure the American captain himself aboard for use as a hostage. Now he must improvise, and the ropes narrowed his options.

"Your pardon, Lieutenant," Renato said, with a bow of the head, "these bonds are cruel upon my wrists."

Goble stood up in the rowboat as two more of his boarding party swung onto the deck. The fourth and final sailor, a fellow who looked villainous enough to be one of Renato's own crew, sat steadying the boat, a musket across his lap. The three sailors on deck, Renato noted with ill ease, had pistols in their hands.

Goble cleared the rail with a long-practiced leap. "My regrets,

Mr. Worthington, but my orders are quite specific. You shall be freed as soon as is practicable."

Renato forced a meek demeanor. "You are very kind. But surely there is no need to come armed aboard my humble vessel. Those evil pirates are long gone, I assure you."

As if in answer, the lieutenant drew his own long-barreled pistol and motioned the grizzled sailor with the rifle to clamber aboard.

Behind Goble's back, LaChaise's piggish eyes flicked pointedly to Goble and back. He was hot to slip his bonds and bury his pistol in the officer's ribs.

Renato shook his head. To play that trump too soon would doom them all.

LaChaise scowled his disapproval. He was like the rest of Renato's crew. Muscle without brains. Renato hoped he could keep the man in check until the proper time.

"Paschelke," Goble said, "you, Britt and Richter will examine the lower decks. And take care that nothing finds its way into your pockets. Mr. Horvat, you will remain here. See that you stay alert."

The three first named moved quickly toward the hatch, while the man called Horvat gripped his musket and peered owlishly about the deck.

Goble approached Renato, the big pistol hovering before him like the head of a snake. The man's beard was white, and tied off into three puffs of hair. The first, nearest his chin, was the size and shape of a lemon. The second was more elongated, like a dill pickle, while the third resembled a man's finger. He stepped carefully around the foremast, his eyes seeming to take in everything at once.

Renato felt a firm tug on the ropes binding his wrists. For a moment, his hopes soared, but the fussy bastard had merely been checking the knots.

Renato said, "If you won't free me, will you at least offer me drink? I'm desiccated near to death."

Goble looked him full in the face. Behind the man's eyes, Renato saw an involuntary shudder. But there was something else—a hint of recognition. Had they met before?

A wave of dread washed over him. A younger version of this fellow had stood with Lafitte and the other gunners in saving New Orleans, and his skill had rivaled that of the pirates.

As the lieutenant leaned closer, the third puff of his beard—the one shaped like a finger—pointed at him accusingly. "Do I know you, sir?"

"I cannot claim that honor," Renato croaked. "But about that thirst…"

"Mr. Horvat." Goble's hand beckoned. "Bring your canteen." The sailor approached warily. "Sir?"

"Mr. Worthington is thirsty. You will kindly accommodate him."

Horvat shuddered. "With my own canteen, sir? Must I?"

"That's an order, sailor."

Resigned to his fate, the man took the canteen from his belt and held it an inch from Renato's lips, clearly wishing to avoid contact.

Taking the hint, Renato tilted his head back. But as the canteen moved closer, he craned forward, catching the neck between his lips. Reveling in the look of horror upon Horvat's face, he sucked greedily—but had no sooner begun than he retched and spewed, causing the navy men to jump. It was bad enough the stuff was warm and tasted of rusty metal—but it did not even contain spirits! This pathetic excuse for a seaman carried nothing in his canteen but water.

"You've given him too much." Goble's voice was stern. "Now see to the girl as well, but take care to go easy."

Renato's blood turned cold. If they got a glimpse of Quayle's stubbly chin, all would be lost. And even now, Horvat was raising a hand to pull the wig from Quayle's face.

"You're too kind," Renato said, his mind racing. "Few men have the courage to succor such as she."

The sailor paused, angling an eye at Renato.

Goble arched an eyebrow. "Odd words, sir, regarding your own daughter."

"True enough," Renato said heavily. "She was a lovely lass once, but that was before…"

"Before?"

Renato knew the look of a man with information he did not wish to share. He assumed that expression now.

"Speak, man." The lieutenant tapped the pistol against his leg. "Before what?"

"Before…" Renato's voice fell to a whisper, "the pox."

"Smallpox?" The word exploded from between Goble's teeth.

Horvat lurched back as if stung.

Renato pressed the heel of his boot against Quayle's ankle, and ground it home.

Quayle emitted a delightfully womanish squeal, driving the two men further away.

A grumbling arose from *Medusa*'s deck—a single word echoed from every throat.

"Mr. Goble!" Bentley's voice slashed through the din. "Is there pox aboard that ship?"

Goble stared at Renato with haunted eyes.

Renato moved his head slowly from side to side. "She is well past it now, and no danger to anyone. Still, it's as well not to touch her."

In the silence that followed, Quayle saw fit to add another squeal.

"Lieutenant!" The sailor Paschelke's face appeared above the hatch cover. "Sir! They carry slaves!"

CHAPTER 32

"What in heaven's name?"

THERE HAD BEEN no further shots, and this worried Bowie more than if there had. He barreled down the trail of broken and trampled grass, heart drumming in his ears.

Dark visions swirled through him: Gaudily painted warriors with spears dragging Mariette off to their camp; hard-faced women kicking her and plucking off her clothes; a shaman preparing to slice off a strip of flesh.

Reason told Bowie he should fear for the others as well. But the truth was, Mariette had been in his thoughts more with each passing day. It was only now, in this moment of panic, that he was forced to face it.

Suddenly, above the crashing of his own body through the grass, he caught the sound of running feet. A bent figure appeared, racing toward him at full tilt. Bowie shouted a warning, tried to swerve, but the runner crashed headlong into his chest, expelling a cloud of foul breath.

Before him on the sandy ground, head quivering like a sack of angry bees, lay the scrawny pirate Sharky.

"What's happened?" Bowie demanded. "Where are the others?"

Sharky pointed back up the trail he had plowed in the grass. And when Bowie looked, the man bolted past him and was quickly eaten by the grassy jungle.

After a moment, he detected new sounds ahead. A gruff, commanding voice, and subdued replies.

Following the voices, Bowie peered through the grass at a firepit ringed with log benches. And it was here he found his friends. But they were not alone.

Surrounding them were four Mexican lancers. And with them, astride his great black stallion, sat the Mexican sergeant Guiterrez. All were decorated with bruises and bandages, and one had his arm in a sling, but their weapons were steady in their hands.

Andre, Sam and Mariette knelt at the edge of the firepit, hands above their heads.

"SLAVES!" THERE WAS ice in Captain Bentley's voice. "Can you explain that, Mr. Worthington?"

Renato was all innocence. "Most assuredly, sir. We rescued those poor souls from a plantation on the Mississippi coast, and are taking them to Boston, and freedom."

Lieutenant Goble stood above him, scowling. Another damned abolitionist.

"Lieutenant, sir!" Seaman Horvat knelt at the edge of the gaping hole where the mainmast had been. You should see this."

Shaking like a dog after a bath, Goble strode to the spot.

"Something queer here, sir." Horvat touched his musket barrel to the scorched and jagged edges of the hole. "Have you ever known cannon shot to open such a rent?"

Frowning, the lieutenant examined it from all sides. "Mr. Worthington! You said you were attacked by pirates. How did this damage come about?"

Renato took pause. That was a question he, too, wished answered. It had been sabotage, to be sure, but how or by whom he was unable to fathom. He was inventing a plausible lie when a hubbub erupted from the lower deck. A hoarse shout was followed quickly by sulfurous curses, the rumble of feet, and the sharp bark of gunfire. Goble and Horvat gripped their weapons as wisps of smoke drifted through the hatch.

Bellows and groans roiled up from below, accompanied by the smacking of fists upon flesh, but there were no more shots.

"Mr. Goble!" Bentley bellowed from *Medusa*. "What in heaven's name is happening over there?"

A score of fierce-eyed sailors had rifles trained upon *L'Intrepide*'s deck. And above them, seeming close enough to engulf Renato in its gaping mouth, perched the 18-pound swivel gun. Now, Renato knew, he stood on the knife-edge between life and death.

A pirate bobbed up from the hatch. Seeing Goble, Horvat, and the guns aboard *Medusa*, the man quickly disappeared.

"Who goes there?" Goble demanded. "Step up, carefully now, and show yourself."

"Not bloody likely," came the reply, followed by a chorus of rough laughter.

"Paschelke! Britt! Richter! Report!" The lieutenant's words were like the cracking of dry branches.

"Paschelke here, sir! Britt is wounded, Richter dead. There be pirates here!"

More rough laughter followed, with mocking repetition of the line, *There be pirates here!*

Goble's glare slammed against Renato. "Mr. Worthington! What is the meaning of this?"

LaChaise again caught Renato's eye, his face afire with eagerness.

Renato granted him a brief nod. "It means, Lieutenant, that your life and mine are now inextricably bound."

CHAPTER 33

"The first nice thing."

"ENOUGH OF YOUR stalling," the Mexican sergeant growled. "You will tell me what I wish to know—and quickly—or we will stick you like the pigs you are. And we will begin," he added with a crooked smile, "with the pretty señorita."

Bowie must act immediately, or forever regret it. He stepped boldly into the clearing. "I'm late to the party," he announced, "but ready to dance."

The sergeant's eyes flashed fire. Leveling his pistol at Bowie, the man kneed his horse closer. His face bore angry scratches and a purple mouse beneath one eye.

"I rejoice at our reacquaintance, Señor. At first, I was only interested in killing you. But that was before I learned of your quest for gold." He paused, his beetle-like eyes scuttling over the group. "Now I intend to relieve you of your map. *Then* I will kill you."

Bowie forced a laugh. "Gold? You've been listening to tall tales, Sergeant. Not uncommon in this country."

"Dissembling will avail you nothing." Gutierrez ran a soiled white handkerchief under his black-stubbled chin. "I have the story from my cousin Joaquin, who had it directly from one of your own party."

One of their party. There was only one it could be.

"That sniveling weasel, Sharky? If it would earn him a drink, he'd swear his mother was the Queen of Spain."

The sergeant almost smiled. "I take your point. But if I accept your word, it avails me nothing. I would merely kill you and be on my way. On the other hand, if the treasure is real, it will benefit me greatly."

A clicking sound brought their attention to the far end of the clearing. There stood Pacal, windmilling his arms at the lancers.

"Who is that man," Gutierrez demanded, "and what is he jabbering about?"

"He's nutty as a squirrel. Ask him yourself."

"If he does not subsist, I will have him shot immediately."

"Sergeant," Bowie said, "that's the first nice thing you've said to me."

The lancer nearest Pacal aimed a pistol at him, and the brown man flopped cross-legged to the ground. For the moment, he was blissfully silent.

"Now," Gutierrez said, "as to this map. I intend to have you searched, one at time, until I find it." His tongue slithered across his lower lip. "We will begin with the girl—unless, of course, you prefer to surrender it at once."

Bowie did not know where Mariette had secreted the map, but the thought of her forced to disrobe before these eyes filled him with a red rage. If he was slated to die, he preferred it to be on the attack, taking some of his enemies with him.

While Gutierrez issued instructions to his men, Bowie looked pointedly at Andre and Sam. Holding the gaze of each in turn, he flicked his eyes significantly at the lancers, indicating which each should go for. Andre gave the briefest of nods. Sam merely yawned, betraying no interest, much less agreement.

To Mariette, Bowie shifted his eyes downward, indicating she should drop to the earth. She shook her head. Bowie repeated the signal. Another shake, and her eyes darted toward one of the lancers. Bowie gave up.

At the sergeant's order, a man advanced his horse toward Mariette. "Take care not kill her—yet—or your own life will be forfeit."

Tensing his muscles, Bowie gave the others a short nod. Tearing the knife from its sheath, he burst forward as if shot from a cannon. The sergeant's pistol remained steady, its large black eye staring directly at him. He ran with jerky strides, expecting at any moment the bone-crushing impact of the pistol ball.

A chorus of hisses came from several directions at once, but Bowie kept his legs churning, eyes fixed on the sergeant.

Gutierrez smiled. His finger whitened on the trigger. Then he lurched upright, twisting at an odd angle, and crashed face first to the sandy earth. Between his shoulder blades stood a thin wooden shaft nearly a yard long.

Bowie dived to the ground at the man's side. Snatching the pistol from limp fingers, he scanned the direction from which the shaft must have come, and saw nothing but tall grass swaying in the breeze.

The sergeant's lips were torn back, exposing broken and pitted teeth, and his eyes fixed on eternity.

Bowie swung about, anxious for the others. Mariette knelt over a body at the foot of a riderless horse. Andre and Sam gaped at the two dead Mexicans on the ground before them. The final soldier lolled back in his saddle, feet still hooked in the stirrups.

Each of the lancers had one of the javelin-like shafts protruding from his body.

CHAPTER 34

"Five minutes to decide."

"INEXTRICABLY BOUND?" Lieutenant Goble's pistol pointed at Renato's nose. "I'm afraid you must explain yourself, sir!"

By the time he'd finished speaking, LaChaise and Moring had slipped their bonds and risen with drawn pistols.

Captain Bentley barked, "You men will drop your weapons immediately, or we shall open fire."

"Fire away, damn you." Renato's Yankee accent was gone. "Your own men will be among the first to die."

Bentley hesitated.

Renato did not. "Mr. Faraday, you may bring the other prisoners on deck."

A sailor emerged from the hatch—the white-haired man Goble had called Britt. Behind him, pistol in hand, came Faraday. Britt moved with difficulty, a crimson stain decorating the leg of his uniform. Paschelke followed, the blade of a scar-faced pirate digging into his back. Behind them, the rest of Renato's crew scrambled onto the narrow deck.

"Mr. Faraday." Renato jerked his head. "Cut these bonds. Quickly."

Faraday's face flashed fear, regret and resignation, all in a matter of seconds. But he produced a knife and began sawing Renato's ropes.

Quayle, still in girlish voice, squealed, "Mine too!"

"Bugger you, you little tart." Faraday freed Renato's legs, while the other pirates sniggered.

Bentley watched, scowling. "This will gain you nothing. If you offer further harm to my men, I will blow you out of the water."

"I doubt that very much." Renato pried the pistol from Goble's grip and jammed the barrel under his beard. "Ever seen a man shot from this angle, Captain? The ball plows through until it bursts out the top of the skull, making a most glorious fountain of blood and brains. It's particularly fascinating if the brains belong to someone you know."

Bentley's mouth was a grim line. A chorus of curses issued from *Medusa*'s crew.

Renato smiled. "Not your cup of tea, perhaps, but one you shall surely swallow, unless my demands are met."

Bentley's voice was like an echo from a cave. "I have no interest in your demands. I merely wish to know one thing—your real name."

Renato puffed his chest. He moved to twirl his mustache, then, finding it no longer there, performed a deprecatory wave. "Have you not guessed it? You have the ill luck to address the Last Great Terror of the Gulf, the infamous Renato himself, the very man you pretended no knowledge of. What say you now, sir?"

Bentley glowered at him a long moment, and Renato could almost hear the grinding of teeth.

"I can now state, with absolute certainty, that my first assessment of him was correct—a petty villain with delusions of grandeur. The buccaneers of legend would not deign to sneeze upon him."

Renato found himself momentarily without words.

Bentley raised his voice. "As such, I shall address you no longer. You men, you would-be pirates. This deranged braggart has no doubt bullied you into committing acts you would otherwise never contemplate. Someone must pay for the evil done here today, but it need not be you. Surrender this Renato person to me now, and the rest of your lives will be spared. You have five minutes to decide."

Renato felt the eyes of his men upon him. He glanced at Faraday, then surveyed the others—and felt a stab in his vitals. To a man, they appeared to him as strangers. Their faces denoted thought, an ability he'd believed beyond them.

CHAPTER 35

"Damned if I know."

BOWIE HUGGED THE ground, expecting more shafts to fly.

The others had followed his lead, laying as flat as possible. But while Mariette and Sam were slim enough to be almost invisible, Andre's great girth presented an easy target.

For long seconds, no one moved. Bowie strained to catch the slightest sounds from the surrounding fields. He heard only the nervous breathing of the horses and the steady gurgle of the creek.

He fought to make sense of the situation. This was not the Karankawa way of fighting. Those painted savages came straight at you, spears held high, screaming to curdle the blood. The Kronks in this area were said to be behaving strangely, but a complete shift in battle tactics was unthinkable.

Likewise, he was baffled by the peculiar shafts extending from the dead men's backs. They were too long to be arrows, too short for spears. No Indians of his experience were known to employ such weapons. But whoever they belonged to, his party's prospects appeared bleak.

A sharp cackle broke the silence. Pacal was back on his feet, strutting toward the nearest lancer. With an angry clicking, he unleashed a kick, and the man's head jerked upright before flopping back to earth. With wild abandon, Pacal continued his tirade, delivering vicious blows to other parts of the dead man's anatomy.

Bowie watched, waiting to hear that hissing sound, and see the brown man pitch to the earth with a shaft in his back.

Instead, Pacal made a beeline for the next lancer. This time, his kicks elicited a moan, and the body heaved of its own accord. With a sharp cry, Pacal fell to his knees at the man's side. A blade glinted as his fist, plummeting downward again and again until the lancer's cries ceased. When the brown man rose, his arm was bathed in blood, and he held a still-pumping heart in his hand.

Mariette sobbed. Andre swore.

Pacal's head rotated, snake-like. His dark eyes gleamed as he marched toward his next victim.

"Pacal! *¡Alto!*"

Bowie's command had no effect. He fired the sergeant's pistol, raising a geyser of sand at the brown man's feet.

Sibilant hisses poured from Pacal's mouth, and Bowie had no doubt he and all his ancestors were being damned.

When the little man ran out of steam, Mariette called, "Pacal, please!"

While it was doubtful he understood English, he seemed to understand her tone. Crossing arms over his chest, he curled his legs and corkscrewed to the ground, Indian style.

Bowie shook his head, at a loss to understand why the little blister was still alive.

"Andre! You see any way to get out of this with our skins?"

"Damned if I know what to think, Jim Boy. But I can't lie here forever. I'm getting a pain in me sackerillyack."

A rustling of grass came from the far end of the clearing, and large shape flew out of the jungle, thudding to the earth.

Andre said, "What in Satan's name was that?"

No one answered. The thing had been roughly the size of a man, but something told Bowie it was not human.

Pacal rose fluidly and clacked to himself as he strode off toward the mysterious shape. With a glad cry, he bent low, then rose with a great weight on his back, and trudged toward the firepit.

The thing was now visible as the body of a deer. Bowie could find no words.

Andre grunted and hove to his feet. "I've had enough layin' about," he told anyone within hearing. "If ye've a mind to kill me, do it now or hold your peace."

More silence.

"Damnedest bunch of ambushers I ever saw," Andre said. "First they kill our enemies, then offer us supper. By my lights, it'd be downright rude not to accept."

CHAPTER 36

"Our tails in a crack."

"**M**Y PATIENCE GROWS thin," Captain Bentley patted the barrel of *Medusa*'s 18-pounder, now trained to blow a swath across *L'Intrepide*'s deck. "Surrender your captain or die."

Renato's pistol was slick with sweat. He tightened his grip and jammed the barrel deeper into Lieutenant Goble's neck. "Steady, men," he told his rogues. "It's a bluff. A gentleman such as he would never sacrifice members of his own crew."

Renato spoke with a conviction he did not feel. The American captain was precisely the type of prig who would sacrifice all to an abstract principle of law.

"No! He'll do it!" Faraday stood white-faced near the foremast, several of his toadies around him. "What are we waiting for? Renato would throw us over in an instant to save his own precious hide."

"Shut yer cake hole, Faraday!" This from LaChaise, at the center of a smaller group on the quarterdeck. "You've been hot to surrender since we sighted their sail, doubtless 'cause you fear the cap'n's vengeance."

"And what of your motives, LaChaise? Your crimes may be grievous enough to warrant a noose in New Orleans, but not all of us are so desperate."

Renato lent only half an ear to the debate. Whether blown to bits by *Medusa*'s cannon, or hanged from her yardarm was of little consequence. His five-minute respite was nearly gone, and he still had not the glimmer of a plan to save himself.

Bentley waited with an open pocket watch in his palm. His sailors wore expectant grins, eager for come what may.

"We've had our tails in a crack before," LaChaise's friend Moring growled, "and Cap'n Renato always pulled us out."

"Aye," admitted a Faraday man, "but that was before we took on them Voodoo worshipers, and was beset by demons."

Others grunted agreement. While the fiercest die-hards sided with LaChaise, the mood of the majority had swung to surrender.

Renato's mind raced. He still had no viable plan. His eyes roved the deck, seeking something he could put to advantage. All he had to work with was the captive boarding party, a crew of mutinous ingrates, and the power of his own cunning.

"Your time is up!" Did he detect a gloat in Bentley's tone? "Give me your captain—*now*—or face the consequences."

Renato seethed. It was bad enough to die, but to be outwitted by *an honest man* was galling beyond belief.

Faraday's party shuffled forward.

Renato dug the pistol deeper under Goble's chin, forcing him up on his toes.

"You might as well concede," the man said. "Your men are giving you up."

"If that's to be, I have nothing to lose by pulling this trigger. Rest assured—if I go to Hell, I will not go alone."

Goble sniffed. "You do not scare me, sir. I am confident my place in eternity will be far cooler than your own."

Renato snarled. His luck had truly left him. The last man he would ever have the pleasure of killing was not afraid to die.

Taking care that Goble's body shielded his own from *Medusa*, Renato swung to face the approaching pirates. Their ugly faces were grim. Those at the fore flinched under his glare, but did not falter. The men in the stern—all but LaChaise—now approached as well, having surrendered to the fatalist mentality of the pack.

Renato pushed Goble aside, leveling the pistol first at one group, then the other.

At his feet, the ghastly apparition that remained of Princess let out a plaintive yowl. Then Quayle began blubbering, and a devilish new plan burst full-blown into Renato's brain. The Fates were with him still. He had one last gambit to keep the Grim Reaper at bay.

"Halt!" The command carried every ounce of his authority, and the men were conditioned to obey. "LaChaise, release that poor maiden from her bonds." In answer to the man's vacant stare, he jerked his head at Quayle. "Bring her to me at once."

LaChaise moved to obey. The other pirates remained frozen, mouths agape.

"See here!" Bentley shouted. "You men made the right decision—now you must carry it out!"

Having slit Quayle's ropes in a single motion, LaChaise made the frilly-clad bosun kneel at Renato's feet. Thankfully, Quayle still had the sense to keep his face averted.

Renato leaned close to Quayle's ear.

"Hear me, you guttersnipe. No matter what happens, continue to play the maiden in distress."

"Aye, Cap'n," Quayle whispered, "but what—"

"LaChaise. Lively now! Grip this lass tightly, for she'll be sure to struggle." And with that, he drew a wickedly curved dagger from his belt.

Quayle let out a shriek, too realistic to be feigned.

"You pirates!" Bentley's tone was fraught with concern. "This is your last chance! Disarm that maniac at once, or we open fire!"

Renato's crew paid no heed, their fierce eyes fixed upon Quayle. The prospect of seeing the man killed had fired their bloodthirsty souls, driving all else from their minds.

Smooth as silk, Renato said, "You must forgive me, Captain,

as I was forced to deceive you. This young lady, lovely as she is, is not truly my daughter. She's the sole survivor of a merchant brig we took off Belle Isle. I'd been saving her for a special occasion, but present circumstances demand a sacrifice."

The ships were close enough for Renato to see a steady twitch in Bentley's jaw.

"I should like to introduce you," Renato said, "to the most loyal member of my crew." He inclined his head, indicating the black-scabbed cat. "Her name is Princess, and she has not eaten in days. Among the many delicacies she enjoys are human eyeballs."

He waved the dagger close to Quayle's face, producing a girlish gasp. Then Quayle broke down altogether. His pitiful whimpering left Bentley white-faced, fists clenched at his sides.

"And the eyes are just an appetizer," Renato said, relishing his words, "for there are other select portions my Princess enjoys."

Bentley's voice was tight as a wire. "Such savagery will not save you."

"Perhaps not. But it will satisfy my curiosity. I recognize in you, Captain, a man who would trade four of your own men for the glory of bringing me to justice. The question now is this—is your sense of duty more precious than the life of this innocent girl? Would your conscience see her cut to pieces and devoured before your very eyes? That sight, I assure you, will be seared into your memory for the rest of your days."

Bentley's jaw twitched violently.

Behind Quayle, LaChaise all but drooled with anticipation.

Allowing the blade to catch the sun's rays, Renato brought the point ever closer to Quayle.

Bentley's twitch now rocked him to the waist.

Renato's heart had ceased to beat. Sweat trickled down his scarred cheeks, salt stinging his cracked lips.

Men on both ships held their breath. The world was silent but for the gentle creak of timbers and the soft slap of waves against the hulls.

Bentley's eyes flared to white-hot intensity, then dimmed as if a flame had been extinguished. His jaw hung slack.

Renato's heart resumed its beat. "Mr. LaChaise, grip her tightly now! We shall take the right eye first."

Quayle's scream made even Renato's hair stand to attention. The blade quivered a hairsbreadth from the little man's eyes.

A hoarse cry ripped from Bentley. "Stop!"

Renato pretended not to hear.

"For God's sake!" Bentley screamed. "Stop this at once!"

As if coming out of a trance, Renato stilled the blade and turned languidly toward *Medusa*.

The breath of both crews came out in a *whoosh*.

Bentley stood slumped, hat twisted in his hands. "What," he began, but his voice strangled to a stop. "What…are your demands?"

Renato told him, the words clipping out as if to a drumbeat. The men of *Medusa* sucked in their breath. A variety of emotions played over their faces. Shock. Despair. Anger. Disbelief.

Captain Bentley, head sagging, went into muted conference with his officers. When he returned to the rail, the man had aged half a lifetime.

"I accept your terms," he said heavily, "with one proviso, and this is non-negotiable. My man Richter was murdered aboard your vessel. I cannot in good conscience return without the guilty party. You will surrender his killer to me, or the bargain is off."

Behind Renato, the pirates began to grumble. It was against their code to give up one of their own. Renato cared not a fig for the code, but understood the power it had over them.

Bentley shouted, "Paschelke! Britt! Which of those black-guards killed Richter?"

Paschelke shrugged his shoulders. Britt said, "It was dark there, Captain, and all was confusion. We've no way to tell."

The crew of *Medusa* took their own turn at grumbling.

Renato saw his destiny click back into place. "Fear not, Captain. I can name the culprit for you. Only one man on this ship would be so craven as to shoot poor Mr. Richter in the dark." He paused, savoring the moment, as both crews hung on his words.

"That man," Renato said, raising a finger, "that yellow-bellied, back-stabbing, misbegotten cur is…" His listeners hung spellbound as he brought the finger slashing down. "Mr. Faraday!"

Faraday's face blanched. He backed away, steadying himself against the rail. His mouth formed a word that might have been "No!"

LaChaise drowned him out. "Aye! Faraday it was, Cap'n, sure as Billy-be-damned."

"He's right!" shouted another. "Faraday done it, an' no mistake."

Others hooted agreement, and on the instant *L'Intrepide*'s rogues were transformed into a pack of slavering jackals. Just like that, Faraday had been tried, convicted and sentenced to death.

Renato grinned across the waves at Bentley, who stood frowning, hands on hips. After a moment, the man nodded assent.

Renato swelled up, nearly overcome with the magnitude of his triumph. His mind swam with visions of untold riches, everlasting fame and the exquisite vengeance he would visit upon Andre, Mariette and the man he hated most in all the world—Mr. James Bowie.

CHAPTER 37

"The stubbornest humans."

WHILE SAM SKINNED the deer carcass, Bowie stepped into the tall grass surrounding the clearing. After a few moments he summoned Andre to join him.

"What do you make of this, old man?"

The ground was covered with footprints, too short for a full-sized man, too wide for most women or children. They were peculiarly matched to the broad, stubby feet of Pacal.

Andre grunted. "Looks like me daughter's little friend was doin' a war dance. The man's crazier than a bed bug. Could we not find a way to make him vanish, and tell Mariette he simply wandered off?"

"I heard that." Mariette herself pushed through the grass. "And the answer is *no.*"

She stood with hands on hips, black tresses falling carelessly over her shoulders. Her lips were pursed, her eyes warm and languid. Bowie had never seen her so fetching. She's the daughter of a friend, he reminded himself, and even if she were not, Karankawa country was no place to bill and coo.

"Don't know about you two," Andre said, "but I'm hungry enough to eat my boots." And with that, he vanished into the tall grass.

Mariette's smile grew warmer.

Bowie had to wet his mouth before speaking. "Me, too," he said roughly. He took the girl's hand and led her quickly back toward the firepit.

The deer was barely on the spit when a familiar voice boomed, "You're cookin' me a snack! What're the rest of you gonna eat?"

Strap Buckner's head and shoulders were visible above the grass long before he swaggered into the clearing. From one hand dangled the renegade Hinkle, and from the other the wild-eyed figure of Sharky.

Buckner dropped both to the earth and planted a wash-tub-sized foot squarely on Hinkle's back. "This rascal said something about gold." He laid a glare on Bowie. "I believe you've somethin' to tell me."

Bowie almost smiled. He had a strange liking for the man. "His exact words," he said, "were, *They're after the gold—and the girl.*" Striding forward, he jerked Hinkle's head from the ground. "We know who *they* were. Why did you tell them?"

"It wasn't me," he blubbered. "That rascal Sanchez did it. I just come to warn you."

"And why would you do that?"

"I was hopin'," he said, "for a taste of the gold."

Bowie let the man's head fall back. Then, with assistance from Andre and Mariette, he told Buckner of their encounter with the Mexican soldiers.

There was disbelief in the big man's eyes until Bowie yanked one of the strange shafts from a lancer's back and presented it for inspection.

"Two of those fellows," he told Buckner, "appeared to have non-fatal wounds, but died within minutes. The things were probably dipped in poison."

"That's no arrow," Buckner said. "How'd they shoot it?"

Bowie shrugged. "They just flashed across the clearing, fast and straight as rifle balls. No living man could have thrown them that hard."

Strap Buckner cleared his throat, and all eyes swung to him.

"Pardon," Bowie said. "No living *mortal.*"

Buckner nodded.

"So how do you explain it?" Mariette asked. "There were half a dozen Indians out there with the strength of Samson?"

Bowie squinted at Buckner. "Any Indians like that in these parts?"

"Not a chance. I've been all over this territory huntin' an opponent my own size. Most of them cussed Kronks ain't much bigger than you. And see the way that point's chiseled? No Karankawa done that, nor Tonkawa, nor even Comanche."

"So how did it get here?" Mariette asked.

"Actually, there are numerous possibilities." Sam looked up from his cooking. "Most indigenous tribes, regardless of their pride and almost universal enmity for their neighbors, occasionally bow to the necessity of trade. This particular item could have traveled many leagues, over the course of several centuries."

"For all your fancy talk," Andre said, "all you're really sayin' is they wasn't Kronks."

"The question, then," Bowie said, "is who killed the soldiers? And if they could handle them so easily, why did they spare us?"

Buckner frowned. "There's another question needs answerin'. One that concerns gold. Don't think for a minute I was fooled by that fairy tale about a captive brother."

Andre gave a start, and Bowie saw him wet his lips, ready to uncork a new lie.

Mariette laid a hand on the big man's arm. "We will tell you everything. Truly. But first, would you join us in eating? Whatever Sam has done to that venison, it smells delicious."

IF ANY AROUND the fire feared for their lives, they hid it well. Strap Buckner ripped great hunks from a haunch of venison as easily as a normal human might nibble a turkey leg. On the big man's left, doing his best to keep pace, sprawled Andre. Bowie himself abandoned all manners and devoured his food Indian fashion. Even Mariette showed her hunger without shame.

Sharky had been allowed to join them, but took a haunch and

ate by himself away from the fire. Hinkle was thrown occasional scraps, while Sam watched in silent amusement, arms crossed and legs outstretched. Pacal had attacked the carcass before it was cooked, devouring a huge amount of raw flesh, and vanished once again into the wilds.

"Compliments to the chef," Buckner said between smacks. "Never knowed venison to taste so good. How'd you do it?"

Sam laid a finger aside his nose. "Magic."

Both Buckner and Andre halted in mid bite, eyeing the black man with suspicion. After a long moment, Buckner snorted and resumed eating. Andre followed his example, but with less gusto.

Despite his inner warmth, Bowie was not entirely at ease. The mysterious slayers of the Mexicans seemed to be aiding them, a notion he found more disturbing than an outright threat.

The log he shared with Mariette seemed to grow shorter as the meal progressed. At first there'd been at least a foot of space between them. Before long, her knee was brushing his leg. Now he felt the warmth of her thigh pressed firmly against his own. If they remained here much longer, she'd be full in his lap.

If Andre took note of this, he gave no sign. He lolled on the log, obviously in his cups. The old pirate had been eager to sample Ianitello's moonshine, and pronounced it acceptable.

Having downed as much of the liquor as Andre would permit, Sharky now swaggered about, slashing the grass with the sword he had taken from the body of Gutierrez. Reeling up behind Sam, he lashed out with the blade, cleaving the air scant inches above the black man's head.

"Ho, Nubian varlet! On your feet! I would test your mettle!"

Sam eyed him without favor. " 'O, that men should put an enemy in their mouths, to steal away their brains!' *Othello*, Act 2, Scene 3."

"So!" Sharky's thin chest expanded. "You dare insult a bold buccaneer. Taste my steel, dog!" The sword flashed out again, on a much lower arc.

Sam shot from the log and spun to face his attacker. Across

the seat of his trousers was a wide slash, exposing a dark swath of gleaming backside.

Sharky jumped back, nearly dropping his weapon, while Sam stretched down to scoop up a battered frying pan.

With a whoop of terror, Sharky bolted for the other end of the clearing, his enraged foe hot on his heels.

"Isn't that charming?" Mariette said. "They're making friends."

Bowie could not restrain a laugh. Looking to Andre, he said, "Say, old man, could you spare a shot of that eel juice?"

Andre hugged the bottle to his chest. Then his face softened. "Only for you, Jim Boy."

Bowie said, "What about you, Strap? Care for a dose?"

"I may be forced to dine with pirates," Buckner said, "but I'll be damned if I'll drink with them, too." One impossibly long arm sailed out to backhand Andre in the face, knocking him off the log.

Bowie soared to his feet, fists clenched.

Mariette knelt at her father's side. "You brute! Have you no shame, picking on a man half your size?"

"A quarter my size," Buckner growled. "But if it's an apology you want, ask him."

Bowie said, "I thought we'd settled this matter."

Buckner's eyes smoldered. "Maybe you'd like to settle it again."

"Look," Bowie said, "we know about Renato's pirates taking the girl, and the Kronks storming your settlement. But you drove them off and no one else was hurt. Why can't you forget the matter?"

"There will be no forgettin'. Your pirate friends just sailed merrily off, leavin' others to pay in blood."

The emotion in the big man's voice took Bowie aback. There was more than anger here. It was as if they'd caught a glimpse of the big man's soul.

Mariette obviously felt it too. In a small voice, she said, "What happened to them—and to you?"

Buckner's face colored, as if he'd revealed more than he intended. He turned to Bowie. "You people," he said, "are the stubbornest humans I've yet to meet."

Bowie held back a grin. "Not counting yourself, of course."

"Four days after the pirates left," Buckner began, "the Kronks retaliated by attackin' two of the settlers' cabins."

The heaviness in the man's voice weighed on Bowie as well, and he resumed his seat.

"One of those cabins belonged to Tor Kjelstrom and his wife Lavonne. They were raisin' four fine girls. Nearby was the cabin of Leland and Iris Littlewood."

Bowie nodded, but the big man appeared to be staring off into the past, oblivious even to the fire before him.

"The menfolk were off huntin' when the Injuns came. It was hell on earth for those six women. The Kronks showed 'em no mercy, butchering Sarah, Polly, Lavonne and three of the girls. They thought they'd killed the fourth as well, but little Becky survived by playin' dead, even when one of the devils yanked an arrow from her belly."

Mariette put a hand to her mouth. Her eyes glistened with tears. "What happened to her?"

"By the time her pa got her into Matagorda, she was nearly gone, but the womenfolk nursed her back to health. She's there still, and mostly recovered, save that she still walks a little catawampus. Old Tor Kjelstrom is still about, as well, though I've seen dead men look more alive."

"And that," Bowie said, "is why no one in Matagorda will talk about it."

Buckner nodded. "It's not a thing we discuss. The toll on those two—and others—has been too great already."

"And you," Mariette said softly, "were one of those others." It was not a question, and Buckner did not respond. "One of those girls was special to you."

Buckner hung his head. No one spoke.

After another minute Andre groaned loudly, struggled onto his elbows. "Wha' happen'?"

Buckner's head rose, his eyes once again hard. "So you can imagine my displeasure at seeing two of that rotten crew return, doubtless to stir up the Injuns again."

"That's not why we're here," Bowie said.

"But here you be, headin' straight into the Kronks' new holy ground. If that don't annoy 'em, I don't know what will."

Mariette laid a hand on her breast. "These men, my father and Sharky included, are here because of me."

Buckner snorted. "So I heard. To rescue your imaginary brother."

Mariette's face turned pink. "I must apologize for that. It was my father's idea."

Andre gave a start, then assumed a guilty look.

"We're after gold, it's true," Mariette said. "But my father invented that 'brother' story to mask his shame." She flashed Andre a scornful glance. "He abandoned us, you see—my mother, my three sisters and me—to fend for ourselves in the slums of New Orleans. We managed to scrape by until my youngest sister took sick, and mother was forced to stay at home. Then she took sick as well, and my sisters and I were on the verge of demeaning ourselves. I had, in fact, approached a certain gentleman with a particularly shameful proposition. Lucky for us all, he took pity on me and gave me an old treasure map. You've heard of him, perhaps? His name is Dominique You."

Buckner grunted. "That I have, young missy." Incredible as it seemed, Buckner's anger had all but melted away. "So you seek this gold only to save your mother and sisters from depravity."

Mariette nodded humbly.

"But what of this adventurer, Bowie? Is he, too, interested only in this noble cause?"

"Mr. Bowie is an old family friend, and a true gentleman. If you know anything of him at all, you know a body could have no finer champion."

Bowie tried to appear modest. He was again staggered by the girl's uncanny ability to prevaricate. The parallel of four daughters was a true masterstroke.

The big man beamed down at Mariette. He seemed entirely taken in.

"I would consider it a great favor, Mr. Buckner, if you would aid us in our quest."

Buckner bowed his head. "I will aid you if I can, little missy, but not as a member of your company. For now, I must return to my homestead."

"To your…wife?" Mariette said, a catch in her voice.

Buckner blushed furiously. "Uh, no ma'am. There's no such critter as that. I must see to my animals, is all."

"Then I trust we'll meet again," Mariette said. "Soon."

"Mayhap we will." Buckner seemed thoroughly embarrassed. "Now I really must be off." He grasped Hinkle by the scruff of the neck and strode toward the edge of the clearing. There he turned, gazing wistfully back. "If you've a mind to spend the night here, you'd best stay close to the fire. This area is rife with wolves, not to mention tigers."

"Tigers?" Sam's tone was scornful. "There are no tigers within ten thousand miles of here. They do not exist in the Western Hemisphere."

"Remind yourself of that," Buckner growled, "when you wake to one gnawing on your gizzard." Then, with a touch of his hat, he turned and lumbered into the grass.

CHAPTER 38

"Fishes love witnesses."

R ENATO SURVEYED THE deck of his fine new ship. All about him, men rushed to make *Medusa* ready to sail.

Amidships, three men struggled to maneuver Renato's portrait-in-progress down the hatch toward the captain's cabin. In the stern, four others jockeyed his church pew into position against the rail.

Renato glanced across the waves to the forlorn group on the deck of his former ship. Bentley clutched the rail as if he might otherwise collapse, while at his side, straight as a spar, glowered Goble. Further back, amid a knot of slump-shouldered sailors, stood the tightly-bound form of the traitor Faraday.

The thought of this delicious and well-deserved revenge produced an unstoppable smile. The movement stung Renato's tortured face muscles, but was worth the pain.

The past hour had been a busy one. With the ships lashed together, the exchange of crews had been smoothly accomplished. Bentley's men were ordered to leave their arms behind on *Medusa*, and, once aboard *L'Intrepide*, found themselves staring down the barrel of the 18-pounder. Renato's men had quickly transferred everything of value, including food, gunpowder, and the spoils of recent conquests. Renato's paints and canvasses, his chest of personal treasures, his goose-feather mattress, and the finer items of his wardrobe were already in his new cabin.

Renato stroked the iron barrel of the 18-pounder as he might the leg of a woman. Had he been possessed of so fine a weapon earlier in his career, the Lafittes would already be consigned to the dust of legend. He hoped Rayón was watching to find him in possession of such a fitting instrument of revenge.

He smiled grimly as his black flag climbed the mainmast. He now resembled the grinning skull more than ever. The flag unfurled, catching the westward wind. It was a good omen, for it was in that direction they were bound.

LaChaise approached, clutching a bundle of red and white cloth. "Beggin' yer pardon, Cap'n. What of this cursed flag of theirs? Shall I wrap it 'round the cannonball we uses to sink 'em?"

"No, Mr. LaChaise, you may stow it with the rest of our collection. It may prove useful."

"Aye, sir. Are we ready to fire, then?"

"No. I wish to make sail at the soonest possible moment."

LaChaise's mouth hung open. Then a slow smile appeared. "Ah. Ya wishes us to put off a ways, allowing them buggers a shred of hope before we blasts them to bits. You're a sly one, Cap'n, an' no mistake."

"Mr. LaChaise, let me be perfectly clear. We shall not be firing upon the Americans."

"But Cap'n! If word gets back to New Orleans of what we done, all our necks'll be in a noose. An' it's like ya always says— the fishes loves witnesses."

"That they do. But I have my reasons for allowing those men to live. Whether those reasons are clear to you is of no consequence. Is that understood?"

If it were possible for the man's fist-like face to grow any tighter, it did so. "Aye, Cap'n, but—"

Renato's hand drifted toward his pistol. "But?"

"But... I was so lookin' forward to firin' this monster."

"Once we catch our quarry, you will have ample opportunity."

Renato turned away. LaChaise was right. Once word of today's activities reached New Orleans, the navy would launch such a manhunt as had never been seen. Had he hoped to continue in his current profession, he would surely have consigned Bentley and his crew to the bottom of the Gulf. But he would soon be retiring from the sea, and pictured *Medusa*'s fine cannon mounted on the battlements of his castle.

Besides, he wished the tale of today's events to reach the States, where it would soar across the nation on the wings of *The Niles Register*, making the deeds of Bowie and Lafitte pale by comparison.

LaChaise had moved away, using threats and curses to hasten the men, and Renato congratulated himself on his choice of new quartermaster. Then LaChaise looked back at him. For a moment their eyes locked, and Renato's blood turned to ice. He forced his lips into a wicked grin, but the feeling of dread would not leave him. There was something deep in this man's eyes that made his own dark dreams seem benign by comparison.

And as LaChaise walked past, Renato noted something else. The man had a distinct odor—the dense, fetid aroma of a charnel house.

Still somewhat disconcerted, Renato turned for a final word with Bentley and Goble. "Time to bid you adieu, gentlemen. I trust you will have an unpleasant voyage home. Should you ever have the misfortune to encounter me again, I promise to reacquaint you with your fine gun."

Bentley's eyes burned bright. "If we meet again, you black-hearted scoundrel, I will be certain not to give you the chance."

"And see that you remember my name. Renato. R-E-N-A-T-O, known to all as the Last Great Terror of the Gulf." Renato touched his brim in mock salute, then threw back his head, allowing himself a long and lusty laugh.

"Mr. LaChaise, you will get us underway at once."

"Aye, sir. On what heading?"

Two days past, Renato's answer would have been vague. But the long hours strapped to the mast had given him time to think, and that near-death experience had brought unusual clarity. In his mind, he had relived many of the pivotal moments of his career, among them the instant he first beheld the treasure map. The details were now as distinct as if he held it in his hands. He knew precisely where to go—an obscure inlet behind a barrier reef on the southern Texas coast, a place settlers had dubbed Karankawa Cove.

"West by Southwest," Renato said, well pleased with himself. "We are bound for Matagorda Bay."

PART III
FATE

CHAPTER 39

"A lion among wolves."

BOWIE WATCHED AS Sam chopped grass with the sword he'd appropriated from Sharky. His intention, he'd announced, was to create a mattress to lay next to the fire.

Sprawled on a nearby log, Andre wore a vague sneer. The old man would have likely prepared a mattress also, but his fierce pride would not allow him to follow the lead of a slave, particularly one as annoying as Sam.

Shading his eyes against the fiery orange ball in the West, Bowie let his imagination soar out beyond the horizon. Three hundred miles inland was San Antonio, the most civilized city in Texas. There was opportunity there, a chance for a second start at life. He wished he were headed there now, instead of moving deeper into this lair of cannibals.

Born and raised on the frontier, Bowie found life in the wilds invigorating. He felt perfectly at home in buckskin and homespun, and could live off the land as well as any Indian. But from his first visit to New Orleans, he'd been captivated by the glamour and bustle of the city. He'd quickly acquired a taste for fine clothes, good food, and the company of elegant women. But if he did not have the wilds to return to, he would not find the city half so interesting. To be content, he needed both extremes, and everything in between.

San Antonio, from all he'd heard, might be just the haven he was looking for. The city itself was graced with fine haciendas, inhabited for over a century by wealthy and influential Spanish families. And surrounding it on all sides was wild country, teeming with Indians and legends of lost mines. It seemed a place he could take root, and satisfy his roaming feet at the same time.

Whether Texas remained a state of Mexico, sought to join the United States, or managed to become an independent nation, there were great fortunes to be made. In this new land, a man was what he made of himself. There was a new aristocracy waiting to be born, and he felt Texas calling him to be part of it.

He felt a gentle touch on his arm.

"You're drawn to her, aren't you."

"Her?"

"Texas." Mariette stepped to his side, and he felt the points of contact at calf, thigh, hip and forearm. "I've seen the look in your eyes. It's enough to make a girl jealous."

Lit by the setting sun, her face seemed to glow from within. She had never looked more beautiful.

"I'll not deny the attraction," he said, and saw her eyes sparkle. After a moment he remembered he was speaking of Texas, and forced himself to look away. "There's land for the taking. More land than in Louisiana and any six states combined. It needs the right man to shape it, to mold it to his purposes. Hardly the sort of treatment a woman would envy."

"You underestimate yourself," she said. "That's precisely what some women need."

"But not you, I'll wager."

"That," she said, arching an eyebrow, "is for you to find out."

From high above their heads, in the crook of a cottonwood, came the sound of snoring. Sharky had walked up the tree agile as a monkey, and his angular limbs melded into the tree so effectively, that if not for his ragged shirt and britches, he would have been entirely invisible.

"Doesn't he know," Bowie said, "that cats climb trees?"

"Where are we sleeping tonight?"

Mariette's question caught him off guard. He felt as if he'd swallowed his tongue. But he sensed she was laughing at him.

"I'm making a bed near the fire," he said, "and I suggest the same for you."

Mariette gave him a beguiling smile. "Is that an invitation?"

Bowie felt his face flush. He did not trust himself to words.

"In any case," she said, "I accept. You may do with me as you will."

Bowie cleared his throat. "Come, there's just enough light left." He scooped up an ax and led her just beyond the clearing, to another copse of trees. His eyes swept the landscape, finding nothing amiss.

He began chopping branches from a cottonwood.

"Tell me a little about yourself, James."

She always addressed him by his given name, and he liked the sound of it. "I'm just a man with a knife," he said, hearing a touch of bitterness in his voice.

"I doubt that very much. I've heard you mention brothers. How many do you have?"

"Three, at last count. All more respectable than myself. Though none so handsome," he said with a wink.

"And sisters?"

"Two. Both older and wiser."

Mariette found a seat on the grass next to the creek. "Bowie," she said, stretching out the sound. "What sort of name is that?"

"Scottish. My great-grandfather came to the new world to start a new life. Said he was descended from Rob Roy himself."

"And you doubt that?"

Bowie grinned. "I've never known a Scotsman who wasn't."

"Hm," Mariette said dreamily. "This Rob Roy must have been a very virile fellow."

To hide his embarrassment, Bowie broke off a leafy branch and tossed it to the earth. "It may interest you to know I was named for a king."

"Really?"

"James VI of Scotland, who later became James I of England."

"King James," she said. "I like the sound of that. Every woman secretly longs to be a queen."

"My father had his own claim to fame. He helped old Francis Marion and Thaddeus Truitt chase the British out of the Carolinas."

"Marion—the Swamp Fox? I *am* impressed. What of your mother?"

Bowie attacked a second likely branch. "They met during the war, when she was a volunteer nurse. There's a story my father loved to tell. Shortly before I was born, he was arrested for shooting a horse thief. When my mother got word, she grabbed the shotgun off the mantle, climbed in the wagon and whipped the horses into town. The way the story goes, she leveled that gun at the sheriff and gave him the choice of freeing her husband or meeting St. Peter. That sheriff couldn't get the cell open fast enough, and promptly grew forgetful of the charges. He never bothered my father again."

Mariette's laugh was lovely. "She sounds wonderful."

"That she is," Bowie said. The second branch came off in his hand, and he flung it atop the first. "What of your own family? Assuming, of course, that the tale you told Buckner was another fable."

Mariette smiled. "You mean my three imaginary sisters? That was wicked of me, though I did actually have a mother."

Bowie sobered. "But no longer?"

"She passed over a year ago. Consumption, the doctors said."

Bowie tried to picture the type of woman who would couple with Andre, even an Andre of twenty years ago, and did not find the image pleasing.

"I know what you're thinking," Mariette said, and Bowie immediately felt guilty. "You're wondering what kind of woman would take Andre to her bed, much less marry him. Those were different times, when freebooters were well-respected in New

Orleans. Jean Lafitte, as you must know, was much admired by the people."

"But he was still an outlaw," Bowie said.

"The governor had a price on his head, it's true, and the navy pursued him, but mostly because he was an embarrassment. I understand you knew him. Were you not impressed?"

Bowie tossed another branch on the pile. "He was a lion among wolves."

"My mother thought him the most handsome man in the world."

"I thought we were speaking of Andre."

"Lafitte kept a mistress," Mariette said, "a lovely quadroon by the name of Catherine Villard. My mother was one of her dearest friends."

Bowie turned, appreciating her beauty with new eyes.

She blinked at him. "Did you not suspect I was of mixed blood?"

Bowie attacked the tree again. "I'm waiting to hear of Andre."

Mariette let out a small sigh. "On one of Lafitte's visits to Catherine, he brought Andre along. My mother happened to be visiting also."

"So Lafitte introduced them?"

"He praised Andre as one of his most trusted associates."

Bowie added a leafy branch to the pile. "It comes clear at last. Since the great man was already taken, your mother accepted Andre as a substitute."

"In her heart, I believe she loved them both. At any rate, she considered Andre a good catch, and he provided her a fine little house on Rampart Street."

Bowie found himself wanting to believe every word, and struggled to forget the lies she had told Buckner and the colonists. "He was still a pirate," he said, his voice gruff. "He couldn't have been around much."

"Sadly, no. But my mother was an attractive woman, and

enjoyed the company of other gentlemen. My father understood this, and the arrangement suited him as well."

Bowie held his face impassive.

"You disapprove."

Bowie blinked. How could she read him so easily? "It's not for me to judge." He added more branches to the pile. A few more cuttings and there would be enough to make her comfortable. He paused at the thought, wondering when her comfort had become so important to him.

"You like to think yourself wild and untamed. But you're not, are you? You're really quite old-fashioned."

Bowie felt his cheeks growing warm. "Just because I wasn't raised in New Orleans, it doesn't make me a hayseed. You'd be surprised at some of the things I've seen and done."

"Oooh. I love surprises. Tell me."

"Not now." He bent to gather branches. "It's time we got back to the others."

Mariette flounced to her feet. "Fine. But you'll have to catch me first." And before Bowie could stop her, she lifted her skirt and scampered off upstream, grinning back at him.

"Come back!" he ordered. "There's no telling who or what is out there."

"Don't be silly. I have you to protect me!" Reaching the base of a great live oak, she stopped, her back to the trunk, eyeing him coyly.

As he neared the tree, she feinted left and right, as if about to dart away again. He refused to make a lunge. "I should take you over my knee."

"Yes," she said. "You should." Springing forward, she draped an arm around his neck and pressed her body close to his. Her other arm trailed up, toying with the hair on the back of his neck.

"It's dangerous to be this far from the others," he said, his voice hoarse.

"Yes," she said, "it is." She pulled him closer, and he inhaled the scent of her. She smelled like budding clover.

"There could be Indians out here. Or a pack of wolves."

"Yes," she said. "Or worse." Her lips melted into his own. Her tongue darted through his teeth like a flicker of fire. Her small breasts pressed against his chest.

She leaned back, bursting the buttons from his shirt to bare his chest. "So many scars," she said, running her fingers over his souvenirs of the Sandbar Fight. "I like a man with scars."

Then she grew heavier, and was pulling him down to her. Feeling oafish, he allowed this, and she continued to sink lower, until he was forced to his knees. At last she settled into the grass beneath the oak, her knees up, singing softly to herself.

She began working the buttons of her blouse. Bowie leaned into her, kissing the hollow beneath her chin, and recognized the song: *Sailing, Sailing, Over the Bounding Main.* As he continued down her throat she moaned softly, pulling his head still lower. She had stopped singing, but the tune still thrummed in his head, reminding him of her parentage.

"We can't," he whispered. "Andre is my friend."

She laughed softly. "Don't worry about him. He's not…" she paused, her hands now working at his belt, "not the type who'd begrudge us our pleasure."

The belt came undone, as did his trousers. He touched her thigh, and found warm, yielding flesh beneath the skirt. He ran a hand up her leg, encountering no petticoats, no garments at all. Nothing but the sweetness of Mariette herself.

"Sweet Lord," she said with an impish grin. "I thought your *knife* was big."

CHAPTER 40

"Dead as a fried oyster."

THE NEW VIEW from his pew pleased Renato greatly. *L'Intrepide* had been a fine mistress, and served him well. But the great gun stretching nearly half the length of *Medusa* filled him with a sense of power beyond that of the world's most dangerous buccaneer. It made him feel like a god.

Beside him, Princess shared the view, and the scratchy gargle that passed for purring indicated she, too, was content.

Renato glowered as a plump form suddenly blocked his view.

"Beggin' your pardon, Cap'n Renato, sir."

"What is it now, Quayle?"

"The men wished to thank you, Cap'n, for takin' the slaves aboard."

From where he sat, Renato could see two of the lanky Haitians in the bow, goggling at their new surroundings. One of the blacks swung about, returning his gaze. Though he put no stock in Voodoo, there was something disconcerting in the man's eyes, and despite himself, Renato shivered. The past few hours had taken a greater toll on his nerves than he had realized.

"I seek neither the crew's approval, nor their gratitude. It was merely a matter of practicality."

"As you say, Cap'n. All the same, the men's relieved you're honorin' their promise." During his period of delirium and deposal, the men had promised the Haitians freedom at next landfall. For this consideration, the crew believed the curse had been lifted.

Renato gave a noncommittal grunt. He would have been pleased to be rid of the black pariahs, but he'd been captaining long enough to know precisely how far his men could be bullied. Leadership, he had learned, was largely a matter of exploiting men's fears. This crew of rogues had learned to dread his wrath more than death itself, but it would not do to test that against their fear of the supernatural.

As for the slaves, the choice was not difficult. In the hands of the navy, they would be delivered to the docks of New Orleans, where they would be sold at auction. In Texas, they would be technically free—free to be eaten by cannibals, most like, but at least they would bring no profit to the U.S. Navy.

Renato became aware that Quayle still stood before him.

"You've said your piece. Why do I still smell you?"

"I—I've more to report, Cap'n." Quayle shifted his feet, rubbed his hands on filthy brown trousers.

"Out with it, then. What's amiss?"

"Well, sir, it's like this. When the men was moving your mattress into the cap'n's cabin, they come across a case of Burgundy."

Renato brightened, his tongue already anticipating the taste. But Quayle was not finished. "And?"

"And you see, Cap'n, before I could get there, one of the hands had made off with a bottle." Quayle winced, as if expecting a blow.

"And this man's name?"

"Nesmith, Cap'n."

Renato did not recognize the name. Nor should he. Such trivialities were beneath him. "Summon Mr. LaChaise!"

LaChaise arrived in moments, head bobbing in obeisance.

"As quartermaster of this crew," Renato told him, "your first assignment is to prepare a man for punishment."

LaChaise's little eyes gleamed. "Aye, Cap'n. Which man be that?"

Renato turned to Quayle. "The miscreant's name again?"

"Nesmith, sir."

LaChaise flexed his arms, causing the muscles to writhe like snakes. He was halfway to the hatch when a skinny, slack-jawed pirate staggered up onto the deck, a near-empty bottle in his fist.

"Nesmith! Stop where ya are."

The skinny man's jaw snapped tight, eyes rolling in terror. He reeled away, stumbling toward the bow.

LaChaise stormed after him. Men pressed themselves against the great gun barrel to allow him passage.

Reaching the bow, Nesmith peered around the foremast, rocked as if the ship were caught in a buffeting storm, and raced back down along the opposite rail.

LaChaise tore around the mast, nostrils seeming to snort fire. His ape-like arms bruised the air behind Nesmith's back.

The wretch was halfway to the stern when his toe caught a rope and he staggered, crashing to the deck.

LaChaise lifted him into the air and shook him like a rag doll. "I'll teach ya to run from me, ya drunken sod!"

Renato rose, affording himself a better view. Down the length of *Medusa*, men's faces bore the bestial appreciation of another man's pain.

With a final shake, LaChaise dragged Nesmith by the neck up the steps to the quarterdeck. Reaching the pew, his arm windmilled up and around, slamming him down at Renato's feet.

"The prisoner," he said, his voice rasping, "is ready for punishment."

Quayle dropped to one knee, lifted Nesmith's head and laid two fingers along his throat. "He's past ready," he said, looking sidelong at Renato. "He's dead as a fried oyster."

Renato gave the briefest of nods. "Very well, Mr. LaChaise. You will dispose of this garbage at once."

LaChaise caught the end of the rope the man had used for a belt, and with a flick of the wrist sent the body sailing over the rail. The resulting splash put period to Nesmith's sordid career as a buccaneer.

As Renato turned away, Princess leapt from the pew and bounded toward him, her blackened paws barely touching the deck. Renato extended a leg to facilitate her customary scramble up his side.

To his shock, the little beast sailed past him, leaping instead onto the filthy trousers of LaChaise, climbing rapidly up his jacket. Before Renato could close his gaping mouth, his faithful Princess perched on the new quartermaster's shoulder and gave him a nip on the ear.

Renato turned away, his mind in turmoil. The cat admired brutality above all else, and was an excellent judge of character. This could mean only one thing: His once loyal pet now considered LaChaise even more wicked than Renato himself. And that, he thought grimly, meant one thing more.

LaChaise would have to die.

CHAPTER 41

"The maddest thing ever."

BOWIE'S THOUGHTS DRIFTED. He had rarely felt so content. But on the far edge of awareness, he heard what sounded like someone sawing wood. He must be dreaming, perhaps of the time he and his brothers owned a sawmill.

But as the sound grew in volume, he knew it was not a dream at all. His eyes snapped open and he peered into the darkening sky.

The settlers had not given them a saw, and he could not imagine the Kronks using such a tool. The only other explanation brought him to his feet, spilling Mariette yelping onto the grass. He quickly fastened his trousers and jammed feet into boots. His shirt was a lost cause, and he tossed it aside.

The sawing sound came again, and Bowie knew for sure. It was the full-throated roar of an angry jaguar. It was followed by a pistol shot.

Dusk had come while they lay spent, and he would soon have only moonlight—and the screams—to guide them back to the clearing.

"Haste, girl! Your father needs us."

"Meaning you and your knife, I suppose."

Bowie settled the knife securely into its sheath, and plunged the sergeant's pistol into his waistband. He was ready.

Having quickly fastened her skirt, Mariette worked at the buttons of her blouse. Bowie could not understand how they could be so difficult to fasten. They had certainly come undone easily enough.

The cat in the clearing let out a ferocious growl. It was growing impatient, a feeling to which Bowie could relate.

Mariette shook out her hair and combed it back with her fingers. "Well," she said, "what are we waiting for?"

He swung away, gliding swiftly toward the clearing. The cries of the cat grew louder, more terrible, and were now intermingled with the frightened whinnies and snorts of the horses.

Bowie cursed himself. He'd known this stretch of coast was fraught with danger, and allowed this temptress to befuddle him.

Reaching the clearing, he found the situation much as he'd feared. The firelight illumined a great spotted cat, well over seven feet long, prowling back and forth before the fire. A glistening smear on its haunch attested to the marksmanship of Andre, who stood with his back to a tree, pistol at his feet and rapier in his hand.

Behind the tree crouched Sam. "Come away from there, old man! You can't fight that animal with a sword!"

"And I can't fight him without it," Andre growled back. "Tell me again there's no tigers in Texas."

Sam gave a haughty snort. "Ignorant to the last. Tigers have stripes, do they not? Do you see stripes here? This animal is of the genus *Panthera onca* of the Felidae family, commonly known as the jaguar."

Bowie marveled that the two could continue to bicker even in the face of death.

The jaguar took a tentative swipe at Andre. Quick as lightning, the rapier flashed out, and the cat snarled, drawing a wounded paw to its mouth.

Bowie drew the long dragoon pistol from his belt, cocked it in near silence and sighted carefully. There were only two sure ways of stopping such a beast—a bullet to the brain or a shot straight to the heart.

The jaguar went into a crouch, hind legs tensed to spring. He could wait no longer. He centered the barrel on the animal's head and squeezed the trigger.

The blast filled the air with smoke, and the beast's head jerked—but a moment too soon. Instead of piercing the skull, the ball skipped off the side, digging a furrow in the sleek fur. The cat's terrible scream spoke of rage and pain. As Bowie stepped into the clearing, baleful yellow eyes fixed upon his throat.

"Jim Boy! Nice of thee to ante in."

Bowie saw the animal's mind working, judging which meal looked most tasty and offered the least trouble. The beast's wounded ear twitched angrily. It swung about and fell into a crouch, muscles coiled. It had chosen Andre. In another moment the man would be engulfed in a maelstrom of teeth and nails.

Bowie's hand went to his sheath, and the knife sprang into his hand. He filled his lungs and charged. Rising from deep within and spilling from his mouth was a war cry that would shame all the savages on the frontier. That scream, Bowie's father had boasted, had frozen the hearts of King George's redcoats in the Carolina swamps, allowing the rebels to rout many a larger force.

Startled, the cat reeled to face him.

Bowie saw death in those hellish yellow eyes, but there was no stopping now. Pouring every ounce of fury into his scream, he brought the knife arcing down on a trajectory to split the animal's skull.

A split second before impact, the jaguar whirled about and bolted for the far side of the clearing.

Bowie stormed after it, letting the rest of the scream rip from his lungs.

The cat was a blur of black and gold as it dived into the dark sea of grass. Bowie rolled to a stop, taking in deep draughts of air. He silently thanked his father, and hoped he had been watching.

Andre huffed to a halt at his side. "By God, Jim, that was the maddest thing I've ever witnessed."

A soft hand slid around his arm. "James! Whatever were you

thinking? If you'd gotten yourself killed, I'd have never forgiven you."

"With all the screamin' we heard earlier," Andre said, "me and your fancy-tongued valet feared you two'd been eaten by that monster's mate. From them scratches on your chest, ye had quite a tussle. That how ye lost your shirt?"

Bowie felt his face flush, saw Mariette beaming up at him.

A fresh volley of roars ripped the night, not more than twenty yards into the jungle. With the snarls of the cat came the cries of a human being in mortal terror.

He started toward the noise. Mariette clung to his arm. "James, stop! You've done enough!"

"What I've done," Bowie said, "is turn a wounded man-killer loose on someone else. I wouldn't even wish that on a Kronk."

Gently disentangling himself, he started forward again. But the commotion in the grass had dwindled to nothing, and the cat's cries faded into the distance.

Whoever had been out there was at best half dead, if not half inside the animal's belly. Bowie did a quick about-face, dashing to the fire for a torch.

"Don't go, Jim Boy. Whatever's out there, it can wait 'til morning."

"Maybe it can," Bowie said, "but I cannot."

He plowed into the tall grass, holding the torch high. He'd taken only a few steps when his nose began to twitch. The sweet, metallic scent of blood. And another smell, even less welcome. The fetid stench of death. Taking shallow breaths, he followed his nose into a circle of mashed and trampled grass. There was a fearful amount of blood, as if someone had held a bucket and spun about.

His boot struck something yielding, and he stared down at a bare human foot projecting from a clump of mesquite.

There was something familiar about that foot. Holding his breath against the smell, he bent to examine the body. There was no immediate sign of feeding, but the chest and stomach had been slashed open, leaving a mass of pulpy flesh.

Still, the shape of the body was plain to see. Short legs, small feet, sloping shoulders and sinewy brown arms. Bowie moved a hand over the face, wiping away the mask of blood. The ravaged features were wide and flat, as was the head itself.

Bowie looked away, raising his eyes to the starry sky. He had fervently wished for this little madman's demise, but now that it had arrived he felt a peculiar sense of loss. For better or worse, Pacal would never annoy anyone again.

CHAPTER 42

"One hellacious wallop."

RENATO EXTENDED THE telescope, making a slow sweep of the sea between *Medusa* and the distant coast of Texas. The morning sun made everything sharp and clear, and his practiced eye found no hint of sail. He could not believe Bowie and the others aboard *Lucinda* could have recovered the treasure and vacated the area so quickly, so they must still be within Matagorda Bay. And with the bay's only mouth now dead ahead, they stood no chance of escaping him.

Laying the spyglass aside, he relaxed on his pew. His burns still plagued him, relieved only slightly by the grease Quayle had found in the navy ship's galley. He would need all his strength for this venture into cannibal country—and the seizing of the treasure he had waited five long years to claim.

The treasure was his by right. He had earned it with courage, cunning and the lives of half his crew—and nearly lost his ship in the process. But in the end, as in so many things, he had been denied his due by the despicable Jean Lafitte.

Renato thought he'd seen the last of the pompous fellow seven years past, when Lafitte fled Campeachy with his tail between his legs. Fearing retribution from the American and Mexican governments, Lafitte had shifted his operations to Cuba and points east, and his forays into the Gulf had become increasingly rare.

Then, early in 1823, Renato learned that the president of Colombia was again issuing letters of marque—authorizing privateers to prey upon the shipping of other nations. Lafitte himself had accepted such a commission, and been granted a well-provisioned ship by the Colombian government.

With the news, Renato had set sail at once for Cartegena. It was always preferable to hold a letter of marque, however dubious, than risk being caught and tried as a lawless pirate.

L'Intrepide had reached the northeastern tip of Yucatán when he encountered Lafitte in his new forty-ton schooner, the *General Santander*. Brimming with flattery, Lafitte had begged him to join in his latest venture—pursuing the prize of a lifetime.

The Spanish galleon *Lady of Cadiz* was about to depart the Gulf with gold enough for he and Renato to live like kings. Ordinarily, Renato would have told Lafitte to go bugger himself, but the lure of the enormous prize had been too great. He and Lafitte chased the *Lady of Cadiz* deep into the Gulf, enduring several days of heavy weather before finally catching her along the Texas coast.

Renato paused his recollection, stretched his legs out on the seat of the pew, and gazed out over the dark green water. *Medusa* was now very near the spot *L'Intrepide* had been when Lafitte signaled to let the game begin. The sea before him was placid now, where then it had been wild. Over the past five years, he had replayed the battle so many times that it was as vivid as if it were happening at this very moment.

The plan was for *L'Intrepide* to fly the hated tri-color flag of Spain, tricking the galleon into thinking her a friend. Even now, Renato could hear the boom of *General Santander*'s bow chasers, and see geysers of water erupting on either side of *L'Intrepide*'s stern. And once again, he was back in the battle…

Renato cursed luridly. Lafitte was only pretending pursuit, it was true, but those shots had been too close for play-acting.

Renato bellowed orders, and soon *L'Intrepide* was skimming the waves, with *General Santander* struggling to keep up.

All the while, the *Lady of Cadiz* came into sharper view. She was triple-masted, her square-rigged sails climbing high into the stormy sky. Adorning her center sail was a huge blood-red cross. The Spanish deemed themselves to be the wrath of God. They would see wrath today, and likely their god as well.

Renato was relieved to find the *Lady* alone. She'd been guarded earlier by a heavily armed frigate, but the ships had apparently been separated in the storm.

When sighted, the *Lady* had been toiling less than a mile off the Texas shore, doubtless seeking a friendly wind to take her eastward. Renato could sense her captain's uncertainty. The man would be wondering if *L'Intrepide* was indeed a Spanish vessel in need of assistance, or some enemy employing an age-old ruse.

From behind came the crash of another gun, as Lafitte continued his part in the masquerade. This time, the ball fell just off *L'Intrepide*'s stern, dousing Renato with cold salty water. Wiping his face with a sleeve, he resolved to settle with Lafitte for good and all once the prize had been secured.

The close shot, however, appeared to convince the Spaniard of *L'Intrepide*'s peril. With a flurry of activity, the *Lady* came slowly about, ignoring Renato's approach, and presented her port side to the *General*. A dozen black barrels trundled from the twin rows of her gun ports.

A burst of orange flame announced the first ranging shot. Renato grinned as a waterspout plumed a hundred yards short of the *General*. The Spanish gunner's aim was good, even if he did not yet have the range. Lafitte would soon have a taste of his own medicine.

Renato's head tilted back as they neared the *Lady*'s stern. The galleon was huge compared to his tiny schooner, her upper deck high as a three-story building. Mustachioed faces in high-peaked hats peered down at him, and more than one face registered alarm. With *L'Intrepide* now under their very noses, the Spaniards could not help but recognize her crew as pirates.

"Fire as you bear!" shouted Faraday, and the first gun roared. Through the smoke, Renato saw a gaping hole open in the *Lady*'s stern. Then the next gun spoke, followed quickly by the third, and the scene was obscured by smoke.

Now it was Lafitte's turn. The plan was for the *General* to close on the *Lady*'s port side, while *L'Intrepide* reloaded for a strike from starboard. Caught between the fire of two faster, more agile ships, the galleon's superior gunnery would be effectively neutralized.

Smoke still roiled from the *Lady*'s stern, obscuring Renato's view of the *General*. "Damn it, Sharky! Where in blazes is Lafitte?"

The gnarled man in the crow's nest pressed an eye to his spyglass. "Half a mo', Cap'n!"

L'Intrepide had now cleared the galleon's stern. From high above came the crack of muskets, and Renato heard the balls zip through his sails and thud into the deck. The *Lady*'s starboard gun ports now snapped open, and the snouts of her great guns began to poke out. Renato shuddered. Each was an 18-pounder. At this close range, those iron monsters could not be angled low enough to strike *L'Intrepide*'s deck, but should they come to bear, she would be blown to pieces in a matter of seconds.

The rain came steadily now, and the sky grew darker by the second.

More musket balls zinged from the Spanish deck. A man near Renato said "Whuff!" and threw his hands to his face, blood gushing between his fingers.

"Hard a-port!" Renato roared. "And get those guns reloaded!"

A new round of explosions thundered from the galleon. Renato ducked instinctively, then realized they came from the *Lady*'s far side, as she lobbed balls at *General Santander*. Answering fire came from Lafitte, but he was too far off to present more than an annoyance. Devil take the man! He'd sent Renato in to do his fighting, then laid back in relative safety, hoping to reap the spoils.

L'Intrepide completed her turn at last, and the ship straightened into a course along the *Lady*'s side.

"Prepare for broadside!"

Above, from the *Lady's* gun ports, Renato saw match fires gleaming. An instant later, two guns belched fire. Despite the fact they were aimed well overhead, Renato flattened himself to the deck. One ball caught the jib line, sending the small triangular sail fluttering over the starboard bow. The other passed squarely between *L'Intrepide's* two masts, ripping a huge rent in the mainsail. The next three guns fired almost as one, and balls whistled overhead, parting lines and chipping hunks of wood from spars and yards.

Climbing to his feet, Renato surveyed the damage—and could not resist a grin. If this was the best the Spaniards could do, he might yet win the day. And at that moment two more of the *Lady's* guns spat flame. As if the very heavens were exploding, a great crack sounded, and the foremast burst apart. The upper half hung in the sky a moment, then plummeted like a huge spear, dragging lines, sails and spars in its wake. Two men leapt from the starboard side, just ahead of the wreckage, while a handful of others were swept into the foaming sea.

Renato clung to the mainmast as *L'Intrepide* lurched. Above him, the wind howled through the rigging. The storm was now almost upon them. He glanced to port and saw they had drifted to within six yards of the *Lady's* hull.

The men manning the port side guns had thrown themselves to the deck, using the guns as cover.

"Up, you vermin! Back to the guns! Now is our chance!"

Those pirates still alive and conscious staggered back to their feet.

"Aim for the waterline!" Renato bawled. "Fire all guns!"

With a great hammer-crash, the first gun spoke, followed in quick succession by the others, and the 9-pound iron balls hurtled point-blank into the *Lady's* exposed hull. Renato covered his head as a shower of splinters and wood chunks fell around him.

As the rain of debris ceased, Renato raised his head. Two

great holes gaped in the galleon's hull, each wide enough to sail a jolly boat through. Water rushed in in torrents, and men howled with fear from the decks above. The *Lady of Cadiz* was doomed.

L'Intrepide passed almost within arm's length of the gaping hull before veering away. As they cleared the *Lady's* bow, Renato lips curled back in a snarl. There, half a mile in the distance, sat the *General Santander*, untouched and unharmed. On her deck, without doubt, stood Lafitte with his telescope, calmly surveying the results of the battle.

Renato shook himself, saving his rage for later. Having lost her foremast and various sails, *L'Intrepide* was barely maneuverable through the storm-tossed waves. It would be all she could do to limp away from the sinking galleon.

With the *Lady of Cadiz* already beginning to list, Lafitte was on the move, tacking to approach the galleon from the bow. Even at risk of losing his prize, the man was too cowardly to present himself before the *Lady's* guns.

But the Spaniards were in no mood to resist. Men raced about the sloping deck, shouting curses as they struggled to lower boats. As Renato watched, the broad tri-color of Spain trailed down the mast, and the thin white flag of surrender climbed into its place.

On board *L'Intrepide*, men were busy hacking away lines still clinging to the fallen foremast. The great length of wood hung suspended over the starboard side, and now, in concert with the deepening waves, threatened to capsize the ship. Renato took up an ax and chopped furiously alongside his men, pretending the rope was actually the neck of Lafitte.

By the time the wreckage had been cleared away, the storm had carried *L'Intrepide* a good half mile away. *General Santander* had attached grappling hooks to the *Lady's* starboard side, which now listed at a perilous angle. The two ships rocked in the rough sea, their hulls banging and scraping.

Through his telescope, Renato saw Lafitte in the *General's* stern, directing the movement of cargo crates from the *Lady's* hold to his own. A squat-bodied figure in a gaudy red shirt swung over the *Lady*'s rail, slithered down a rope and dropped heavily to the *General*'s deck, racing immediately to Lafitte's side. Even through the driving rain, Renato recognized Andre, one of Lafitte's favorite toadies. After a moment of animated conversation, Lafitte's back stiffened, and an instant later he was climbing hand-over-hand, following Andre up the rope to the galleon's deck.

Renato strained at the scope, trying to follow their progress. Something was definitely afoot. For Lafitte to personally board a captured vessel was almost unheard of. Renato could only surmise the treasure had been found.

Long minutes elapsed before Lafitte reappeared. By this time, the *Lady*'s upper deck had sunk nearly to the level of the *General*'s. If the grapnels were not released soon, the brig would be in danger of sinking along with the galleon. Close on Lafitte's heels came Andre and three other crewmen, struggling with a heavy burden. As they manhandled it over the *Lady*'s side, Renato's heartbeat quickened. It was a long black chest, seemingly of polished ebony, with gold-chased trim. This, then, was the fabulous treasure trumpeted by Lafitte.

For a long moment the chest hung precariously between the two ships, and Renato thought it would surely spill into the sea. But with Lafitte's coaxing, the men guided it to a rough landing on the *General*'s deck.

As the chest disappeared into the hold, Lafitte turned his attention back to the *Lady of Cadiz*. At the rail of the sinking galleon, two of Lafitte's rogues bracketed a short, nearly naked man with skin the shade of a coconut. The man's skull had a peculiar flat quality. Renato found him unlike any human being he had ever seen.

With seemingly little effort, the pirates tossed the brown man bodily over the rail, and the fellow landed light as a cat on Lafitte's deck. It was only then, as the little man turned angrily toward his captors, that Renato saw his hands were shackled behind his back.

In a rush, the rest of Lafitte's men leapt over the side, and the hooks were hastily removed. *General Santander* immediately began to pull away.

As the *Lady of Cadiz* slipped farther into the sea, her survivors leapt from the decks, swimming frantically for her bobbing boats.

L'Intrepide continued to drift, while Faraday and the men fought vainly to regain some degree of maneuverability. If Lafitte now came to their aid, they might still be towed to shore before engulfed by the storm.

But to Renato's chagrin, *General Santander* put on full sail and aimed her bow due east. Having left Renato to do the fighting, Lafitte was abandoning him altogether.

Renato called down the curses of all the gods he knew. And for the first time in his life, his prayers appeared to be answered. The *General's* sails bucked and filled, pushing her backward. The wind, already rough, turned decidedly violent, and beat back toward the Texas coast with increasing fury. The gray sky turned nearly black, sending great whitecaps over Lafitte's deck.

Not even a ship as seaworthy as the *General* could long survive such a beating. As Renato nodded with satisfaction, Lafitte turned toward shore, running with the wind past the disappearing hulk of the *Lady of Cadiz*.

But pleased as he was with Lafitte's failure to escape, Renato faced an even grimmer fate. The full rage of the storm had now overtaken *L'Intrepide*, and the helpless schooner was tossed from wave to wave like a piece of driftwood. Their one hope was to batten down and pray they would not be split asunder.

"Cap'n! Cap'n Renato, sir!"

Renato ignored Quayle's pleading cry. As *General Santander* sped toward the distant shore, he clung fiercely to the rail, cursing the treacherous bastard who, having tricked and robbed him, was now leaving him to die.

"Cap'n Renato! What is it, sir! What's amiss?" This time, Quayle's annoying cries were accompanied by rough hands on his shoulders.

Renato snarled, preparing to swat the little man down. But the snarl died in his throat as he stared up into the scowling face of LaChaise. Swinging his head about, he beheld Quayle crouched at the far end of the church pew.

Renato blinked his eyes, struggling to readjust his thinking. He was back aboard *Medusa*. The sky was clear and the sea was smooth. Lafitte, the storm, and the *Lady of Cadiz* were once again five years in the past.

Renato fixed Quayle with a menacing glare. "For your sake, Quayle, I hope this is important."

"Beggin' your pardon, Cap'n, we feared you'd been possessed by demons. You was screaming something terrible, spouting such curses as to curdle our blood! An' besides, Mr. LaChaise was needin' to consult you on our course."

"That's so," LaChaise growled. "We've sighted Matagorda Bay. You never said if you wanted us to enter or stand off the coast."

Renato pulled himself erect. "You were correct to inquire, Mr. LaChaise. You may proceed to the bay mouth with all possible speed, but do not enter."

LaChaise stomped off without an acknowledgment, while Quayle bowed gratefully away, leaving Renato to his memories.

Even after all this time, he was amazed *L'Intrepide* had survived that storm. After drifting for nearly a week, they had come ashore a hundred miles from their original position, just north of Galveston Island. Not long after, word had come that Lafitte had died at sea, killed by a splinter while battling an unknown foe.

Robbed of his revenge, Renato had focused on the treasure. He'd made it a point to seek out men who had been with Lafitte on *General Santander*, even taking that toad Andre into his crew. While no man seemed willing or able to relate the full story, all agreed Lafitte had been forced to leave the black box behind on the Texas coast, and all—all but Renato—believed it hopelessly lost.

Three more years passed before word came that Lafitte had died again, this time of fever on the coast of Yucatán. Renato could only suspect the great coward had concocted the earlier tale to escape his vengeance—but whatever the truth, the man now surely burned in Hell.

And at last, retribution was nearly within Renato's grasp. With the treasure finally in his possession, it would be he, not the precious Jean Lafitte, who would be remembered as the greatest pirate ever to sail the Gulf.

"Mr. LaChaise! I shall be in my quarters. I am not to be disturbed until we reach the mouth of the bay."

RENATO HUMMED A bawdy ditty as he performed his morning toilette. The song, involving a bishop, a blindfold, a milkmaid and a cow, had been a favorite of his step-father Beluche. Though the pain in his scorched face and limbs was still intense, Renato was in high spirits. This was too important a day to be spoiled by anything so common as pain. This was the day he would fulfill his destiny.

From his chest of personal treasures, he extracted a small brown bottle with a blackened cork. Applying a minute amount of liquid to a fingertip, he dabbed it carefully behind his charred ears, then dried his finger by wiping it down his blistered throat. This was the French cologne that, according to Renato's mother, his father had employed. It was a manly scent, reminiscent of blood orange and tobacco, and far too sophisticated for his ill-bred crew, from whom it was kept strictly secret.

Returning the bottle to its place, Renato proceeded to the next step of his daily ritual. This too was something best kept from the crew, with the necessary exception of Mr. Quayle. Fishing a purple velvet bag from under his bed, he loosened the drawstring to remove a broad china bowl with two handles. The outer circumference was decorated with exquisitely rendered red and white roses, while the rim was adorned with delicate gold leaf. Renato could not resist a smile, for this was no mere bowl. It was a true work of art, one he had personally appropriated from the cabin of a French countess—a chamberpot fit for a queen.

For the crew, it was enough to squat over one of the two rude holes extending over the stern, but such was beneath the dignity of a captain. As far as Renato was concerned, it was best the men believed him above such needs at all. For that reason the pot's existence was known only to Quayle, whose duty it was to empty and clean it.

The gruff voice of LaChaise rumbled down through the thick oak planks of the deck. The man seemed to take an unholy delight in giving orders. It was not uncommon for a newly promoted officer to enjoy his authority, but LaChaise's arrogance reminded Renato altogether too much of his own.

Positioning the pot with care, he hunkered over it and began his business. He found his mind exceptionally clear at such moments, and took the opportunity to formulate plans for the day ahead. With *L'Intrepide*, he could have sailed directly into Matagorda Bay without fear of becoming mired on the shallow bottom. But *Medusa*, by virtue of her enormous gun, sat lower in the water, requiring a less direct approach.

A heavy creaking disturbed his thoughts. An upward glance found dust motes swirling from the cracks in the deck. He wondered vaguely what was happening up there, annoyed that he did not yet know the sounds of his new ship. He had captained *L'Intrepide* so long that her every nuance had become as familiar as the workings of his own body.

Shutting out the noise, Renato returned to his meditations. A quiet approach in the jolly boats, he reasoned, might allow them to reach the treasure site without alerting either Bowie's party or the pestiferous Karankawa. With luck, he'd be back on *Medusa* with the treasure by nightfall, free to destroy his enemies at his leisure.

With a start, he became aware of still another noise—a harsh, sputtering hiss that seemed to originate directly over his head. This was a sound he could not fail to recognize, but his shouted curse was engulfed in a mind-numbing roar.

It was as if the hands of a giant had clapped him on the ears. At the same moment, the ship lurched to starboard with force enough to turn the cabin nearly on its side. Renato clung desperately to the handles of the chamberpot as it went sliding toward the starboard bulkhead. Just as he was about to crash into the wall, the ship heaved violently back to port. His world turned upside down, Renato lost his grip on the bowl and tumbled pell-mell back across the room, the pot shattering somewhere above his head. The bowl's contents showered down upon him as *Medusa* rolled a third time, slamming him back to starboard.

The deck still rocked, but at an increasingly slower pace, as the ship struggled to right herself. Renato scowled horribly. Paints, canvasses, clothing and wine bottles were strewn in mad fashion over every inch of the cabin.

Even before the deck ceased to sway, Renato snatched up a spare shirt to clean himself and began clawing into his trousers. He was still fumbling at the buttons as he raced through the narrow corridor and up the ladder to the main deck.

Clearing the hatch, the rotten-egg smell of burnt powder was strong in the air. Dark smoke still rose from the barrel of the big 18-pounder. Renato's head swiveled in all directions, expecting to see *Lucinda* or another enemy vessel. But the waters were clear. The men's backs were to him as they laughed and gestured toward the Texas shoreline.

LaChaise stood in the stern, a spyglass fixed to his eye. The glass was aimed at a point of land near the mouth of Karankawa Cove. Following LaChaise's line of sight, Renato spotted a cloud of yellow dust hanging above an unnatural gap in the tree line.

"Mr. LaChaise! What the blazes possessed you to fire that gun?"

LaChaise continued to study the shoreline for several seconds after Renato's words had faded into the breeze. When he finally lowered the glass, his brutal features were twisted into a travesty of a smile.

"Top of the mornin', Cap'n, sir. I'se pleased to report we got 'em."

Renato felt his jaw drop. He snapped it shut, squared his shoulders, and filled his chest with air. "Got whom?"

"Why, the hostiles, o' course. We sighted a band of the red devils gawkin' from that neck of land yonder, and figured as you'd want 'em tellin' no tales of our arrival." The smile widened. "I can assure ya, Cap'n, them particular hostiles will be tellin' nothin' to nobody."

Renato felt the rage rising within him. His hand strayed to his belt, but found it empty of hilt or gun butt. Feeling the men's eyes upon him, he attacked with the only weapon at his disposal—scorn. "Mr. LaChaise, did it not occur to you that by firing that gun you have announced our presence to every man and beast within fifty miles? Instead of entering the cove and securing the treasure unobserved, we can now expect to fight every step of the way, with the Indians on one side and Andre's party on the other. I trust you are proud of yourself."

The man's smile was undiminished, but a sharp glint appeared in his eyes. "Oh, I am indeed, Cap'n, and thankee for sayin' so. This 'ere gun packs one hellacious wallop, does she not? I only hopes a few more of them rascals pokes their heads out of the bushes for us."

Renato hesitated. The damned maniac was toying with him, daring him to make an outright challenge. "I'm afraid that won't be possible, Mr. LaChaise, as you'll be accompanying me ashore. You will detail six men to remain with the ship, and get the rest into the jolly boats." When LaChaise did not respond, Renato added, "At once!" and the man finally began barking orders.

Turning away, Renato crooked a finger at Quayle and waited as the little man scurried forward. "I have a special assignment for you," he said, careful not to be overheard. "You shall have the honor of cleaning my cabin."

Quayle looked at him askance. It was a common enough order, but something in Renato's tone seemed to give the fellow pause. "I understands, Cap'n."

"Not yet, you don't," Renato said, pleased to envision the man's coming horror. "But you will."

CHAPTER 43

"Me mouth still waters."

BOWIE PICKED HIMSELF out of the mesquite and looked around for his horse. The mustang was twenty feet back down the trail, stomping and snorting as Sam fought to grip its reins. At the moment of the blast, Bowie had been turned in the saddle, trying in vain to raise a smile from Mariette. All at once her horse had bolted ahead, his jackknifed, and he'd found himself soaring through the air.

The shirt he'd scavenged from the largest of the dead Mexicans had fit him like a second skin, and was now ripped at the seams.

Mariette looked down at him with a grin. Andre and Sharky arrived just as Sam came up with the mustang, and they too regarded him with amusement. Thanks to the Mexicans—and their mysterious slayers—all now had their own mounts.

Bowie growled, "Anyone see the lightning before that thunderclap?"

"That were no thunder," Andre said. " 'Twere a ship's gun, without doubt, an' nothing less than an 18-pounder."

"A ship?" Bowie clapped dust from his trousers. "Renato?"

"Not bloody likely. *L'Intrepide*, if she's still afloat, sports nothin' near so big."

Swallowing his disappointment, Bowie climbed back into the saddle. Above all else, he still longed for the chance to personally deliver Renato to his doom. But the cannon blast raised a new concern. If not Renato, who?

It had been a trying morning. Mariette had been decidedly cool toward him, in marked contrast to their heated encounter of the night before. She had insisted on a Christian burial for Pacal, which the men provided with ill grace, considering it wasted on a heathen. The chief effect of the brown man's passing had been to remind them all of the thin line between life and death in this wild country. At any moment, all knew they could be set upon by cannibals, mauled by beasts, or pierced by sticks hurtling out of the brush.

And now, to make matters worse, they had a cannon to contend with.

"If not Renato," Bowie said aloud, "Who?"

Andre scratched his belly. "Leaves me jiggered, and that's a fact. That gun was close, not more than two miles off, puttin' it somewhere near the mouth of the bay. And that's a puzzle."

Guiding his horse back into the lead, Bowie resumed the course along the trail. "Out with it, old man. Why a puzzle?"

Andre fell in line close behind. "It's like this, Jim Boy. No ship large enough to carry eighteens would attempt to enter that shallow bay. Anything too heavy is sure to run aground. Lafitte himself learned that lesson, to his sorrow. It's what lost him the treasure."

Bowie brought the mustang to a halt. "You *know* how the treasure was lost?"

"Oh, aye." Andre kept his sorrel plodding ahead. "I was there, you see."

"And why am I just hearing this now?"

"Well…" Andre drew the word out until his voice faded. "Ye just now asked, did ye not?"

Bowie suppressed his anger. Andre was, first and last, a pirate. To be frank and forthcoming was simply not in his nature. "Yes," he said, "I've asked. And this time I expect the whole story."

For the next quarter hour, as they progressed warily toward the cove, Andre painted the highlights of the tale: How Lafitte had recruited Renato, and how they'd found and defeated the *Lady of Cadiz* amid a mounting storm.

"Renato was overeager," Andre said, well into his story, "and closed with the galleon too soon. Afterwards, *L'Intrepide* was barely able to limp away, and Lafitte was forced to salvage the treasure before the *Lady* went down. Just as he was about to offer Renato aid, and his share of the booty, the wind come up somethin' terrible and forced us toward shore."

"And what did this booty consist of?"

"Ah, Jim, it was a sight to behold. Crates stuffed with all manner of golden objects. Plates and statues, gold-plated shields, and crowns set with gems big as your fist. Me mouth still waters to think on it."

Bowie turned an eye on Mariette. "That dagger I saw in New Orleans. It was part of that horde?"

When she offered no reply, Andre said, "That it was."

"And what of the rest? Did Lafitte leave all that behind?"

"Oh, no. Not that lot, he didn't. He sold and bartered away the gold, and hid the jewels I know not where. What he left was a single black chest. Polished ebony, it was, and trimmed all in gold. Lafitte allowed no one to see its contents, but later—in his cups—told me it was worth more than all the rest by many times over."

Bowie sighed, wondering how much of this to believe. "So how did he lose it?"

"Well, the wind had come up so fierce Lafitte feared we'd be ground to bits against the reef. Our only chance was to make for the mouth of Matagorda Bay, hopin' it would offer a bit of shelter. It did, too, after a fashion, but we wasn't more than halfway up afore our hull scraped bottom, and we was caught neater than you please. We worked through the night, tryin' every trick we knew to free the ship, but nothin' availed. And by morning, when the storm had calmed considerable, we had another problem."

Bowie raised his eyebrows, drawn into the yarn in spite of himself.

"There at the mouth of the bay, bristlin' with guns, sat a proud Spanish frigate, doubtless the one assigned to escort the treasure ship. Outgunned us by a thrice, she did, and we was in dire straits, 'specially as we was still stuck aground. The Spanish commander was wise enough not to enter the bay, and sent four heavily manned boats at us, meanwhile takin' long-range shots from beyond the reef. Lafitte feared we'd be captured sure, and couldn't bear the thought of losin' that ebony chest. So he did what he had to."

"Which was?"

"He chose a party of five men, trusted swabbies all, and set 'em down in a jolly boat. They was to bury the chest in a likely spot ashore, returnin' as soon as may be. One of 'em was a fair mapmaker, and charged to make a record, so's Lafitte could reclaim the prize later."

"So what went wrong?"

"Well, them Spanish boats was nearly upon us when the storm heaved up again. Turned out we'd been caught in the eye, you see, and once it passed we was right back in the hell of it. The waves climbed twenty feet high, even there in the bay, and their boats flew about like tenpins. Out beyond the bay mouth, the Spanish frigate was dancin' a jig on the wavetops. One moment her flags was halfway to the clouds, and the next she was hull-up, bein' dashed to bits on the rocks. Lafitte's *General Santander* was in a fair way to crack up too, until a big wave washed over us, wrenching our hull free of the bottom. We slipped into deeper waters, where we dropped anchor and rode out the rest of the storm. Time it was over, more'n half our men had been swept away, and the bay was awash with bodies."

"And what of the ebony chest?"

Andre shrugged. "That jolly boat never returned. Lafitte waited three full days, frettin' and fumin' like a demon. He'd have had every man ashore searchin', but our other boats had all been lost in the storm, and we daren't approach in the ship without runnin' aground again. Finally, as the men were growin' surly enough to threaten mutiny, Lafitte agreed to leave. But he swore he'd get that chest again someday, no matter the cost."

"And did he?"

"Not far's I know. Sometime later, we got into a tussle with a British squadron, and he was sorely wounded. The crew was told he'd died of his wounds, while only me and the surgeon knew the truth. Under cover of taking on provisions at the *Isla Mujeres*, we set him safely ashore with a few of the choicest gems. And that was the last time I seen him. Two years passed before I managed a return, and the natives said he'd died of fever. Even showed me his grave, they did. I left half a bottle of good rum sittin' on his marker, by way of tribute, though some bug-eater likely guzzled it as soon as me back was turned."

"So that's what we're after," Bowie said, half to himself. "An ebony chest worth more than a shipload of gold." His voice, he realized, had taken on a dreamy quality, but he no longer cared. The lure of the treasure had him at last in its grip.

"That is all very well," Sam said, "but let us not forget the cannon fire. Whatever it portends, it cannot be good."

Andre made a sour face. "Much as it pains me, I must agree. That gun means trouble."

"I hate to mention this," Mariette said softly, "but we may have another problem. Look!" She aimed a slim finger to the southeast, just above the treetops. There, extending high into the sky, was a thin purple ribbon of smoke.

"Kronks." Andre spat the word like an oath.

"Kronks," Bowie agreed. "Calling all kith and kin to supper."

CHAPTER 44

"Goin' to sculp a few?"

"**R**OW, YOU DOGS! I'll have an ear off each of you if we don't beat LaChaise to the point." Renato perched in the stern of the jolly boat, a jewel-mounted cutlass in his hand, while four men heaved on the oars.

Twenty yards off the larboard side, LaChaise's crew struggled to propel the other boat.

Satisfied his rowers were properly motivated, Renato glanced back at the shore of the bay, where the slaves still milled about in confusion. He could not resist a smile. He had promised to free them at first landfall, and had done precisely that. The fact that it had much to do with strategy, and nothing at all with mercy, was a detail that pleased him no end.

The slaves appeared unwilling to venture into the brush, but at the same time afraid to remain where they were. Renato gave not a fig whether they lived or died. He cared only that they distract the Karankawas long enough for he and his men to make landfall inside the cove.

The map, still vivid in his mind, had placed the treasure midway down the cove's northern shore, a spot marked by a small, peculiarly shaped inlet.

Meanwhile, *Medusa* would continue blasting from the bay, persuading the Indians she represented the main threat. The most troubling aspect of the plan was leaving Quayle in command of *Medusa*, but he was a less dangerous choice than LaChaise.

At the next deafening roar, Renato glanced back to see a great cloud of smoke belching from the ship. An instant later an 18-pound ball screamed through a copse of trees not thirty yards from the slaves.

Renato's rowers faltered momentarily, then, faced with his wrath, worked their oars furiously, widening their lead on the other boat. LaChaise's curses came too late, and Renato's crew cleared the point, entering the cove a good three boat-lengths in the lead.

"Cap'n!" The hunchbacked man in the bow, whom Renato had attempted to christen Caliban, but the men insisted on calling Hump, pointed wildly into the northern sky. "Look!"

Renato's confidence died in his breast. Rising high above the treetops was a column of smoke. While the Karankawa normally numbered no more than forty to a band, half of those women, there was no telling how many the smoke might bring. He had faced these Indians before, and while he considered them little more than beasts, he was forced to admit they were fierce and canny fighters.

"Hard to starboard! Make directly for that fire."

Hump gave an eager laugh. "We goin' to sculp a few of the buggers, are we, Cap'n?"

"Yes. All of them, if need be." But he was not at all certain Karankawa scalps would be the only ones taken this day.

The men strained at the oars, and the boat made good time. From beyond the bay came the periodic explosions of the 18-pounder. Quayle, in his first command, was performing well. Once this adventure was concluded, Renato mused, perhaps he would reward the man with some token of appreciation—something along the lines of a patched but serviceable chamberpot.

Behind them, LaChaise's curses burned the air. His rowers were less skilled, and all his threats could not impel them to sufficient speed.

Renato scanned the shoreline. He still saw no Indians, but

had a growing unease, a feeling that unseen eyes followed them from the shadows.

Tense minutes crawled by, and the men grunted and sweated with exertion. When at last they were within two hundred yards of land, Renato breathed easier. It appeared they had gone undetected after all.

And it was at that moment, as if the Fates had been waiting for his hopes to rise, that a horde of gaudily painted savages burst from the trees. Separating into four groups, they piled into dugout canoes and pushed off from shore.

Renato yanked two silver-chased pistols from his belt. His throat was dry, and his pulse hammered, reawakening the pain in his limbs. Each of the Indians carried a longbow and sheath of arrows. Renato had seen the effect of those weapons, and had no wish to face them now.

The dugouts flew over the water with alarming speed. Renato's eyes roved from one to another, watching for the Indians to take up their bows. Land was still a hundred yards off when a warrior snaked a hand over his shoulder for an arrow. The movement was deft enough to deceive any ordinary man, but to a master of deceit such as Renato, it was blatant as a war cry.

"Ship oars!" As the men snatched up their guns, Renato leveled his own two pistols at the nearest dugout. "Aim low, and make every shot count!"

The Kronks, as if obeying the same order, raised their weapons. The nearest savage, his arrow nocked, rose slightly as he bent his bow.

"Fire!" Renato's first shot took the crouching Indian high in the breast. The blast of his second was drowned in a ragged volley, as guns exploded all around him.

CHAPTER 45

"God's bollocks!"

THE BARK OF pistol fire brought Bowie's group to a halt. They had grown accustomed to the distant cannon blasts, but this new sound was closer, presenting a more imminent threat.

More shots followed, and Bowie recognized the bellow of muskets adding to the din.

"What do you make of it?" He asked Andre.

"Someone's in one hell of a battle. And they's not all Indians."

Mariette pushed her buckskin up next to Bowie. "What's happening?" There was an excited gleam in her eyes. Rather than being frightened by gunfire, she seemed almost aroused by it.

"Someone out there has Indian trouble. They may need our help."

"*Our* help? I forbid it! We're here for gold, not to fight other people's battles."

Bowie just stared at her.

Mariette's lips were tight. "Just who do you think is out there?"

Andre answered for him. "If it ain't pirates, it's maybe a merchantman, a new load of colonists, or even a navy ship."

"Or more Mexican soldiers," Mariette said. "We certainly owe *them* no help. Whoever it is, they can keep the Indians busy while we slip in and make off with the treasure."

The distant gunfire had become more sporadic.

Bowie shook his head. "I'll not stand by and watch those

savages feast on…" he was about to say *white men*, but saw Sam eyeing him, and finished with "civilized folk."

Before he could act, a movement in the brush caught his eye.

"Hell and damnation! Did ye see it, Jim Boy?" Andre had drawn his pistol, now pointed at the same spot.

"What was it?"

"A flash of yellow-gold, crawling with big black spots. That cursed tiger again."

"Jaguar," Sam said archly. "The tiger, otherwise known as *Panthera tigris*, is indigenous only to—"

"Stow it, Sam! Did you see it or not?"

The black man drew up in a huff but offered no reply.

"I did," Sharky said, his voice shaky. "You interrupted its feeding, Cap'n Bowie. Now it's hungry again."

Slipping from his mount, Bowie stole a glance at Mariette, making sure she was sheltered behind them.

Sharky let out a squeak. "There! Just beyond that tree."

There did, indeed, appear to be an unnatural waving of the grasses at the base of a cottonwood. Hearing a low, saw-like growl, Bowie cocked his pistol. He wished the cat would charge and have done with it. His clanging nerves made him fit to leap out of his skin.

Long seconds later, the growl was repeated.

He sensed motion behind him. "Steady, lass. He won't get past us." He wanted to turn and comfort the girl, but dared not. The cat might charge at any moment, and he would have only one shot at it.

Tasting blood, he realized he was biting his tongue. Still the jaguar did not attack. What was it waiting for?

From somewhere behind came a scream, stopping as abruptly as it began. He whipped about. "Mariette! What—?"

His throat tightened. His heart seemed to stop. The trail behind him was utterly empty. Mariette was gone.

Andre called over his shoulder, "God's bollocks, Jim, what's amiss? Do ye expect me to handle this hell-cat by meself?"

Bowie listened into the distance, hoping for another scream to guide him, but heard nothing. To rush blindly into the brush would be foolish. After a moment he leaned down, plucked a large stone from the ground and hurled it at the spot they'd been watching. The stone crashed deep into a thicket, but there was no other sound, no hint of movement.

Andre's mouth hung slack. "What—what happened to the cat?"

Bowie hung his head, his stomach tasting of bile.

"There was no cat," he said. "It was a trick, and we fell for it like simpletons. Mariette has been taken."

CHAPTER 46

"You rutting bastard!"

RENATO SIGHTED CAREFULLY and squeezed his trigger. The powder flashed, the pistol kicked in his hand, and he was rewarded by the sight of still another savage tumbling into the cold waters of the cove. He threw the empty gun at Hump, huddled on the floor and struggling to load the other pistol.

"Hurry, fool! Your scalp's at risk, too!"

Renato flexed his hands. The guns were growing hotter with each shot, and he felt blisters on his palms. The past few minutes had been as bloody as any in his memory. The Kronks were hellishly good with their bows. One of his men was dead, and another wounded so badly he may as well be. LaChaise had fared even worse, with two men killed and one out of action.

But thanks to Renato's leadership, their first volley had killed nearly half their attackers, and the second all but emptied two of the dugouts.

Having dumped their dead and dying over the side, the pirates had room to crouch low and fire over the gunwales. But the Kronks now sat back and lobbed arrows high into the air, where they rained down into the open boats.

As Renato snatched a loaded pistol from Hump, another fell out of the sky and split the skull of the man in front of him. Renato drew a bead on the sole occupant of the third canoe, and grinned as the Indian clutched his throat.

Of the two remaining dugouts, one had lost half of its crew.

A pistol spat from LaChaise's boat, and one of the two survivors slumped over the side. Renato turned his attention to the fourth canoe. This group had played the wisest game, keeping their distance and presenting only their prow as a target.

From behind came another shot, and LaChaise's men cheered as the final Indian fell from the third dugout.

The warriors in the last canoe gave an angry shout. Laying aside their bows, they took up oars and flew over the water toward Renato.

Accepting another pistol from Hump, he sent a ball hurtling toward them. But with uncanny instincts, the four savages leaned sideways, two left and two right, allowing the shot to pass harmlessly between their heads.

Renato swore. With the Kronks growing closer by the second, he had no choice but to ask for help.

"LaChaise! Prepare for a volley!"

The reply was a spate of distant laughter. Chancing a look, he saw the other boat twenty yards off and moving toward the mouth of the cove. The dog was leaving him to die!

"LaChaise! Come back, you rutting bastard!"

"And why would I be doing that, Cap'n?"

Renato's mind whirled. There was only one thing that might appeal to such a brigand. "The treasure!" he shouted. "You'll get an extra share!"

This got the man's attention. LaChaise spoke gruffly to his men, and they rested on their oars.

The Karankawa canoe was now less than thirty yards away. "Damn it, man! Hurry!"

"To my way of thinkin', Cap'n, an extra share just won't do." LaChaise scratched his chin in a parody of thinking. "I believe I requires a full half of the loot."

"Half! You're mad, man! But because I like you, I'll make it an eighth!"

A bowstring twanged. An arrow appeared in the shoulder

of Renato's last remaining rower, and the man began squalling like a hog.

Renato gave him a savage boot in the ribs. "Quiet, wretch! I'm negotiating here."

"Half," LaChaise called, "or I sails away with yer fine new ship."

The Indian dugout was within twenty yards and closing.

"A quarter!" Renato howled. "No more!"

Another arrow whizzed by, inches from Renato's head.

"Good-bye then, Cap'n! And luck to ya."

"Half!" Renato shrieked. "Half, damn you! Now get back here and blast these devils!"

LaChaise did not reply, and the Kronks were now so close he could see the sharpness of their teeth.

"Here, Cap'n!" The hunchback thrust two loaded pistols into his hands.

The Indians approached head-on, with only the lead man presenting a good target. Damning LaChaise to Hell, Renato sighted his first gun carefully and fired. The Indian's head jerked back in a halo of blood. He timed the second shot perfectly, but the second man held his dead companion before him like a shield, and Renato's ball thudded into lifeless flesh.

On came the canoe, now nearly within arm's reach. As Hump cowered in the bottom of the boat, and Renato's last rower scrabbled for a cutlass, Renato plucked a dagger from his belt. He would fight tooth and nail rather than allow himself to be eaten.

A red hand gripped the gunwale. A painted face rose above the side. As the warrior jumped, Renato sprang up, his dagger thrusting for the man's heart—and a second Indian appeared, climbing over the wounded rower.

Just as all appeared lost, Renato heard gunfire. The head of his opponent disappeared in a shower of blood. The other savage jerked spasmodically and fell into the water, while the Kronk in the canoe slumped over his oars.

A lusty cheer erupted, and Renato swung to see LaChaise's boat a mere ten yards away.

The brute's bulldog face was wreathed in a horrible grin. "It appears, Cap'n, that you and me have a bargain."

Renato could only clench his teeth and nod. He cast his eyes past the floating corpses to the shore, but could find no further sign of savages. Then he caught a flash of spotted skin moving swiftly through the brush. A Mexican tiger, no doubt. But after facing a horde of wild Indians, a mere tiger would be child's play.

"Very well, Mr. LaChaise. I suggest we collect the treasure—*our* treasure—and be rid of this cursed cove as quick as may be." *But on my oath*, he added silently, *you will not live to spend it*.

CHAPTER 47

"You intend to let them die."

CONCERN FOR MARIETTE still crowded Bowie's mind, and his impulse was to charge forward, killing anyone and anything in his path. In his youth, he would have done just that, but experience had taught him the value of a cool head. They were now deep within territory the Karankawa considered sacred ground, and death might lurk behind every tree.

After investigating the scene of Mariette's abduction, they had come away with more questions than answers. The sandy earth where she was last seen revealed small footprints identical to those found yesterday around the firepit—tracks they had attributed to Pacal.

The ground behind the cottonwood bore the same prints, with no indication a cat had been present.

Sharky had been unable to contain his fears. For the past ten minutes he'd been wailing and moaning, convinced Pacal's ghost had returned from the netherworld to take vengeance on them. Sam had merely snorted, while Andre strove—with little success—to convince Bowie he put no credence in the notion.

Bowie himself was too busy worrying about earthly enemies—and the fate of Mariette—to be concerned with spirits. If the time came that he encountered a ghost, he would deal with it. Until then, he would concentrate on evils he could fight with his knife, his fists and his guns.

The gunfire from the cove, after a brief but thunderous

barrage, had abruptly ceased. Whoever had been fighting the Kronks was now dead, victorious, or taken prisoner.

Within him brewed a storm of grief, loss and guilt. Just as he and Mariette had grown closest, she had begun to pull away—and before he could discover why, he had allowed her to be captured.

The rapid slap of feet upon the earth, growing louder by the second, sent the group to cover behind a stand of live oaks. Fifty yards in the distance, two men burst from the brush, running for all they were worth.

The men were thin, muscular, black as ebony, and bathed in sweat. They were visible for mere seconds before being swallowed up by the brush, but before Bowie could puzzle over their presence, another group shot into view. More black men, but their breathing was labored, and several were nearly spent. Bowie counted six men, and wondered if this group pursued the first, or if they were chased by someone—or something—else.

The answer was quick in coming. Wild cries and whoops rose from the jungle, and a score of Kronks poured onto the path. They were tall, well-built warriors, skin burnished bronze beneath streaks of blue and black paint. Each carried a spear, and many brandished naked daggers.

Unlike the blacks, they ran seemingly without effort, and their faces reflected confidence almost to the point of amusement. They seemed content to merely chase their prey.

When the parade of Indians had passed, Sam sniffed haughtily. "As I recall, Jim, you vowed not to abandon 'civilized folk' to the cannibals. Does that extend to those of African descent, or is 'civilized' a term reserved for Caucasians?"

Bowie frowned. "I'll not deny aid to any man. Not even those who try my patience," he said pointedly. "But those poor devils will have to wait their turn."

"In other words," Sam said, "you intend to let them die."

"I intend to get Mariette back. If we aid others in the process, all to the better, but until she's safe all other matters, including that damned treasure, are secondary."

CHAPTER 48

"Yer captain is afeared of slaves."

"GOD'S BLOOD, CAP'N! These hummingbirds won't leave me be."

"Those aren't birds, you twit. They're mosquitoes." Renato had already made the mistake of swatting one of the pests from his neck, earning a stinging reminder of his scarred and tender flesh.

"Wait 'til you see the grasshoppers," another man snorted. "Them buggers are big as jackrabbits."

The surviving pirates lay in the shade of a golden-boughed cottonwood, catching their breath and reloading their weapons.

Besides himself, LaChaise and the hunchback, only two pirates had come unscathed from the battle. One of LaChaise's men limped from an arrow that had passed clean through his calf, while Renato's last rower still had an arrowhead lodged in his neck. The group had plenty of weapons, but the fight had consumed an alarming amount of powder. What remained must be used sparingly.

On reaching shore, their jolly boats were well-hidden, and three more dugouts found and destroyed. They had then followed the nipple-shaped inlet toward the spot Renato had seen marked with an X.

LaChaise sprang to his feet, brushing cottonwood tufts from his breeches. The mosquitoes swarming about his head seemed to bother him not at all. "Time to get about collecting my treasure."

Renato rose slowly. In truth, he was not anxious to discover the treasure until he had devised a way to free himself of this upstart.

Twirling his saber, LaChaise extended a hand, palm up, toward Renato. "I believe I'll carry the map from here on."

" 'Twould be a heavy burden, I fear. The map is in my head."

LaChaise's hand curled into a fist. "Then I suggest ya move quickly, before I opens yer skull and removes it."

Seething, Renato led the way deeper inland from the cove. The map indicated four blazed trees roughly north, south, east and west of the X. Once those trees were found, lines drawn between them would converge upon the burial spot.

LaChaise and the others lumbered through the brush like a team of oxen, and several times Renato had to halt and caution them to silence.

He was considering various means of bringing about LaChaise's demise when the first of the map's trees loomed up before him.

The marker might have escaped his notice had he not been imagining LaChaise dangling from a noose, and glanced up in search of a suitable branch. There, shoulder-high on the trunk of a great elm, was the blazed image of a turtle.

Renato quickly averted his eyes. Until LaChaise had been dealt with, it was best the others knew as little as possible.

From its position on the map, the turtle tree was the most easterly of the four. Somewhere to the west, then, would lie the snake, with the bird and fish to north and south. Renato took his bearings from the morning sun and proceeded west, eyes roving continually in search of likely trees.

They had covered no more than thirty yards when the vegetation began to fall away, and they reached the edge of a long, wide clearing.

Renato stopped as if frozen in place. LaChaise growled, "What—?" but immediately closed his yap.

"This ain't good," one man breathed, voicing the thoughts of all.

Stretched out across the clearing were well over a score of grass-covered huts. They were constructed of willow branches, each large enough to house six to eight Indians.

The sight prickled Renato's skin. The Karankawa traveled in groups of no more than forty, women and children included, rarely remaining in one spot more than a few weeks. The present village looked to accommodate more than a hundred, and had a look of long use, if not permanence.

Strangest of all, at the edge of the village stood a great wooden structure, rising at least twenty feet into the air. A half dozen tree trunks rose from a wide circular base to converge at the peak, where they were joined by bands of leather. In mad fashion, it resembled nothing so much as a church steeple. Having long been courted by friars of the Spanish missions, the Kronks were no strangers to churches. But that they would see fit to build one of their own was beyond imagining.

At first the village seemed deserted, but as the pirates stood staring, the air carried the sound of laughing children. Moving to his left, Renato saw them dancing about naked while long-haired Indian women busied themselves with camp labors.

LaChaise let air hiss between his teeth. He bulled forward, turning when the others did not follow. "Well, get moving, ya apes. I'm wanting my treasure."

Renato stood his ground. "Something's off here. Where are all the warriors?"

"We killed 'em, remember?"

"We killed four dugouts full. A village this size would accommodate several times that number."

"Well, they ain't here now." LaChaise shook his head disdainfully. "The once-mighty Renato—afraid of women and children. Lucky I'm here to protect ya."

Renato raised a hand. "Quiet!"

From somewhere to the north—and not far off—came the crackling of bushes and pounding of feet.

He spun about, darting back the way they'd come. Well ahead

of the others, he dashed around a stand of trees and dove into a thick patch of mesquite. The others scrambled for a nearby stand of hackberry trees, disappearing just as two runners burst into the clearing.

Almost immediately, LaChaise barked a laugh and stepped into the open. "Here, you black scoundrels! How'd you escape them savages?"

Renato stared, astounded to see two of the Haitians this far inland—and still among the living.

The other pirates emerged from cover, beckoning the slaves to approach.

"Stay down, fools!" Renato called.

LaChaise curled a lip. "Hear that, men? Yer great captain is even afeared of slaves."

More footsteps thundered out of the north. Caught in the open, the pirates reached for their weapons, but relaxed on seeing more Haitians.

Renato stayed hidden. These men weren't just running, they were running *from* something.

LaChaise picked up one of the scrawnier blacks and shook him, to the great amusement of the other pirates.

And that was how they stood when a horde of wild-eyed Indians poured out of the jungle, catching them flat-footed.

CHAPTER 49

"Cunning, dastardly and dangerous."

BOWIE HATED MOSQUITOES. Given the choice, he would sooner face a pack of wolves or a family of alligators. But the bugs were certainly fond of him. The buzzing, biting mass swarmed about him tight as a sweater—and his knife was useless against them.

Even more irritating, the pests had no interest at all in Sam, providing the black man no end of amusement.

The two lay flat on the sandy earth, barely concealed in a field of foot-tall grass. Spread out before them was the Karankawa village, and at its end rose a huge wooden teepee.

The camp appeared empty, but at the far end of the clearing, a hundred yards beyond the teepee, a large group of Indians milled about on a small hill topped by two ominous-looking stakes.

Bowie tugged McQuiddy's telescope from his belt. He was thankful, this once, for Andre's habit of appropriating items not his own. Closest to the hilltop were at least twenty painted warriors. Edged around them were the women, and running wild on the outskirts were a great number of children. Recalling the tiny footprints at the scene of Mariette's abduction, he tried without success to imagine these waifs as kidnappers.

Off to one side was a group of prisoners held at spearpoint. Bowie was not at all surprised to see the eight black men he had observed earlier.

"What have you ascertained?" Sam whispered, but before Bowie could reply, something else caught his eye.

He gripped the telescope so tightly the metal began to bend. Behind the blacks were several white men clad in pirate fashion. Heart pounding, he scanned the area in search of Renato, then studied each of the pirates in turn, gnashing his brain to recall if he had seen any aboard Renato's ship. He could not be certain.

With great care, he searched the group for Mariette's dark tresses, but of these there was no sign.

"Have you found her?" For once, the black man had discarded his highfalutin language. He seemed genuinely concerned with Mariette's fate.

A faint sound issued from the village, and a tall warrior emerged from a nearby hut, striding in their direction. Bowie pressed himself lower to the ground, easing the knife from its sheath.

Like most of his tribe, the Indian wore his hair in three waist-length braids festooned with scraps of bright cloth. He had reached the outskirts of the village, and Bowie was about to risk all on a charge, when the man ducked into another hut.

Bowie waited, barely daring to breathe. At last the man reappeared, and stalked off toward the group on the distant hill

"Something—or someone," Bowie said, "is in that hut."

Sam goggled at him. "Surely you do not intend going in there."

"If I'm discovered, you'd best be ready to run."

"You have nothing to fear on that score."

Sprinting at half his height, Bowie reached a position where the hut hid him from view of the far hill. He looked about, heart pounding. For a moment, he thought he'd seen the flat brown face of Pacal scowling at him from the side of a nearby hut— but he now saw nothing. *There are no such things as ghosts*, he reminded himself. But despite the heat, he felt a chill.

Praying he would not encounter a shrieking woman or a frightened child, he ducked his head under the grass roof, where a rancid odor smote him with the force of a fist.

Ringed about him were several baskets, and three clay pots.

He dipped a hand into the largest pot, and lifted his fingers to his nose. And gagged. It was some sort of animal fat, and not from an alligator, which he would have recognized from the Louisiana bayous. At least it was not a cooking pot filled with human stew.

The smaller pots contained blue and black dye. The man must have come here to apply war paint. Disappointment washed over him. This was bringing him no closer to finding Mariette.

Stepping outside, he came face to face with a Karankawa warrior rounding the corner of the next hut. The two men stopped, scarcely a yard apart.

The man towered a good four inches above Bowie's six feet, allowing him to glare down beneath beetling brows. High on each cheekbone, flanking a wide flat nose, were blue tattooed circles, and his lower lip was pierced by a short length of cane, signifying an accomplished warrior. The man's lips pulled back, baring a set of strong white teeth. Then the teeth parted, and Bowie sensed the man was about to summon friends.

Before the Indian could utter a sound, Bowie's right hand shot out, closing about the savage's throat.

The Indian's own right hand went instantly to Bowie's wrist, attempting to break the grip, while his left sought Bowie's eyes. Bowie exerted all his strength, but it was like trying to strangle a steel cable. They had reached a stalemate.

With a fierce grin, the warrior released Bowie's wrist and whipped a short double-edged blade from his sheath.

Bowie had no choice. He needed his right hand, even if it allowed the Indian to call a hundred Kronks down upon him.

He released the man's throat, but the hand refused to move. The Indian had clamped it between chin and chest, holding it fast.

The man smiled, knowing he had the advantage, and raised his dagger.

In that instant of certain death, Bowie heard a thump, and blinked, amazed, as the Indian's eyes glassed over. The dagger slipped from limp fingers, and the man fell forward, collapsing on Bowie's chest.

Bewildered, he thrust the slack form aside. And standing before him, a heavy branch in his hands, stood Mr. Samuel Frost Gideon. His face wore a satisfied smirk.

Bowie wasted only a moment on surprise. "I'll thank you later," he said. "Let's hide this fellow before we're discovered." Grasping the warrior's wrists, Bowie began dragging him toward the brush. Sam tossed the club aside and bent to take the legs.

After much grunting, they reached a suitable spot behind a stand of oaks.

"Is this aborigine deceased?" Sam asked.

Bowie knelt quickly beside the man, feeling for a pulse.

"Not quite," Bowie said. "When you get around to hitting a man, you do a good job of it."

"Forgive me if I do not consider that a compliment."

Bowie took a moment to study the man who had so nearly ended his life. Aside from a dirty breechcloth, the savage wore only a necklace of shells and a wristband of soiled deerskin. Unlike the first warrior he'd seen, this one's hair was thin, and reached only to his neck. The blue circles on his cheekbones were joined by more blue lines, extending from the corners of his eyes and mouth, and downward over his chin. More designs in blue and black ran down his arms and across his chest.

The fellow's skin glistened with more than sweat. He was covered with the rancid animal fat Bowie had discovered in the hut.

"From the Carcharhinidae family," Sam said. "Primitive peoples have been known to apply it as an insect repellent."

When Bowie just frowned, Sam added, "Shark fat."

Leaves rustled nearby, and Bowie peered anxiously into the surrounding trees. Had he caught a glimpse of jaguar hide, or were his eyes playing tricks?

Hearing no further sounds, he looked thoughtfully up at Sam. "Why, Mr. Gideon? Why did you help me?"

"I have hopes of returning to civilization," the man said, "and your ship offers the best opportunity."

"Oh." Bowie felt somehow deflated.

"And," Sam said, "despite your dreams of avarice, I judge you to be a reasonably honorable man. The world may be marginally better off with you than without."

A tart response was on Bowie's lips before he noticed the man's impish grin.

"You realize what this means, don't you?"

"That we of the black race are no less violent than our inferiors?"

"It means," Bowie said, "that you just saved my life. By my reckoning, you've more than earned your freedom."

Sam nodded gravely. "I must agree, and happily accept."

Bowie felt a sudden release, as if it were he, not Sam, who had just gained his liberty. "So. As a free man, what are your plans? A return to Matagorda, and the ship?"

"Perhaps. But not immediately. I must confess I find this treasure talk intriguing. I believe I may stay and claim a share for myself."

Bowie grinned. "Which proves, of course, that you of the black race are just as greedy as the rest of us."

"Perhaps." Sam said softly, and displayed the most genuine smile Bowie had yet seen from him.

"But first," Bowie whispered, "we have to get Mariette back. Are you willing to help?"

"I insist upon it."

"Then you can begin by trussing this fellow up tight as a turkey."

"And what will you be doing, if I may ask?"

"Making preparations. I believe I have a plan."

Sam looked at him curiously. "Is it cunning, dastardly and dangerous?"

"All of that," Bowie said, "and then some."

"Dangerous for you, or for me?"

"Me, mostly."

"In that case," Sam said, "I most heartily approve."

CHAPTER 50

"Cap'n Renato! Save us!"

RENATO LEANED AGAINST the trunk of an ancient oak, breath growling in his chest. Eight hours alone in the wilds, wary of every sound and sign, was an experience totally alien to him. He'd been born to skim over the sea, not crawl upon the land like a worm.

While LaChaise and the others had been caught flat-footed by the Kronks, Renato had lain prone in the brush for nearly an hour, barely venturing to breathe.

Circling west of the village, he'd finally been rewarded by the image of a snake cut high on the trunk of a great live oak. The second tree. Somewhat rejuvenated, he had moved south, finding the fish—a hundred yards from the edge of the Indian camp.

Now, north of the village, he'd at last come upon the sign of the bird cut deep into the bark of an elm.

He now had the final piece of the puzzle. Having already plotted the line between the bird and the fish, he now had merely to determine the line between the turtle and the snake.

The Kronks were busy gathering wood and brush near a hill not far from the camp. Atop the hill were two thick posts, at least eight feet tall, and Renato had no illusions as to their use.

He wished the Kronks had bound their prisoners' mouths as well as their limbs. The near constant praying of the Haitians was grating on his nerves, and he could only hope the pirates' shouts of "Cap'n Renato! Save us!" were thought directed at some white man's deity.

Feeling safe for the moment, he sought to relocate the turtle tree. The line between the fish and the bird had run directly through the village, offering the troubling possibility that the treasure lay somewhere beneath. He hoped the bisecting line between the turtle and the snake would place the treasure out of the camp but away from the gathered Indians.

At the edge of the village, a hundred or more yards from the hill, stood the strange structure he had noticed before. He stared at it, shaking his head at the madness of man. For what purpose could these savages have erected a giant steeple of logs?

Continuing his search, he was puzzled that the turtle tree could elude him. He had kept it in sight earlier, but now it was nowhere to be found. Shaking his head, he passed to the other side of the crude steeple.

And there it was. A curse escaped his lips. The turtle was directly across the clearing from where he now stood. He had not seen it from the snake tree because the log structure had been in the way. Which meant, of course, that the steeple was directly between the markers. The line between the first two trees had likewise passed through the steeple, so there was now no doubt. Either the treasure had been buried inside the building, or—more likely—the building had been erected over the burial site.

Savage voices carried from the hill. Men applied torches to opposite sides of the ring of brush, and the two fires raced to meet each other. Within seconds a flaming circle surrounded the posts.

As if on cue, a figure in fantastic dress stepped into view. The man—if indeed it *was* a man—wore a flowing cloak of feathers, and as he moved, a rainbow of colors shimmered in the firelight. Atop his shoulders sat a nightmarish green head, twice as large as a man's, and fashioned in the shape of a reptile.

Renato knew what was coming next, and cursed his luck. Much as he would have enjoyed this rare entertainment, he must use the distraction to investigate the treasure site.

Tearing his eyes from the scene, Renato scurried crablike toward the steeple. But he froze as a voice boomed over the clearing, and the snake-headed man came marching toward the village, followed by two torchbearers.

Renato swallowed his curses. His only chance was to scuttle back the way he'd come, praying the savages were too caught up in their pageantry to notice him.

Staying low to the ground, he ran, expecting an angry shout or a twanging bowstring. But he made the edge of the clearing and galloped another twenty yards before tripping over a log and crashing into a thicket.

If the savages had not seen his retreat, they had surely heard his fall. He peered through the brush to see one of the torch-bearers pointing excitedly in his direction.

Renato shivered, ready to bolt deeper into the night. The odds of evading these savages on their home ground were slim, but he'd grope at any chance to avoid becoming their dinner.

CHAPTER 51

"I'm sorry."

BOWIE HAD SEEN something move. A hunched, gray shape running in fits and starts against the darker gray of the night. And it was no ghost, unless ghosts trampled through the brush as loudly as living beings.

One of the torchbearers accompanying the advancing priest had heard this too, and clearly wished to investigate. Bowie hoped he would. He'd be more comfortable knowing the supposed ghost had been laid permanently to rest.

Bowie lay behind a clump of acacia near the southern edge of camp, trying not to squirm. After shedding his civilized clothing—and making other adjustments to his appearance—he'd taken a cue from the Kronks and applied shark fat liberally over his body. He couldn't decide which was worse—the insects or the stench.

The torchbearer drew a long-tongued dagger and started toward the edge of the clearing. Almost immediately, Bowie heard a crackle of brush, and a peculiar, whinny-like sound issued from the darkness.

Bowie knew that sound, the cry of a screech owl, and though he did not see the bird itself, the cry faded off into the distance.

The warrior stopped, shaking his head, while his fellow torchbearer laughed. The man loped back to his companions, and the three resumed their stately march toward the village.

Bowie stared off toward the brush. Had this been another

deception? He could not say, but he was certain the gray shape he'd seen had been neither an owl nor a jaguar.

The Indians' course had taken them directly to the tepee-like structure at the edge of camp. Here they stopped, the priest ducking inside.

Meanwhile, cheers and jeers went up from the group around the fire. Two bound men were being dragged toward the stakes. One was a hulking, pinch-faced pirate, while the other was the largest of the black men. The Kronks invariably chose the strongest of their enemies to devour first, deeming them the greatest source of power.

The noise from the hill was horrendous. The black man chanted, the pirate spat a string of sulfurous oaths, and the audience kept up a raucous yipping and cawing that would rival a Kentucky bear-baiting match.

Bowie's every instinct was to help the victims, but he steeled himself and focused on finding Mariette. Since her abduction, he felt as if his heart had been ripped from his body, and he would not be whole again until she was back at his side.

"I'm sorry," he whispered, but whether to the men tied to the stakes or to himself, he could not say.

After a short time, the priest emerged from the log tower, lugging something extremely heavy. A man squatted to assist him, and in the flickering light, Bowie caught a brief flash of gold. From inside the building, the other warrior produced a long straight pole. After much grunting, the pole rose into the air high above the priest's head, and the three men began a slow march back toward the fire.

In the light of the torches, the purpose of the pole became clear. Riding its peak was a bizarre golden statue, more than two feet in height. At the top was the head of a serpent ringed with rows of carved feathers. The lower portion coiled in tight curves, like the body of a snake.

The similarity to the priest's costume was unmistakable.

As the procession neared the fire, the main body of Indians

fell silent, prostrating themselves before the idol. The priest and his escorts passed into the circle of fire, and there, between the staked prisoners, transferred the pole to a hole in the earth.

The priest raised his arms, his feathered cloak forming two great shimmering wings. From his lips came a low, haunting chant, rising steadily until it reached a shriek.

Bowie growled. He had no desire to witness what was coming next. He was about to resume his search when he caught another flash of motion—a blur of gray flitting from hut to hut in the direction of the giant tepee.

Could it be Mariette—or whoever had taken her? He had to know. He had a duty to the girl, and a need to reclaim something of his lost self.

The dark figure appeared again, merging at last with the darkness of the great tepee.

With a grim smile, he drew the knife from its sheath and waited for the figure to reappear.

CHAPTER 52

"My destiny awaits."

HEART RACING, RENATO pressed his back against the dark side of the steeple. Another close call. And yet, here he stood, on the threshold of his destiny. What an ordinary man might perceive as luck, Renato recognized as the workings of Fate. This was his treasure, and this was his time.

His one regret was that the Kronks had made off with that golden statue. It must represent only a small portion of the riches taken from the *Lady of Cadiz*, but Renato wanted it all. Once the main body of loot had been secured, he would find a way to recover the statue as well.

Whoops of excitement echoed from the hill, and Renato saw the priest approaching LaChaise with a dagger. The savages howled their approval, while the black on the other stake stood stoically, seemingly unafraid. On any other day, Renato would have paid much for such entertainment. But not today. Not with the wealth of kings within his grasp.

Lifting the leather flap, he ducked his head and stepped inside.

BOWIE CROUCHED LOW beside a grass hut. A full minute had passed, and the figure had not reappeared. Who was this intruder? And was it possible he bore the scowling face of Pacal?

Howls of delight erupted from the campfire as the priest in the robe-of-many-colors danced close to the big pirate, his dagger flashing in the firelight. Blood spurted, and the pirate bellowed like a bull elk.

Bowie turned away. He had to find Mariette, before he and all his party suffered the same fate.

He was still troubled by the existence of this strange structure, but if the savages were holding another captive, this seemed a likely prison.

Drawing strength from the knife in his hand, he moved silent as a shadow toward the great teepee.

JUST INSIDE THE steeple, Renato stood transfixed. Moonlight filtered through the cracks to illuminate a bizarre scene.

Fixed to the walls were canvasses of stretched deer hide bearing images of fantastic beasts. To his painter's eye the execution was childlike, but all depicted snakes with feathers, aping the design of the golden statue.

What fired his blood was the object on an altar in the center of the room. A lacquered ebony chest, lavishly trimmed in gold.

Renato's pulse thundered in his temples. This was the chest that had haunted his dreams—the prize he had seen transferred from the *Lady of Cadiz* to Lafitte's ship. The chest was smaller than he remembered, but large enough to hold more diamonds, rubies and emeralds than he had ever imagined.

Slowly, almost reverently, he reached for the golden latch. His fingers had just brushed metal when his nose began to twitch. A rancid odor, growing stronger by the second. He knew that smell. Karankawa!

Focusing on the cracks between the logs, he saw a dark form pass the side of the building. He flattened himself next to the entrance, hand gripping a Spanish dagger that had already sent a score of men to meet the Devil.

"Come join them," Renato said without sound. "My destiny awaits."

BOWIE PAUSED, HAND on the deerskin flap. He'd heard a scuffling from somewhere in the village. The sound came again, closer. And there, sharp in the moonlight, he beheld the scowling face.

For an instant, he was so shocked he nearly dropped his knife. Then the face ducked behind a hut and was gone. But the image remained fixed in his mind. Flat features, a squarish head, and an expression of extreme disdain. The face of Pacal.

It was impossible. But whoever or whatever this thing was, it may have knowledge of Mariette's whereabouts. Anything solid enough to scowl at him could be pricked with a knife. And he had just the knife for the job.

SEEING THE DARK shape glide away, Renato moved quickly to the ebony chest, grasping the lid in both hands. Heart hammering, he raised the lid and peered inside.

And stared in disbelief.

The chest held nothing but a purple velvet cushion—a cushion with the unmistakable imprint of the golden statue now raised above the Indians' ring of fire.

So the idol was indeed a part of his treasure. But it could not possibly be all. He thrust his hands deep into the box, rummaging beneath the cushion. There must be more. *There must.*

But there was not. Nothing but the bare boards of the chest.

In a berserk fury, Renato sent the chest crashing to the ground. He knocked over the stump that had formed the altar, and clawed the crude paintings from the wall.

A snarl tearing at the back of his throat, he fell to his knees and began clawing at the earth with his bare hands.

BOWIE CIRCLED THE hut where he had seen the face, finding nothing. Where moonlight touched the earth, he discerned the imprint of short, wide feet at the base of the hut, but the tracks led off into utter darkness, impossible to follow.

New cries erupted from the hill. The priest's blade flashed

again toward the pirate. As the man writhed and roared, the priest plucked a glistening red mass from his victim's chest.

Bowie tried to look away, but he, too, seemed bound in place. Raising the grisly trophy high over his head, the priest lowered it to his mouth, ripping off a portion with his teeth.

A sharp sound behind him, almost a laugh, brought Bowie spinning to see a dark form flit away deeper into the camp. He surged after it, but had taken no more than a stride when another sound, this time a definite cackle, came from the hut he had just left. A scowling face regarded him from the opposite side—and just as quickly, it was gone.

Bowie swore under his breath. To chase these phantoms was folly. The only person he really sought was Mariette, and the most likely place to find her remained the giant teepee.

CHAPTER 53

"Find your tongue, or lose it."

THE EARTH WAS not hard, but the digging was difficult. The sandy dirt slid back into the hole as fast as Renato could scoop it out.

So consumed was he that he did not immediately register the smell. There was no gradual strengthening of scent, as before. By the time he noticed it, the rancid odor filled the entire enclosure. He was no longer alone.

Continuing to dig, he scraped a handful of sand close to his waist. Quick as a snake, he tore the dagger from his belt and swept the blade in a wide arc behind him. With it went the handful of sand, straight for the intruder's face.

With seeming ease, the man stepped out of range, allowing the dagger to sweep past, then moved back in, catching Renato's wrist in a grip of iron.

Renato took stock of his opponent. He was a wide-shouldered brute, even for a Kronk, with a deep chest and a flat, hard stomach. Like others of his tribe, blue lines and circles decorated his face and body, and he was naked save for a dirty breechcloth and a primitive necklace tight about his throat. But instead of the usual long braids, this man's hair was cut in almost civilized fashion. His eyes glared hate from under heavy brows. He was altogether one of the meanest looking savages Renato had ever seen.

BOWIE WONDERED IF he were truly awake, or trapped in some mad nightmare. Having just been taunted by

288

a ghost, he now faced a creature without a face, a monster with eyes like two hot coals that seared into his soul. He'd scoffed at tales of things from beyond the grave, but here was just such a horror, armed with a dagger and possessed of uncanny fighting skills.

The man's mottled face appeared to have been melted half away, leaving only scraps of charred flesh and hair attached to the bone. It was a wonder the man was able to see and breathe, let alone fight.

Rising from his knees, the horror aimed a boot at the Bowie's midsection. Quick as lightning, Bowie's knife slashed through leather, the horror let out a screech, and the boot was quickly withdrawn.

RENATO GOGGLED AT the knife. The blade alone was half the length of a man's arm, and deadly as a razor.

The Indian's teeth were bared in a grimace. They were white and perfectly formed, and Renato could easily imagine them tearing into his liver.

Delivering a vicious head butt, he tore his wrist loose and swept his dagger toward the Indian's belly.

Incredibly, the savage anticipated the move, catching Renato's blade on his own. For long seconds, they stood face-to-face, noses nearly touching. The Indian had pale blue eyes, indicating a touch of white ancestry. Those eyes burned with an intensity Renato had rarely seen except in a mirror.

His dagger caught, Renato sought to draw his sword. But again, the man was too quick, pinning his arm to his side. He felt his bones grind together in the savage's powerful grip.

Then the Indian spoke.

"I don't wish to kill you," he said, speaking English with a Southern drawl. "All I want is the white girl."

Stunned, Renato could only repeat, "White girl?"

"Black hair. Brown skirt. Her name is Mariette."

Mariette. Andre's daughter. *The map thief.* "How could you

know…" He studied the man's features more closely. The wide forehead, heavy brows, the fierce blue eyes, and most of all—the deeply cleft chin.

Realization flooded through him. His brother Rayón screamed from beyond the grave. One word escaped his lips, both a name and a curse.

"Bowie!"

BOWIE NEARLY LOST his grip.

He had not expected his disguise to bear close scrutiny, but that this blackened creature—appearing more dead than alive—should guess his identity, smacked of the supernatural.

Then the monster spoke, in a voice as noxious as its appearance. "You murdered Rayón, and you shall pay the price."

Rayón! This, then, was not a ghoul, but one of Renato's crew.

In one swift motion, he freed his knife and pressed it tight beneath the pirate's chin. A thin stream of blood coursed down the length of the shining blade.

"Where is Renato? Speak quickly or die."

The man stared at him, his expression impossible to read.

"Find your tongue, man, or lose it."

To Bowie's astonishment, the pirate began to laugh. The laugh had a bitter, mocking quality that made him want to slit the rogue's throat and be done with it. But something stayed his hand.

"Aye!" the pirate said. "I can tell you where Renato is. But you may not like the answer."

"Liking has nothing to do with it. Where is he?"

"He's just outside. Release me and I'll show you."

Wary of a trick, Bowie held the knife in place. Stepping behind the fellow, he relieved him of the dagger and guided him toward the doorway.

Once outside, the lipless mouth appeared to be smiling at him. "I'll keep my bargain. Release me, and I'll deliver Renato to you."

Bowie withdrew the blade from the pirate's throat, holding it steady. At the first sign of treachery, he would lop the fellow's head off.

"Now. Where is he? And who are you?"

"He is here," the pirate said with a flash of blackened teeth, "and I am he!"

As Bowie gaped, the man darted just out of reach, and a hand flashed to his waist, drawing a cutlass.

Bowie jumped back, the blade missing his throat by inches. It was only then, when his wits became unstuck, that the meaning of the man's words reached him.

This living nightmare was Renato himself!

RENATO COULD NOT believe his luck. Bowie had been stupid enough to allow him into the open. And now the murderer of Rayón stood before him armed with only a knife, while he, the greatest swordsman on this side of the world, held his favorite cutlass.

A feint for the groin caused Bowie to lower his blade, and a quick thrust bit deep into his shoulder. Bowie grunted, ducking the riposte meant for his head, and assumed a fencer's stance, presenting the knife as if it, too, were a sword.

Renato grinned. This would be child's play.

"*En garde.*" Renato pressed forward, his blade weaving a steel curtain before him. No man had ever survived such an attack, and this American clodhopper would be no exception.

BOWIE RETREATED BEFORE the flashing blade. He blocked a thrust and lunged for the heart, but Renato recovered, and the two blades clanged together, sending bright sparks into the night.

Bowie continued to parry, watching for an opening, but Renato was canny enough to present no such opportunity. It was press and press again, allowing him no chance to counter. He had to try something else.

"You begin to bore me," he said with feigned nonchalance.

"You are even less skilled than your poxy brother, whom I gutted like a fish."

Renato's eyes flared. His careful attack exploded into savagery, pressing his full weight into every hacking swing.

Choosing his moment, Bowie dropped his guard, presenting an irresistible target. Renato took the bait, his cutlass whistling down like a butcher's cleaver—and Bowie sidestepped, catching the blade on his own.

The force of the blow nearly tore the knife from Bowie's hand, but he twisted upward, locking the two weapons together. With a final twist, the sword came free of Renato's hand. But sweat had washed shark fat down Bowie's arm, making his fingers slippery, and he lost his own grip as well.

Both weapons sailed off into the darkness.

HIS CUTLASS GONE, Renato flew at Bowie bare-handed. With the spirit of Rayón coursing through him, he possessed the strength of two men. He caught Bowie in a bear hug, lifting him from his feet. A fierce lunge sent him toppling backward, where they thumped heavily to the earth.

Renato groped for a stranglehold. Pinned beneath him lay the butcher of Rayón. He had sworn vengeance on his brother's grave, and that vengeance was finally at hand.

WITH RENATO'S FINGERS clawing at his throat, Bowie kicked and heaved. Now he was on top, then again on the bottom, as he and the pirate rolled frantically about, battling fang and claw like savage beasts.

Gone were thoughts of Mariette, Pacal, the Indians and the gold. His world was a red storm of rage. Hovering behind Renato's twisted face was the pitiful image of the blonde girl, spurring him to greater fury. Each blow he delivered was for her. Each gouge, bite and kick carried her wrath along with his own.

A great roaring filled his ears, as if a host of Renato's other victims had joined the girl, urging him on to the kill.

RENATO HEARD THE shouting through a crimson haze. He clamped his hands to Bowie's face, thumbs probing for the eye sockets. In a moment the man would be blind, and he'd have the gibbering fool at his mercy.

A hand clamped about his forearm, and he almost lost his grip. Then someone grasped his other arm, and he was lifted bodily into the air. Snarling, he turned to see who dared interrupt his vengeance. And his stomach fell.

Ringed close about him, eyes gleaming from painted faces, stood a score of Karankawa warriors.

Renato attempted a smile, and a man smote him heavily in the chest, jabbering in his savage tongue. He was being questioned, but the words meant nothing to him. Voice rising, the Indian struck him again, his tone even more demanding.

Bowie, meanwhile, was pulled to his feet by a pair of warriors. But instead of confining him, they treated him with consideration. The reason hit Renato like a blow. These ignorant savages thought him one of their own!

Nodding sheepishly, Bowie turned away, slipping through the ring of warriors.

"Stop him!" Renato shouted. "He's an impostor! He's a white man!"

The Kronks cocked their heads, examining him like a peculiar insect, and Renato realized his mistake. He'd been speaking English. The only civilized tongue these creatures had was the Spanish taught at missions.

He opened his mouth to try again, but a warrior lashed out, delivering a backhand blow to his jaw.

After that, Renato knew no more.

BOWIE EASED THROUGH gaps in the crowd, chin pressed to his chest.

No one had attempted to slow his progress. A few more yards and he would reach the edge of the group, and from there it would be an easy lope into the outer darkness.

He'd nearly reached his goal when a young woman stepped into his path. She was short, with wide hips and fat breasts. Bowie tried to slide past her, but she moved with him, running a smooth hand down his arm. He could go no further without bowling her over.

The girl spoke a few soft words, her tone warm and coy. Good God, she was flirting with him!

Grunting his appreciation, he tried to step past her.

Before he could escape, she wrapped both hands about his arm and clung to him. Stretching up, she whispered words doubtless intended to fire his blood.

When he failed to respond, she spat an ugly word and released him. Then she stopped, staring from her blue palms to his pale skin.

Throwing herself on him, she cried out, calling for help.

And before he could shake her off, Bowie found himself surrounded by a dozen angry warriors.

CHAPTER 54

"You and I are much alike."

RENATO AWAKENED TO pain, a thing to which he had become accustomed. But now, his ears rang with ghastly screams, and the burns on his face and body seared as if he were being barbecued over a campfire.

He cracked his eyes open, fighting the sting of smoke. Beyond the flames, demonic faces bobbed in and out of the darkness.

Once before Renato had awoken to believe himself in Hell. This time he found the notion harder to dispel. Then he saw the fantastic figure in the feathered cloak and snake mask prancing about with a bloody dagger, and he remembered. The empty treasure chest, the fight with Bowie in disguise, and his capture by the savages while Bowie slithered away.

He knew precisely where he was, and wished he were in Hell after all. He stood bound to a stake at the center of the Karankawa fire ceremony. He had seen LaChaise struggling on this very stake, and knew it could not be dislodged.

The flames were a good two yards away, apparently not intended for cooking, but the heat was intense.

From the post above him, the hideous idol glowed like a thing alive. It mocked him now, as if it alone knew the secret of the treasure, and it alone had guided him here to his doom. He had failed at every task. Failed to avenge his brother. Failed to destroy Andre and his daughter. And worst of all, failed to secure the treasure that was his destiny. He had trusted to the Fates, and they had abandoned him.

He rolled his head, expecting to see a slave at the other stake. And got a shock. Because bound there, every bit as helpless as he, was the murderous bastard Bowie.

Bowie glowered at him, and Renato returned the look in full measure. The man's chest heaved, his arms swelled, and his entire body quaked as he strained against his bonds.

"Should I get free," Bowie roared above the noise, "you won't have to worry about the Kronks!"

Despite himself, Renato was impressed. The man's ferocity was almost akin to his own.

"I am forced to admit," he shouted, "that while you could never hope to be my equal, you and I are much alike."

BOWIE COULD NOT believe his ears.

"Alike? You're mad! I am nothing like you!"

"Face it!" Renato shouted back. "You're nothing but a land-bound buccaneer, gutting those who stand in your way! You are as much a pirate as I—merely much less successful!"

Bowie was stunned at this effrontery, not least by the niggling feeling there was truth in the charge.

He slumped against the stake, his fury spent. Whatever the truth, it was too late to redeem himself.

Renato had apparently lost interest in him, his eyes fixed on the golden idol. How like the man—that even now, when any moment might be his last—his thoughts were for the riches he desired above all else.

Bowie himself had all but forgotten the treasure. His concern for Mariette's safety had pushed such thoughts away.

The feather-clad priest pirouetted before him, cloak swirling as if about to take wing and fly. Passing his dagger through the flames, he lashed out, and Bowie felt white-hot agony blaze across his chest.

Renato's face lit with something akin to ecstasy, and Bowie clenched his teeth, choking back the pain. He would not give Renato the satisfaction of a scream.

RENATO GLOATED AS Bowie's face became a mask of pain. Blood poured over the man's belly, down his legs. It was almost worth being caught, to have such a fine view of the man's torment.

Still, unless Fate provided another chance, Renato would be the next to die. Might there be a chance? There was no one left to rescue him but Quayle and the men on *Medusa*.

Impossible as it was, the thought had given him hope, and Renato clung to it like a drowning man.

"Quayle!" he bellowed. "What are you waiting for? Attack!"

The snake man, dagger poised for another cut at Bowie, turned to Renato instead.

"Quayle, damn your eyes! Where are you?"

The dagger tore through Renato's already aching flesh, and a scream exploded into his lungs. His mouth filled with sound, but he kept his lips clamped shut. He could not show weakness where Bowie had not.

Through the pain, he saw the truth of things. Quayle was not coming, and even if he did, he'd find nothing but charred and discarded bones.

RENATO'S SHOUTS HAD given Bowie a momentary reprieve, but the priest was already returning, eager to carve a steak from his gizzard.

Something told Bowie this would be the crucial blow. Dark eyes gleamed through the snake mask. The dagger passed through the flames, and began to rise.

The earth seemed to tremble, a sound he could only assume was the rushing of his own blood.

RENATO FOCUSED ON the priest, willing him to thrust his blade deep into Bowie's heart. Then he felt tremors beneath his feet, and his ear quivered as if from thunder. The Indians' howls diminished until even the priest turned to look.

Renato blinked. A huge creature came lumbering toward them. The thing was too big to be human, and the flame-red hair dancing about its head gave it every appearance of a super-natural being.

Murmurs of astonishment floated through the tribe. At the priest's command, six warriors rushed to flank the giant, spears at the ready. The creature strode past them as if they were so many shoots of grass.

As the giant came nearer, Renato saw he pulled three captives behind him on a rope.

The first was a lanky, broad-shouldered black man, clearly no Haitian. Next was one of Renato's own crew—a sniveling cur known as Sharky. He'd last seen the man before the explosion on *L'Intrepide*, and recalled his own delight in assuming the wretch had been lost at sea.

But it was the sight of the turtle-like figure in the rear that brought Renato's blood to a boil.

Andre! Andre the traitor. *Andre the thief.*

BOWIE'S HOPES SOARED as big Strap Buckner approached the fire, but the sight of his captives caused his jaw to drop, along with his prospects.

At the priest's shout, Buckner rolled to a halt and stood smiling at him. He replied in Spanish, his voice betraying no hint of fear.

"You know me, great chief. I am called Kokulblothetopoff, which in the white man's tongue means Red Son of Blue Thunder."

The priest answered with a noncommittal grunt.

"I come to the Karankawa in peace. The settlers of this region wish no trouble with your people."

Several warriors snorted.

"I speak truth," Buckner insisted. "These men are foul pirates, enemies of the white settlers as well as yourself. They have brought anger and strife among us, and deserve what punishment they receive."

"You have killed many of our people," the priest replied. "You are our fiercest enemy."

Buckner nodded. "I have fought your people, it is true. But I now wish peace between us. As proof, I bring this gift." He paused, sweeping an arm behind him. "I caught these three pirates sneaking into your territory, plotting devilment. They are yours to do with as you will."

Bowie could take no more. "Damn you, Buckner!" he roared in English. "Sam's no more a pirate than I! And these others are no threat to anyone. How can you betray us to these cannibals?"

Buckner turned slowly, bringing the full weight of his glare upon him. "You were warned. You were told not to come here and disrupt the peace. What happens to you now is on your own head."

Buckner spoke with such scorn that Bowie was taken completely aback. He wished he had his knife—and half a minute of freedom—to repay this treachery. But the blade hung at the hip of one of his guards, and he would never hold it again.

The priest said, "I know the ways of the white man. You expect something in return."

Buckner nodded. "You are wise indeed. I ask a single favor— the release of the white woman, she of the slim shape and raven hair."

The priest addressed his tribe in their own tongue, receiving brief replies.

Bowie's hopes rose. If Mariette were freed, it would ease his guilt, and his passing.

"You are mistaken," the priest replied. "There is no white female among us."

The big man's brow clouded, his shoulders quivered, and he seemed about to erupt like a volcano. Finally, he got himself under control. "If you speak it, great chief, it must be so."

The Kronks were renowned liars, but Bowie's instincts told him the priest was telling the truth. That Mariette was not in the hands of cannibals was a blessing, but who had taken her, and why? And where the devil was she now?

The same questions were obviously working their way through Strap Buckner's brain. Having said his piece, he stood his ground as if he had no notion what to do next.

The priest snapped another command, and a large shape moved along the outer edge of the gathering. The warriors flanking Buckner grinned and rolled their eyes.

Bowie himself almost smiled as a young Indian woman stepped timidly into the light. Despite her obvious youth, she had the height to equal—and girth to dwarf—any of the Karankawa warriors. Compared to Buckner she was almost petite, but by any normal standard she was huge, with wide hips, a broad belly and breasts the size of powder kegs.

"A man needs a woman to warm his hut," intoned the priest. "As token of our bargain, we give you Tulipita, which in our language means Little Flower."

Buckner gulped so loud Bowie thought he'd swallowed his tongue. A single drop of sweat, big as a goose egg, appeared on his brow and ran its course down his cheek.

"I am honored," he said at last, his voice a croak.

The priest nodded, and a warrior took the rope from Buckner's hand, yanking the prisoners forward.

Bowie tried to catch Andre's eye, but the man kept his head down. Sam, likewise, averted his face, and Sharky cringed so low his elbows scraped the ground. The three were herded quickly though the gaps in the circle, and out the other side.

Without another glance at Bowie, Buckner strode back toward the village, the commodious Little Flower close upon his heels. The warriors behind had to leap aside, as he did not slow, or even seem to notice them, and he and the girl were soon swallowed by the darkness.

CHAPTER 55

"You prefer that thing to me?"

RENATO WAS UNSURE what surprised him
more—that the giant had walked unarmed into a swarm
of murderous savages, or that the savages had let him leave,
presenting him with a woman to boot.

But one fact was not lost upon him. The Kronks could be
bargained with.

"Great chief," he said in Spanish, "I too have come in friendship. Like your big friend, I wish to offer gifts."

The snake priest turned, examining him through the slits in
his mask. For the first time, the man's dagger lay loose in his
hand, and his stance was not threatening.

Renato felt heartened to continue. "I, too, offer sacrifices. A
half dozen or more, waiting upon my ship. In exchange for my
freedom, I will gladly deliver them to you."

The priest grunted, which seemed his all-purpose response.
Renato wondered if his offer had been accepted, but did not
wonder long. The Indian raised his dagger and brought the hilt
swiftly down, striking him a savage blow on the bridge of the
nose.

BOWIE HEARD RENATO'S spiel, and the resulting
yelp of pain, without giving it much attention. His mind still
reeled at the enormity of Buckner's betrayal.

Could the man have been motivated by his infatuation with
Mariette? He found this hard to credit, but stranger things had
been done in the name of love.

He shook the thoughts away. It would be only moments before the festivities resumed. The best he could hope was to die in a manner befitting his legend.

But did that really matter? Who would tell the world how the famous James Bowie met his end? Not the Indians, surely. And if Strap Buckner were still in the area, he would keep silent to hide his complicity. That left only Mariette. Might she be watching, and somehow escape? That was a hope he could cling to, the only hope left to him now.

Bowie gazed calmly at the grim mask of the priest. He no longer felt fear. Even his anger had drained away. All he had left was regret, and a calm certainty that his time had come.

RENATO'S NOSE HURT like the very devil, but so did every other part of his body. All that mattered was the pleasure of witnessing Bowie's death before facing his own.

Strangely, Bowie almost seemed to smile. Either the oaf was too dull-witted to be afraid, or had become completely unhinged.

Then came a change in the air. A false note penetrated the screams, something that spoke of shock and alarm.

Renato pushed the sound aside, willing the priest to act. Instead, the man turned to face the village.

Well beyond the circle of fire, other blazes added their brilliance to the night. Even as Renato watched, more flames sprang up out of the darkness.

The camp was catching fire!

BOWIE COULD NOT believe his eyes. At least half a dozen huts were in full blaze, with others flaring up as if by magic. The Indians jumped to their feet *en masse* and rushed away toward the camp.

Barking a command to his guards, the priest raced after them, his feathered cloak swirling behind. Save for the guards, Bowie and Renato were now alone.

"Andre!" Bowie shouted. "Sam! Are you alright?"

"More than alright, Jim Boy." Andre's voice came from the patch of darkness beyond the flames. "Give us a moment."

Growling, the guard with Bowie's knife stalked toward him. Then something hissed out of the night. The man made a gurgling sound and fell on his face in the dirt, a long shaft quivering from his back. The second guard scarcely had time to shout before he too jerked and sank to the earth.

And into the circle burst a small brown man in a jaguar-skin tunic.

Bowie's scalp prickled. Pacal! *Pacal, or his ghost.*

But close upon his heels came a second figure, nearly identical to the first. *Two* Pacals. The same wide faces, the same flattened skulls. Then from behind them came two more. And for the first time in his life, Bowie truly doubted his sanity.

RENATO PROBED HIS memory. There was something familiar about these repellent little men.

Two of the newcomers shimmied up the post holding the golden idol, while the others worked at the base, straining to tip the pole backward. Their intent was clear. They meant to dislodge the statue from its perch and make off with it.

"Stop!" Renato roared. "That thing belongs to me!"

The brown men spared him not a glance. Seething, he switched to Spanish. "That's my treasure! Mine by right of battle!" At the words, the image of the ebony chest from the *Lady of Cadiz* flashed through his mind. And with it, the memory of the small brown captive Lafitte had taken from the Spanish. In some bizarre fashion, these creatures were connected to his treasure.

"Which of you was aboard the *Lady of Cadiz*?" he demanded. "Which of you knew that bastard Lafitte?"

Then still another figure ran into the circle, and Renato nearly went mad.

"Bitch!" he screamed. "Whore!"

BOWIE HAD LONGED for just this vision, and feared it might be an illusion. But as soft hands caressed his face and a tender voice spoke in his ear, he ceased to care.

"James, I am so sorry."

Mariette's hair was tangled and matted, her blouse gray with dust and her skirt smeared with mud. If she were a vision, she would look better than this. *She must be real.*

"Mariette. I tried to—"

"I know, James, I know." She pressed her mouth to his, and her lips were delicious.

Between kisses he gasped, "Mariette, that Indian at your feet. He has my knife."

"Your *knife?*" Her tone hardened. "You still prefer that thing to me?"

"Of course not. Just cut my bonds. Quickly."

Mariette made no move toward the blade. Bowie feared she might be in shock.

"Please," he said gently. "Hurry."

An odd look came into her eyes. "James, I—" her voice broke, and she pressed fingers to her temples.

Bowie fought the impulse to shout. The Kronks could return at any moment. "Mariette," he said, with all the tenderness he could muster, "I want to live. All the more now that you and I…"

Bowie found himself unable to finish. Her eyes were wide and wet. She caught at her throat and nodded as if reaching a decision. As she retrieved the knife, the blade caught reflections from every side, flickering like a flame in her hand.

She moved to step behind him, but jerked to a halt, her arm caught in a fierce grip. The knife fell to the earth.

Bowie looked past her into a scowling brown face. *Pacal.* And this was no ghost, but the little madman in the flesh.

While the four men in jaguar skins resembled him, their faces were smoother and softer—younger versions of the man

Bowie knew. This one's chest was bare and his trousers torn, but he showed no sign of having been ravaged by a jaguar.

RENATO WATCHED ENTHRALLED as Bowie went mad. The lout's lips peeled back in a grimace fierce as the rictus of death. His heels dug into the earth, shoulders bulging as he thrust his weight from side to side. Incredibly, the stake began to move.

The brown man clutching the girl spat a few harsh clicks, and the others redoubled their efforts on the post. In a matter of moments, it came crashing to earth. Two of the jaguar men scrambled to tug the idol free, while the others spread a length of animal hide on the ground. Rolling the statue onto the hide, they took a firm grip, lifting it between them.

With a grunt, the bare-chested man made for the rear of the circle, tugging the sobbing girl behind. But through the passage came Andre, who stood gaping at them.

Renato shouted, "Stop them, fool. They have your daughter!"

Andre looked from the brown men to Renato and back, confusion on his face.

Issuing a quick command, the leader spun on his heel, dragging the girl through the opposite side of the circle. Two men followed with the idol, while the others brandished daggers, forming a rear guard to discourage Andre.

The old man croaked, "Mariette!" But by then the five men and the girl had vanished into the night.

CHAPTER 56

"Should have told thee."

BOWIE STILL STRAINED against the stake. It had shifted, but not enough. He had failed Mariette once again.

Half the village roared with flames, the shrieks of women adding to the fury. Then new cries of rage rose from the men. The absconding of their idol had been noticed.

Someone was speaking to him.

"Jim Boy! Rouse yourself!"

"Andre?"

"I'm here, Jim. Time we was going."

Bowie's mind cleared. "My knife. She dropped it."

"Aye," Andre said. "I'm powerful sorry, Jim. Should have told thee everything."

Bowie squinted at him. *Everything?* But he said, "The knife, damn it. Quickly."

The old man scooped it from the ground. "Aye. But then, I owe thee the truth."

"Agreed. But later."

The whoops of angry Indians grew louder. Fully half the warriors had abandoned the village fires to chase the thieves.

Bowie felt the pressure of the blade as Andre applied it to the strips binding his wrists.

Then he heard a growl, and a bloody nightmare burst into the circle.

"LaChaise!" Renato shouted. "This way! Free me!"

It was the fist-faced pirate, the man the priest had cut to the bone. Bowie could see blood hemorrhaging from the great cavity in his chest, but still, unbelievably, he had the strength to walk. Heedless of Renato's cries, he barreled directly toward Andre.

And Bowie knew why.

"He's after the knife!"

Andre turned just as the brutish pirate slammed into him, and the two went down in a tangle of struggling limbs.

"LACHAISE!" RENATO WAS beside himself. "Belay that, damn you! Free me and I'll kill them myself!"

The two men grappled frantically in the dirt, kicking, gouging and snarling like wolves. With each turn, Bowie's blade flashed in the firelight, but Renato could not tell which man had control.

He found himself rooting for Andre to win. The old man would be less likely to butcher him where he stood.

"Kill the bastard, Andre! Slit his throat!"

An arm rose above the tangled bodies, the knife firmly in the grip of one man or the other. Then the blade fell like a streak of lightning. A hoarse voice cried out in agony.

After a moment, a hunched figure rose on unsteady legs, its face glaring at him with evil intensity.

"Good work, LaChaise!" Renato said quickly. "That scoundrel needed killing."

The crazed pirate raised the blade, a thing of blood and fire. Stepping over Andre's body, he shambled toward Renato.

"You've done me a great boon!" Renato's voice sounded alarmingly shrill. "You'll be justly rewarded!"

But LaChaise continued to advance, mouth twisted in a horrible sneer.

And Renato tasted fear.

ANDRE LAY GASPING at Bowie's feet, his lifeblood staining the earth.

Rage coursed through Bowie as he bucked against the stake, twisting his wrists against the partially cut leather.

The man called LaChaise had nearly reached Renato. Whether he meant to kill him or free him was unclear, but Bowie could not permit either. If Renato were freed, Bowie would be as good as dead. If Renato died by any other hand, the blonde girl would go unavenged, and Bowie would be haunted by her spirit forever.

The leather bit deep into his flesh, muscles swelling until fit to leap from his bones.

At last the cord snapped, and Bowie burst from the stake, hurtling onto LaChaise like a stampeding buffalo. The big pirate stumbled forward, the weight of both men slamming into Renato. As Renato cursed and squalled, Bowie locked an arm around the man's throat, straining to break his neck. But LaChaise jabbed backward with the bloody knife, and Bowie had to jump free.

LaChaise spun about, wheezing, blood pouring from his chest. His lips were flecked with red, proof not all the bleeding was on the outside.

The knife made a sweeping arc, and Bowie dropped into a squat, the blade cropping an inch from his hair. Springing up, his right hand caught the pirate's wrist. Clutching the elbow with his left, Bowie raised a leg and slammed the man's forearm down across his knee. The bones broke with an ugly crack, the knife slipping from limp fingers.

Plucking the handle from the air, Bowie felt a surge of energy. All his rage welled up within him, and he swung the blade like a scythe, cleaving through LaChaise's neck and passing out the other side. The big man's body hung a moment as if suspended before crashing to the dirt. His head flopped sideways, clinging to the trunk by a length of gristle.

Bowie sank to Andre's side. Sam was there, one hand propping the old man's head, the other pressed to a widening stain in his side. Andre's eyes flickered, and he drew breath in shallow, wet gasps.

Bowie gripped Andre's hand in his own. "Your killer will be in Hell to meet you."

Andre's lips seemed to grin. "Jim Boy. So sorry. Should have told thee long ago."

"Don't try to talk."

"Have to. Ye're a better man than I. Deserve to know the truth."

"The truth about what?"

"Pacal. The treasure. All of it."

"Don't strain. Just tell me what you can. What about Pacal?"

"He knows everything," Andre said. "Get him. Get the key."

"The key? What key?"

"That golden idol. The key to the treasure."

Bowie didn't know what to make of this, but found he didn't much care. "That's not important now. What matters is getting Mariette away from Pacal and his devils."

"Mariette. She's not—" Andre coughed wretchedly, blood foaming at his lips.

"You have my word, old man. I'll get her back. I swear it on my soul."

Andre squeezed his hand with new fervor, all his life force channeled into that grip. "Forgive me, Jim. Mariette, she's not…" Andre tried again, the effort costing him greatly, "not my daughter." He wanted to say more, but his breath bubbled and the words were lost. His eyes burned brightly a moment, then faded like the drawing of a curtain.

RENATO CURSED THE crackling flames and howling Indians that had obscured Andre's dying words. The possibility he had told Bowie something of the treasure's location spurred his fury to new heights.

Cradling Andre's head, the slave lowered him gently to the ground and stood, staring at Bowie with obvious concern.

After a moment, Bowie passed a hand over the old man's face, closing the vacant eyes. Another sign of weakness. Renato relished the look of dead, staring eyes. It still rankled that LaChaise had stolen his chance to send Andre on that last journey, but at least he'd been there to enjoy it.

The black man laid a hand on Bowie's shoulder. "Jim. Time we were going."

Jim! The slave called him Jim. Truly, Bowie's weakness knew no bounds.

The slave persisted. "We must think now of Mariette."

At the name, Bowie shook himself and pushed heavily to his feet. He turned from Andre to cast eyes upon the nearly headless corpse of LaChaise.

Renato caught only a portion of that scorching glare, but was almost glad his limbs were bound. Otherwise, much as he loathed to admit it, he'd have been tempted to run.

Then Bowie turned that same glare on Renato. When he spoke, his voice was like a death rattle. "We have unfinished business, you and I."

Renato put up a bold front. "That we do. And it can only be settled man to man."

Bowie growled, taking a step forward.

Renato said quickly, "So you'd kill a helpless man. As I thought, you've not a spark of honor."

Bowie's eyes were twin points of fire. "No honor is lost in slaying a rabid beast. Still, if it's a fight you want…"

"Jim!" The slave thrust himself between them. "This is not the time. Mariette needs us."

Bowie seemed about to swat the man aside. But the slave spoke again, his voice almost a whisper.

"She has no one else now."

Bowie's eyes cooled. "I'll deal with you later," he told Renato, "provided there's anything left of you."

"Coward," Renato snarled. "You've not the stomach to face me, now or ever."

Bowie bared his teeth, and Renato's hopes rose.

But the meddling slave clasped Bowie's shoulder, whispered, "Mariette," and the spell was broken.

Renato damned the Fates once again as Bowie turned and dashed from the circle, the black man at his heels.

CHAPTER 57

"An oaf with a pigsticker."

THE INDIANS' TORCHES flickered through the trees, moving rapidly in pursuit of Pacal and his lookalikes. Bowie could only follow, hoping to snatch Mariette away from one party or the other.

Sam, running close behind, said, "Why did the old man deem it vital to tell you Mariette was not his offspring?"

Bowie shook his head. Whoever she was, she needed help, and quickly. It was inconceivable she had been Andre's wife or mistress. And if she were some other relation, why would Andre lie?

A faint sound brought him to a halt. He peered into the darkness, hearing only the babble of a small stream.

Sam touched his arm, said, "One moment," and ran toward the sound. Bowie stood perplexed until the man returned, hands cupped before him.

"What—?" Bowie gasped as Sam slapped something cold and wet against his chest. The slash opened by the priest's dagger stung like hellfire, but after a moment the pain subsided to a small degree.

"A mud pack. We must halt the loss of blood, and prevent festering of your wounds."

Sam was right, of course. But Bowie heard himself say, "That's enough. Mariette's in trouble."

"And if you bleed to death, she will remain so. Cease your

squirming so I can finish." As he worked, Sam added, "I regret the death of your pirate friend. I had grown fond of him as well."

"He'll be missed," Bowie said shortly. It was too soon to voice his feelings. "How did you and he get free?"

Sam coughed. "Our capture was a ruse. Andre was in favor of more direct action, while Mr. Buckner felt we should simply extract Mariette and abandon you to the aborigines. But since we did not know her whereabouts, your somewhat obedient servant posed a stratagem he hoped would induce them to produce her."

Bowie eyed the man with new respect. "That showed a good deal of courage. I'm in your debt."

Sam nodded. "It was a fortunate byproduct that we were able to aid you in the process. Luckily, Mr. Buckner was not averse to starting that conflagration in the village."

"That was him? I've misjudged the man. But why is he 'Mr. Buckner,' when you insist on calling me 'Jim'?"

Sam's teeth gleamed in the moonlight. "When a man is the size of an elephant, I call him whatever he desires."

"DAMN YOUR EYES, Sharky. You'll free me at once, or I'll have you keelhauled!"

The little weasel had come stumbling out of the brush shortly after Bowie's departure, still whimpering something about demons. From his bedraggled appearance, Renato guessed he had run at least a mile into the wilderness before skulking back, as afraid of the dark as he was of the Indians.

"I—I can't, Cap'n Renato, sir. Cap'n Bowie would kill me sure."

"And you think I won't?"

"Beggin' your pardon, Cap'n, but you's tied up. Cap'n Bowie's not, and there's something 'bout you that makes him almighty testy."

"I will get loose, I promise you, and when I do I will personally deliver you to those demons you fear so much!"

Sharky looked like a man being strangled by invisible hands. "I—I have to be going now. Cap'n Bowie will be looking for me."

"Curse you, man! Bowie's no captain! He's an oaf with a pigsticker."

"Yes sir, Cap'n Renato. Whatever you say. Luck to you, sir."

As the gnarled wretch turned away, another voice hissed out of the darkness. "Shark! Shark, old pal! You wouldn't leave *me* here, would you?"

Sharky swung his head around. "Hump? 'Zat you?"

"Right enough. Be a good lad, won't you, and loosen my bonds a bit?"

"Oh Lordy, Hump, I don't know."

Renato was tempted to shout *Do it, fool!* but judged he'd profit more from silence.

"Listen Shark, remember that wager you owes me? Cut me ties and we'll forget it. What say you?"

Renato held his breath, awaiting the weasel's decision.

"Well…"

Sharky moved into the darkness beyond the flames. Someone grunted, and a moment later came Hump's voice. "Thanks, old pal."

Others piped up. "Do me, Sharky. You owe me twenty, remember?" and "I've two gold coins in my pocket. Free me and they's yours!"

"Naw, naw, I can't!" Sharky's voice was a squeal. "I must find Cap'n Bowie." And with that his shadow slunk off into the night.

When Renato spoke, his voice was full of honey. "Oh Hump, my dear. I've been meaning to speak with you. It seems the position of quartermaster has once again come vacant."

BOWIE CROUCHED BESIDE Sam in a copse of stunted elms. The mud had fallen off, and his chest leaked badly, staining his legs with blood.

Ahead, the Kronks were now beating the bushes. They

sounded increasingly agitated, a feeling Bowie shared. Five men and a girl could not long evade them, especially burdened with a heavy statue.

He pondered Andre's dying words. Whatever secrets Pacal held, Bowie intended to find them out. And then the little man would pay.

"May I inquire as to your strategy?" Sam asked. "I admit I am perplexed."

Far to their right, Bowie saw movement. Six dark forms flitting in and out of the shadows, moving steadily southwest.

"I know where they're going," he told Sam, who simply stared. "And I mean to get there first."

And with that, he bounded into the brush, moving swiftly but silently toward Karankawa Cove.

GUIDED BY THE stars, Renato marched toward the jolly boats. It was time to get back to *Medusa* and plot a new course of action. Behind him, straggling along like frightened sheep, were Hump and four other survivors of the landing party.

"Keep up, damn you, or I'll leave you to the cannibals."

"Cap'n, sir!" Hump's voice sounded at his elbow. "I hears something up ahead."

Renato stopped, straining his ears into the darkness. The only unnatural sound was a faint clicking. He was about to dismiss it when he heard a distinctly female sob.

A moment later, the moonlight revealed figures moving along the water's edge. One gave a glad cry, and clumps of brush were tossed into the air. They had discovered one of his hidden boats.

Two of the jaguar men struggled with the statue, while their bare-chested leader tugged at the wrist of Andre's wayward daughter.

Renato smiled. The pirates had only one weapon between them—a dead Indian's dagger—and that carried by Renato himself. But even barehanded, five desperate pirates would be more than a match for these stunted brown men.

As they broke through the brush, the jaguar men reached over their shoulders for long wooden sticks. Faster than Renato would have believed possible, the sticks were fitted with thin shafts. He had seen the effect of those shafts on the Indians, and ducked quickly behind a burly seaman.

An instant later, as his human shield collapsed, Renato leapt forward, reaching one of the jaguar men before he could reload. The Indian dagger sank to the hilt in the little man's gullet, while the pirates fell upon another, pummeling him with mallet-like fists. Two more of the little demons retreated into the brush.

Renato lunged for Mariette and the older man, cursing as they eluded him. But square in their path stood his would-be quartermaster.

"A sack of gold, Hump, if you catch the girl!"

The hunchback took a wide stance, making his face fierce, while Renato charged from the rear.

Mariette's captor looked forward and back. With a hiss, he thrust the girl at Renato and bounded toward Hump. Just as it appeared the two would collide, the brown man swerved aside and scampered into the jungle.

Renato caught the staggering girl, snaring her wrists. "We meet again," he said. "Did you miss me?"

Mariette stared up at him, her confusion clear. She could not reconcile the voice with his altered appearance. "You!"

Renato dragged her toward the boat. "Hump! Get that golden monstrosity loaded and prepare to shove off immediately. And be sure the other jolly boat will be of no use to our enemies."

As the men went about their tasks, Mariette became a human tornado, kicking, twisting and biting.

"I could kill you now," Renato growled, "but I'd prefer to take my time aboard ship."

Mariette ceased her struggles. "If you want the treasure, you won't kill me at all."

"You know where it is?"

"I do, and you'll never find it without me."

"Tell me now, damn you, or I'll split you open and leave your corpse for the Kronks."

Mariette gave a harsh laugh. "It's nowhere near here. But once on your ship, I can guide you to it."

Renato seethed. It was not his way to bargain with women, but the Indians' cries were growing louder.

"You will," he said, "depend upon it."

He tossed her into the boat, where one of the men held her fast, then quickly followed.

They had just shoved off when he saw Bowie and his slave burst from the bushes onto the narrow beach.

BOWIE STUMBLED TO a stop. Pain hammered his chest, and he felt light-headed. The priest's handiwork with a dagger, on top of the punishment received from Buckner, had further aggravated his pierced lung. The image of the boat gliding from the shoreline was hazy, as if seen through a fog, but two faces stood out like beacons. Renato and Mariette.

"Sam! We have to save her!" The words sapped more of his energy, and he leaned on his knees, taking in great gulps of air.

"You require rest. And medical attention."

Bowie shook off the fog. "I'm going, before it's too late." He planned a running dive into the water, but his vision blurred and his left leg collapsed under him.

From the east, the whoops of the Indians grew ever closer.

He felt Sam's steadying grip on his shoulder.

"We can stage a rescue later, Jim. Your first task is to survive."

He was still shaking his head as two young Pacals flew out of the brush onto the sandy shore. The little men looked quickly at the receding boat, at its demolished mate on the water's edge, and finally at Bowie and Sam.

Sam said, "Time to go," and yanked Bowie upright with surprising force, propelling him back toward the trees.

The brown men plucked strange, notched sticks from their

backs, resting them lightly on their shoulders. In a flash, each had fixed a shaft into the notch.

Bowie stumbled along, praying he and Sam would reach cover before the shafts thudded home.

RENATO GRINNED AS the jaguar men readied their weapons. His position at the rear of the boat accorded him an excellent view.

It was time to watch Bowie die.

Instead, the little savages pivoted on their heels and sent the shafts hurtling directly toward the jolly boat.

Renato nearly swallowed his tongue. Leaning back, he yanked the girl in front of him, and heard two sounds almost simultaneously. A solid thunk and a meaty smack, followed by a hoarse gasp.

One shaft quivered in the gunwale, while the other lodged in the neck of a burly pirate. The man struggled to pull the shaft free, but blood already gurgled from his mouth.

At almost the same moment, a chorus of bestial cries erupted from shore. The Kronks had arrived.

The jaguar men were enveloped in a cloud of arrows. One stiffened and pitched onto the sand, while the other dodged away. A good dozen warriors stormed after him, rolling like a tide along the shoreline. Bowie and the black man were nowhere in sight.

Some of the remaining Indians loosed futile arrows at Renato's boat, while others scurried about, their dismal howls signaling the discovery of the smashed dugouts and jolly boat.

Renato ran his tongue over cracked lips, tasting both triumph and defeat. He still lived, while his brother's slayer faced certain death.

It was not the victory he so fervently desired, but it would serve. He could be content knowing Bowie would never get vengeance for his precious blonde girl, and torment his dead spirit further by forcing him to watch Mariette suffer the same horrendous fate.

FROM A STAND of live oaks, Bowie watched the boat glide further away. He drew the knife from its sheath, drawing strength from its touch.

"I'm going for Mariette."

Before he could move, an iron grip clamped his shoulder, and he felt rooted to the spot.

"Mariette?" The word was a whisper, but carried the force of a strong wind. "What about her?"

Sam was staring upward. Towering above them—almost blotting out the stars—was big Strap Buckner.

"Renato has her," Bowie said. "And he's getting away."

"Then why are we standing here?"

"I was formulating a plan."

"And?"

"It's simple. We smash through the Kronks and swim after them."

Buckner nodded approval. "I'll smash. You swim."

Something in his tone made Bowie raise an eyebrow.

"Swimming," Buckner growled, "is too much like bathing."

Sam said, "This is sheer suicide." When no one answered, he spoke again. "But if you will provide me a weapon, I will endeavor to help."

Strap Buckner moved a hand toward his belt, then looked at the hand strangely, as if surprised to find something in it. He opened his fingers and shook them, allowing a crumpled shape to fall to the earth.

Bowie peered down at a dark form in soiled white trousers. Pacal.

"He looks dead. Is he?"

"Does it matter? I nearly stepped on the bugger in the brush, and he tried to bite me." Buckner drew a double-edged blade from his belt, handing it to Sam. It was a deadly-looking thing, known on the frontier as an Arkansas Toothpick.

Bowie nodded appreciation to them both. Then he turned and charged toward the water, the others pounding close behind.

He'd taken only a few steps when his vision blurred, and the land moved beneath him like the waves of a rolling sea.

"No!" he shouted.

But the earth swallowed him up, along with the moon and stars, and he knew no more.

PART IV
DESTINY

CHAPTER 58

"A plucked goose."

RENATO SHOULD BE pleased.

He sat once again in the stern of his fine new ship. The roll of *Medusa*'s deck was liberating after the stubborn rigidity of the land. The salt breeze whipped at his wounds, a bracing reminder he had once again cheated death, while his enemies were either cold meat or satisfying the appetites of the Kronks. Mariette was his captive, awaiting his vengeance, and would guide him to the greatest treasure of the age.

But something was wrong, something that made him feel not quite himself.

"Don't fret, Captain. Gold cures all ills, and you'll soon be richer than Midas." The girl's lilting voice did little to comfort him. It had, in fact, the opposite effect. Was this witch able to read his thoughts?

He brought her into focus, lounging demurely at the other end of his pew. Among his collection of captured finery, she had found powders, rouge, and a flowing gown of plum-colored taffeta. The color suited her, and the pearl necklace made her eyes shine like the morning sun on the wave crests.

On her lap sat his own fire-scorched Princess, enjoying her caress. He'd hoped the pair would be instant enemies, but instead they had formed a sort of feminine bond, and were now all but inseparable.

Normally he would never allow a prisoner such liberties. But there was a certain satisfaction in seeing her fancied up. A farmer like the late James Bowie might have likened it to fattening a hog before slaughter.

"If the treasure was never in Texas," he said, "why did we thrust ourselves into the jaws of those stinking cannibals?"

"I've explained all that. We needed the key. Without it the treasure is beyond reach."

"And how is it you know all this?"

Mariette turned to survey the sky. "That cloud," she said, pointing. "Does it not resemble a plucked goose?"

Renato kept his eyes fixed upon the girl. She continued to evade his questions. Why he had allowed her to play her games so long he was at a loss to say.

"How long do you think you can keep the treasure's location from me?"

"Oh look," she said. "The goose has lost its head." Her tone was playful, and she wore a smirk.

Renato backhanded her across the face. The slap resounded across the deck, drawing the eyes of every man aboard.

Mariette spilled out of the pew. She lay on the deck, sobbing, but Renato felt little satisfaction.

The men continued to stare.

He glared down at the girl. "If it's sympathy you want, you may lay there until your bones rot."

"I know you didn't wish to hurt me." Mariette's words were too hushed for any but him to hear.

"I didn't wish to *kill* you. Not yet."

"You needn't explain. Your men must believe you to be in charge." She parted her hair to expose a wink. "Was my performance convincing?"

Renato turned away. Damn the witch! She was playing with him. Worse, she pretended to understand him. He should put his pistol to her temple now, and have the truth from her. But for some reason he did not.

Perhaps the privacy of his cabin would allow him to sort his thoughts. He was halfway to the hatch when he heard the girl's grating words.

"You heartless bastard!"

Renato felt the beginning of a smile, but battened it down. Descending the steps, he saw her face, haggard and hateful. But at the last moment her lips formed three silent words. Words that put him once again at sea.

"I forgive you."

CHAPTER 59

"I fear he'll live."

BOWIE WANTED THE dream to end. Wild, screaming faces. Flashing daggers. An endless parade of blood and pain. And flickering through it all, the image of Mariette receding into the darkness with the leering face of Renato at her side.

Then the dream changed, and he found himself flat on his back, ringed by eight black figures adorned with feathers, beads and paints of gaudy colors. From their mouths came an eerie, senseless chanting.

The chant devolved into a single word, growing louder and more fervent with each repetition. A word that to Bowie was utter nonsense. "Ogu! Ogu! Ogu!"

A heavy crash, seeming to shake the very earth, brought the chanting to an end.

"Cease that infernal racket! Vamoose, all of you!" The bellowing voice could belong to no one but Strap Buckner. So he too was an inhabitant of this dream.

The black faces were replaced by the huge freckled features of Buckner himself. "Hm," he said. "What do you think?"

Another face appeared. Sam's. "His disposition has not improved, but his color seems to be returning."

"I agree." Buckner sounded less than pleased. "I fear he'll live."

"Look on the bright side," Sam said. "At least he no longer smells like a shark."

Perhaps this was not a dream after all.

"Go 'way," Bowie said, his voice little more than a moan. He was in a dusty room with rough-hewn walls and an impossibly high ceiling of thatch and mud. "What is this wretched place?"

Buckner scowled.

Sam wore an amused grin. "Mr. Buckner has been so generous as to give up his own bed, until you either recovered, or..." He let the last words go.

"How long?"

"Two days," Sam said.

"And then some," Buckner added.

"Mariette!" The realization he was truly awake brought the girl once again to the forefront.

Buckner grimaced, his face fearful to behold.

Sam shook his head. "With Renato. Or so we hope."

"When you collapsed," Sam said, "there was nothing we could do but retreat. We were fortunate to escape with our lives."

A serpent of smoke drifted over the bed, causing Bowie's nose to twitch. "What is that godawful smell? And was that troop of black lunatics really here, or did I dream them?"

"I've swept them out a dozen times," Buckner said, "but they always return."

"They were calling on the Loa, Jim. For assistance in reviving your spirit."

"The who?"

"The Loa. Not gods, exactly, but powerful spirits, each with unique abilities and proclivities. It is really quite fascinating. You should—"

"Damn it, Sam! What the hell are you talking about?"

"That's *Mr. Gideon* to you. Your infirmity does not excuse rudeness. Those men are followers of Voodoo. Formerly prisoners of Renato, whom he abandoned in the wilderness."

"Voodoo!"

"There is nothing to fear from it, Jim. Really. Once you delve beyond the more sensational aspects, such as zombies and curses, it is a religion like any other."

"Zombies! Is that what they've done? Turned me into a zombie?"

"Certainly not. As I understand it, you would have to be dead first."

"And how do you know I wasn't?"

Sam looked at Buckner, who shrugged, then back at Bowie. "Well, you are alive now, are you not?"

"So it seems," Bowie said. "That's what worries me. In any case, what in Hades are those men doing here, with us?"

Sam appeared somewhat embarrassed. "We came across them on our retreat. They were hiding in the brush, along with Sharky, hoping to evade recapture by the Indians."

Buckner nodded toward Sam. "They look upon him as their savior."

Bowie found a grin of his own. "It's a curious thing, Mr. Gideon, but each time I look at you I see more than the time before."

Buckner grunted. "If he's so bloody wonderful, maybe he can tell us where that barbecued pirate has taken Miss Mariette."

Sam coughed gently. "I cannot pretend to possess that knowledge, but I know someone who does."

"Who?"

"Our little friend Pacal. He has been quite anxious to speak with you, Jim. He claims to know precisely where Renato and Mariette are going, and will tell you under one condition."

"Then spit it out, man."

"He insists he be allowed to accompany us on the journey."

Bowie recalled again what Andre had told him. *Pacal knows everything.* But he also recalled the brown man's treatment of Mariette. "What's to prevent me making that promise, then snapping his neck?"

"I put that question to him myself," Sam said. "For some reason, he thinks you a man of your word."

CHAPTER 60

"Through playing games."

R ENATO FOCUSED ON the canvas before him, striving to shut all else from his mind. Another day had passed, and he still had no idea what troubled him.

The painting was one he had last worked on only days ago, days which now seemed a lifetime. There stood the old Renato—dashing and devil-may-care—flanked on either side by untold riches. It was everything he had ever wanted.

But that was then. A dream of that former Renato.

Something was different now. Something was missing from this ideal future, and he could not fathom what it was.

"Do you know what that picture needs?"

The girl's voice, inches from his ear, made him jump.

"Yes," he said, "I do." He waved a brush at the upper right corner. "You, hanging from a gibbet, with flies feasting on your carcass."

Mariette cocked her head as if giving the idea serious thought. "I was going to suggest that adorable pussycat perched on your shoulder, but you know best. You are so much more imaginative than I."

Today she wore a gown of sea-green brocade trimmed in black lace. The bodice was tight and the neckline low, revealing more cleavage than it seemed possible for her to possess.

The scratchy gargle that passed for the cat's *meow* turned his head, and he goggled to see her clad in a tiny dress—fashioned from the same fabric as Mariette's.

At the sound of footsteps, the girl said, "Thank you, Mr. Quayle. Just in the nick of time."

Renato stared as she accepted two crystal goblets, and handed one to him. The scent was unmistakable. His private hoard of Burgundy.

"Quayle!" he bellowed, but the bosun's head was already disappearing through the hatch.

Mariette sipped from her glass. "My compliments, Captain. This is really quite excellent."

Renato knocked the goblet from her hand, and it crashed to the deck, forming an angry red stain. It looked like blood, and he found himself wishing it was. *Hers.*

He raised his own glass. The wine was an elixir, soothing and stimulating at the same time.

"You're welcome," the girl said, in her faintly mocking tone.

Eyes narrowing, Renato looked beyond her. The men of the afternoon watch followed her every move, seemingly intoxicated by her presence.

"Mr. Hump! We carry too much weight. You will prepare a list of the three most expendable hands, and we shall offer the sharks a little sport."

"A list, Cap'n? Such a thing as requires writing? Beggin' your pardon, Cap'n, but surely you knows—"

"Enough, Hump! You are excused."

The little man backed away, but every man on deck now attacked his work with new-found relish.

"Impressive," Mariette said. "Where did you acquire such skill at handling *men?*"

Renato caught the peculiar emphasis on the final word. She was mocking him again.

He glared at her, and was again surprised at how small she was—making it all the more fantastic she could trifle with him and live.

"We are through playing at games, you and I."

"I am shattered, Captain. I had been anticipating a late-night hand of whist."

Scarred and blackened fingers closed upon her arm. She winced, her face contorting, and he felt the odd impulse to release her. She was so soft, so fragile, and yet so aggravating.

"Where are you taking me, wench? Where?"

"To your treasure, Captain, as I've told you."

Renato applied more pressure. "Name the place. Now, or I snap your bones."

"I like a man," she said, "who knows what he wants, and will stop at nothing to get it."

Once again, Renato was all at sea. He felt the urge to release her, even comfort her. But the eyes of the men were upon him, and he could not appear weak. He willed all his rage into his muscles, steeling himself to break her arm.

But his fingers fell slack, refusing to obey. Renato wanted to scream, to lash out at whatever force possessed him. But he saw nothing to strike at, nothing but Mariette, and even that pleasure seemed denied him.

A smile formed on her lips. She was maddeningly beautiful, but equally unfathomable. And somewhere deep within, beneath the layers of scorn and unfulfilled vengeance, Renato felt the smallest hint of admiration.

"Deck there! Sail fine on the lee bow!" The lookout's call broke the eerie connection between them.

"My telescope, quickly!"

The glass in his hands, he caught a speck of white against the pale sky.

"What do you make of her?" he demanded of the lookout.

"Rigged fore-an-aft, Cap'n, but a small 'un. A ketch, mayhap, or a schooner."

That could mean anything. A trader. Homesteaders bound for Texas. Even a naval vessel.

"What think you, Cap'n?" Hump had materialized at his elbow. "Fat pickings for we'uns, perhaps?"

"Perhaps."

"Deck there! She's raised her colors, Cap'n! Stars 'n' Stripes. I knows her now, Cap'n. The schooner *Kassandra*."

American. Was the navy after him again, so soon? "Then we will do likewise. Mr. Hump, get that American flag aloft immediately!"

Renato grinned. There was little chance the Americans had learned of *Medusa's* new ownership. They would perceive her to be a friend, right up to the moment an eighteen-pound ball blasted through their hull.

"More flags breaking out, Cap'n. Signals!"

Renato handed the telescope to Quayle. "You're familiar with their signals. What does she say?"

Quayle made a croaking noise. "I don't understand, Cap'n. The signal reads, *Enemy in Sight*."

Enemy? What enemy? "You're daft, man. The sun has fried your brain."

"Another signal, Cap'n! *Prepare for battle*."

"Damn you, Quayle, if you're mistaken—"

"Deck there! Another sail, on the larboard quarter! Looks like a frigate, Cap'n!"

A frigate. Rigged for battle, she might carry as many as twenty guns. With the added firepower of *Kassandra*, *Medusa* would stand little chance.

This could not be happening now. Quayle and the lookout must be wrong.

Quayle swiveled about, focusing on the new sighting. "He's right, Cap'n! Another American. And she's acknowledged the signal. They're comin' for us sure!"

CHAPTER 61

"A man of honor."

"**W**HAT'S WRONG WITH you, man? A girl's life is at stake!"

To emphasize the point, Bowie jabbed a finger into the puffy chest of Captain McQuiddy.

The two stood nose to nose in the bow as *Lucinda* rocked at anchor in Matagorda Bay.

"If that demented pirate has her," McQuiddy said, "she's already dead. I'll not risk my ship to rescue a corpse."

From the other end of the ship came a rumbling roar, like the challenge of an enraged bear.

McQuiddy's face went white. "And I'll not be bullied by you or that man-mountain Buckner."

McQuiddy and his crew had been busy in their absence. Having made repairs, *Lucinda* was ready to sail. The question now was where she would go.

"What of your agreement with Dominique You? I understood you had put yourself at the girl's disposal."

"Aye," McQuiddy snapped. "And now that she's lost to us…"

The words died as Bowie's hands flew to the man's throat. Shouts burst from the sailors as McQuiddy flopped about like a fish on a line.

The protests stopped at the sound of a thunderclap. Buckner had brought his enormous hands together, and now turned them into fists. "The first to move," he boomed, "will be first to die."

Bowie loosened his grip, allowing McQuiddy to suck air.

"I suggest you cooperate, Captain. And order your men to do the same."

"No," McQuiddy gasped. "I won't. I'll not go chasing a wild goose. Particularly not to parts unknown, at the whim of your pet firebug."

Bowie scowled. Pacal was a sore point with him as well. The brown man refused to disclose their destination until they were well at sea. But Mariette needed help, and Renato needed killing.

Bowie eased the knife from its sheath. He steadied the blade beneath the man's chin.

"You will take us where we wish to go, or this deck will be awash with blood. Your blood. You have ten seconds to decide."

Bowie was reminded of bullying Tamarand's man Smythe, and instantly ashamed. That incident now seemed long ago and far away, and he was startled to realize how much his priorities had changed. His dream of political power now paled beside visions of Mariette and his long-awaited reckoning with Renato.

McQuiddy's answer carried to every man on deck. "I've heard stories of you, Mr. Bowie. You are loyal to your friends, and hell to your enemies. But you are a man of honor, not a murderer."

"You're betting your life on that?"

"Aye. I am."

Bowie cursed his luck. This was what came of having a reputation. If exaggerated, you had to live up to it. If accurate, it made you predictable. This man had called his bluff, leaving him only one course of action.

"I could simply take your precious *Lucinda*," he said bitterly, "but as I'm *a man of honor*, I will purchase it instead."

"Purchase it?" McQuiddy was incredulous. "Do you know what a vessel like this is worth?"

"Less than the life of one slim girl."

When McQuiddy merely goggled, Bowie said, "Mr. Gideon, a piece of paper, if you please. Write 'I.O.U. one boat,' and I will sign it for our fat friend here."

"That would be 'one ship,' Jim."

"Just write it."

"This is robbery!" McQuiddy sputtered. "If you ever set foot in the States again, you'll be hanged for piracy."

"Perhaps."

"In any case, this will avail you nothing. My men will not sail with you, and without a crew you won't make it out of the bay."

Bowie turned to see Sharky climb over the rail, guiding the first of the Haitians.

"But I do have a crew, you see. I brought my own."

Sam thrust the paper and pen into his hand, and Bowie sheathed his knife to scrawl his name. Then, as McQuiddy continued to bluster, he stuffed the note into the man's mouth.

"Now, *Mr.* McQuiddy, get the hell off my ship." Bowie turned to the seamen. "You men. Any willing to remain with us will be heartily welcome. And should we come out of this with gold in our pockets, which is not unlikely, you shall receive equal shares."

At the word *gold*, several men had jerked to attention.

"Don't listen to him!" McQuiddy squalled. "Any who help him will join him on the gallows!"

The deck tilted as Strap Buckner surged forward, lifted McQuiddy by the hair, and dropped him over the side. The man's screech ended with a great splash.

The sailors moved to the rail, climbing quickly down to the waiting boat. Bowie watched them go, knowing his chance of success went with them. He would have manpower, but only one experienced hand. And that hand was Sharky.

Two of the seamen hung back, talking quietly in the stern. One, a well-muscled fellow with fuzzy side-whiskers, approached with hat in hand. He wore no shirt, but had a green sea monster tattooed on his chest. "My name's Wilson, Mr. Bowie. Me and my partner Young, we sort of took a liking to Miss Mariette. We'll go along, if you'll have us."

Bowie stuck out his hand. As the man shook it, Young chimed in. "And if, as you say, there's gold to be had, we'll help with that as well."

CHAPTER 62

"I know what you're planning."

"**H**OW WE GOIN'** to beat 'em, Cap'n?"

"Is that my Burgundy I detect on your breath, Quayle?"

The little man shrank away as if he had vanished into smoke. But his question remained.

The navy ships grew ever closer. Given equal conditions, *Medusa* could outpace any schooner or frigate afloat. But the Americans had approached while Renato and his crew were distracted by that minx Mariette. She would pay, once the danger passed. *If* it passed.

Renato had already discarded a dozen clever stratagems as unworkable. For once in his career, he would be happy to take flight. But with the wind against him, that was not an option. To stand and fight was equally hopeless. The frigate, identified as the U.S.S. *Blain*, carried two 18-pound long guns and sixteen 32-pound carronades. A direct hit from any of those guns would turn *Medusa* into a cloud of bloody splinters.

"What'll we do, Cap'n?"

"Aye, Cap'n. We don't wanna die!"

"Silence, you jellyfish!" Quartermaster Hump sounded almost cheerful in his newfound authority. "Cap'n's never failed us yet."

Renato tried to shut out the voices and think, but his head seemed awash with gruel. Something was dangerously wrong. Perhaps he had not yet recovered from his ordeal with Bowie and the Kronks. Or worse, that savage priest had cast a spell to sap his will.

Until he regained his old power, he would be hard pressed to survive in his present occupation.

"Once we find the gold," Mariette said, close to his ear, "you can retire from all this."

Renato stiffened. "If we survive this day, you and I shall have a reckoning."

"Oh, we'll survive. I have perfect confidence in you."

Renato didn't know whether to strike her or curse her. But of one thing he was sure—her closeness left his brain more fuddled than ever.

He spun away and strode back to the stern, plumbing his bag of tricks. *Kassandra* was already in range of the 18-pounder. He could extract some small satisfaction in destroying the smaller ship before the frigate arrived. But that was all. His corpse would be hanging from the *Blain*'s yardarm before the sun went down.

This time, Mariette's French perfume reached him before she spoke. "I know what you're planning, Captain. It's magnificent."

Renato waited, daring her to continue, fearing she would not.

"You intend to run right at *Kassandra*. To the Americans it will seem the last act of a desperate man. But in truth…" She leaned forward, whispering into his ear.

Renato's eyes stretched wider with each word. Was she indeed a witch, to be so well-versed in naval strategy? By the time she finished, he had regained his composure.

"You walk a dangerous path," he said, "with this mind reading trick of yours." Then he began shouting orders. "Mr. Hump! Bring the ship about and set us on a collision course for that schooner."

Hump stared open-mouthed until Renato added, "At once!" after which the little hunchback hopped into action.

"Quayle! Select two strong men and follow me to the galley. There is much to be done!"

CHAPTER 63

"Where in blazes are we going?"

FOR A TIME, it seemed *Lucinda* might never make it out of Matagorda Bay. McQuiddy's former crewmen had warned him the channel was shallow, and insisted on frequent soundings. Instructing the Haitians to handle the sails was another challenge. The fact they could not speak English meant Sam had to translate Wilson and Young's instructions into French. Young improved this considerably when, fetching pen and ink from McQuiddy's cabin, he drew a series of sketches illustrating each man's task.

Bowie tried to follow the lessons for a time. But the listing of sails alone—staysails, topgallants and a dozen others, soon had him yawning. After what seemed an age, they at last won free of the bay, plunging into the choppier waters of the Gulf.

Bowie turned to Sam. "Well? Is that little parasite ready to talk?"

At the moment, the brown man sat atop the foresail yard, peering anxiously into the eastern sky.

"I shall inquire." Sam sauntered to the base of the foremast, calling up the question. Pacal's answer was lost in the breeze, but his manner said *No.*

Bowie wished Strap Buckner had agreed to accompany them. The big man may have had success squeezing answers from Pacal.

At length, Pacal came slithering down the mast, and Sam guided him to Bowie.

"So," Bowie said in Spanish, "where are we bound?"

Pacal made clicking noises.

"None of that," Bowie said, touching the butt of his knife. "I know you understand me."

With a start, Bowie realized the Haitians had stopped working, and stared at him from hooded eyes. He had noticed similar looks before, but never with such intensity. He owed them no debt, but they seemed to believe otherwise.

Pacal made a sour face, then spoke in Spanish. "Among my people, I am a holy man. I am also a king."

"Very well, Your Holiness—or Highness if you prefer—where in blazes are we going?"

"To my home. It is known to your people as Yucatán."

"Yucatán!" Bowie bent forward, his face inches from Pacal's. "Listen, little man. I didn't go to the trouble of acquiring this ship just for your benefit. You agreed to lead us to Mariette and Renato."

"And so I shall. You will find those you seek in Yucatán."

Sam said, "If I may inquire, sir, what interest would Renato and Mariette have in visiting your homeland?"

"Gold." Pacal spat the word as if it were evil.

"You refer to Lafitte's treasure, I presume? We were led to believe it resided in Texas."

"The treasure was never Lafitte's, and the bulk of it has never left my country. We went to Texas to recover the key."

Bowie said, "That's what Andre called that ugly statue. The key to the treasure. What did he mean?"

Pacal looked smug. "You people are large, but your brains are small."

Bowie eased the knife half out of its sheath.

"He was correct," Pacal said quickly. "Without the key, the treasure is lost to us all."

"I understand that much," Bowie gritted. "Now tell me what the hell it means."

Pacal's flat eyes darted about the ship as if seeking a place to hide. Finally his shoulders slumped, and he stared vacantly at his feet. "My people ruled the land for a thousand years. We built great cities and served our gods well. Then others came. First the Aztecs, whom we absorbed, then the Spanish, who sought only wealth. Determined to safeguard our gold, my ancestors locked it away in a great temple."

To Bowie's surprise, this talk of riches held little interest for him. "How does this help us find Mariette?"

Pacal ignored the question.

"The secret of that temple was passed through the generations, from father to son, awaiting the day our people will rise again and take our place in the world. My father passed the secret to me. I am the current guardian of the treasure, and I have failed. Failed my father, my ancestors, and my people."

Bowie wondered how much of this to believe. "So you have a temple full of gold. Why do you refer to that statue as the key?"

"Because that is what it is. The temple is one huge vault, requiring the key to open it."

"And now Renato has it."

Pacal's face fell, tinged with something like despair.

"But how will he find the temple, and know how to use this key?"

"The girl," Pacal said with a choke. "She knows."

"Mariette? How could she? There was nothing about it on the map."

The brown man grimaced. A light burned in his eyes, then just as quickly faded. As if reaching a decision, he snapped his mouth shut and strode off toward the bow, where he sat Indian-style, gazing out toward the eastern horizon.

And no matter how many questions were put to him, he would say no more.

CHAPTER 64

"You should see this!"

BALLS SCREAMED OVERHEAD as *Medusa* plunged headlong toward *Kassandra*.

Renato leaned over the hatch to the lower deck. "We need that stove lit now! What in Satan's name is taking so long?"

Through the hatch, Quayle hove into view wrestling a huge bucket of lard. "Not much firewood down here, Cap'n!"

"Then burn something else, damn you, as long as it's not from my quarters!"

Renato staggered as a ball slammed into the hull. *Kassandra*'s little sixes blasted away at an astonishing pace, pummeling *Medusa*'s prow and filling the air with grape. *Blain*'s 18-pounders had been busy, too, and coming near to finding their range. Some inner sense warned him to duck as a huge ball scorched the air above his head. Seconds later another plowed into the sea just short of the stern.

He must have been mad to adopt the plan of that traitorous girl. For all he knew she may be hoping for an American victory.

Quayle piped up again. "We tried the spare sail, Cap'n, but it don't want to start. Fabric's too thick!"

Mariette appeared at Renato's side. "They need something more flammable."

Before he could respond she was wiggling out of her gown, her thin shoulders pale as bone. The dress slipped easily over her hips and into a ring at her feet. As if struck dumb, Renato stared open-mouthed at a slim form in scanty underthings.

"Here," she shouted, kicking the gown onto Quayle's head, "burn this!"

Dropping the dress into the lard bucket, Quayle raced toward the galley. Moments later, the whoosh of flames sounded from below, followed by tendrils of smoke.

"Smear more lard on that canvas," Mariette called, "and feed it slowly. Any wool blankets or sailor's clothing will do as well!"

The difference was dramatic. A pungent cloud soon billowed from the hatch.

Renato rushed to the bow, alarmed to see they were little more than two cables from *Kassandra*. But for the first time, the navy guns faltered in their rate of fire. With thick dark smoke now pouring from *Medusa*'s hold, she must have been a fearful sight.

The Americans would believe *Medusa* would soon be engulfed in flames—and if the two ships met, *Kassandra* would share the same funeral pyre. Nothing struck fear into seamen like a fire-ship.

Aboard *Kassandra,* sailors raced madly about, hauling lines and leaning on the tiller in an attempt to veer from *Medusa*'s path. But Renato could already see terror in the Americans' eyes.

And the *Blain* was powerless to help. She was too far off to intervene, and could not use her guns for fear of striking *Kassandra*.

"Prepare to board!"

The pirates rushed forward, stuffing their belts with knives and pistols, filling their hands with axes and short swords.

"You'd be safer below," Renato told Mariette. "I need you alive until I know where we're bound."

The girl laid a slim hand on his arm. If she was at all embarrassed by her near-nakedness, she betrayed no sign. "Yucatán, dear Captain. We are bound for Yucatán."

Renato stared, the implications of this flashing through his mind. Then he heard the men roaring, and saw they were nearly within reach of *Kassandra*.

The pirates' grapnels flew out to catch the other ship's rail. A few brave sailors lined *Kassandra*'s side, but most still raced about, unnerved by the imminent collision with the vessel they believed to be a fireship. Wood shrieked as the two ships met. The smoke from *Medusa*'s hatch rolled over *Kassandra*'s deck, followed immediately by Renato's screaming pirates.

Rifles and pistols banged, making bright flashes in the smoke. Men cursed and screamed. Renato caught only glimmers of swords and axes, but could picture the scene clearly. His pirates were scything across *Kassandra*'s deck, striking at anything in blue.

At his side he heard a thin growl, and turned, expecting to see Princess. But the sound had come from Mariette. Beads of sweat covered her near-naked body, and her face was lit with an unholy light as she reveled in the sight of men fighting and dying. She had never looked more fetching.

More quickly than he had imagined, he heard the shout, "She's ours, Cap'n!" and the grotesque face of Hump emerged from the smoke.

"Do you expect a medal? Get busy and proceed as ordered!"

Hump vanished, shouting orders, and Renato strode to *Medusa*'s foremast, grasping the line that held his twin-skulled flag. It pained him to lower it, but he reminded himself the success of Mariette's plan demanded it.

At the same time, he knew, signal flags raised by Hump were bursting out above *Kassandra*, assuring *Blain* that the dastardly pirates had been subdued.

A QUARTER OF an hour later, the smoke finally gone, blue-clad figures moved about *Medusa*'s deck as if inspecting the swivel gun, while others climbed through *Medusa*'s rigging, working to repair damage.

More blue-clad men worked aboard *Kassandra*, mopping up blood and pushing bodies over the side.

Approaching on a leisurely tack, the *Blain* grew ever closer, gun ports closed, her officers taking their ease on the poop.

While small in comparison to a genuine ship-of-the-line, the frigate's deck rode high above those of the schooners.

"Cor, Cap'n! You should see this!"

"You know damn well I can't, Quayle. So just tell me." Renato, also clad in blue, kept to the shadows behind *Kassandra*'s mainmast. It was doubtful the frigate's telescopes could discern faces at this distance, but one so scarred as his would be sure to attract notice.

"It's that scary-tall Cap'n Bentley," Quayle said, "and that stiff-necked loo-tenant of his."

"Aboard the *Blain*? Are you certain?"

"Oh, Aye, Cap'n. I got far too close a look at them two back on *L'Intrepide*."

Renato grinned. It was doubly lucky he had hidden his face.

The *Blain* now presented her stern to *Kassandra* and her apparent prize. From her poop a row of pompous officers peered down their noses at the schooners.

At Renato's order, the men examining the 18-pounder laid their weight against the barrel, swiveling it to point directly at *Blain*'s exposed stern.

No longer fearing identification, Renato snatched the scope from Quayle's hands. The shocked faces of Bentley and Goble jumped out at him as they realized they'd been duped again.

As they watched in horror, Hump applied a match to *Medusa*'s gun. Flame blossomed from the barrel, and the huge iron ball blasted the length of the ship, scattering men and guns like ten-pins. Bentley and the others ran for their lives as half the poop deck plummeted into the sea.

And just as the Americans thought the worst was over, *Blain*'s mainmast came crashing down, dragging sails and men with it. As the smoke about the stern cleared, streams of red ran from a great scorched hole, as if the ship itself was bleeding.

Something soft touched his arm, and Renato found Mariette at his side, her smile as horrific as his own.

CHAPTER 65

"I may go mad."

"**W**HAT DO YOU make of it, Wilson?"
The weathered seaman lowered the telescope and squinted at Bowie beneath shaggy brows. "It's as I thought. The *Blain*. Been through a hell of a battle, and no mistake."

"Renato?"

"Don't see how. She's twice the size of *L'Intrepide*."

"What's that's smaller ship?"

"A navy schooner. Doing her best to pick up survivors."

"The damage looks severe, those sailors may require our aid."

"A kindly thought, Captain Bowie, but sure you want to risk it?"

"Risk what?"

"They'll be asking difficult questions. Like where's Captain McQuiddy, and why is his ship now manned by this crew of... dark-skinned gentlemen."

"All that can be explained."

"Aye, perhaps. But them navy salts might hold you on suspicion of piracy, slave-trading, or both."

"We can't just leave fellow-Americans in distress."

"Mariette is an American too, Jim." Sam appeared at his elbow, as silently as ever. "Besides, that vessel does not appear to be in danger of sinking."

Bowie nodded, relieved to have an excuse to follow his heart. "Very well, Wilson. We stay on course."

For three straight days the winds had been friendly, push-ing them along at a good clip. The Haitians could now manage such basic operations as taking in sail without tripping over one another. At times, Bowie had come on deck to see them smiling and laughing, but upon sighting him they invariably clammed up, watching and waiting.

"What ails those fellows?" he demanded of Sam.

Sam spread his hands. "Alas, they refuse to confide in me. They say only that they are waiting. For what, I do not know."

"Well, whatever it is, I wish it would happen. If I have to endure these dour looks much longer, I may go mad."

Still aggravated, Bowie's eyes fell upon Pacal, lounging in the bow.

"And what of our unwelcome guest? Has he revealed any of Mariette's role in this?"

"Every time I mention her name, he reverts to clicking. Sadly, Mayan was not among the tongues my former master had me tutored in."

"This master of yours—why did he provide you such learning? It seems excessive for a house servant."

"Oh, but I was much more than that, Jim. I was raised as counselor and companion to the old master's son." When Bowie raised his eyebrows, Sam nodded. "Much to my master's dismay, the boy was born slow in the head, so I was educated in his stead. I was to be the young man's brain, so to speak."

Sam's features softened as he spoke, obviously reflecting on more pleasant times. "Then what were you doing with that pig of a barkeep in New Orleans?"

Sam's face fell. "The poor lad became involved in a duel, and his body was delivered to the plantation with a bullet in the brain. The old master began to whither, and was dead within the year. His heirs wanted none of me, and sent me to auction, where I went to that miscreant."

Bowie shook himself. Sam's case was an unusual one, but in the end not unusual enough.

"Jim," Sam said quietly, "once this is over, are you still determined to run for Congress?"

"Of course," Bowie said automatically. "Why wouldn't I be?" But he heard annoyance in his voice. In truth, he had not thought of those aspirations in several days.

"Politicians were frequent visitors at my old master's home. They were shallow creatures, arrogant but insecure."

"And that's what you think of me?"

Sam slipped into an outrageous dialect. "I'se only a poor darky, Massah. What would I know?"

"What would you say if I told you I wanted to faithfully represent the people of Louisiana?"

"Would I be speaking as a poor darky, or as a man whose opinion you value?"

Bowie looked at him keenly. "The latter."

"Then I would ask this: Do you truly believe the man you are buying this election from would allow you to be so altruistic? I am familiar with his breed, as well, and they abhor such notions."

Bowie bristled. "You don't believe I could be my own man?"

"You clearly are. But could you truly be your own congressman?"

Bowie felt an unreasonable anger. Not at Sam, but at the disillusion of a long-cherished dream.

Seeking an outlet for his feelings, his eyes returned to Pacal.

The little man reacted not at all to Bowie's approach.

"It's time we talked of Mariette," he said in Spanish. "What hold do you have upon her?"

When the man did not reply, Bowie grasped his shoulder and spun him about. "Speak, damn you! Who hired you to accompany her? What was her true connection to Andre?"

Pacal spoke two words in Spanish, words suggesting Bowie perform an impossible act.

"Enough!" Bowie's left hand caught the man by the neck, sweeping him off the deck and holding him with legs kicking wildly. His right hand held ten inches of razor-sharp steel. "Talk, or I'll skin you like a raccoon."

Pacal let out a squeal that must have been heard on the *Blain*.

When Bowie's ears stopped ringing, he heard a skittering on the deck behind him, and something pounced upon his back, ripping through his shirt with teeth and claws. Dropping Pacal, he got a handful of hair and swung the creature over his shoulder, slamming it to the deck, where he imprisoned it under his boot.

There, squirming like a trapped animal, was one of the Pacal lookalikes he'd seen in Texas. The little monster sank claws into his leg and Bowie raised the knife to cut him off at the wrists.

"No!" Pacal screamed. "Don't!"

As Bowie stared, the brown man clicked urgently until the fellow ceased his struggles.

"Where the hell did he come from?" Bowie demanded.

"He was hiding. He is very good at hiding."

Bowie was shocked. "He's been with us since we left Texas?"

"Since we left New Orleans," Pacal admitted. "With one of his cousins."

"And where is this cousin now?"

Pacal looked infinitely sad. "Dead. In Texas."

"Give me one reason I shouldn't toss him to the sharks."

"Please." Pacal's voice had a wheedling quality. "He is my son. His name is Chak."

Before Bowie could wrap his brain around that, he sensed a commotion on the deck behind him.

The Haitians were grouped around him in a rough half-circle, chanting and rolling their eyes like men possessed. "Ogu! Ogu!" They said again and again, in tones both jubilant and reverent.

Bowie shot a look at Sam. "What the devil are they on about now?"

"It would appear your wish has been granted, Jim. Whatever these gentlemen were waiting for, they wait no longer."

CHAPTER 66

"A great favor."

RENATO FELT STRANGE. So strange, in fact, that he could not decide if the feeling was good or bad.

He was beset by a warmth that had nothing to do with the heat of the day. It came from somewhere within, and seemed to radiate outwards, encompassing everyone and everything around him. This included Mariette, who now posed on the pew in the stern.

That was alarming enough, but even his interactions with Quayle and Hump had lacked their customary derision and contempt. Thankfully, the men had seemed more fearful of him than ever, and made themselves scarce. And this, at least, he minded not at all, for it left him alone with the subjects of his latest painting.

Mariette, in a red silk gown and a necklace worth a king's ransom, sat with one finger poised bewitchingly on her lower lip, while her green eyes reached out as if probing the depths of his soul. On the girl's lap lay her constant companion, Princess.

Renato's right hand moved, applying brush strokes to the new canvas, but he could not bother himself to look. His eyes were for Mariette alone. For some reason, the more he looked upon her, the less he wished to look away.

At the moment, his attention was torn between the Mariette before him and the one in his mind's eye—the wanton who had occupied his bed the night before. The battle with *Blain* and *Kassandra* had aroused her to such a degree that she had practically dragged him to his cabin and ripped the clothing from his back.

"How much longer?" the Mariette before him asked. "This posing is thirsty work, and Princess and I are dying to *see*."

Renato blinked. "Patience, my dear. You have fired my muse, but it cannot be rushed." But even as he spoke, he felt his brush fairly flying over the canvas, as if compelled to serve her.

"As I recall," she said lazily, "you did not mind being *rushed* last night."

And indeed he had not.

Renato had had many women, and not all of them by force, but last night's encounter had been like nothing in his experience. She had been equal parts wind and fire, unleashing a passion that all but consumed him. First she was atop him, writhing, squealing and urging him to ever greater efforts. Then she was below, seemingly submissive, but merely gathering energy for another assault from above. He could hear her, taste her, feel the tautness of her skin as she—

"Ahoy, Cap'n!" The lookout's cry wrenched him back to the here and now. "It's Tulum, dead ahead, an' no mistake!"

Mariette uncurled from the pew, the cat in her arms, and followed the man's outstretched arm.

The spell broken, Renato turned about, where he could barely discern a squarish structure crowning a distant spit of land.

Their encounter with the U.S. Navy had left them with damaged rigging, ripped sails and a demolished bowsprit. The delay had infuriated him, but its one saving grace had been the opportunity to spend more time with Mariette. Her astonishing performance in his bed had inspired him, and he'd insisted on painting her portrait—the first ever of a subject other than himself.

He no longer wanted to kill her, but he was left with new, and more troubling emotions. She had made him feel—as never before—like a man, but at the same time somehow unmanned him.

Now they had reached Tulum, which she called the starting point for the final leg of their journey.

This was a place Renato had never visited, nor had he wished to. And the nearer they came, the less he liked it. Glowering down from a lofty perch was a huge gray castle, radiating an aura of extreme age. Flanking the castle were smaller structures, all connected by a high stone wall. The place had a hoary, unclean look, a breeding ground for fears of ghosts and witches.

He turned suddenly at Mariette's voice. "Now!" she cried, "let us see!"

Renato checked his canvas. The last time he'd looked, it was blank. Now it was not, and he stared in wide-eyed wonder at what his hand and brush had wrought.

He was up in an instant, snatching the painting from the easel and bawling for Quayle.

Thankfully, the man appeared before Mariette could reach him, and Renato thrust the canvas into his hands, making sure the surface was turned away.

"You will stow this in my cabin at once!" he ordered. "And no one is to see it—least of all *you*. If I even suspect it, we shall revisit that idea of feeding your eyes to the cat."

Then Quayle was gone, and Mariette stood before him fuming.

"Why did you do that? You know how anxious we are!"

"It—it does not yet do you justice," Renato heard himself say. Had he actually *stammered*? "You will see it when it is worthy of your attention."

She looked slantwise at the cat. "What do you think, my dear? Shall we allow the artist more time to achieve perfection?"

The beast's eyes turned to examine him, and Renato saw only disdain.

"Quickly," he said. "Let's get ashore. Our treasure awaits."

THE FARTHER RENATO got from the sea, the more irritable he became.

"If you cannot keep up," he called to the men straggling behind, I'll be pleased to lighten your load."

"Why thankee, Cap'n," Hump replied. "That would be most kind."

Renato drew the cutlass from his belt. "You'll be much lighter on your feet if relieved of those fat ugly heads."

The two struggling with the golden statue put on a sudden burst of speed, shouldering the others aside in their haste.

"You certainly know how to motivate your followers." Mariette's tone was playful, as always, but no longer irritated him. He longed to hear more of it.

He said gruffly, "How much further to this damned treasure house?"

"Do you tire of my company already? I was so enjoying our walk."

Renato averted his face to hide his confusion. It was two hours past noon, and they followed an overgrown path northwest through the jungle. The flat landscape was dusty and sunbaked, and the earth burned through the soles of his boots. And yet, Mariette's presence made it somehow bearable.

"Cap'n Renato!" Quayle's squeak was extra thin in the dry air. "There's someone up ahead."

Heat waves rose from the white dust of the path, making things shimmer and dance. But there, just off the trail, sat a tousled figure in a faded red dress.

Renato gripped his cutlass. "Hump! Send men ahead to scout the surrounding woods. This may be a trap."

"I don't like it," Renato told Mariette. "Why would this person be waiting on the trail?"

"Why not? We are intruders here. The trail belongs to the local people."

The little hunchback had reached the slouching figure, and stood waving. "Just an old woman, Cap'n! She's alone."

At close range, she did not look much like a woman. Through

her tangled hair, a very rat's nest of twigs, leaves and dirt, Renato saw a large hooked nose and coarse dark skin.

"You," he said in harsh Spanish. "Rise and address your betters!"

The gray head shook as if awakening from a nap. Ever so slowly, the crone produced a gnarled cane and rocked forward, her body bent like a drooping tree.

"You startled me, good sir." The sound from her flaccid lips was high-pitched and grating. "I get few visitors here."

"We mean you no harm, good mother." Mariette spoke in English, and her tone was gentle. "We seek a great temple left by the ancient dwellers of this land."

The old woman cackled. "Then you are in luck, girl." Her English was oddly accented. "This land is littered with temples. Walk a league in any direction and you are likely to stumble upon one."

Renato bristled. "This particular temple is said to contain a great treasure."

The woman's mouth formed a large O. A gray tongue flapped in an out like that of a frog catching flies. "Then I shall do you a great favor, and tell you nothing."

Renato's sword pricked the front of the old hag's dress. "I will not be toyed with, woman."

"Please," Mariette said softly. "Perhaps she will explain."

"Thank you, my dear, I will. That temple is not difficult to find, but you would be wasting your time. The Maya believe the place is protected by the gods."

Renato was growing impatient. "How do you know of this temple?"

"There are few secrets from one who has lived as long as I."

"If you wish to live another day, I suggest you guide us to it. At once."

"Please help us, mother. We *will* gain entrance, and when we do, you shall be amply rewarded." Mariette turned her face to Renato. "*Won't* she?"

"Oh, certainly," Renato said, favoring Mariette with a broad wink. "Without doubt."

Mariette walked at the crone's side, providing a supporting arm and conversing in comforting tones.

Renato tuned them out, imagining the many uses he would find for a temple full of gold. His daydream was interrupted by an annoying bleat from Quayle.

"There's someone out there, Cap'n! I seen 'em zip from tree to tree. First on our left, and then again on the other side."

"Animals, Quayle. This may be Yucatán, but it's still the same earth."

" 'Tweren't no animals, Cap'n, 'less they walks on two legs."

"Enough, Quayle. You'll say no more of this—to anyone."

The last thing Renato needed was for the men to be spooked by wild talk. Still, he would have to keep watch on their surroundings. If there were enemies lurking, he wished to know it before finding a spear in his back

CHAPTER 67

"Ain't bloody likely."

"**B**LAST MY EYES," the seaman Young wheezed. "That's *Medusa*. What's she doing here?"

Bowie twisted the telescope, bringing the ship into closer view. The triangular sails were similar to those of *L'Intrepide*, but on the deck was a huge cannon, out of all proportion with the small schooner.

Bowie seethed. Had Pacal's story been merely a ruse to gain passage home?

The Haitians began jabbering, pointing angrily at *Medusa*, and with Sam's interpreting, Bowie soon had the story of Renato's ship exchange with the U.S. Navy.

So they were on the right track after all.

He turned to examine Tulum. Perched upon that awesome crag was a massive gray pyramid, topped by a square stone temple. The crumbling walls had the look of extreme age.

"Most seamen avoid it," Young said, "believing the place accursed."

Bowie could understand why. He would not have been surprised to see a hundred Pacal-like heads appear over the walls, loosing a storm of fearful shafts across the water.

He returned his attention to *Medusa*, asking Young, "Could that ship be deserted?"

Sharky pushed forward. "Beggin' your pardon, Cap'n, but Renato wouldn't never go ashore without someone guardin' his means of escape."

Bowie grimaced. This would further delay his reunion with Mariette. And with Renato.

He fingered the butt of his knife, recalling all Renato had to answer for.

I'm coming for you, you black-hearted bastard. And this time, there will be hell to pay.

CHAPTER 68

"Destiny can be fickle."

THE PIRATES FLOPPED on their bellies, faces submerged in a small brown stream. Renato eyed the crone, seated upon a flat rock and kneading the sole of one very large foot.

"What more has she told you?" he asked Mariette.

"One thing of interest. Apparently, the Mayans believe life on earth follows a great cycle, and they await the next cataclysm."

Renato pretended to know what a cataclysm was. "And when might that be?"

"The year 2012, at which time the skies will grow dark, the seas will scour man from the earth, and the slow crawl to civilization will begin again."

Renato snorted. "She must be mad."

"She didn't say she believed it. Only that the Mayans do. More to the point, they believe their treasure temple is impenetrable without the key, and see no need to stand guard over it."

Renato licked his lips. Things were going his way again at last. He strode to the old woman's side. "You must have lived here many years."

"More than I care to remember."

"Did you ever encounter that washed-up poseur, Lafitte?

The woman perked up considerably at this. "Lafitte! *Si! There* was a man! He was once my lover, you know."

Renato choked, attempting to mask it with a cough.

"Ah, you may scoff, but I have not always been as you see me now. I was one of the great man's favorites."

Renato scowled. "There was nothing great about him."

"Then you did not know him as I did, Señor. But then, of course you did not." And she proceeded to make the most hideous sound, which Renato finally identified as a giggle. And to add further annoyance, Mariette joined in.

"He was a braggart and a thief," Renato persisted. "He was utterly without honor."

The old woman laughed. "But naturally, Señor. He was a pirate."

"He is still much admired in New Orleans," Mariette said. "If he ever returned, I believe they would make him Governor."

"He will *never* return," Renato said hotly. "He's worm food now."

The old woman shrugged. "There will never be another like him."

Renato bit off another retort. A thought had just occurred to him. "Did he spend much time here, in this jungle?"

"Oh, but of course. He visited the temple many times. He so longed to discover a way to reach the gold."

"But he never did."

"Sadly, no. If he had, I might now be a queen."

Renato grinned. At last he knew why Lafitte had chosen that god-forsaken *Isla Mujeres* as a place to retire. He had discovered the temple's location, and hoped to find another way in.

But the repulsive old woman was right. There would not be another like Lafitte. There would be one far greater, who would triumph where Lafitte had failed.

"Cap'n Renato!"

"What is it now, Hump?"

"I don't like it, Cap'n. My humps tinglin' like crazy."

"If you ask me to scratch it, you cretin, I will kill you where you stand."

"It means something ain't right, Cap'n. Somethin' ain't natural."

The nearly incessant chirp of birds had stopped. He could not even hear the buzz of insects. And the steady salt breeze coming off the ocean had vanished entirely. Renato's spine twitched, but he shrugged it off.

"You are worse than the old woman, Hump. This is a jungle like any other."

But moments later, his words proved a lie. Their boot heels rang suddenly upon stone, and they discovered themselves to be walking a flat, raised causeway.

The old woman answered their startled looks. "A Mayan road. We have reached the outskirts of the city."

"City? I thought there was merely a temple."

"Oh, there are temples, and much more. According to legend, this was once the mightiest of Mayan cities, abandoned centuries before the Spanish came."

Minutes later, drier of throat and shorter of patience, Renato caught sight of something against the glow of the dying sun. The distinct shape of a building, impossibly high in the air. It seemed to sit atop the distant line of trees, held as if by sorcery.

"We must camp here," the old woman said.

"Now?" Renato said. "Why? We've an hour of daylight left, and I'm anxious to meet my destiny."

The crone lay a finger aside her nose. "You should be less anxious, Señor Captain. When you have lived as long as I, you will know destiny can be fickle."

CHAPTER 69

"Good night, Ogu."

"WALK THIRTY MILES?" Bowie was horrified. "Don't you people have horses?"

"If we had," Pacal replied bitterly, "the Spanish would have taken them."

"The Spanish? Are they going to be a problem?"

Pacal shook his head. "They grow fat in their houses at Valladolid, a day's ride from the northeast. There is little to interest them here."

Bowie and his party were at last on land and eager to proceed, only to learn the temple was still a full day's travel away.

The pirates found drunk on *Medusa*'s deck were left in the care of Wilson and Young—along with the ships—and they now stood on the edge of the jungle behind Tulum.

Pacal and Chak ignored all questions regarding the city, save to say it had no connection to the treasure. As they prepared to leave, Chak slung a long, narrow sheath onto his back, containing the shafts and stick Bowie had seen used so effectively.

He made an attempt at conversation. "What do you call that thing?"

Chak merely sneered, but Pacal said, "It is called an *atlatl*, and has been used by my people for longer than any man remembers."

"An impressive weapon. Could you teach me to use it?"

Without hesitation, the brown man said, "No." Then he set off at an easy trot into the jungle, and Bowie could only follow.

Sam loped easily at his side, his long legs eating twice the ground of Bowie's. Behind them came the Haitians, still whispering about the mysterious Ogu.

The past day had shed no further light on the Ogu question, save that the men now afforded Bowie every possible respect. Before eating, they prostrated themselves, begging him to accept their food, and their eyes rarely left him.

By the time Pacal called a halt, the moon was high in the sky, and Bowie was ready to collapse.

"Two hours," Pacal said, indicating beds of grass along the side of the trail.

Bowie heard the whispered name again.

"Ogu."

"Ogu, Ogu, Ogu!" he roared, wheeling upon the Haitians. "I've had my fill of Ogu! Who the hell is he?"

The men's faces shone in the moonlight, their eyes large and round.

Sam spoke a few words of French, earning no response. He repeated himself, this time with heat, and one man answered.

Bowie watched the back and forth, wanting desperately to sink into the grass, but determined to see an end to this business.

When Sam turned to face him, his lips bore a peculiar smile. "Well?"

"It would seem, Jim, that these gentlemen believe you have been 'mounted'."

"Mounted!"

"It is their term for one who has been possessed by a Loa. In this case, the warrior spirit Ogu, one of the most powerful in their belief system."

"They think I'm possessed?"

Sam could not contain his amusement. "Only in a good way. The Loa Ogu is associated with blood, fire, lightning and the sword. It was he they summoned to inhabit you in Mr. Buck-

ner's cabin, and they watched for the spirit's presence to mani-
fest itself."

Bowie looked from Sam to the Haitians and back, at a loss
for words.

"When you went into a rage the other day, drawing your
knife on Pacal's son, it was proof you are now under Ogu's spell.
It may amuse you to learn that Ogu is also something of a male
fertility god."

"That's it! That's enough! Tell them there is no one inhabit-
ing this body but James Bowie. That I have always been as I am
now, and require no assistance, in love or war, from any damned
Voodoo spirits. Well, tell them!"

Sam turned to the Haitians, speaking slowly and patiently.
The black men listened, nodded at him, nodded at Bowie, and
receded into the darkness, seeking places to bed down.

"Thank you, Mr. Gideon."

"Oh, you are quite welcome."

Something in Sam's tone gave Bowie pause. "You did tell
them what I said?"

"Oh yes. I told them the great and powerful Ogu is pleased
by their eagerness to serve him."

Bowie narrowed his brows, tightened his lips. He felt ready
to explode.

"They may come in handy, Jim. You must admit, we should
employ every means available to aid Mariette."

"Damn your hide. If I still owned you, I'd sell you to Pacal.
For a coconut."

Sam merely looked smug as he lowered himself onto the
grass.

"You began this quest, I believe, seeking riches as a means
to power. Though riches still elude you, you have achieved half
your goal."

"Voodoo nonsense is hardly the kind of power I had in mind,"
Bowie growled.

"Perhaps not," came the reply, "but is it any less illusory?"

Bowie did not know what to say to that. But despite the aggravation, his eyes were heavy, and he was nearly asleep when Sam's quiet voice came out of the darkness.

"Good night, Ogu."

And as Bowie passed into slumber, he could almost swear he heard the black man giggle.

CHAPTER 70

"The Maya are tricky devils."

I N   T H E   M O R N I N G light, the secret of the building in the sky was revealed.

A small temple sat atop a colossal gray pyramid. At first glance, with the roots of trees entangled in its sides, it appeared a natural mountain. But there was no mistaking the regular shape of tiers, or the flights of crumbling stairs proceeding up the side. Compared to this, the great stone castle of Tulum was little more than a henhouse.

Mouth dry as dust, Renato said, "Is that where the treasure lies? Is that entire building full of gold?"

The crone emitted her annoying laugh. "Alas, no, Señor. But the treasure temple is not far now. And its size will not disappoint you."

For the next hour, one wonder followed quickly on the next, as more vine-covered buildings materialized out of the jungle.

In the utter quiet, the voice of the old woman was audible to all.

"The Mayan name for this mighty city is unpronounceable, but the Spanish called it Cobá."

"Mighty, perhaps," Renato said, "but the Spanish did conquer it."

"Oh, but this city was never conquered. The Maya abandoned it of their own accord"

"So why did they leave their gold?"

"There was dissent among them. The Mayan king believed

Cortez to be the reincarnation of their god Kukulkan, whose sign was the feathered serpent, and wished to lay all his possessions before him. The priests were more wary. They decided to leave their greatest treasures here, where the invaders would not think to search."

"Little good it did them," Renato said. "There is no one left to spend the gold."

"The Maya still exist," the old woman said. "They are merely waiting."

"And now they have waited too long." Renato laughed. "Their gold will soon be spent. By us." But inwardly he said, *By me.*

BOWIE WAS UP with the dawn, shaking Sam and the Haitians back to life.

The two hours had passed like so many minutes. Pacal and his son sat as he had last seen them, cross-legged and scowling at their unwelcome guests.

Not for the first time, Bowie noticed Chak eyeing him with open contempt. He still marveled that the little monster had managed to stow away on *Lucinda* without being discovered. But if Sharky was to be believed, the exploits of his friends aboard *L'Intrepide* had been even more remarkable—stealing the pirates' food and engineering the explosion that scorched Renato past all recognition.

In any case, Bowie found this junior version of Pacal even more ill-tempered than the original, and longed to be rid of both at the earliest opportunity.

"THAT'S THE ONE!" Renato eyed another great pyramid rising from the jungle ahead. "Speak, woman. Tell me that's the one."

"You are ever wise, O Captain. That is indeed the temple you seek."

Like the first pyramid, this looked more like a mountain than a man-made structure. But patches of smooth stone were visible beneath the vegetation, and with no temple on top, it rose to a peak. Flanking one side were smaller buildings forming a sort of gateway. Renato was strangely reminded of a cathedral.

The men's exhaustion of the night melted away, and even those lugging the statue found new energy.

Reaching the pyramid, the entire company streamed toward the entrance, a wide stone arch with a descending flight of stairs. And here, for the first time, was evidence of recent visitation. Vines and brush had been cut back, allowing them to descend with relative ease.

In no time they stood in the shadow of the entryway. But that's all it was. A small enclosed space, leading nowhere.

The wall was a riot of carvings. Snakes, birds, skulls, and large-nosed men in fantastic dress contorting their bodies in painful ways.

"Where is the lock for this key, woman? If you have lied…"

"Fear not, Captain. I am not fool enough to trifle with such as you. The lock is within reach of your right hand."

Renato peered skeptically at that area of the wall. "Do not toy with me, crone. Show me this lock while you still have your head."

With a cackle, the woman ran a hand over a carved circle nearly a foot in diameter. "This is the place you seek. This is where you insert the key."

The circle was cut no more than half an inch into the stone, and protruding from its center was the glaring head of a serpent. Its mouth was open, displaying rows of teeth, and ringing its neck like petals were sharp, triangular feathers.

Renato snorted. "How can the statue possibly fit into that?"

The old woman shrugged. "That is all he told me."

"Who? That bastard Lafitte?"

Her answer was a serene smile.

Mariette turned a thoughtful eye on the idol. "Bring it," she ordered, "and turn it upside down." And such was her ring of command, that the men obeyed, resting the head of the statue at Renato's feet.

Staring up at him was the hollow base, a ring of gold roughly the same size as the stone circle. He was bending to lift it when the old woman spoke again.

"As a gracious leader, should that honor not fall to one of your loyal followers?"

Something in the way she spoke carried a warning. "Caffrey," Renato said, naming the biggest man among them, "I believe she speaks of you."

Caffrey stared stupidly as two men thrust the statue into his arms, its head buried in his belly, while the hollow body extended toward the wall.

"Place it against the circle," Renato said, his voice hoarse.

Caffrey hunched forward until the base nestled into the depression of the stone circle. It was a perfect fit.

"Now what?" Renato demanded.

The woman gave another shrug. "If he knew, he did not tell me."

"Push," Renato said, and Caffrey strained forward, grunting.

Nothing happened.

"Kelley," Renato said, "Meech. Help him." And two men stepped behind Caffrey, bracing their legs and placing hands upon his back.

"Again," Renato ordered. "Push."

The three heaved together, grunting with exertion, and there came a crack of stone, as something gave way. Something clicked, and Caffrey screamed.

Renato jumped back, unable to control his reflexes. When the scream subsided into a gurgle, Caffrey slumped forward, unconscious or dead. But he did not fall.

Renato stared at the growing crimson pool between the man's legs. Swallowing hard, he bent to look. Protruding from the wall—and up into Caffrey's belly—was a long metal spike.

He turned on the crone. "You knew of this?"

"The Maya are tricky devils," she said indifferently.

"A key," Mariette said, unfazed by the man's death, "must be turned."

Renato pointed to Kelley and Meech. "Take hold of that thing." When they hesitated, he lay a hand on his cutlass, and the two complied.

With great reluctance, they stepped to either side of Caffrey and wrapped hands around the idol.

"This time," Renato said, "you will turn it, like a key."

With terrified faces, the pair braced their legs, flexed their arms, and began to turn.

After much scraping and grinding, there came another click, then a great rumbling of stone, and they were enveloped in a cloud of foul-smelling dust.

When the dust cleared, a portion of the wall had separated itself from the whole. The opening was wide enough to admit two men walking abreast. A rancid odor stung Renato's nostrils—the stench of a room unopened for hundreds of years.

Mariette peered into the darkness. "We will need torches."

"Get them," Renato barked. "Quickly." By the time they arrived, he was nearly beside himself with impatience.

"Who goes first?" Mariette asked.

Renato stopped with one leg halfway through the opening. "The crone."

With no sign of fear, the old woman accepted a torch and stepped into the blackness.

Renato held his breath.

Then came her voice. "Come, Captain. It is quite safe."

He followed, annoyed, but as the torches lit the scene within, all else was swept from his mind.

CHAPTER 71

"Your hand is dirty."

THE HARD SLAP of feet against the earth pounded in rhythm with the pain in Bowie's chest. He judged they had covered more than ten miles the previous night, and a similar distance already today. If they did not reach the temple soon, he feared his wounds would reopen. And he still had much to do.

Ahead, Pacal turned from side to side as if seeking something in the jungle.

Bowie looked about, spying nothing unusual. The same vine-draped trees, the same thick brush he'd seen for many miles. Then a chorus of screams arose around them. There was a blur of movement, and onto the trail spilled a group of small men brandishing axes, clubs and hoes.

Pacal and son stopped in their tracks.

More armed men emerged from the jungle, until the company was entirely surrounded. The newcomers' expressions said they were eager to tear into Bowie's party at the slightest provocation.

Pacal raised his hands and spoke in a loud, commanding voice. Immediately, the new arrivals lowered their weapons, but their faces did not soften a whit. That these men were Mayans was obvious, but while their features were uniformly broad, their heads were round rather than flat.

"It is as I thought," Pacal told Bowie. "Those we seek have gone into the city." And reading Bowie's expression, added, "Including the girl."

"And this little army didn't stop them?"

"These people are farmers, not fighters. In normal times, it is forbidden for them to enter the old city. Protecting the treasure is the job of the Jaguar Society."

"So where are these jaguar men?"

"You saw them in Texas. Three were my nephews, two my sons. Now all but Chak…" he hung his head, "have gone to meet the gods."

"So what happens now?"

"Until the treasure is safe again, we are all Jaguars." Then, raising his voice, he addressed his people in their own strange tongue.

His words galvanized the crowd. There was much cheering and brandishing of weapons.

"I don't doubt their commitment," Bowie said, "or their ferocity. But Renato's men are born killers, with swords and guns. You will need our help."

"Sadly," Pacal said, "I believe that is true."

"There are conditions."

Pacal growled, but waited without speaking. Chak merely glared.

"Mariette is not to be harmed. She leaves with us."

Pacal nodded.

"And Renato is mine. I will deal with him in my own fashion, but you may rest assured he will die, and his passing will not be pleasant."

Pacal's nostrils flared. "He killed one of my sons."

"As he has killed many others. But the vengeance I owe him is long overdue." Bowie laid a hand on his knife, and his voice took on some of the blade's steel. "I will not be denied."

Pacal gave a short nod. "I must witness his death."

"Agreed."

From behind came the raspy voice of Sharky. "Uh, Mr. Pacal, sir. One more thing. If we help save your treasure, may we not have a small reward? Just enough to line our pockets?"

Bowie stared. That the man had brains enough to master Spanish shocked him no end.

Pacal gripped the hilt of his dagger. For a moment it seemed he would dart back and plunge it into Sharky's breast. With air hissing through his teeth, he said to Bowie, "Is this, too, one of your conditions?"

Bowie looked at his companions. The Haitians, who understood little if any Spanish, stared curiously back. Sam appeared mildly interested. "For myself, I want only a life—and a death. But these others have traveled far and suffered much. A pittance of gold would be just compensation."

Pacal sighed. "We waste precious time. Yes, we have a bargain."

Bowie extended a hand.

Pacal stared at it. "I have no gold to give you now."

"Do your people not shake hands to seal a contract?"

"My word is good," Pacal said. "And your hand is dirty."

RENATO'S HEART THUNDERED like a succession of cannon blasts. His breath came in short, violent bursts and his scarred body tingled in every nerve.

Within the mountain-sized pyramid was an inner mountain of treasure, stacked high enough to brush the ceiling. There were golden statues of all descriptions. Jewelry set with agates, amber and fire opals. Weapons and death masks made from jade. Even benches and thrones fashioned entirely of gold. It was more than his eyes could take in, more than his mind could conceive.

From the doorway, some fool shouted, "Cap'n! Do ye hear that? Sounds like men cheering!"

Renato had no time for such nonsense. "Then clean out your ears, you halfwit! The city is deserted. And even if there were men hereabouts, what would they have to cheer about?"

The fool at the door said no more, and Renato quickly erased him from his thoughts.

Within minutes, his pockets were heavy with treasure, his packsacks full to bursting. And still, he longed to caress each crown and statue, fondle each goblet and bowl. Other objects were indefinable, some so bizarre as to have been fashioned by a lunatic, but each more desirable than the last.

Here was more wealth than he had ever imagined. But fantastic as it seemed, he wanted one thing more. The missing element in his future happiness, the final factor that had eluded him these days past, was suddenly crystal clear.

"Mariette!" The old woman's shriek echoed off the sloping stone walls. "Look!"

Renato picked his way along the edge of the golden mountain to where the crone huddled over a massive chest worked with intricate and grotesque designs. Behind her stood Mariette, face glowing bright as any torch.

"This is incredible," the old woman shrilled. "These may be worth more than the gold!"

Renato hastened his pace, his tongue slaking dry lips. More valuable than gold?

He stopped, inhaling Mariette's scent as he stared into the open chest. He rolled his eyes and blew out a great snort. The thing contained nothing but folded lengths of rough-looking paper—paper covered with odd symbols and abhorrent drawings.

The hag turned an insolent eye on him. "Apparently," she said, "you know not what you see. These are books, called codices, and they contain the accumulated wisdom of the Mayan people."

Renato sneered. "What wisdom? The wisdom to build stone temples and carve hideous images? What did it get them? A pyramid full of gold they could not spend. Such wisdom had best remain lost."

The old woman clacked her tongue. "I once thought as you do. When I was young and stupid."

Renato's cutlass was halfway from its scabbard when Mariette laid a hand on his arm. "Please. She means no offense."

Still bristling, Renato slammed the blade home. "Why suffer her insolence any longer? She is of no use to us now."

Mariette's smile was deliciously wicked. "She is old," she whispered, "but strong. She can carry much gold."

Renato studied the girl with frank admiration. Her instincts were impeccable, nearly equaling his own. He addressed his men. "Gather everything you can. It's time we returned to the ship."

He had already formed a plan. Get back to *Medusa* with all the treasure they could manage, returning immediately for another load, and another. When the ship could hold no more they would sail for a civilized port, where more men could be recruited, more ships purchased or stolen. Horses and wagons would be brought. There was enough here to fill a dozen Spanish galleons.

He quickly outlined the plan to Mariette.

"Exactly as I envisioned it," said the crone.

"You? What would you know of vision?"

"Apologies, my lord. I merely meant that in some ways you and I think alike."

"Do you know what I'm thinking now?"

"Why no, Señor."

"Then you may count yourself lucky." Feeling Mariette's eyes upon him, Renato turned away. The old hag's time would come.

Minutes later, they were back on the causeway, toiling in the direction of the coast. The men were so heavily laden they were already beginning to tire, and would soon be forced to lighten their loads. They would discover just how much they could carry, and they would carry it as many times as necessary. Or they would die.

Renato's spirit soared. With nothing but the wealth now in hand, he would be rich for life. And when he at last claimed the rest of his due, he would be the most powerful man in all the world.

He stole a glance at Mariette. She would make a fine queen. And she had been right about the old woman's capacity as a beast of burden. The crone hauled more treasure than most of the men, and with less difficulty.

A sharp hiss interrupted his thoughts. Not five feet in front of him, Quayle squeaked, staggered and crashed heavily to the causeway, a shaft protruding from his chest. As Renato stood staring, another man cried out, pitching sideways off the road.

"Take cover!" Renato roared. "And protect the gold, or I'll kill you all myself!"

CHAPTER 72

"Renato said you were dead!"

RENATO! BOWIE SAW him scuttle over the edge of the causeway, and marked his position. But a second later, he spotted Mariette, just disappearing around the side of a great pyramid. She was clad in an oversized seaman's coat, and in the grip of a thick-boned old woman in a ragged red dress.

Pistol balls spanked the leaves above Bowie's head as the pirates answered the Mayans' attack. Heedless of flying lead, Pacal's army of farmers stormed across the road, brandishing their tools and howling like maniacs. Making the most of the distraction, Pacal and Chak flattened themselves to the road and wriggled like snakes toward Renato's position.

Bowie found Sam at his side. "Mr. Gideon! Please ask your Voodoo friends to assist those peasants. And remind Pacal that Renato is to be captured, not killed. I'm going for Mariette."

"Aye Aye, Captain Ogu, sir."

"If you like that name so much," Bowie said, "I'll be pleased to carve it into your backside."

"Ouch."

With a grim smile, Bowie crab-walked over the causeway and hurried through the jungle toward the massive pyramid.

PEERING FROM HIS position of cover, Renato felt a jolt run through him.

Bowie! Alive, and here in Yucatán!

Renato gnashed his teeth. What did the Fates want from him

now—to punish his brother's killer, or to escape this mad land with his future queen?

From nearby came ragged shots and a bevy of strange war cries. The attack was focused on his gang of pirates ensconced on the opposite side of the causeway. Stashing his treasure sacks in a clump of brush, Renato drew his cutlass, rose to half his height and slipped away after Bowie.

Behind him came an angry clicking, and he whirled to face two scowling demons. With a start, he recognized them. Like that accursed Bowie, he had left them for dead in Texas. The older one was poised to throw a dagger, while the younger readied his stick weapon.

So the Fates had him by the tail again. Damn the Fates! They would toy with him no longer. He would take what he wanted and kill whom he liked, and Providence could dance to his tune.

Thrusting his cutlass before him, he charged headlong to the attack.

"MARIETTE? ARE YOU there?"

Bowie edged along the side of the pyramid, certain he had glimpsed the red dress through the maze of green. If the old woman was near, Mariette should be, too. And if that haggard creature was holding the girl against her will…

The thought faded as palm leaves parted and Mariette emerged from the trees. "James."

Overcome with relief, Bowie swept her up and crushed her body to his own. Their lips met in mingled relief and desire.

He could not help noticing she was remarkably heavy, and parts of her were lumpy and hard. Returning her to the earth, he stepped back for an examination. Adorning her throat were dazzling necklaces, and upon her head a gem-studded crown of gold. The pockets of her seaman's coat bulged with odd shaped objects.

"It would appear you found your treasure."

"We found the gold, but—" her voice caught, and he realized she was crying. "Oh, James. Renato said you were dead!"

"I'm not altogether certain he was wrong. But what of Renato? Did the bastard harm you?"

She suppressed a sob. "James, it was horrible. But all that matters now is that we're together."

Bowie made to speak, but she put a finger to his lips, covering his mouth with her own.

Wild cries and gunshots sounded in the distance. Bowie heard them dimly, knowing he had unfinished business. But for the moment, he did not care.

RENATO KICKED, CUFFED and pummeled the two brown demons, using every trick in his repertoire. But he was losing.

His mad charge had saved him from their weapons, but the little beasts had sprung upon him, engulfing him in a whirlwind of fury. Somehow in that melee his sword had vanished and he was reduced to bare-knuckle brawling.

The brown men were wiry and agile as wildcats, and fought with every available appendage. Worst of all were their teeth, slashing like tiny daggers through his scarred and blackened flesh.

With the young demon chewing on his arm and the older one ravaging his leg, Renato thrust a hand into his clothing, groping for something he could use as a weapon. Wrapping his fingers around a heavy cylindrical object, he raised it like a club.

Instantly, the younger man released his arm. The older man withdrew from his thigh and stared up with bulging eyes. The two exchanged words in their savage language, their expressions a mixture of reverence and astonishment.

Renato waited no longer. He brought the heavy object down full force, hearing a satisfying crunch as it crushed the older man's skull. The young one cried out, but only until Renato's backswing smashed him full in the face, knocking him into a bristly sedge, from which he did not arise.

Curious, Renato peered at his bloody weapon. It was a golden staff, half the length of his arm, fashioned in the shape of a snake. Upon its body, instead of scales, were a multitude of feathers. Another of those damned serpents. It was fitting this had been the last thing either man would see.

Clutching the blood-smeared staff, Renato raced after Bowie. The muscle-bound churl had left a trail a child could follow. Renato's rage increased with each stride, until he stopped bolt upright on a scene that jarred him to his heels.

Bowie kissing Mariette. *His* Mariette.

BOWIE BLINKED DAZEDLY as the girl stiffened and pushed away. An instant later, his face stung to a ringing slap.

"You cad!" she shrieked. "You bounder!"

Bowie rubbed at his cheek. He could make nothing of this. Then from behind came the howl of a tortured beast, and he found Renato nearly upon him.

A bloody cudgel whistled past his head, ripping his shirt and plowing a furrow down his arm. He slammed a fist into Renato's midsection, but his knuckles caromed off more solid objects, and he felt the snap of bone. His hand afire with pain, he realized too late that Renato's clothing, like Mariette's, was stuffed with treasure.

Renato's golden club came blazing back toward his skull. Bowie ducked under the blow, ramming his head into the pirate's face, and felt the snap of crushed cartilage. Renato staggered back, stunned, still clinging to his weapon.

Bowie did not like his chances. His left arm was numb, his right hand shaky. And despite his shattered nose, Renato was more dangerous than ever. He had seen the man enraged before, even beside himself with fury. But this was a Renato beyond imagining. His eyes flamed with the unholy light of a berserker, and a stream of bloody spittle poured from his charred lips.

Mariette watched as if transfixed, eyes bright and shiny.

Bowie recalled the slap. She had seen Renato watching,

and ended their embrace. The conclusion was too fantastic to consider, but he could find no other.

She had feelings for this monster.

And the monster was jealous.

RENATO SAW BOWIE through a red haze. This was the man he had ached so long to kill. The man who slaughtered his brother. But that crime paled compared to his latest offense. Now the wretch meant to steal Mariette, the only woman ever worthy of him.

Bowie's left arm hung limp. His right hand dripped blood. A bum arm and an unsteady hand were all that stood between Renato and his queen-to-be.

He swung the golden club again, and Bowie sidestepped, lashing out with a boot. Renato felt the impact in his groin, knew he was in pain. But pain was meaningless now. Only hate had meaning—hate and the crazed yearning he had come to realize was love.

Renato readied the staff for another strike. Bowie was breathing heavily, growing weaker, while Renato felt more powerful by the minute.

Then he heard a voice. A voice both familiar and impossible.

"Renato! Drop your weapon at once! I command you!"

BOWIE FOUGHT THE impulse to turn. The voice stabbed at his memory, but the face eluded him.

The effect on Renato was remarkable. His mouth hung slack and his eyes grew large as billiard balls. His right arm fell to his side, the cudgel loose in his grip. He seemed to have forgotten Bowie entirely.

Bowie stepped aside for a look at the newcomer. And he, too, had cause to stare.

There stood the woman in the huge red dress. As he watched, the dress was ripped open, exposing a worn leather vest, a hairy chest and ragged breeches shorn at the knees. The dress fell to the ground, revealing faded tattoos up and down each muscled arm. Then a tousled wig was tossed aside, exposing swarthy but handsome features and iron-gray hair tied with a ribbon.

The woman was now a man, and the man's eyes held a sardonic gleam.

"My compliments, Mr. Bowie. A pleasure to see you again."

Bowie could only stare as Renato spat the name.

"Lafitte!"

CHAPTER 73

"Which do you choose?"

RENATO FELT THE earth reel beneath his feet. Lafitte—*alive!*

There had been debate as to the place of Lafitte's burial, even the manner of his passing, but all believed the man was well and truly dead.

Yet here he stood. Thicker of waist and grayer of hair, but this was he, beyond all doubt. The same arrogant ring in his voice. The same superior glint in his eyes. The same ability to strut without moving, as if posing for a portrait.

And the fiend had played him once again for a fool.

Lafitte said, "Time is short, gentlemen. Explanations must wait."

Renato heard the words, but clung to the hope this was some mad nightmare.

"If we wish to live," Lafitte was saying, "we must put our differences aside. The Mayans are slaughtering Renato's men, and will never allow the rest of us to leave with their gold."

"Speak for yourself," Bowie said. "I have a bargain with Pacal."

"As do I," Lafitte countered, "but I am not fool enough to trust him."

Renato felt the world begin to stabilize. These men were discussing survival, a subject close to his heart. They didn't know Pacal was dead. Could that work to his advantage?

His eyes roved to Mariette, her small fists quivering at her sides. She appeared ill at ease, but as maddeningly alluring as ever. All her flush-faced attention was centered on Bowie.

And she had kissed him.

Could she actually prefer that backwoods bumpkin to him? Was it Bowie she truly loved? At the first sign of such, he would be ready, and in that moment the bumpkin would die.

BOWIE SAW RENATO staring trance-like at Mariette. He seemed oblivious to all else.

"I've no love for Pacal," Bowie said. "He's foul-tempered, unpredictable and borderline insane. But I'm still inclined to take him at his word."

Lafitte made a sour face. "And what of you, Captain Renato?"

This brought no response.

Bowie's knife hand twitched. The pain was brutal, but he was now able to move his fingers, and feeling was creeping backing into his left arm.

"Renato!" Lafitte's voice cut like a blade. "Speak, blast you! We must work together, or we're all dead."

Shaking himself, Renato scoured Lafitte with a glare. "I will never fight at your side." His scorn shifted to Bowie. "Or his. I will see us all in Hell first."

"Renato, please." Mariette's voice was soothing as a lullaby. "Would you doom me to die as well?"

As Renato faced her, his resolve seemed to melt. Bowie marveled at her effect upon the man.

"Before I agree to anything," Bowie said, "there's something I must know." He turned to Mariette. "Forgive my bluntness, girl, but where do your affections lie? Assuming we survive this, which of us do you choose?"

RENATO'S BREATHING STOPPED. His heart ceased to beat.

After long seconds, Mariette turned from Bowie to *him*, returning his steady gaze. She no longer flinched at seeing his scorched face. Surely she now saw past the mask to the man who loved her. Conflict and misery were written large upon her features, and it tortured him to see it.

She looked again to Bowie. Renato's fingers tightened around the staff. Two steps and a swing would end her indecision.

Then she spoke, nailing him in his tracks.

"If I must choose…" her voice cracked, faltered.

Renato's heart was fit to burst.

When Mariette spoke again, her voice was brittle. "If I must choose, I choose my father." And she stepped close to Lafitte, linking her arm with his.

BOWIE RECOILED AS if struck by a viper.

Renato stood rooted to the ground, his body twitching. He seemed about to split asunder.

Lafitte's daughter!

Bowie cursed himself for a fool. The thing had been plainly before him. The girl's knowledge of the map. Her patronage by Lafitte's oldest friend. Her wild and reckless nature. Her staged abduction in Texas. Andre's dying apology. All the clues had led to this. Her final betrayal.

He had been used from the start—by Lafitte, by Andre, and most of all by Mariette, whom he had almost come to love.

"In that case," he said, surprised at the coolness of his voice, "I will take my chances with Pacal. Mad as he is, he's more trustworthy than the three of you combined."

"My father is dead," snarled a new voice. "And your chances with me are slim."

RENATO FELT STRANGELY detached, watching as from a dream as the young demon emerged from the jungle. Behind him marched Sharky, Bowie's slave and a gaggle of Haitians, prodded by an army of brown men armed with farm tools. Several in that army wore scraps of bloody pirate attire, including Hump's vest. His own men, then, were already dead.

Surely that demon should be dead as well, as should the

Haitians. But Renato felt no surprise. Every ounce of shock had been drained from him.

"Chak! You speak English?" Bowie, ever the simpleton, spoke the obvious. "What's the meaning of this? Your father and I had an agreement, which my men and I have honored."

The brown man displayed a hideous sneer. "My father was too trusting. And he died for it, at the hands of this swine." He leveled an arm, and Lafitte and Mariette swung to stare at Renato, horror on their faces. The other natives fanned out to surround them.

Renato cared not at all. His heart had turned to ashes. Part of him wished to strike out, to rend and kill. But he knew not whom he hated most—Lafitte, for his repeated deceit, Bowie, for his brother's murder, or Mariette, for making him the ultimate fool.

"The girl comes with me, Chak, as do my men." Bowie's voice was firm. "And Renato is mine to punish. I care not what happens to Lafitte."

Chak's scowl was wider than his face. "You are powerless here, big man. These pirates defiled our sacred temple, as did the female. For that they shall die by my hand—not yours. You and the rest," he swept an arm to indicate Sam and the others, "may leave, provided you go quickly, taking nothing of the Maya."

"No—no gold?" Sharky whimpered.

Chak spat a few harsh clicks, and one of the farmers buried an ax in the scrawny man's back.

"Now go!"

CHAPTER 74

"I cannot save her."

BOWIE FELT A numbness around his heart. Mariette had chosen her own fate. Everything about her had been a lie.

As for Lafitte, Bowie sensed the old's pirate's hand behind this whole affair. Whatever doom awaited him now was of his own making.

But the fate of Renato was another matter entirely.

Seemingly of its own accord, Bowie's knife sprang into his hand. He covered the distance between them in a bound, and had the blade at the Renato's throat before anyone could prevent it.

"He comes with me," Bowie gritted. "I have sworn to take his life by my own hand, and in particular fashion. I assure you, Chak, he will regret every sin ever committed, including the killing of your father and brother."

Chak regarded him coolly. "I can see you are a man who cares little for his own life. But I suspect that disregard does not apply to the lives of others." He clicked a few words, and his warrior-farmers closed in around Sam and the Haitians.

Bowie examined the faces of his companions. They betrayed no fear, and might go to their deaths without complaint, but he could not sacrifice them to salve his own conscience.

"You will surrender your weapon and go," Chak said, "or none of you will ever leave at all."

With a sigh, and a silent apology to the blonde girl, Bowie

lowered his blade. He pushed Renato roughly away and stood glowering at Chak. But in truth, most of his anger was directed at himself. Since the moment this quest began, he had failed at every turn.

One of Chak's men held out a hand, and Bowie surrendered the knife without a fight, feeling a part of himself go with it

RENATO WATCHED BOWIE and the others led away. He still felt hatred for the man who had killed Rayón, but it was now a muted thing, overwhelmed by the enormity of Mariette's betrayal. Even his hatred of Lafitte paled in comparison.

He offered no resistance as his wrists were bound, and the three of them were prodded like cattle toward the great hoary pyramid with the temple at its peak. The climb, without use of hands, was a torture in itself, but he endured it in silence.

When at last they reached the top, they were shoved roughly into the small temple, to find the demon called Chak awaiting them. But this was a Chak he had never before seen. The man's outfit was bizarre beyond belief. A cloak of golden, black-spotted hide flowed from his shoulders, and covering his face was the hollowed-out head of a jaguar. It was only through the beast's gaping jaws that Renato saw the evil features of Chak himself.

The rest of the man's attire would make a rich man weep. A golden breastplate engraved with a hundred tiny skulls—a girdle of gold plates and brilliant gemstones—and gold bracelets in the shape of coiled serpents.

The man's eyes bored into Renato as four men gripped his limbs and slammed him flat on his back atop a stone altar.

Chak's hand gripped a dagger of razor-sharp obsidian, its golden handle fashioned in the shape of a two-headed snake. "You," he said, his voice dripping venom, "the killer of my father, will be the first to die."

BOWIE HUNG HIS head as he walked the causeway back toward Tulum and the sea. Sam made occasional remarks meant to cheer him, but he was beyond cheer. Behind them, the Haitians were strangely silent. There was no talk of Ogu now.

An eerie chanting followed them, floating down from the square structure atop the tiered pyramid. Some foul and ancient ceremony was taking place there. Bowie tried to close his mind to it, focusing on the road to the ship, to sanity and an end to this disastrous venture.

His rage at Chak still burned, for his refusal to honor Pacal's word, and for the senseless killing of Sharky. But he was equally angry at Mariette, at Lafitte, and at himself. Though he was certain Lafitte had been behind it all, it was he himself who had taken the bait and been reeled in like a fish, and he who must live with the consequences.

God's own terror, Andre had called him. He felt like God's own fool.

Three small but determined peasants had been assigned to escort them to the coast. Chak had deemed these sufficient once Bowie and the others had been stripped of their weapons. And save for Bowie's knife, those weapons were now far beyond reach. The big blade had caught the fancy of their farmer escorts, who turned it this way and that as they walked, admiring their reflections and catching rays of the sun.

Sam trudged along at Bowie's side, speaking too softly for the guards to hear. "If you wish to return for her, the Haitians and I await your command. These Mayan gentlemen are too preoccupied to offer much resistance."

Bowie shook his head. "Part of me wants to, but I cannot. Mariette used me. She wove us all into her web, even Renato. If someone must pay for this fiasco, who better?"

"But Jim, the Mayan sacrificial ceremony is barbaric. Victims are tied spread-eagled to an altar and forced to watch as—"

Bowie clapped hands over his ears, shutting out the rest. When the man's lips were finally still, Bowie dropped his arms and said, "I cannot save her. Besides, I am half-convinced Chak and his people are justified."

"Then what of your promise to the that golden-haired ghost? Will your broken heart blind you to your oath?"

Bowie said nothing. The words stung. Were they true? Was the pain of lost love clouding his judgment? He dropped his eyes to his feet, marking their steady progress toward the sea.

And from the temple behind came a piercing cry, so ghastly as to chill the heart. Even a heart as cold as Bowie's.

RENATO'S THROAT BURNED with the rattle of his scream. The descending dagger had stopped just above his heart, where the madman Chak carved a jagged X in his flesh.

He shot a glance at Mariette, slumped against a wall next to Lafitte. He regretted the scream, hoping she would not despise him for it. His feelings for the girl still confused him, and now, with death imminent, they would never be resolved. He would never know whether she preferred him or that oaf Bowie—or despised them both. Perhaps it was best he die clinging to the belief she had for a brief time been truly his.

Renato fought to control his terror. Lafitte had been almost jovial as they were prodded to this sacrificial temple, describing in horrendous detail the treatment they could expect. At the time, Renato had doubted him as a matter of course, but now knew the man had not exaggerated.

Raising the golden staff—the same staff Renato had used to bash the skull of the little beast's father—Chak broke once more into his repellent chant.

Renato averted his eyes. He could understand being slaughtered to avenge Pacal's death, even for stealing the Mayan gold. But to die on the altar of some feathered snake was an insult to his legacy. It cheapened his death to be sacrificed to a god so patently ridiculous.

Chak's followers took up the chant. Some were adorned in equally rich costumes, while others had merely fastened scarlet and emerald plumes to their rags. Renato recognized the blood-lust in their faces. He had seen it often enough in his own crew.

Chak raised his dagger. This time there would be no reprieve.

This time, Chak would not halt until the still-beating heart had been ripped from his chest.

The dagger reached its zenith. Renato steeled himself. This time, he would not give the little savages the satisfaction of a scream.

Chak's eyes gleamed with a hatred to rival Renato's own.

And into the temple burst a group of otherworldly figures. Their cries were high-pitched and haunting, like spirits from beyond the grave.

Renato craned his neck. The newcomers moved so quickly it was hard to focus, but their bodies were dark, their faces gleaming white as bone. Their arms swayed up and down as if summoning gods from on high. They began to shout, "Ogu! Ogu!"—doubtless the name of some savage deity.

Chak and his followers stared in bewilderment. Then something hit the rooftop with a dull thud. Came a sharp blast, and the ceiling shook as if on the verge of collapse. The dust of ancient stone filled the air like smoke.

And most of Chak's followers went mad, bleating in terror as they raced to escape.

BOWIE CROUCHED AT the side of the small temple. He grinned as the terrified farmers came flooding out as if devils were after them. After a moment the devils themselves burst out, wailing and jabbering imprecations to their patron Ogu.

Bowie waved them on as they chased the Mayans down the side of the pyramid. The Haitians, aided by glowing paints from their *gris-gris* bags, had done well. As had Sam, making a bomb from a clay pot and the contents of their powder horns.

Now it was Bowie's turn. His chest still ached from the climb up the pyramid. The sides were so overgrown it had been like scaling a mountain. But he could not give in to pain. Easing the knife from its sheath, he turned and roared into the temple.

Strapped to a stone slab in the center lay Renato, his scarred face bearing a look of complete astonishment. Against a wall to one side stood Mariette and Lafitte, bound but apparently unharmed. While most of the Mayans had fled, Chak and five warriors remained, evidently those hardest to scare. Now, realizing they had been tricked, they bared their teeth and charged.

Bowie's knife swept out, opening his nearest attacker from chin to brisket. Another came at him from behind and he turned, swinging the blade up with tremendous force. The man howled as his right arm leaped into the air—the hand still gripping a club—to skid across the stone floor. A third warrior surged forward just as Sam burst through the entrance, and fell beneath Sam's Mayan ax.

Bowie slashed the bonds holding Renato's feet, then dashed to the head of the slab, freeing his hands. "This," he said through gritted teeth, "is not the way you die."

As Renato scrambled free, Bowie saw Sam struggling with the last two warriors. Sam had lost his ax, and one man held his arms while the other sought an opening for his spear.

Bowie was about to throw his blade when Sam shouted, "No! Mariette!"

Bowie spun to see Chak gripping the helpless girl by the neck. The fiend's other hand rose above his head, clutching a golden dagger—a twin to the weapon he had seen a lifetime ago in New Orleans. Lafitte, bound at Mariette's side, was helpless to act.

He swung back to Sam. One of his attackers had tightened his grip. At any moment the other would plunge his spear into the black man's chest. Sam's eyes flicked from Bowie to Mariette, his meaning clear.

Bowie was torn. Mariette's face was drawn, her eyes locked onto his, pleading for life. Chak's face shone with malevolence. Only an instant had passed. Only an instant remained. Sam or Mariette? An impudent slave he had come to admire—or the girl who had betrayed him, but still held a piece of his soul.

There was no time to think. Barely time to act. His wrist flicked back, shot forward, and the blade blazed through the air to bury itself in a fierce Mayan heart.

Bowie spun desperately about. Chak was about to strike.

Mariette's eyes seared into his, full of hatred now, and the knowledge he had chosen Sam over her.

Bowie darted forward, knowing it was too late. Time seemed to slow, heightening the pain of his decision, and his helplessness to save this woman he had almost loved.

Chak's blade had barely reached her breast when a dark shape hurtled into him, sending the dagger flying. Chak smashed into a far corner of the temple, the dark shape mauling him like a panther. Snarling, shrieking, bone-splintering noises erupted from the corner in a cacophony of fury.

Bowie reached Mariette's side. Blood flowed from a shallow gash in her breast, and he felt a flash of relief. Then she spat full in his face.

"Pig!" she said. "You prefer that slave to me!" Clearly, any feelings she had for him were gone.

And in that instant, he knew himself free of her as well.

Mariette turned to peer into the corner, where the sounds of struggle had finally ceased.

Wiping spittle from his eye, Bowie saw a ravaged figure stagger out of the shadows. Its hands and teeth were red with gore, but its eyes were bright. They fixed on Mariette with obvious relief.

"My hero!" she cried. "My dear Captain Renato! I knew you would not fail me."

CHAPTER 75

"Justice."

THE LONG TREK through the jungle should have been a great moment, a triumphant return with a king's ransom in gold. Instead, Renato's arms were bound, and a black man led him with a rope about his neck, while his most hated enemies traipsed along free-as-you-please.

Although he'd now had time to think, the events of the previous day left him confused. Why had Bowie, a man with every reason to despise him, returned to save him from Chak's altar?

Even more baffling, why had he himself risked his neck to rescue Mariette? While Bowie was busy with the Mayans, he might have slipped away, returned to the treasure temple and made his way back to *Medusa*. But he had sacrificed everything for the life of one fickle girl—and she the daughter of a sworn enemy.

Mariette, smeared from head to toe with blood and dirt, somehow retained the bearing of a queen. At his side, she would have been that and more, and her betrayal still stung him to the quick.

Since leaving the ancient city, Bowie had been tight-lipped, barely acknowledging his presence, but Lafitte missed no opportunity to torture him. The old braggart waved his arms about as he recounted his masterful plan to steal the Mayan gold. The fact his great scheme had come to nothing seemed to faze him not at all.

The story, stripped to its essentials, was not long in telling.

The Spanish, as all knew, had plundered the Yucatán for nearly two centuries, finding little if any treasure. Finally, five years hence, they had come upon a strange statue and several chests of gold, and planned to send it, along with a captured Mayan king, back to Madrid to amuse King Ferdinand. This much Lafitte had learned from his spies in Mexico. But from natives at his sometime base on *Isla Mujeres*, he'd also heard mutterings that the statue was the key to a much greater treasure.

Renato knew the next part of the story. Resorting to his usual treachery, Lafitte had briefly captured the chest containing the key, only to lose it again.

"Had you not tried to cheat me," Renato put in, "we would have had the key long ago—and the treasure."

Lafitte answered with a grin. "A man who trusts a pirate is a fool. And a pirate who trusts another pirate is the greatest fool of all."

And as if this passed for an apology, the man continued to brag. "After scouring the Texas coast for the chest's hiding place, I eventually came here, bringing Pacal with me, and exhausted other means of opening the temple."

"And faked your own death," Renato said bitterly, "rather than enlist further aid from me."

"I bided my time," Lafitte replied, "awaiting word the casket—or the map—had been found. When my spy Sharky reported the map was coming to you, I formed a shaky alliance with Pacal, and sent him to Dominique with the plan to relieve you of it. Pacal insisted on accompanying Mariette, and sent some of his followers to bedevil you. I understand they performed quite admirably."

Had his hands been free, Renato would have killed the man with a single blow. "But for all your cleverness," he retorted, "you failed to account for the presence of Bowie."

"On the contrary, I insisted Andre recruit him. Aware of your blood feud, I knew he would make things hot for you, and if he managed to kill you along the way, so much the better. The crux of the plan was to get at least one ship and crew to Karankawa Cove to retrieve the key, and deliver it here to me."

Renato could scarcely credit his ears. "And you trusted those little brown demons to share the treasure with you?"

Lafitte displayed a condescending smile. "I promised Pacal the lion's share, of course, but planned to relieve him of it when the time came." Then his tone grew winsome. "And I might have succeeded, but for one oversight. It never occurred to me that both you and Bowie might survive the journey, bringing your battle all the way to Cobá. I underestimated him—and overestimated *you*—and both errors are now upon my head."

"And for that I shall be ever grateful," said the grating voice of Bowie himself. "Doubly grateful, in fact, for I believe the Governor of Louisiana still has a bounty on that head."

So the clod had been lurking nearby, eavesdropping all along.

At that, Lafitte fell silent, leaving Renato to his own regrets.

What he found particularly galling was that the only ones with gold in their pockets were the Voodoo men, whom he himself had rescued from the sinking merchantman. With the Mayan leaders dead and their followers scattered to the winds, Bowie had let the former slaves retrieve a portion of the booty Renato and his men had removed from the temple.

All that saved him from madness were the occasional comforting words and sympathetic looks from Mariette. Those small attentions, which he once would have scorned, were everything to him now.

At last the party spilled onto the white beach beneath Tulum, to see *Medusa* and *Lucinda* riding easily at anchor.

Bowie turned his cold blue eyes upon him, and Renato felt his hackles rise. "What do you want of me, damn you?"

The others turned to stare, and all conversation ceased.

Bowie's voice was quiet, but his answer seemed to echo and re-echo within Renato's head.

"Justice."

BOWIE HEARD THE first of the jolly boats crunch into the sand behind him. Grasping the rope about Renato's neck, he marched him down the beach and thrust him roughly into the bow. He turned to find the rest of the group on his heels.

"Renato and I are paying a short visit to *Medusa*. The rest of you will proceed to *Lucinda* and make ready to sail." Bowie ran a hard eye over the group, intending to brook no argument. "I will not tarry long."

As Sam translated for the Haitians, Lafitte said smoothly, "I would much prefer to accompany you. This bears every sign of a rare and delicious entertainment."

"I, too, wish to witness this performance." These were the first words Mariette had spoken to him since leaving the city, and her voice was like a winter frost.

With cries of "Ogu! Ogu!" the Haitians clambered into the second boat and began rowing with great enthusiasm toward *Medusa*.

Bowie grimaced. He would prefer this final act to play out solely between Renato and himself, with the golden-haired girl looking on in absentia. But in the end it mattered little, so long as the deed was done.

Once assembled on *Medusa*'s deck, the group stood tensely, eyes roving between he and Renato, who sat bound at the base of the great swivel gun. They seemed to expect a speech.

"Devil take you all," Bowie said. "This is not some sideshow staged for your pleasure."

"Still," Lafitte said, "we are here. After all we have endured together, will you not offer some hint of your intentions?"

Bowie looked to Sam, who raised his eyebrows and shrugged.

"Vultures," Bowie said without heat. "Some of you know of the longstanding differences between this jackal and myself." He raised his voice to be heard above Renato's snarl. "Following the death of his equally rabid brother, Renato vented his rage on a girl whose only offense was to offer me a smile." Renato roared another protest, earning a boot to the chin. "At the time, I was too busy chasing riches to avenge her, a failing I now regret. But I swore that one day Renato would suffer the same vile fate he visited upon that girl. That day has come at last."

"N O O O O !"

Renato recognized the cry as his own, and tried to shut it off. But the noise kept coming.

Of all possible deaths, this was one he had never imagined for himself. It had been fitting for the blonde whore who had betrayed Rayón, but would hardly do for The Last Great Terror of the Gulf.

Bowie had whispered orders to his lanky manservant, and the man was already instructing the Haitians in the loading and priming of the great 18-pounder.

Renato chanced a look at Mariette, and saw Lafitte speaking softly into her ear. He looked quickly away. He did not wish to see her expression when she learned what he had done to the blonde wench. He had reveled in his choice at the time, and recalled it fondly ever since, but under Mariette's eye the act made him feel small, even despicable.

All too soon, Bowie hauled him up from the deck and sliced through his bonds. Like a scene from a nightmare, the slaves manhandled him into position facing the barrel of the huge swivel gun.

"It's all a lie!" Renato roared. "It never happened."

Bowie glowered at him, his face inches away. "You're calling Andre a liar?"

Renato forced a laugh. "Are you daft? He was a pirate!"

The slightest shade of doubt appeared in Bowie's eyes.

"Andre was the king of all liars," Lafitte put in. "But not in this case. I heard the tale from a dozen tongues, including that of my good friend Dominique, and it disgusted even me. Had I witnessed it I would have killed you myself."

Bowie growled swift orders, the manservant translated, and the Haitians pressed Renato's belly tight against the mouth of the gun. They pulled his arms and legs forward, hugging the barrel, and looped ropes around them, making them secure. After long hours in the sun, the iron barrel was hot as a griddle, and he heard his flesh sizzle.

Renato stared down the length of the great cannon, dreading what was to come. He would be forced to watch as the fuse was lit, the powder ignited and the huge iron ball blasted through him, leaving naught but bloody appendages.

He looked again to Mariette. Her eyes were shiny, but whether from tears or anticipation he could not tell. He was still astonished by his rescue of her. He had heard of such feats, and considered them empty heroics, grandstanding to gain respect otherwise undeserved. But something in the act had left him with a pleasurable sensation, almost a measure of pride. Perhaps it was best he would never see another day. Death would be a mercy if he had become that thing he most despised—a fool who cared for others.

CHAPTER 76

"Now we are even."

BOWIE STOOD BEHIND the gun, staring into the hollow features of the man he had hated so long. Finding little satisfaction there, he glanced quickly around the group. "I suppose it would be pointless to ask you all to leave."

Lafitte smirked. Sam gave a small shake of the head. The Haitians' eyes gleamed, and they began chanting "Ogu! Ogu!" until Bowie silenced them with a glare. Wilson and Young stood frowning, arms crossed over their chests. Mariette reacted not at all.

"Then we shall waste no time on ceremony."

A terse order was relayed, and two Haitians leaned into the gun, turning the mouth toward the open sea.

Bowie struck the long match against the base of the gun and positioned it above the fuse. The face of the golden-haired girl swam before him, for what he hoped was the final time.

"I told you we are much alike," Renato sneered. "Now we have the proof of it."

Bowie's hand shook, but he clamped his teeth and made to apply the match.

"Cap'n Bowie!" Wilson's voice was like a shot. "Sail on the lee quarter!"

RENATO CRANED HIS neck to see white sails rounding the southern tip of Cozumel Island. The U.S.S. *Blain*, without doubt, and already turning toward the cliffs of Tulum.

Bowie studied the approaching frigate. Even at this distance, he saw her gun ports opening, and the stubby mouths of the carronades being run out, bristling like rows of blackened teeth.

"This must be quickly done," Bowie said, "before they can prevent it."

"If you fire now," Lafitte said calmly, "they'll think you're shooting at them. Their carronades will blast us to bits."

"Not if we fire in the opposite direction."

At Bowie's order, the barrel was swung around to face Tulum. This granted Renato a small reprieve, but he knew it would benefit him little.

While Bowie and the others were distracted, Mariette drifted toward the front of the gun, where she spoke quietly to Renato.

"I owe you a debt, Captain." She pursed her lips, blowing him a kiss, and he imagined it landing upon his cheek. From the folds of her blouse she produced the obsidian dagger with the two-headed snake and sliced the ropes binding him to the gun. "Now we are even."

BOWIE HEARD A great splash. Spinning about, he saw Mariette at the port rail, staring into the bright blue sea. The huge gun barrel stood stark and naked behind her. Renato was gone!

Following the girl's gaze, he saw the pirate surface ten yards off the side, stroking furiously toward *Lucinda*.

Without a word, Bowie clamped the back of his blade between his teeth and dived in after him.

Though Bowie considered himself a strong swimmer, his best efforts gained him nothing. When Renato hauled himself over *Lucinda*'s rail, Bowie was still a good twenty yards behind. Immediately, the man was scrambling about the deck, no doubt seeking a weapon.

Continuing his rapid strokes, Bowie fell without conscious intent into the rhythm of the Haitians' chant, "Ogu! Ogu!"

Renato disappeared through the hatch, and had not yet

returned when Bowie reached *Lucinda*'s rail, thrusting a leg up and over.

He had barely reached his feet when Renato sprang into view, a cutlass shimmering in his hand.

"COME," RENATO SAID, "The sooner this is over, the sooner you'll see your precious blonde wench again." Without taking his eyes from Bowie, he tossed the sword into the air, allowing it one complete revolution, and caught it deftly by the grip.

Bowie took his knife in hand. "I see her every day," he said. "And today will be the last."

Renato felt renewed. All the advantages were his. The deck of a ship, any ship, was his home ground. Add to this the fact that Mariette wanted him to live. Best of all, she would witness this final confrontation, and recognize him as the better man. Once Bowie was disposed of, there was still the matter of Captain Bentley and the *Blain*, but he had escaped tighter snares.

Renato waited for Bowie to make the first move. He knew the feel of the deck, knew where it was safe to step and when. Bowie was rumored to have fought a number of outrageous duels, but Renato would wager the man had never faced a foe aboard the cramped, rocking deck of a small sailing vessel.

As expected, the fool came at him like a wild bull, heedless of the ship's pitfalls. Renato played the matador, sidestepping easily as his cutlass forged a red gash across the back of Bowie's britches. "Ole, Señor Toro!" He laughed as the great oaf stumbled into the ratlines, nearly garroting himself.

A chorus of jeers carried across the water. The *Blain* was coming about now, turning her starboard guns to address the smaller ships. Her crippled masts and missing sails made her sluggish, but the guns would soon come to bear. Sailors hung from her yardarms and lined her starboard rail, peering at the scene aboard *Lucinda*. Renato would give them a good show, and write the finale in the blood of the famous James Bowie.

That alone should be enough to splash his name over the pages of *The Niles Register*.

BOWIE GATHERED IN his rage. He must stay focused, or he'd be joining the golden-haired girl permanently. He must treat Renato as a skilled opponent, rather than an object of vengeance. Taking deep, even breaths, he strove to clear his mind of all but the challenge before him.

He focused on the skills he'd honed with his brothers—the cut, thrust, back cut and parry. With each move came the graceful footwork and twisting of his torso to maintain balance and flow, always with an eye for attack and counterattack.

Those hours of practice and play had saved his life more times than he could count, and he willed those skills—those *instincts*—to wash over him now.

With a cool eye, he assessed the deck—what Rezin's training manuals termed the field of combat. He had best stay close to the mainmast, forward to the hatch and aft to the quarterdeck. Outside that area he would encounter ropes, barrels, the big iron capstan, and any number of other obstructions, denying him freedom of movement.

He relaxed into his favored fighting stance, right leg forward, right arm half-extended. His left arm was chambered at his side, left hand balanced for use when needed.

Now, at last, he felt the blood of his Scottish ancestors coursing through him. He was no longer the enraged beast, no longer even a man with a knife. He and the knife were one. He had felt this way only once before, in his log-bound fight to the death with Rayón, and it was fitting he feel it again now.

RENATO WATCHED THE man with growing scorn. Bowie had stood quivering, then closed his eyes as if trying to escape a nightmare. He now appeared frozen with fear, positioned—no doubt by merest chance—in what resembled the classic Italian stance of sword fighting. This was the method ingrained in Renato by his stepfather Beluche, and to see this yokel aping it was an abomination.

Renato approached, cutlass extended, and the sight of his blade, three times the length of Bowie's, buoyed his confidence.

But he was somewhat disappointed. Though flames flickered behind Bowie's eyes, he betrayed no awareness of Renato's presence. Had the lout's wits fled him completely, along with his courage?

Renato had wanted an epic battle, full of action and fury to entertain his audience. As it was, he would likely just slaughter the fool where he stood.

Renato advanced, and, as Bowie seemed too petrified to move, went forward at the charge, prepared to send the fool's head flying from his shoulders.

BOWIE REMAINED CALM. Though Renato came at him full tilt, his movements appeared slow, as if running underwater. The cutlass rose across his body, then swept into a wide arc, on a leisurely journey toward Bowie's neck.

There was no need to plan a defense. Bowie's muscles knew what to do. Knees flexed, he smiled inwardly and waited until the proper moment.

RENATO STAGGERED, CAUGHT off balance as his cutlass cleaved nothing but air. The coward had squatted with left leg extended, just in time to avoid the blade. And now, almost faster than the eye could follow, he swept the knife up and around in a vicious counterattack.

Jerking his head to avoid the blade, Renato felt a tug near his jawline, and saw a shriveled and blackened ear sail over the rail. Cheers erupted from the *Blain*, mingled with cries of "Ogu!" from *Medusa*.

Renato breathed deep. He had escaped death by the slimmest of margins. Using his momentum, he pivoted lightning-quick to his right and delivered a perfectly-timed cut toward Bowie's head.

BOWIE WATCHED RENATO complete the slow turn. As the cutlass inched toward his head, Bowie rose, blocking the stroke on the heel of his blade.

The force of the blow ran through him, but seemed only to feed his power, and he followed by turning his torso, raising his arm above his shoulder and thrusting straight for Renato's heart.

RENATO COULD SCARCELY believe his eyes. By dumb luck, the man had executed a perfect *punta mandritta*! But there no time for amazement. He flung up his left hand to deflect Bowie's blade, and saw three fingers leap into the air as the point ripped on through his coat and drew a line of fire across his chest

BOWIE LAUNCHED INTO a series of figure-eight movements he had learned as a boy.

The drill trained fighters in approaching the eight angles of attack—the head, neck, waist, hips, groin, and back up the other side. Bowie had turned the exercise into a fighting technique, and swept his blade in tight arcs, seeking his next target.

READYING HIMSELF FOR a lunge, Renato stopped, open-mouthed. He recognized the drill he too had perfected in his youth. But this was no drill. Bowie's feet were in motion, flowing left, right, forward and back—each step executed with perfect ease, seeking an angle Renato could not defend. And neither could he attack, for the speed of Bowie's blade placed it everywhere at once.

Then Bowie had made his choice, and the blade came streaming toward Renato's hip. The attack came from his right, and his left hand, already maimed, was powerless to help.

BOWIE DREW THE blade deep into Renato's flesh, striking bone and raking it through to the other side. In its wake came a flying river of blood, and he allowed himself a grim smile of satisfaction.

Renato squealed, almost dropping his sword. And as the man floundered, Bowie raised the knife in a high arc, inverting the blade and plunging down on line with the center of Renato's forehead.

THROUGH BLINDING PAIN, Renato saw the knife point arrowing toward his face. Too late to swerve, he thrust his body backwards, crashing to the deck while the point of Bowie's blade missed by inches, carving a furrow from front to back atop his skull.

Another attack was already coming. Renato brought his legs up to defend himself, and as much by luck as design, buried a boot in Bowie's groin.

BOWIE'S INNER CALM fell away like a shroud. He staggered back, blinking through the pain, and heard boos and catcalls from the *Blain*. Renato's movements were now faster than his own, and he could only stare as the pirate, dripping blood from high and low, scrabbled to his feet, looking for all the world like the Grim Reaper coming to collect a soul.

THE BATTLE JOY surged like music through Renato's veins. Bowie had done his best to kill him—and failed—and he now felt invincible.

While Bowie stood dazed, Renato sent a thrust hurtling toward his heart. The sword had nearly reached its mark when Bowie's blade chopped down, parrying the blow and deflecting the point into his own thigh. The pain in the man's face was terrible to behold, but less terrible than his rage. Already, the great knife was coming for Renato's throat.

Wrenching his sword from Bowie's leg, he swept it up in time to catch the knife on his guard, a scant inch from his jugular. The force of the blow pushed him back, nearly to his knees, before he got his footing.

Bowie's eyes were points of blue hellfire, his lips pulled back in a fearful grimace. The man was once again a wild beast—a beast whose strength was fading.

Though Bowie was weakened, Renato had tasted the depth of his skill, and knew his best course was to steer him out of his preferred area of combat.

BOWIE POURED ALL his strength into his arm. His rage knew no bounds, but could only take him so far. Knowing it was now or never, he pushed on with all his might.

Renato was giving way, moving backward and to the side, and Bowie rejoiced. *Huzzah!*s and *Ogu!*s filled the air as Bowie gathered his last reserves and pushed—just as Renato's resistance vanished, along with Renato himself.

Bowie staggered as the force of his drive sent him crashing headlong into the barrel-sized iron capstan. His chest hit with stunning force, and he bounced back, reeling against the starboard rail. Renato had tricked him.

Through waves of pain, he peered across the deck, and found the man resting against the opposite rail, his back to *Medusa*.

The roaring from the spectators was constant now, but above the din Bowie caught Sam's deep shout. "Mariette! No!"

Renato's eyes flickered at the name, but remained fixed on Bowie.

On *Medusa*'s deck, Lafitte and Mariette had their shoulders to the barrel of the great swivel-gun, pushing it around the bow. Sam and several Haitians toppled into the water as the gun came swinging about. From the touchhole came the telltale sparks of the fuse.

As the barrel came to bear on *Lucinda*, Lafitte and the girl scampered to the far side and dived headlong into the bay.

Bowie gripped the rail, balancing his weight. "Renato," he called, "Mariette has a message for you."

"I know," Renato rasped. "She hates you. She wants to see you dead."

"Beyond doubt," Bowie said. "But she feels the same about you."

As puzzlement filled Renato's face, two things happened at once: Flame blossomed from *Medusa*'s gun, and Bowie spun to leap over the rail, plummeting toward the water.

He was still in the air as the huge ball smashed into *Lucinda*, transforming the ship into a boiling cloud of splinters. He hit the water just as the ship's timbers snapped, and a massive spar hurtled out of the sky, smacking against his skull.

For an instant, he saw the smiling face of the golden-haired girl. Then there was only darkness, and the welcoming warmth of the sea.

"Fate finds a way."

BOWIE SAT BOLT upright, bathed in sweat and blinking into the gloom. Wherever he was, it reeked of blood and death.

"Where am I? Speak up, damn you! Am I dead again?"

"It was a near thing," said a voice at his side. "But it happens you are not."

"Mr. Gideon!" Bowie collapsed back onto the bed. "My God, I was afraid I'd wake up in Hell."

Sam's face loomed out of the darkness. "Afraid? You? The greatest knife fighter in the Western Hemisphere?"

Bowie peered up at him. "Who said that? Who have you been talking to?"

"Just some of the naval gentlemen here on the *Blain*. I had no idea I was in such illustrious company."

"Forget that talk," Bowie said gruffly. "It's mostly a nuisance." He tugged at a sheet, wiping sweat from his face and neck. "I've never feared death in battle. But a gypsy once told me I would die in bed. I never quite believed it, but still…"

"I fail to see the problem," Sam said. "When my time comes, that's precisely where I want to be. Preferably with company." And the black man winked.

Bowie laughed, then winced from a dozen pains. Glancing down, he spied bandages covering most of his body. "Curse you, I'm in no condition for humor. You say this is the *Blain*.

Why does it smell like a charnel house? And how long have I lain here?"

"This is the second day. We are in a room off the surgeon's quarters. The sailors refer to it as the orlop deck."

"The surgeon? It was that bad?"

"Apparently. Though it could have been worse. He wanted to bleed you."

Bowie stared, aghast.

"I let it be known that if he tried, our Voodoo legion would cast a spell on him. He did a great deal of grumbling, but subsequently left you alone."

Bowie held back a laugh. "Then I'm indebted to you once again. But truly, the odor in here is enough to kill a man. Can we not have some air?"

Sam opened two of the gun ports. Immediately, a salt breeze moved through the room, and Bowie took a deep but careful breath.

Through one of the ports, he saw triangular sails. A schooner.

"What ship is that?"

"*Medusa*."

Medusa! The events aboard *Lucinda* came rushing back, and he nearly shouted. "Renato! Where is he?"

"Dead. Or so everyone thinks. Didn't you see him perish?"

"I was busy when the ball struck. Trying to stay alive."

"I was in the water aside *Medusa*," Sam said, "but had an excellent view. *Lucinda* appeared to erupt right at Renato's feet. After that everything was chaos. One of the Haitians claimed to have seen a miniature zombie swimming toward shore, but that could hardly have been Renato. I find it inconceivable he could have survived."

Bowie felt a heat growing within him. He rose painfully to his elbows. "Help me up. I want to search for myself."

Sam shook his head. "I have absolutely no regret to inform you that at latest report, we are already halfway to New Orleans."

Bowie slumped. He closed his eyes, trying to picture the golden-haired girl, but her face would not come into focus.

"If the ship was such a wreck, how did I survive?"

"Apparently you were dragged under by the mainmast. The Haitians and I hauled you to the surface, but we would have likely drowned had the *Blain* not lowered a boat for us."

Bowie was silent for a time, recalling his last moments on *Lucinda*'s deck. "Was it truly Mariette who fired that gun?"

"I saw the match in her hand, just as she and her father swung the cannon around."

"And where are they now?"

"Young claims he saw them crawl ashore and run up the sand to the cliffs beneath Tulum."

Bowie stared out a gun port, seeing nothing.

Sam said softly, "What do you suppose will become of them?"

Bowie shook himself. "As to Mariette, I cannot guess. But I've no doubt Lafitte will live to die again. And again. I wouldn't be surprised if that rascal outlives us both."

A screen at the end of the room slid aside, and a tall man in an officer's uniform strode into the room. From his hand dangled a purple silk bag. Behind him came a bespectacled sailor lugging a stack of canvasses.

As the officer stepped into the light, Bowie saw blond, mutton-chop whiskers and piercing, sea-blue eyes.

The man dipped his head in greeting. "I have been informed, sir, that you are the famous James Bowie, he of the daring battle on the sandbar, and presumed candidate for Congress. It is a pleasure to make your acquaintance."

Bowie waved that away. "That sandbar business was wildly exaggerated, and I fear my political aspirations are dust in the wind. I will, however, be pleased to shake your hand."

When he had done so, the man said, "I've been hoping for an opportunity to thank you. I understand you were instrumental in recovering my ship."

"Your ship?"

"The *Medusa*. I am Captain Charles Bentley, at your service. My first lieutenant, Mr. Goble, is overseeing the cleanup of the mess left by those damned pirates."

"Ah," Bowie said. "Well. Glad to be of help."

"I'm told you were quite well acquainted with that fellow… what was his name, Rateno?"

"Renato. No, not well, but much better than I wished. Are you certain he's dead?"

Bentley bristled slightly. "I had three men with telescopes watching the shore. If he escaped their notice, he was some kind of magician. And we had boats in the water within minutes of the blast, scouring every inch of seabed. The water is remarkably clear along that coast, you know, and against the white sand, a body would be easily seen. All we found were *Lucinda*'s 6-pounders, a small stove and a few metal tools. I can only assume this Renato person was blown into a thousand pieces."

Bowie said nothing. Bentley's hands were balled into tight fists, his arms trembling with emotion. "I wanted him quite badly, you understand."

Bowie realized his own fists were clenched. "I understand perfectly. More than you could possibly know."

"Well. In ridding my cabin of his leavings, we came upon this…rubbish." Bentley jabbed a thumb at the stack of canvasses in the other man's arms. "I was going to order them burned, then thought they might amuse you." He motioned to the sailor. "Mr. Carbon, if you please." And the man dropped the paintings against the nearest bulkhead, obviously glad to be rid of them.

"There is one more thing," Bentley said. "When those pirates stole my ship, there was a case of quite fine Burgundy in my quarters. Remarkably, one bottle remained. I thought you might care to join me in a toast."

"My mouth tastes like the inside of a muskrat. I would kill for a drink of wine."

Bentley opened the silk bag, producing a long green bottle, followed by a corkscrew and two glasses.

Deftly popping the cork, Bentley poured one glass precisely half full and presented it to Bowie.

Bowie held it to his nose, savoring the aroma, while Bentley poured another.

Bentley raised his glass. "To Old Hickory, and the destruction of all pirates."

Bowie said, "What about Mr. Gideon?"

Bentley's face was blank. "Who?"

"My nurse here." Bowie nodded at Sam. "Do you have a glass for him?"

Bentley looked at the tall black man in tattered clothing, and his face went even more blank. "Um, no. I'm afraid I do not."

"No matter, then. He can have mine." Bowie proffered the glass to Sam, who was quick to accept.

Taking a delicate sip, Sam gyrated his lips. "Ah," he said, "a muscular, weighty attitude with a perfumed edge. From the village of Gembry-Chambertin in the *Côte de Nuits*, I presume?"

"Um, er, uh, yes." Bentley said. "Quite." He turned vexed eyes to Bowie. "I, ah, I really should get back to my ship. Here." He extended his own glass, still untouched. "I believe you need this more than I." Then he spun and marched stiffly toward the door, the sailor following at his heels. At the last moment he turned, shooting Bowie a parting salute. "And again, my thanks."

When the screen had closed behind them, Bowie and Sam touched glasses and drank.

The black man appeared about to say something, but Bowie spoke first. "Let's have a look at those paintings."

Sam held one up at arm's length, wrinkling his nose as if it fouled his nostrils. Bowie found it equally repellent. The grotesque figure appeared to be Renato, with a bloody cutlass and smoking blunderbuss. They worked their way through the stack, finding each more gaudy and amateurish than the last. Renato in the high-laced collar and white stockings of a courtier. Renato perched upon a throne, a ruby-studded crown tilted rakishly across his brow. Renato in fur-trimmed purple robes, with some kind of animal crouched at his feet.

"Is that a pig," Bowie asked, "or the world's ugliest dog?"

Sam peered more closely, his lip curling. "I believe it more closely resembles a three-toed sloth."

Second to last in the stack was a head-and-shoulders study of Renato leering straight out of the canvas. The workmanship was no better than the others, but in this one, the painter had at last caught something of the man's true nature. Behind the eyes lurked a dragon thirsting to escape human form.

As Sam held up the final painting, Bowie felt a stab in his chest. It was Mariette, beautiful as life, and considerably more naked than the day she was born. This was the girl he remembered from their night in Texas, when her caress had turned his blood to wine. How Renato had captured her so perfectly was a wonder, but that he *had* explained much of what followed.

"A surprisingly fair likeness," he managed at last.

"So," Sam said, "you wish to retain this one?"

"No. Burn it, if you please, and the quicker the better. But that last one of Renato interests me. Hold it up against the bulkhead, will you, where I may see it from a distance."

With a great roll of his eyes, Sam humored him.

Bowie's hand flashed to the table by the bed. With a flick of the wrist, his knife sang through the air, pinning the canvas to the wall. The blade still quivered where it struck, directly between Renato's eyes.

"Yes," Bowie said. "I believe I will enjoy that one."

He drained the rest of the Burgundy, enjoying the dry burn as it trailed down his throat. "So, Mr. Gideon, I believe you acquired a fair amount of wealth. How do you plan to spend it?"

Sam looked wistful. "I had always anticipated visiting Europe with the young master. Touring the museums, staying at the most decadent hotels. That is now an option. But I have been entertaining another possibility. I may open a dining establishment in the French Quarter."

"That sounds promising," Bowie said. "You could hire your Voodoo chums as waiters."

"I doubt I could tempt them. They are eager to return to Haiti, where they expect to be the eight wealthiest men in the country. About that restaurant, however, I may have a suitable position for you."

Bowie laughed. "As what? A celebrity food-taster? Someone of notoriety to attract the finer element?"

"Well, not precisely. I thought I might capitalize on your ability with a knife."

"I see. Exhibitions of skill, then."

"Yes, you might say that. I shall require someone with a fine touch, you see, for slicing meats and vegetables."

Bowie stared, his heat rising, until Sam clutched his sides and shook with mirth.

"You imp!" Bowie thrust the covers aside, swung a bandaged leg to the floor and tried to rise, but immediately felt lightheaded and was forced to give it up.

"What about you?" Sam asked, regaining control. "What do you plan to do?"

Bowie thought a moment. "I still have a land deal awaiting me in Arkansas. I hope. But eventually, I intend to take root somewhere peaceful. Somewhere like Texas."

"Texas? You found wrestling Strap Buckner and being all but skinned alive by savages to be peaceful?"

"No more of that, thank you. No, I was thinking of San Antonio. It's said to be a quiet and civilized city, free of violence and strife."

"There may be a reason for that," Sam said. "They have yet to experience the galvanizing presence of the famous James Bowie."

"But first," Bowie said, "I need to raise cash, and quickly.

Other than a lifetime supply of aches and pains, I've nothing to show for this venture but debts. With *Lucinda* demolished, I owe McQuiddy a new ship. And your previous owner still has my marker for five hundred dollars."

"What you need," Sam said, "are more well-wishers to cheer you up." With that, he strode long-legged to the door and slid back the screen. Bowie heard him speaking in a foreign tongue.

After a moment, one of the Haitians entered, sniffing the air and looking curiously about. Behind him, the other seven filed quickly into the room, lining up around Bowie's bed.

Bowie felt like a sideshow attraction as they peered curiously into his eyes, poked at his limbs and examined his bandages. After a few moments they shook their heads and began whispering among themselves.

Bowie could take no more. "What the blazes are they saying?"

Sam smiled. "You should be pleased. They are now thoroughly convinced the spirit of Ogu has abandoned you."

"Well, thank God for that."

Displaying no further interest in him, the Haitians began moving toward the door.

Sam spoke sharply to them.

They turned, looking surprised, then apprehensive, clutching at the heavy bags dragging at their belts.

Sam spoke more forcefully.

The Haitians exchanged glances, a variety of emotions playing across on their faces. Uncertainty. Suspicion. Guilt. Even a tinge of fear.

Sam pointed sternly toward the bed, and they all trudged back, fingers fumbling at their belts.

Passing the foot of the bed, each man dipped into his bag and extracted some small object, which he deposited on the blanket. Bowie stared at the growing collection. A jade necklace, a ring decorated with skulls, a medallion bearing the face of a man with a pointed tongue, a golden frog with turquoise eyes, and other items too exotic to identify.

When the last man finished, the Haitians filed out, casting unhappy glances at Sam.

Bowie lifted the medallion by its chain. The scowling visage reminded him of Pacal. "How did you do that?"

Sam looked sheepish. "I'm afraid I was forced to prevaricate. I told them Ogu had ordered me to relay a final message—that you had proved a satisfactory vessel, and he wished you rewarded for it."

"And they believed that?"

"More or less. Mostly less, I suspect, but they feared to risk the consequences."

"I don't know what to say."

"If I might suggest it, perhaps 'Thanks be to Ogu.'"

"Well," Bowie said. "Thanks to *you*, Mr. Gideon, I've almost broken even. That seems to be the story of this enterprise. I had Renato at my mercy, yet failed to kill him. I found love, of a sort, and just as quickly lost it. On the plus side, I may have satisfied the golden-haired girl. I last saw her just as *Lucinda* exploded, and she looked pleased." Bowie paused, gazing out at the sea. "But I do have one great regret. Andre. He was an incorrigible rogue, but I relished his company. I lost a good friend."

Sam was silent a moment. Then he said, "That may be, Mr. Bowie. But Fate usually finds a way to balance things out."

Bowie looked up at him, divining his meaning. "You know, I believe you're right." He extended a hand, and Sam gripped it firmly. "And did I hear you call me 'Mr. Bowie?'"

"You did indeed." The black man's smile was huge. "And you may now address me as 'Sam.'"

JAMES BOWIE

THE EVENTS OF this novel are purely fictional but much of the background is not. The story takes place in a specific month in Bowie's life—May 1828—and all events leading up to it (with the exception of his duel with Renato's brother Rayón and the possible acquisition of a new knife) actually took place.

James was born in Kentucky in 1796, but his parents Reason (or Rezin) and Elve soon moved the family to what later became Missouri, and then to Louisiana. He and his two older brothers, Rezin and John, grew up wild, and were said to wrestle cattle and alligators for sport. He was particularly close to Rezin, three years his senior, who became something of a mentor. As the brothers grew up, they acquired plantations, both together and separately, and engaged in land speculation, some of which involved the forging of Mexican land grants.

James's first known visit to Texas came in 1819 with the James Long expedition, one of several filibustering attempts to free Mexico from Spain. He did not stay with the expedition long, but his friend Warren Hall did, making the acquaintance of the pirate Jean Lafitte. Inspired by Hall's tales of Lafitte's operations, the brothers hit upon the idea of buying slaves from Lafitte and transporting them to the States for sale. James reportedly became quite friendly with Lafitte himself and some of his men. The Bowies' profits were enormous, but the venture lasted only a few months. When Lafitte abandoned Galveston in the spring of 1820, the brothers turned their efforts to land and politics.

The Sandbar Fight, of September 19, 1827, catapulting Bowie into the public eye, was the pivotal event of his life. Though some reports placed it on the Vidalia Sandbar, it actually took place on an unnamed beach above Natchez, Mississippi, on the northern bank of an oxbow bend in the river. The fight was the culmination of longtime hostilities between two groups separated by politics, personal grudges and business interests.

Those hostilities came to a head earlier that year, when a so-called gentleman by the name of Dr. Thomas Maddox repeated some particularly salacious gossip about the sister of Mr. Montfort Wells. In response, Wells fired a pistol ball at Maddox, and Maddox challenged him to a duel. When Montfort Wells was either unable or unwilling to accept, Maddox challenged his brother Samuel Wells, who could not refuse. Bowie stood with the Wells party, which included Samuel's brother Thomas, his surgeon Richard Cuny, Cuny's brother Samuel, and two other gentlemen. On the Maddox side was his surgeon Robert Crain, Alfred and Carey Blanchard and a particular enemy of Bowie's, Major Norris Wright. This was a recipe for disaster. In addition to the enmity between Bowie and Wright, there were personal hatreds between some of the others.

The duel itself proved underwhelming. After Wells and Maddox both fired their pistols and missed—twice—the code *duello* considered honor satisfied. Accounts of the following events differ, but it's generally agreed the next shot was fired by Crain—at James Bowie. After Bowie returned fire, Crain shot and fatally wounded Samuel Cuny. Major Norris Wright and the Blanchard brothers then joined the melee. Bowie was shot at least three times and stabbed seven times with sword blades. He was down, his lung pierced by Wright's sword, when he grasped Wright's lapel and thrust his knife into the man's body. He later said he had "twisted it as to cut his heart strings." Throwing Wright's body from him, Bowie warded off an attack by Alfred Blanchard by slashing him in the side. Over the days, weeks and even decades following, many conflicting accounts were published in various newspapers, and with each retelling Bowie's fame grew.

Two excellent works have been devoted to the subject, and I refer you to James Batson Jr.'s *James Bowie and the Sandbar Fight, Book I* (1992) and *Book II* (2018), and *Mr. Bowie with a Knife* by J.R. Edmondson (1998).

While recuperating from the fight, Bowie was eager to resume his efforts toward a particularly lucrative land deal, and hoped to revitalize his hopes of reaching Congress. Two years earlier, he'd been touted as a replacement for Congressman William Brent, and obtained Brent's agreement to step down and endorse Bowie in his place. But by 1828, one of his major supporters had died, and his new reputation gave others pause.

After several months he was well enough to travel to New Orleans, and soon took ship for Washington to plead his land case with government officials. When he returned around the beginning of May, most of his political support had evaporated, and Brent had reneged on his promise. And that's where the novel begins—in early May 1828, when history knows little of Bowie's activities.

THE BOWIE KNIFE

THE FIRST BOWIE Knife is shrouded in mystery, and after nearly two hundred years of speculation and research, we still don't know exactly what it looked like.

Raymond W. Thorp's book *Bowie-Knife* (1949) lists thirteen different men purported to have made the "original" knife, and there are numerous others. Most of these stories are pure fantasy, but several are still bandied about today.

For many years, the most widely accepted account regarding the original knife—the one James carried at the Sandbar Fight—came from an angry letter written by his brother Rezin.

The letter, published in 1838, was written to a newspaper in response to an earlier account he considered spurious. Rezin's letter included the following passage:

The first Bowie-Knife was made by myself in the parish of Avoyelles, in this state (Louisiana), as a hunting knife for which purpose, exclusively, it was used by me for many years. The length of the knife was nine and one-quarter inches, its width one and a half inches, single edge, and blade not curved.

He then adds:

Col. James Bowie had been shot by an individual with whom he was at variance; and as I presumed that a second attempt would be made by the same person to take his life, I gave him the knife to be used as occasion might require as a defensive weapon. Sometime afterwards (and the only time it was ever used for any purpose other than that for which it was originally destined) it was resorted to by Col. James Bowie in a chance medley, or rough fight, between himself and certain individuals with whom he was then inimical, and the knife was then used only as a defensive weapon—and not until he had been shot down—it was then the means of saving his life. The improvement in its fabrication, and the state of perfection it has since acquired from experienced cutlers, was not brought about through my agency.

How much of Rezin's recollection so many years after that fact is correct—and how much motivated by a desire to improve his brother's reputation—is impossible to judge.

That letter, of course, did not stop the speculation. Some accounts have Jesse Clifft (or Cliffe), a blacksmith employed by Rezin, making the original knife at his instruction. Bowie's eldest brother John—and his friend Caiaphas Ham—believed the knife was made by Lovel H. Snowden, a Louisiana blacksmith, an opinion shared by Bowie authority J.R. Edmondson.

One persistent story features Arkansas blacksmith James Black. So the tale goes, Bowie presented him with a model he had whittled out of wood. Black then made two knives, one following Bowie's design, and one of his own. When Bowie saw the two, he preferred the one designed by Black. The story then descends into melodrama, claiming that Black had discovered "the Damascus secret" of tempering and hardening steel. He jealously guarded that secret until, on his deathbed, he wished to pass it on, but could no longer remember it.

While it's very likely James owned other knives during the eight and half years between the Sandbar Fight and his death at the Alamo, none have been positively identified. Rezin is known to have presented a number of knives to friends, and there are stories of James doing that as well.

In recent years, the knife getting the most publicity is the Musso Bowie, named for Joseph Musso, a collector and film industry artist who bought it at a California gun show in the early 1970s. It's certainly the most fearsome-looking of all candidates, with a blade nearly fourteen inches long, a brass back on the spine, a clip point tip and a curved crossguard. While it's not impossible Bowie could have possessed such a weapon at one time or another, I cannot conceive of him having it in 1828, only six months after the Sandbar Fight. The knife was later sold to singer Phil Collins, and was recently donated, along with the rest of the Collins collection of Alamo artifacts, to the Alamo itself. The knife has come under much scrutiny, and its authenticity is still a matter of debate.

For purposes of this novel, I have largely dodged the issue, straddling the line between history and legend. The notion that Bowie immediately replaced the hunting knife he used at the sandbar is my own, but as he had resolved to carry a blade in polite society, that does not seem unreasonable. It's also doubtful that the knife he carried at that time had a crossguard and clip point blade, but that design has become so ingrained in the public consciousness that it was hard to envision him without it.

J.R. Edmondson, I should note, has found no evidence that either James or Rezin ever owned a knife with a significant crossguard (though at least one traced to Rezin had a very short one). That said, crossguards and clip points had been common features on knives and swords for centuries, so their use in

Bowie's time was hardly an innovation. Stories of James or Rezin adding a crosspiece, and of James making a sheath, appeared in so many newspaper accounts in the century following his death that they have become what the poet William Blake would call "an image of truth."

WILLIAM BRENT & WALTER OVERTON

WILLIAM LEIGH BRENT was elected to Congress as a Republican in 1822, and served three terms. The story of him agreeing to step down in Bowie's stead appears to be true. He was likely no more corrupt than his peers, but by 1828 voters had surely grown tired of him. He was soundly defeated in the election of that year by General Walter Hampton Overton, a hero of the Battle of New Orleans. Brent returned to his law practice, and died in 1848. Overton served only one term and died in 1845.

JEAN LAFITTE

MANY BOOKS HAVE been written on the life of Jean Lafitte, the most comprehensive of which is *The Pirates Laffite* by William C. Davis (2005). That book's spelling of *Laffite*, rather than the traditional *Lafitte*, seems to be currently in vogue with historians. The man himself was known to have signed his name both ways. I stuck with Lafitte, because it was surely the most common spelling in use in 1828.

Sources differ, but according to Davis, Jean was born sometime around 1782 on a peninsula some thirty miles north of Bordeaux, France. His half-brother Pierre, born a couple of years earlier, made his way to New Orleans as early as 1803, where he soon acquired a mistress and a son. Jean's early history is much murkier, but by 1809 he was likely smuggling slaves and other goods—in concert with Pierre's land-bound efforts—in and out of Barataria Bay.

Jean Lafitte quickly rose to folk-hero status in New Orleans. Residents profited from the brothers' prices on smuggled goods (which lacked the duties imposed by the state), and when Governor Claiborne offered a five-hundred-dollar bounty for his capture, he promptly offered a thousand dollars for the capture of the governor.

There are many stories of Jean's supposed death—in battle, of an illness, or sometimes in a hurricane. A persistent rumor said he had a marked grave in Yucatán—or on *Isla Mujeres* off the coast of Cancun.

Davis bases his version of Jean's death on an article found in a Colombian newspaper. In this account, Lafitte was aboard the *General Santander* in the Gulf of Honduras when he was decoyed into a trap by two ships. Whether they belonged to the Spanish or British Navy, or even privateers, was not specified, but a direct hit to Lafitte's ship was said to deliver a mortal wound, and he died the next day, Feb. 5, 1823, at age 41.

I have no reason to refute that story, but the many outrageous lies I've found in old newspapers about James Bowie leave me less than convinced.

There are plenty of outrageous tales about Lafitte as well.

A book I found in a musty old shop in New Orleans, *The Land of Lafitte the Pirate* by Ray M. Thompson (1943) relates the legend that Lafitte rescued Napoleon from confinement on St. Helena, leaving behind a double to fool his guards. After Lafitte was killed battling a British warship, he and Napoleon were supposedly buried, along with John Paul Jones, in an old cemetery near the town of Lafitte, Louisiana. The book has a photo of the grave site, marked by a huge iron cross laying flat on the ground.

In the 1940s, a man named John Laflin (aka John A. Lafitte and various other names) claimed to have a journal written by the famous pirate, supposedly his great-grandfather. The journal eventually found its way to a research library in Texas, and was first published in 1958. The journal says that after his supposed death, Lafitte retired to Alton, Illinois, where he married and raised a family, and was still alive and kicking in 1850. It is now generally considered a forgery, and some experts have opined that the handwriting resembles that of the short passage in the famous diary of Mexican Lt. Col. José Enrique de la Peña, which claims David Crockett was among several defenders who surrendered and were executed at the Alamo.

Catherine Villard met Jean Lafitte through her sister, the longtime mistress of Jean's brother Pierre. She may have borne him a son, Jean Pierre, in 1815, but there's no evidence their relationship was ever formalized.

There is little left in Louisiana to honor Lafitte. A small painting hanging high on a shadowy wall of the Cabildo in New Orleans depicts the two Lafittes with Dominique You and Renato Beluche in a tavern. I had to stand on a ladder to look at it, wishing I'd brought a flashlight. There's a bar called Lafitte's Blacksmith Shop in the French Quarter, reputed to been used in the Lafittes' smuggling operation. Whether that's true or not I cannot say, but the T-shirt and plastic beer cup they sold me are certainly authentic.

The Jean Lafitte National Historical Park and Preserve pays him lip service, but little else. They operate several sites outside the city, the most significant being the Chalmette Battlefield, site of the great Battle of New Orleans. The battlefield sports several cannons on a reconstructed rampart, and it's fun to stand there and imagine Dominique You and his fellow pirates blowing great swaths of destruction through the advancing British lines. As to Lafitte himself, the only thing I found in the gift shop was a refrigerator magnet bearing the name of the park.

The best tribute I found anywhere in the state was in the small town of Jean Lafitte, twenty miles south of New Orleans. The have a very cool animated marionette show depicting the important events in his life. (If you visit my blog at evanlewis. com and enter "Jean Lafitte" in the search box, you'll find pics of the puppet show—and other Lafittiana.) I also saw cop cars emblazoned with *Jean Lafitte Police*, which would surely have made the pirate smile.

SAM

THERE ARE PERSISTENT stories of James Bowie having a slave named Sam. He is sometimes mentioned as accompanying Bowie on his expeditions from Galveston, and more often said to have been with Bowie at the Alamo. I have been unable to discover the source of these tales.

The earliest mention I've seen of Bowie having a slave at the Alamo comes from *The Telegraph and Texas Register* of March 24, 1836, only three weeks after the battle. Published at San Felipe de Austin, the article contains information provided by John W. Smith (reportedly the last defender to leave the Alamo) and a "Judge Ponton," as communicated to them by Susanna Dickinson, who was in the Alamo during the siege and assault. Following a mention of Travis's slave Joe (who is known to have been present), the relevant passage reads, "Mrs. Dickinson and her child, and a negro of Bowie's and as before said, Travis', were spared."

The first mention I've found of a slave named Sam appears in *James Bowie, The Life of a Bravo* by C.L. Douglas (1944). Douglas tells of Rezin, John and James making two slave-trading trips from Galveston. But thereafter, he says, James went without them, taking with him "one of his father's slaves, a strong fellow called Sam, who was about Jim's own age." He goes on to say they made a second journey in the summer of 1819, in which the slaves escaped.

At the Alamo, Douglas says Sam cared for Bowie during his illness, at one point helping to carry his cot, and made sure his pistols were primed and loaded prior to the final attack. Afterwards, he says, "Santa Anna had spared only Mrs. Dickinson and her child, the Mexican women, and the body servants of Bowie and Travis…"

Douglas lists numerous sources in the back his book (none of which I have access to) but offers no hint as to where any particular details may be found.

Sam appears again in Paul L. Wellman's biographical novel

The Iron Mistress (1950). In that book, Bowie finds Sam being mistreated in New Orleans, and buys him for that reason, an idea I have borrowed. The book also depicts Sam assisting him on one of his slave trading trips, but is not mentioned as being at the Alamo. Sam also appears in the film adaptation in 1952.

John Myers Myers's book *The Alamo* (1948) places a Bowie slave at the scene, but calls him "Ham." Lon Tinkle's *13 Days to Glory* (1958) says Sam was released after the battle, along with Travis's man Joe. Walter Lord, in *A Time to Stand*, (1961) acknowledges that early sources mention a Bowie slave named "Sam" among the survivors, but believes this was a mistaken reference to Mexican Colonel Almonte's cook, Ben.

On screen, Sam had a brief role in *The Man from the Alamo* (1953), hovering near Bowie's side, and appeared again in the 2004 version of *The Alamo*. John Wayne's Alamo epic (1960) gave Bowie a slave named Jethro.

There are now multiple Internet sources stating that Sam, along with Travis's slave Joe, were among (or sometimes the *only*) Texian survivors of the Alamo. Trust them at your peril.

Did a "Sam" really exist? Your guess is as good as mine, but if so, we can be sure he was nothing like the character presented in this novel.

DAVID CROCKETT

DAVID CROCKETT SERVED Tennessee for two terms in the U.S. Congress between 1827 and 1831. His growing opposition to Andrew Jackson's policies earned him a defeat in 1831. He managed a return in 1833, then lost again, famously claiming to have told his constituents they could "go to Hell," and he would go to Texas. Which he did.

A fictionalized account of what Davy may have been doing during the Creek Indian War (1813-14) can be found in the novel *Crockett's Devil* by Yours Truly, available from Steegerbooks.com, and various other places for the low, low price of $19.95 ($5.99 for the eBook). Order now! Mr. Truly will be eternally grateful.

RENATO BELUCHE

RENATO'S STEP-FATHER RENATO Beluche (also called Rene) enjoyed a career even wilder than that of my fictional Renato. Born in New Orleans, his father was a French emigrant who ran a smuggling operation out of his wig-making shop. As a boy, he served as pilot's mate on a Spanish warship. When war with England broke out in 1812, he captained a privateer, taking prizes for the United States. He then obtained a letter of marque from Cartagena, becoming a terror to Spanish shipping and taking much of his booty to the Lafittes in Barataria Bay. In 1814 he joined Lafitte and Dominique You as a gunner in the Battle of New Orleans, and in 1815 joined Simon Bolivar's fight against Spain in the Caribbean. By the time this novel takes place he had been appointed Brigadier General in the Colombian navy. After many more rebellions and revolutions, he settled in Panama and established a shipping business. He died in 1860, at age 79.

DOMINIQUE YOU

FREDERIC YOUX, MORE commonly known as Dominique You, was Jean Lafitte's most trusted lieutenant, and sometimes rumored to be his half-brother. He was one of the boldest of Lafitte's rogues. Various accounts have him born either in France or in the French colony of Saint Dominique. It's believed he served in the French Revolutionary Army, and came to the New World in 1802 in an expedition to put down a Haitian slave revolt. Making his way to Louisiana, he joined the Lafittes, captained a ship named *Le Pandoure*, and earned the nickname *Capitaine Dominique* from the French. In 1814, he was captured in the raid on Barataria Bay, but Lafitte secured his release in time for the Battle of New Orleans, where he served with honor. Andrew Jackson was said to remark he "would storm the gates of Hell with Dominique You."

Though all of Lafitte's men serving in the battle were granted clemency, You was one of the few who did not return to piracy. He retired to a house in the Faubourg Marginy neighborhood of New Orleans and became a popular figure about town. Whether or not he remained involved in the Lafittes' smuggling operations—which seems likely—was never proven. When he died, destitute, in 1830, the citizens of New Orleans threw him an elaborate funeral and built him a tomb in an old cemetery. The tomb's inscription reads, "Intrepid warrior on land and sea, in a hundred combats showed his valor. Without reproach or fear, he could have witnessed the ending of the world without trembling." When I visited the city a few years ago I was unable to visit his grave because the cemetery is an area where even cab drivers tremble to tread.

THE U.S.S. *MEDUSA*

THE *MEDUSA* IS my invention, but the inspiration for her is not. In 1821 the navy launched several schooners designed specifically to hunt pirates. A year later, one of these, the *Grampus*, engaged in a fierce battle with the Puerto Rican privateer *Palmyra*—also known as *Panchita*. The 18-pound swivel gun mounted on *Palmyra's* deck caused the navy much consternation, but *Grampus* eventually prevailed, capturing the privateer and bringing her to port. While 18-pounders were commonly used on frigates and larger ships of the line, there is no record of the U.S. Navy experimenting with such a large weapon on a vessel as small as a schooner. But they *could* have. A U.S. Navy ship briefly bore the name *Medusa* in 1869, and again from 1923 to 1950.

STEPHEN AUSTIN

STEPHEN AUSTIN WAS the driving force in bringing American settlers to Texas, and by 1825 he had attracted at least three hundred. He labored for many years to placate both the

Mexican authorities and his fellow settlers, and considering the volatile forces on both sides, it's doubtful any man could have done better. After serving nearly a year in a Mexico City prison for his troubles, he returned to Texas convinced they would have to fight, and served as the first commander of the Texian army. He died of pneumonia in December 1836 in the newly-independent Republic of Texas.

MATAGORDA

AUSTIN WAS GRANTED permission from Mexico to establish the settlement of Matagorda in 1827. It appears the first settlers from the U.S. did not arrive until 1829 or 1830, so I have fudged a bit, giving Bowie and his party a place to meet Strap Buckner and other colonists.

STRAP BUCKNER

AYLETT C. (STRAP) BUCKNER was said to be six and a half feet tall and strong as a bull. He hailed from Virginia, and was one of Stephen Austin's original 300 colonists. He visited Texas as early as 1812, and returned with Long's expedition in 1819. He claimed to be one of the first to settle on the Colorado River, near the future settlement of Matagorda. Despite various disagreements with Austin, Buckner was appointed commander of the local militia, and in 1826 led an expedition to punish the Karankawas for killing the families of two colonists. The Indians reportedly called him "Red Son of Blue Thunder," and offered him a maiden named Tulipita as wife. He was killed in the Battle of Velasco in 1832, but his legend continued to grow—culminating with the tale of him challenging the Devil to a duel.

ANDREW JACKSON

ANDREW JACKSON, SPRING-BOARDED by his victory at the Battle of New Orleans, ran for President in 1824, opposed by John Quincy Adams, Henry Clay and William H. Crawford. Though Jackson won a majority of the both the popular and electoral college vote, no one earned a plurality, and the election was decided in the House of Representatives. The House chose Adams, who appointed Clay as his Secretary of State, to the everlasting ire of Jackson supporters. Jackson beat Adams in 1828 and served two terms. His draconian policies regarding the Indians earned him the ire of Congressman David Crockett.

FRANCIS MARION

THE SWAMP FOX, of course, was a real person, who harried the British in the swamps of the Carolinas during the Revolutionary War, and Bowie's father really did serve with him. Marion's fictional subordinate Colonel Thaddeus Truitt is my invention, playing an important role in the rip-roaring adventure novel *Crockett's Devil*.

THE KARANKAWA INDIANS

THERE IS NO evidence the Karankawas were true cannibals, though it's likely they practiced some form of ritual cannibalism. Like other primitive (and not-so-primitive) peoples, they may have eaten small portions of their enemies' flesh as a means of absorbing their strength and courage. Little is known of their religion, but it's unlikely they would have worshiped the feathered serpent revered by Central and South American peoples—unless, perhaps, a small band of them found a golden idol buried in the earth.

VOODOO

HAITIAN VOODOO (OR Voudou) developed during the years of the slave trade, mixing traditions of African religion with elements of Catholicism and Freemasonry. The Loa (or Iwa) are spirits who sometimes aid humans in return for their service. Ogu (or Oguon) is a powerful warrior spirit. He was originally the god of blacksmithing, and his symbol is a piece of iron (often a sword or machete), which he uses to fight his enemies. He sometimes comes to "mount" humans, endowing them with his powers. It would seem that Bowie's Voodoo crew knew what they were doing.

TULUM AND COBÁ

THOUGH I HAVE visited the Yucatán Peninsula, I did not make it to Tulum or Cobá. I wish I had. While Tulum is easily accessible, Cobá is deeper into the jungle, about a half hour's drive from the beach. The main pyramid, at 137 feet, is the tallest on the peninsula. The entire site constitutes about 30 square miles, and there are many other structures, though— unless you are very lucky—you won't find a temple full of gold.

JAMES BOWIE, CONTINUED

AFTER THE EVENTS in *Bowie's Gold* (should you decide to accept them) Bowie was back in Natchez and soon set out on another journey to Texas. Traveling by steamboat and horseback, he eventually reached San Antonio, where he cultivated the friendship of Vice Governor Juan Martín de Veramendi.

For several years, Bowie traveled back and forth between Texas and the States, speculating in land in both countries. His most notable adventure during this time (at least of those known to history) was a search for the lost San Saba silver mine, in which he, Rezin and a small company survived a battle with more than a hundred hostile Indians.

He married Veramendi's beautiful daughter Ursula in 1831, but lost her three years later to cholera. Following her death, he was drawn into the growing conflict between the colonists and the Mexican government. Arrested on suspicion of revolutionary intent by General Cos, he soon escaped and delivered valuable intelligence to the Texians. He obtained the honorific title "Colonel" when he was elected to command the militia at Nacogdoches, and promptly marched his men on a small Mexican armory, appropriating their muskets.

In 1835, commanding a small force of the Texian army, he beat back a Mexican attack near Mission Espada outside San Antonio. Later, in what became known as "the Grass Fight," he led a cavalry detachment to capture a Mexican pack train rumored to carry silver, only to discover the packs contained grass for horses.

His most notable achievement came in October of that year. In command of ninety-two Texians, he was surrounded by a force of 275 Mexicans. After holding off several attacks, Bowie's men charged and turned one of the Mexicans' cannons on the enemy, driving them from the field. This engagement, the Battle of Concepción, is considered the first real battle of the Texas Revolution.

The battle of the Alamo has been well-documented, and I urge you to peruse one of the many fine books on the subject. I particularly recommend *The Alamo Story, from early History to Current Conflicts* by J.R. Edmondson (2000, with an updated and expanded edition published in 2022). *Very* briefly, with a huge Mexican force rumored to be approaching, Sam Houston sent Bowie to San Antonio with orders to supervise the destruction and abandonment of the Alamo. When that proved unfeasible, he did his best to fortify it and prepare for attack. Upon the arrival of William Barrett Travis in command of regular Texian troops, Bowie was elected commander of the volunteers. More volunteers filtered in, including David Crockett and a group of Tennesseans, and the defenders eventually numbered—according to various estimates—between 182 and 257.

Mexican forces under General Santa Anna began to arrive on February 23, 1836, and eventually totaled around 2,500. Early in the siege, Bowie was stricken with an illness no one could identify, but which attacked his lungs, and he was confined to bed. J.R. Edmondson thinks it likely the injury to Bowie's lung inflicted by Norris Wright at the Sandbar Fight plagued him all his life, and may have played a part in this collapse.

The siege lasted thirteen days, with the final attack coming on the morning of March 6. Stories of Bowie's final moments range from being murdered without resistance to leaving dozens of dead soldiers at his feet. One of the more optimistic accounts comes from a 1937 article by popular Western historian E.A Brininstool: "He was a famous pistol shot and from his sick cot he brought down many of his foes before his ammunition was expended, after which he fought with the knife he had already made famous. It is stated that he slew nearly a dozen Mexicans before a bullet crashed through his head."

James Bowie was a rogue, and unabashedly so, but lived by his own strict code of honor. His death as a martyr, in concert with the legends of the knife that bore his name, made him one of the most famous heroes in U.S. history.

E VAN LEWIS MET Jim Bowie in Walt Disney's third Crockett episode, "Davy Crockett goes to the Alamo," and was mighty impressed with that big honkin' knife. He was soon reading the cheesy Jim Bowie comic books published by Charlton and watching the pretty dang good TV series starring Scott Forbes.

While Davy Crockett merchandise was everywhere—and Lewis amassed a ton of it—there was very little devoted to Bowie. The only toy he recalls having was a kid-sized Bowie Knife made of black plastic.

Years later, having developed an interest in all things Alamo, he began seeking out books on the guy. Along with precious few biographies and several books devoted to the knife or specific incidents, he found only three novels: *The Tempered Blade* by Monte Barrett (1946), *The Iron Mistress* by Paul L. Wellman (1950) and *Bowie* by Randy Lee Eickoff and Leonard C. Lewis (1998). All are fictionalized biographies, covering a wide swath of his life.

Just to be different, *Bowie's Gold* employs Bowie as a traditional hero of fiction, taking inspiration from James Bond, Conan of Cimmeria, Robert B. Parker's Spenser, Bernard Cornwell's Sharpe, and many others.

The author's first sale, to a now-defunct Internet magazine, was a story called "The Devil and Strap Buckner," about a fellow you have now met. His second sale, "Skyler Hobbs and the Rabbit Man," to *Ellery Queen's Mystery Magazine,* received the 2011 Robert L. Fish Award from the Mystery Writers of America. There followed more Skyler Hobbs adventures, and several tales about modern day (and not-so modern day) descendants of Davy Crockett. The author's homage to Dashiell Hammett, "The Continental Opposite," from *Alfred Hitchcock's Mystery Magazine*, was selected for *The Best Mystery Stories of 2016* and nominated for a Shamus Award. Somewhere along the way he also wrote a couple of tales about Jean Lafitte and his fictional partner-in-crime, Andre.

Then came *Crockett's Devil,* a Davy Crockett adventure starring the spirit of Fess Parker. The author hopes you will buy a copy and recommend it to your friends, relatives and everyone else on (or off) the planet.

Lewis lives in the Wild and notorious West of Portland, Oregon with his wife Irene and five ankle-biting dogs, now plotting his next project and world domination. Please wish him luck.

You are invited to visit his blog, *Davy Crockett's Almanack of Mystery, Adventure and the Wild West*, at evanlewis.com. He would be pleased to hear from you at delewis1@hotmail.com.

GARY CARBON IS a Chicago-based artist who grew up on a steady diet of TV, movies, and comic books. The latter inspired him to follow his interest in art and focus on bringing fictional and mythological characters to life.

He's collaborated on such characters as Sherlock Holmes and with multiple publishers on the pulp character the Spider, including Moonstone, Argo Press, and currently, Altus Press with Will Murray, as well as cover and illustration work for *Thrilling Adventure Yarns* by Crazy8Press, and of course with Steve Bryant on *Athena Voltaire*.

Gary works both traditionally in pencil, pen and ink, pastel, charcoal, gauche, and oils as well as digitally. Occasionally he brings characters to life through photography. To see more of his work, visit garycarbonart.com.

CROCKETT'S
DEVIL

"A Disney-esque romp through the Wild Frontier." - Bibliomaniac

"Crackling with energy, and filled with high jinks and high spirit."
- Peter Meech

"Blood and thunder make-believe." - Stephen Mertz

"Careens wonderfully through the frontier landscape of that wild era to the satisfying conclusion." – Will Murray

"Adventure, humor, thrills, and great story-telling."
- George Kelley

"Paced just slower than an Indiana Jones adventure, and leaves you wanting another story."
– Tim Leahy

"Honesty, honor, villainy, brutality, gentleness - all manner of humanity runs through this well-written novel." - Jackie Blain

"A nice blend of fact (lore?) and fiction."
- Dale Goble

"Rootin' Tootin' and Rip-Roarin!"
– Ann Littlewood

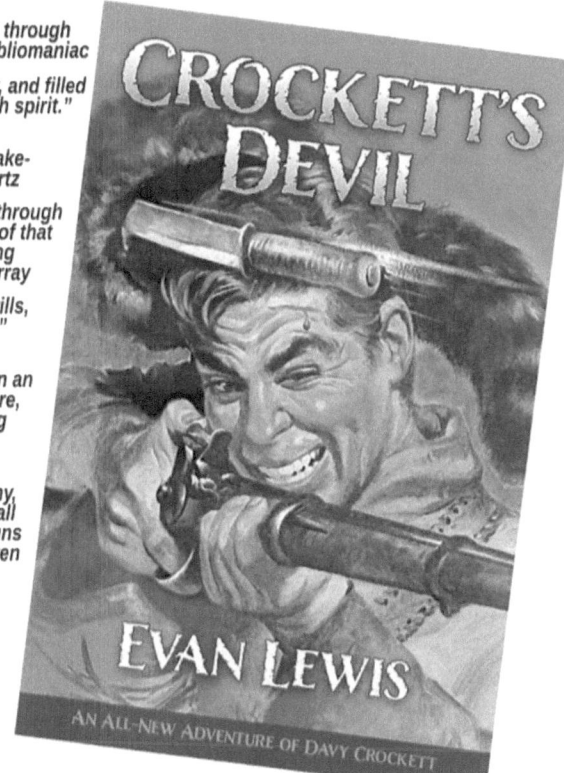

CROCKETT'S DEVIL

EVAN LEWIS

AN ALL-NEW ADVENTURE OF DAVY CROCKETT

INTRODUCTIONS BY EVAN LEWIS